chaco

a tale of ancient lives

MARK A. TAYLOR

SANTA FE

NEW MEXICO

First edition

Printed in the United States of America

Library of Congress Cataloging in Publication Data

Taylor, Mark A.., 1949-
    Chaco : a tale of ancient lives / Mark A. Taylor. -- 1st ed.
      p. cm
    ISBN 0-86534-203-2 : $14.95
    1. Indians of North American--New Mexico--Chaco Canyon--Fiction.
2. Man, Prehistoric--New MExico--Chaco Canyon--Fiction. 3. Pueblo
Indians--Fiction, I. Title.
PS3570.A9452C431993
813' .54--dc20   93-5158
                                        CIP

Published by Sunstone Press
      Post Office Box 2321
      Santa Fe, New Mexico 87504-2321 / USA

CHACO

PART

ONE

CHAPTER

ONE

Roots

The last cottonwood tree in of the city of Chaco stood outside the entrance to Pueblo Bonito. The elders said its roots surrounded the heart of the world, and teachers instructed students to listen for the clacking of its large waxy leaves because it announced the coming of rain. But for many equinoxes The gods had forsaken the city of Chaco and the rain did not come. Yet sometimes late at night when the city slept, the wind God, Yaponcha, snaked down the canyon and made the old cottonwood dance like the mother of many children.

Too many days had passed without rain. The porous red sun and the bone white moon lay alone on the turquoise sky. Almost every day clouds could be seen at the horizon, defining and redefining themselves into oblivion, but they were unwilling to venture out from the mountain tops and bring the rain.

The pueblo Abbotts and Kokopilau astronomers had observed the canyon's cottonwood trees for two thousand solstices. On the day that spring buds cracked, it was time to till the soil. When birds nested in the high branches, it was right for planting. When the yellow leaves carpeted the ground, farmers went into the fields above the city to harvest Mother Corn, called Chochmingwu. And today, hohoya or harvest time, teachers used this last cottonwood tree to teach children a lesson about how shame is never borne from patience.

This old and venerable cottonwood had offered sanctuary to many generations of pilgrims, traders and armies of naked warriors. It had listened to the secrets of Abbotts, but had uttered not a word. It had witnessed the city grow and become a center of power and civility that influenced dis-

---

Author's note: A description of the main characters and a glossary of pueblo terms is included at the end of the book.

distant wandering tribes. Every morning, after the Morning Caller sang out the Cha'tima, the sacred Morning Prayer, from atop Fajada Butte, old men sat at tables under its shade and played the board game Senat. Some of the elders remembered when cottonwoods canopied the entire canyon floor, and grew along Galo Creek and across its narrow flood plain to the canyon walls. But now only one remained. The rest had been cut down and replaced by neighborhoods, plazas and pueblos. The Anaa have an old saying, "Like the granary corn, a little taken every day, no one notices until only a handful remains." Only after the drought deepened and people longed to be cooled in the shade did they realize what they had done.

The last cottonwood's good health and longevity was thought to be a testament to the power and virility of nearby Pueblo Bonito, the greatest of the spiritual pueblos. In the late afternoon, shade from the tree breached the high walls of Bonito and fell onto its plazas, gardens, and on the intricately patterned stone pathways leading to kivas and study halls. Many books have been written at Bonito, plays of profound subjects performed, music of heart and soul composed. Inventions of magic, enlightenment and knowledge spread Bonito's fame far and wide. There were many kivas within its walls; a grand kiva for chanting and the smoking of pipes; another for repentance where the maudlin strings of regret took wing; one for the swell and clash of grief; another for arguments, disputes and the pause of disgust to be witnessed and resolved; and still another for laughter where acrobats, jugglers, tricksters and mimes entertained.

Among those who passed under the protection of the cottonwood were the Special Ones of the twenty-first dynasty of Anaa. Some were charismatics, others possessed great intellect, and still others were aspiring artists. It is said that an Anaa dynasty was only as good as the genius it engendered. Of the four great spiritual houses and the three powerful clan houses, only Pueblo Bonito allowed its Special Ones to pursue a highly unorthodox mode of learning. Students of Bonito choose the path of learning for themselves. This path sometimes conflicted with rules and tenets of Anaa, and many people from the other pueblos believed Bonito's Special Ones were too pampered and had gone too far.

At Pueblo Bonito beatings were rare and only meted out for the most severe infractions. If a student failed in his studies he was sent home instead of being forced to toil at the turquoise mines in the far-off Blue Mountains. Bonito was different from the other houses in other ways as well. Chochmingwu was given to anyone in need, and wuti were consulted on decisions and viewed as equals. Bonito had given Chaco and Anaa life.

The Missed Cha'tima

Hopi stood atop Fajada Butte, waiting to sing out the Morning Cha'tima. He marveled at the purplish-blue pre-dawn light setting afire the sandstone cliffs around the city. In the language of Anaa this light was called Nuptu, The Purple Light of Creation. From Fajada's vantage point he watched as the canyon and the sprawling city below reappeared from darkness of night. Hopi's eyes traced along the winding path of Galo Creek as it cut through the city. It snaked by all seven grand pueblos, in and out of neighborhoods and marketplaces, and disappeared at the other end of the canyon. Very few Anaa had had the honor of seeing the city as Hopi viewed it this morning. Though Fajada Butte stood at the center of the canyon, surrounded by the great city, it was forbidden for anyone except the Kokopilau and their apprentices to set foot on the butte. The price for trespassing was death.

Soon the sun's rays would tip the horizon and reach down into the canyon. As the Caller of the Morning Cha'tima, it was Hopi's duty to watch the shadow of Fajada Butte as it sun-dialed down the canyon cliffs, across the canyon floor to the Tawtoma, or to the place where the sun's rays go over the line. At the precise moment Fajada's shadow reached the Tawtoma, Hopi would usher in the new day by singing out the morning Cha'tima.

There were few greater honors bestowed by Chaco than to be chosen Caller of the Cha'tima. Traditionally, he who makes the calling eventually ends up a pueblo Abbott or high astronomer. Every morning at dawn Hopi stood at the exact place where, for nine dynasties, the Cha'tima was offered to welcome the new day. It was a ritual rich in significance, but it was far more than just a ritual, it was a matter of life and death. Without the sun, the face of the Creator Tawa, the world would cease to exist.

During the 12th dynasty the great astronomer Bask III, having observed a star in the southern hemisphere engorge, predicted the sun's disappearance. With the passing of each night the star grew larger and brighter, until it could be seen during the daytime. Bask III was a shrewd man; he knew this new stellar personality was a wayward comet and probably on a collision course with the Fourth World. Sensing a rare opportunity to extend his power—and that of his fellow Kokopilau astronomers— Bask III told the ruling Anaa clerics that the star was an emissary of the Kokopilau Gods. "Its appearance marks the beginning of a New Order," he told them. He shook his finger and warned, "If you do not consult the Kokopilau before making important decisions, the world will fall into a crack and disappear." The clerics were confused and argued among themselves. The clerics worshiped the sun disk, and they feared that this new star challenged the Creator, Tawa, and would enslave the Anaa.

Every day the new sun grew larger. Mysteriously, it possessed great brilliance—but no heat—further confounding the clerics but confirming what Bask III thought all along. One day the new sun disappeared in the west. Several days later a cloud of colorful mica particles rolled over the land from west to east like a heavy winter blanket. It filled the canyon of Chaco, and the people were convinced the last day of Anaa had arrived. The sun they had long honored was hardly visible through the cloud of particles, and it no longer warmed the land.

The young and old died quickly of a breathing ailment. Chaos reigned, and the tympany of conflict turned to violence. Many hands were submerged in blood and half of the population perished. The order of the 12th dynasty of Anaa collapsed and was overthrown. When the sun finally reappeared, Bask III and his fellow Kokopilau emerged as supremely powerful. Yet, when Bask III died many solstices later, the Kokopilau squandered their authority. Most Kokopilau were not interested in the power of man, but in the power of knowledge. The clerics resented this edict of silence, but they had conducted themselves so poorly, they kept their resentment to themselves. During this darkest period of Anaa's history, religion was inseminated with the science of astronomy.

From that day forward, every morning at the appointed place, known as the Cha'tima Rock atop Fajada Butte, when the sun sun-dialed Fajada's shadow to one of several Tawtoma places, the people offered the greeting of the new day. Not once in all that time, had they missed the Morning Cha'tima.

Hopi, who had made more than a thousand callings, stood on that hallowed place, ready to sing out the sun's praise when he suddenly felt weak. He moved from the Cha'tima Rock and sat down cross legged on a slab of sandstone nearby.

The soft spot on the top of his head pulsated. His breath vaporized, borne into the cool morning air. He repeated the question he had contemplated for seasons. Today, he said to himself, I will find the courage to do it! A thin layer of perspiration covered his brow and he trembled. "Today," he said aloud, "my question will be born into existence with the life of sound. If I am destined to become mist, as my breath is before me now, at least it shall be done."

Hopi stood, squared his shoulders, and set his posture to the eastern horizon. He looked directly into the sun. He opened his mouth, circled his dry lips with his tongue and posed his question. "Oh honorable Gods," he began, thrusting his arms and hands out and up, "if I do not make the Cha'tima Prayer, will the day not begin?"

He closed his eyes and prepared to be struck down. The sun's light shined through his eyelids and created concentric pools of red in his mind's eye. He stood erect, willing to receive the punishment his faithless question deserved. He tried to fix on his mantra, but it was no use. He attempted to link his will, which was extraordinarily strong for a young man, to the Mother Earth, but it was no use. Hopi's personal power or Piu'u, "I am I," was nothing compared to the power of his question. An eternity passed, or was it a fleeting moment? He had no concept of time.

Suddenly from behind him, someone called his name. "Hopi, Hopi! Where are you?"

It was Zuni, his best friend, rushing up Fajada's footstones. He excitedly called out and pointed, "The Cha'tima Rock! The Cha'tima Rock! Quickly!"

Hopi turned away from the sun and mechanically moved to the appointed Cha'tima place. He turned to Zuni who raced up the stairway toward him.

"Quickly! Quickly!" Zuni shouted.

Hopi stared at his friend like a terra-cotta messenger waiting an eternity for the right moment to speak. Only when he saw the fear in Zuni's eyes did he realize that something was terribly wrong. He turned, tilted his head down slightly to make certain Fajada's shadow had reached the Tawtoma line. To his utter amazement and horror, not only had Fajada's shadow touched the Tawtoma, but had submerged its entire circumference. His knees buckled and he nearly plummeted off the high ledge. A fist of fear swelled within his chest and he could not breathe. His question had been given life by his speaking it aloud, but because of it he had missed the morning Cha'tima prayer.

Hopi's question had been answered. Indeed, this would be the end for him, if not for the entire world. His voice trembled but he sang out,

> "May the longtime sun
> shine upon you,
> all love surround you and
> the pure light within you
> guide you on your way."

Not once in the eight dynasties since Chaco survived the black chaos had the morning prayer not been made at the appointed time.

Zuni stood on the pathway, overtaken by fear and watchful not to enter onto the Cha'tima Rock. His mere proximity to his friend Hopi would, in all likelihood, mean his demise also. They faced each other silently. Their eyes were filled with the love they held in their hearts but had never spoken. They were ready for the gnomes of light to pierce them. They waited patiently, knowing that waiting was part of punishment. Finally, after what seemed like a long time, they heard a group of farmers singing as they worked their way up a narrow footpath to the fields above the city, and the sound released them from their daze. Hopi quickly left the Cha'tima Rock and they both hurried down the stairway.

Zuni was certain that by sunset the Wind God Yaponcha would send out his dust devils to whisper the prayers of eternal night and Chaco would plummet into the abyss.

By the time Hopi and Zuni had raced to the foot of Fajada down footstones worn smooth by ancient masters, the wash wuti, merchants, stone masons and farmers filled the streets. Without bidding the other farewell, except for a nod of the head, they parted company. Hopi quickly disappeared into the crowd, and Zuni went north to pray at the open air kiva at Pueblo Bonito.

CHAPTER TWO

Autumn Equinox and the Great Races

All that day pilgrims from outlying communities arrived in the city by the thousands. Making their way down the steep footpaths into the city the devotees of Anaa—as well as non-believers—filled Chaco for the celebration of the autumn equinox. The pilgrims first stopped at one of the seven houses of the sun. They neatly piled their belongings outside the entryway of the house and quietly went inside to pay homage to The gods of Anaa and especially to the Creator, Tawa.

The seven pueblos were equal in the Tawa's eyes, yet because of the imperfections of man, the grand houses of Pueblo del Arroyo and Pueblo Bonito possessed special significance, and most visitors went to pray at one or the other of these two houses. The popularity of these two pueblos was especially evident at festival time and did not go unnoticed by the other pueblo leaders.

Along with the pilgrims came hundreds of red robed priests and young devotees dressed in white 'shamans' loincloths. The youngest devotees had never visited the sacred city and were humbled by the grandeur of the giant pueblos. These uninitiated shamans stood at the spiritual center of the world, and they cried without embarrassment or shame. They walked the streets in a trance and witnessed the contradictions that had become Chaco. They saw opulent pueblos, the Antelope Clan traders attired in rich coats of braided gold and wool, and the abject poverty and squalor of Galo, the City of the outcasts.

After setting up camp, the priests stood on the freshly scrubbed roadways, chanted and played drums. They danced to rekindle old friendships and to make new friends. The Anaa believed that meeting people on the road of life had great significance in death.

The normally well-behaved pueblo students played cruel jokes on the pilgrims. After many Sukops of hard work it was difficult to restrain themselves from poking fun at the backward pilgrims. For their part, the pilgrims were not nearly as stupid as the students believed. Being subject to practical jokes mattered little to them. They were just happy to be in Chaco, and they too saw the humor in their own clumsy behavior.

Many pilgrims came to witness the Great Race of Chaco. Every autumn equinox after the hohoya had been taken, the clans of Anaa celebrated with athletic competition. Fair play was a hallmark of the races, and The gods rewarded the winning clan with bountiful hohoyas and successful hunts. Along with the right to be boastful, there were trade beads, turquoise, concubines and slaves to be won by wagering on the foot races. Fortunes were won and lost, and some desperate souls wagered themselves into slavery for the chance of winning big on the races.

Many unsanctioned competitions were held outside the city on the plateaus. The favorite gamble was on slave fights. Slaves could sometimes win their freedom or possession of a slave for themselves. If they were killed their spirit was set free, so they fought with bravery and courage. Great warrior slaves were often given concubines by their masters as rewards for winning feathers, sacks of trade beads and turquoise. These events were ignored by the pious Anaa, yet in the last few equinoxes even pueblo Abbotts had been known to slip out to witness these gruesome spectacles.

Sacred Bonito

Zuni quickly walked to Bonito, passing through neighborhoods and plazas. Outdoor kitchens filled the canyon with the sweet smell of cooking Concha, a favorite cornmeal tortilla baked between two hot stones and eaten with wine. Concha was also used to make offerings to the dead. Zuni breathed in the fragrance of Concha and wondered if he would soon be making an offering to Hopi. The consequence of Hopi's act would be death. Though they were very different by nature, Zuni admired Hopi's courage to search out his heart. He admired Hopi for the depth of his personal convictions; even when Hopi's ideas were misguided, he was rarely subordinate. In a way, Zuni envied Hopi above all others. If he survived, Hopi would be a high priest, or an astronomer, but he was neither pompous nor did he abuse the power his future calling might afford him. Instead, Hopi preferred to spend his time pursuing answers to the questions which troubled him - and many troubled him.

On the other hand, Zuni—also a Special One of Bonito—was a devoted servant to Anaa. He neither questioned his orders nor hesitated to carry them out. Like this friend Hopi, Zuni was a scholar of great repute. When he spoke his gestures were princely and he was exquisitely handsome. When the tall Zuni strode across a pesta, his posture erect and his shoulders wide, the wuti of Chaco took notice.

As Zuni glided through the intersecting streets and alleyways he was taken up in the joyousness of this grand city. Children played in the street, men stood and talked, and everyone was washed and clean. The houses were neat, the fences white-washed and the wuti wore beautiful blue and purple smocks, silver inlaid turquoise jewelry, and skirts adorned with peacock feathers. Despite Hopi missing the Cha'tima, and the consequences surely to come, Zuni felt lighthearted. He could not help but be happy; festival time had arrived and the famed goodwill of Chaco enveloped him.

At Pueblo Bonito's entryway, under the green canopy of the great cottonwood, Zuni knelt and prayed before entering. As a child Zuni loved the sound of his leather sandals echoing through the fresco-covered, vaulted entryway and today was no different. Every time he heard it, he was home. Zuni was not alone in his love for this special place. For more than forty generations Bonito had been an inspiration to all.

Designed in the shape of the half moon, the pueblo's stucco walls rose more than twenty spear lengths. Zuni moved through the entryway into a large semi-circular courtyard surrounded by five cut-away levels above him. There were kivas, theatres, school rooms, living quarters, sacred Chochmingwu storage bins, more than six hundred rooms in all. Within Bonito a feeling of seclusion, safety and self-sufficiency filled its guests. It was a world in and of itself, a place one could live and worship without worry.

The interior walls of the pueblo were covered with ivy, cooling the courtyard in summer and creating a pastoral forest of loveliness. Spectacular palm trees lined he circumference of the courtyard. Each tree arrived at Chaco as seedlings from Mexico 200 equinoxes earlier and was meticulously cared for by a student who, along with his other rigorous training, carried water from Galo Creek to the trees. It was an honor to care for such an exotic member of the Bonito family, and students earned the right by competing in scholastic achievement.

The surface of the courtyard was a checkerboard of stone pathways and exquisite flower beds. Myna birds roosted in the branches of miniature fig trees. All paths at Bonito converged at the center of the court where an enormous roofless, subterranean kiva welcomed meditation and prayer. At the bottom of the kiva sat a perfectly rounded polished stone, nearly two spear lengths tall. It had been a gift to Bonito from The gods—it was said to have been delivered by a beam of light from the sun.

This kiva was Zuni's favorite place in all of Chaco. He often came here after a night's duty plotting stars on Fajada. It was Zuni's responsibility to observe the Scorpio star quadrant, to make detailed astronomical drawings and to write reports of his observations. It was also his duty to listen for Yaponcha and to note its direction and whether it brought dust devils, the scent of pine, sage, cactus, rain or the rank smell of death. Almost every morning, Zuni went to Bonito to sit in the sunlight and meditate. It was a place of personal power; a place where the light of truth could easily touch his face and warm his spirit.

But today, Zuni's meditation was unsatisfactory. Instead of transcending to a place of peace, he was awash with fear. He worried that something might be terribly wrong with Hopi. Was Hopi, as some of his rivals surmised, slipping away into the oblivion of Piu'u? Would Hopi, like others before him, be burdened with too much knowledge? Surely, Zuni thought, one of the pueblo shamans had noted Hopi's tardiness at Cha'tima. But why hadn't they said anything? More importantly, even if no cleric had observed the transgression, The gods had witnessed it. If The gods had seen this transgression but had done nothing, what did that mean?

Zuni struggled with these confounding questions until he simply decided, 'I shall not think of this subject again for it only serves falseness.'

CHAPTER THREE

Galo and the outcasts

After leaving Zuni at the base of Fajada Butte, Hopi walked to the marketplace where he purchased a stack of freshly baked concha, then went to his quarters where he changed from the gown of Fajada into the rags of an outcast. Then he headed for Galo, the city of Outcasts.

Galo was sheltered below a giant sandstone amphitheater carved out of the cliff face. It perched on the edge of the lowest of three sandstone tiers above Chaco. Galo was cool in the summer and sun-drenched in winter. At sunset, when candles softly illuminated the city below, the crude stone shanties of Galo were still awash in golden light. Visitors to Chaco marveled at Galo's beauty, but residents resented this irony. "An abyss is an abyss!" an old prostitute once told Hopi, wagging a crooked finger in his face, "Appearances are not the truth!"

The beauty of Galo and its prominent location nestled above the center of the city somehow reconciled the residents of Chaco with their anguish over the unfortunate outcasts. In many cases Galo's residents were victims of injustice, prejudice and circumstances beyond their control.

The pathway to Galo was steep and crossed a dangerous rock slide halfway to the top. Hopi walked with the speed and confidence of a great horned sheep. Hopi had visited Galo many times and did not think about the trail, instead a sensation of sadness washed over him. As a young student at Bonito, he and Zuni had accompanied Abbott Amhose to Galo where they offered prayers and gave assistance to the needy. Later at Bonito, as he lay in his clean and safe bed, he could not help but feel angry at gods who created such an inhumane torment for their beloved children. He was also disturbed by the attitude of the people of Anaa who witnessed this injustice everyday but did nothing to rectify it.

Galo was created in the fourth dynasty after Tell, a great grandson of Narmer, wed his brother's three daughters who bore him many children. Of these offspring half were born with horrible disfigurements, some with heads larger than their bodies—these children lived only a few years yet exhibited fabulous mental powers. Others were born without arms or legs or eyes or anuses. The worst had no visible imperfections but, in early adulthood fell sick with demons. Of these children Mitanna was Tell's favorite,

Mitanna was the most beautiful girl in all Chaco. One day as she sat at her father's side while he entertained diplomats from Verda, she suddenly fell sick and frothed at the mouth. The demon inside her was so powerful the guards could not hold her down. She attacked one of her father's visitors, biting him viciously, so Tell, stricken with fear and anguish, drew his knife and pierced her heart.

After his beloved Mitanna's death Tell locked himself in his meditation chapel and did not leave. He refused food or water for many days. When Tell finally reappeared, he ordered Galo built to house his tormented children. The Time Scrolls are in agreement about this; they say Tell stood on his veranda and watched his children as they played on the plateau above. In turn, they observed him and although the situation was very painful, Tell often flew kites to his beloved children bearing letters and gifts.

Over the ages, many unfortunate souls were sent to Galo to live out their lives alone. They were the handicapped, the unbalanced and those who suffered mysterious diseases. The only other alternative was to put them to death. The Anaa were compassionate and so these unfortunate souls were allowed to live and not disgrace their families or The gods of Anaa or the people of Chaco. It was a humane prison if such a thing exists.

Near the top of the trail Hopi was met by Ranal, a talented young musician who had fallen prey to ruminations. Ranal's music was so beautiful it had frightened people. It was not known if it came from good or from evil. When Ranal began talking to the ones that cannot be seen, he was taken before Ammett, the Abbott of Pueblo del Arroyo, who sent him to Galo. Ranal had waited for Hopi's arrival.

"Is there music in the street?" he asked without offering a salutation.

"Yes, my friend Ranal, there is music."

"Is there color and hope?"

"Yes, my son, there is color and there is hope."

"Hopi," Ranal said rolling his eyes, "You missed the Cha'tima! I know this to be true because I watched, I can see you." He pointed to Fajada Butte. "From here we can see and hear everything. There is no place in all of Chaco that the Cha'tima cannot be heard." Saliva appeared at the corners of Ranal's mouth. He jumped lithely from the path to a large stone and back again. "I listened as I always do. I listened with both my ears. You are aware," he said, pausing, "that one of my ears is a true believer . . . Do you believe I am a true believer?"

"Yes, my friend," Hopi said smiling.

"And," Ranal continued, "I listened with my other ear, the one that hears voices, the one that feels the vibrations of my heart, the one that is your friend. I am your friend Hopi, aren't I?"

Hopi, who continued up the path paused, and put his arm on Ranal's shoulder, "Yes, indeed Ranal, you are my friend."

"You missed the Cha'tima! You missed the Cha'tima!" Ranal suddenly sang out while dancing around the sagebrush bordering the pathway, "Will they kill you now?" he asked.

"I don't know."

"Are you afraid?"

"Yes."

"Will you come and live with us? Will you watch life as we do from here, a part of it but apart from it?"

"I cannot say, my friend. It is not my decision." Sensing Ranal's playful mood Hopi continued, "If it were my decision I would live here with you and we would also live out in the desert." Hopi motioned to the south with his striking black eyes. "I would take you, my friend, and we would travel to Mexico. We would eat exotic food and walk the temples under a full moon. We would travel far out on the great blue waters and harpoon fish that defy description. Then, we would travel north to the red canyons of The gods and sleep in the tall sagebrush. If it were up to me, my friend, we would lay in the tall bushes and project our beings out to the furthest star."

"You can't do that!" Ranal exclaimed, frightened but still dancing back and forth, "Only Allander can do that! Even I know that!"

"Yes, you are right, my friend." Hopi replied softly.

The two men crested the last ridge and a crowd of children awaited. They were naked, dirty, unfed and carried the putrefied air of their own defecation. Many were sick or handicapped. Hopi greeted each child individually, calling out his or her name in a loud, clear voice. Hopi looked straight into their eyes. For these children, it was a great honor to hear their name spoken by such a worthy one and they smiled widely. Hopi gave each a concha and wished them a happy equinox. For the most part, these children were not outcasts, but the offspring of outcasts. They had been sentenced by birth to pay for their parents' transgressions or bad luck. Many would leave Galo one day and head south for Mexico taking with them resentment of what Anaa had done. Some would even plan insurrections, fomenting hatred and distrust for the Anaa. But for most, Galo was their home and they knew or desired no other.

Hopi and Ranal walked on past two men struggling to pull a death wagon up the embankment from a ravine. Flies swarmed around a limpid pool of blood in the back of the wagon. It was left there, Ranal told him, by a man who was stabbed the night before. The blood glistened in the morning sun, it was viscous and shined like a polished stone. The man, Ranal added, was a thief and deserved to die.

"If he had not been a thief," Ranal said, "we might have cooked him for the equinox celebration." He waited, gauging Hopi's response.

Hopi said nothing.

"Chaco," Ranal continued, "is the essence of humanity, but life in Galo is meaningless and worthless." He smiled again and waited for Hopi to disagree, but Hopi was not listening. Ranal fell silent, his insecurities swarmed over him like the flies on the pool of blood.

Hopi was shaken by the blood in the wagon. He knew about blood and he knew about death, too. He had seen death three times. The first time was the quiet surrender of a well-traveled soul who exhaled for the last time and a drop of blood mysteriously appeared on his lip. The second time he witnessed the blood-filled heave of a man who had suddenly died in the market place. And the third time he saw the blood of a young girl who had fallen from the cliffs and was broken so badly tiny droplets of scarlet blood surfaced from every pore.

Now that I have committed a grievous sacrilege, will I learn about death, too? Hopi questioned. Will I experience life after the executioner lays me open and my blood flows out onto the stone? Hopi feared the idea of death but surrendered himself to the thought of it. Did the well-travelled old man find peace in his surrender, he wondered? Did the young girl's soul walk away from her broken body into a new life? Death, he said to himself, should come after many years and much life, but not in youth.

Most of Galo's dwellings were shanties just large enough to store what little food and material items the outcasts possessed. From one end of Galo to the other was a distance of only a few hundred steps but every inhumanity could be found within its measure.

Hopi was brought from his contemplation by a drunken man propped against a mud and stone wall.

"Hopi!" the man hollered loudly.

It was Vanga, the stone cutter who had fallen and could not walk anymore.

"Hopi!" Vanga called out again, turning his head cockeyed to get a better look, "I know it is you."

"Vanga, greetings!" Hopi replied.

"Come, please come to me, I must tell you something."

"Yes, good man," Hopi said leaning down and righting the drunken man, "What is it, Vanga?"

"It is very important," Vanga said to Hopi, "please whisper." Hopi lowered his eyes and drew closer. Vanga's grisly face was filthy and a white milky substance beaded at the corners of his eyes.

"Everyone knows what happened today," Vanga whispered, peering over his shoulder to see if anyone was watching, "I tell you this as a friend, you have been good to me."

"Thank you my friend, I appreciate your concern." Hopi said brushing Vanga's matted hair away from his face. Reaching into his pocket, Hopi retrieved a handful of trade beads and forced them into Vanga's hand along with a concha.

Vanga winked and tears filled his eyes.

After Vanga's accident his family nursed him, but his legs failed to heal. Vanga hated his useless legs and his worthless existence. As time went by, he learned to hate his friends and neighbors, his children and ultimately his devoted wife. They did not know the cruelty life wrought, he had convinced himself. This proud man whose powerful apendages once lifted heavy stones or made love like the mightiest of bison was now defeated.

Since being sent to Galo, Vanga became foul and abusive. Single-handedly he pointed out the mendacities and hypocrisies of his neighbors. When Vanga's assessments met with rage, he laughed and dared the offended party to kill him, "Take me by my legs and throw me off the cliff, if you can," he shouted and laughed. "I hope to land in my old neighborhood." And indeed, it was Vanga's dream to be back in his neighborhood with his family. If he could just return to his old life he would tell everyone he was sorry and that he loved them.

Amarna

Hopi's reason for visiting Galo was to see Soya, and her daughter, Amarna. When he arrived at their shanty several men sat on the stoop outside. Many equinoxes earlier, Soya had been banished to Galo for adultery and was forced into prostitution to survive. Her daughter, Amarna, was fifteen and born from an unknown seed. At the insistence of her mother, Amarna had just begun plying her mother's trade. Every season Soya grew older and her customers grew smaller in number. Something had to be done or the two would die of starvation. Even Amarna had argued in favor of becoming a prostitute. Her mother's customers wanted her and she knew it. It was a matter of necessity.

Amarna's skin was smooth and silken, her hair shone blue-black, like a beetle's bottom in the sun. Her youthful breasts were ample and her legs were long and athletic. She was one of the most beautiful wuti in the empire. Amarna soon learned to despise the men who groped her, who explored her, who pinched and defiled her.

Amarna dreamed of living in the city below. She spent many days sitting on the rocks and observing every detail of life in the city. She watched the city people talk to their neighbors, the games the children played, how everyone seemed to laugh, what the wuti wore, how they fixed their hair and how strong the young warriors were. Amarna's dream became more elaborate as time passed; it included a husband who returned to her from cutting stone every night.

Amarna dreamt about the great pueblo kivas and of wearing plumes and handwoven ceremonial gowns to the solstice celebrations. She would walk the clean streets of Chaco, bid greetings to all, and wash the clothes of her husband at the river with the other wives. The wuti would talk of their husbands' strength and courage. She would giggle and turn away when older wuti told of the demands their fat husbands made of them. To herself she would say, 'If they only knew, their envy would be endless.'

In her dream Amarna would listen and she would be heard, but for now when her customers demanded both her body and her attention, she feigned excitement and imagined they were her lover. Since taking up her mother's trade, Amarna's dreamworld engorged. She now held another dream in her heart, a dream so secret even she was unaware it existed. Everytime it tried to display its truth, she refused to acknowledge it. It was a dream of another place and time.

Hopi had gone to Galo to tell Soya he had made arrangements for Amarna to live with a peasant family in the northern city of Verda. He would not allow Amarna to starve, nor would he let her follow her mother's path. If Amarna been born to another family, he considered, she would have enjoyed the benefit of Anaa's protection. If I were in power, Hopi thought, I would embrace the children of Galo, not sentence them to a life of hardship for the crimes of their parents!

He had promised to take care of Amarna, and to have a man such as Hopi responsible for her should have given Soya great comfort. Yet, when he told Soya of his idea she would not consider it. "Surely," he said, "Amarna should not be held accountable for your sins. Can you refuse her the chance to live a life of integrity and happiness?" Soya did not answer. Reluctantly, she agreed to let Amarna leave with him, but only because he would not relent and because he promised to support her, too.

When Hopi realized that the men sitting outside the shack were not waiting for Soya but for Amarna, he was furious. The idea of the child Amarna lying with men she did not love made his heart race. Hopi was a virgin, a requirement of all Anaa's hierarchy until completing their spiritual training, but he was drawn by the allure of the female form. It was not uncommon for wuti to show themselves to men they desired. The female body was celestial and its display was never made without honor, except in the case of widowers or wuti whose husbands had taken up with another. These wuti showed themselves in a more provocative way, sometimes holding their breasts or spreading their legs and rotating their behinds. Hopi had seen these displays and though he was trained at Bonito, and was now an honored apprentice of the Kokopilau, it was impossible for him not to feel a man's feelings.

By the laws of Anaa, Amarna's chance for a life of honor was doomed. Before Hopi could confront Soya, he had to calm himself. A short distance away he sat on a rock outcropping, crossed his legs and meditated. How could the mother of such a child doom her to this fate, he wondered? Surely, The gods will allow Amarna into their hearts. The gods will surely consider the injustice of her circumstances, will they not?

Equanimity and Kaa

Hopi's torment did not last long and was replaced by a feeling of equanimity. He had felt this equanimity for the first time as a child when he was lost in the great cedar forest of the north. From that experience Hopi learned that when he peeled back the veneer to expose the true nature of a situation, he became calm. He would not condemn Soya, but neither would he stand for her subterfuge. If The gods were just and righteous, as he believed they were, Amarna would be forgiven.

Hopi's wisdom had come early. When he was only four Kokopilau calendars old he became separated from his father in the forest of the White Mesa near his home of Grand Gulch. While his father collected firewood Hopi wandered away looking for flint to make arrowheads. When he realized he was lost he was filled with despair and ran farther and farther into the forest. The sun disappeared and little Hopi was cold, so he took refuge under the low limbs of an ancient cedar tree. Soon, he fell asleep on the bed of deep pine needles surrounding its trunk.

For many days thereafter he wandered through the vast track of trees until one morning as he marched along a hand reached down and softly caressed his check. He turned and to his amazement found only a large bough of cedar moving rhythmically back and forth. For a moment he was disappointed, but he was certain this caress was meant for him. It was a loving and soothing caress, the touch of a mother. But how could this be? He sat down and began to cry, but around him the trees began to jostle and sway in a hypnotic dance. Soon, the entire forest took up the dance, tilting and rolling and swaying in unison. This gesture of love made him happy and he no longer felt alone. Hopi relinquished his fear of death and surrendered his life to nature. The twisting limbs of the large squat trees swayed back and forth making the natural world a giant cradle, and little Hopi, the newborn Messiah of nature.

Hopi continued on, sometimes traveling day and night. He ate what was generously offered, roots and grasses, bark and moss, insects and pinenuts. He drank from Koritvi, pot holes in the sandstone. He slept under bushes or hidden by rock outcroppings. One night he awoke to find an owl perched on a branch above his head. The owl spoke to him, "I am Hoodee, your invisible friend."

"How can you be invisible if I can see you?" Hopi asked.

"If I were not your friend, you would not see me."

Hoodee told Hopi stories about the great river of life and the domes and spires and canyons where no man had ever been. "It is the place gods play games with light." Hoodee said.

At Hoodee's direction, Hopi walked through the cedar forest. He rested in its shadows, crossed its plateaus and descended into deep canyons where he found stone houses of the ancient Gods. He called out to them, but his words made no sound. Instead, his words went from his mouth and piled in front of him one on top of the other until they were taller than a tree and he was forced to walk around them. His words were objects in a forest where the unexplainable resided, and Hopi soon learned to swallow his words and to communicate without them. Though he was no larger than a wild boar, everything became the same size to Hopi. All creatures were equal in size and importance, as if equanimity was the root of all things.

In the canyons Hoodee taught Hopi to fly. It was simple; he merely learned the technique of separating his will or 'Kaa,' from his body and he could fly. Hoodee told him birds do not need this technique because they have wings, but the only wings humans possess are of the mind. These wings, the spirit of Kaa, are very powerful, but most men do not know that they even exist. By the time a man becomes full grown his wings are shriveled like an appendage never used," Hoodee said sadly.

Hoodee instructed Hopi to lay on the slickrock and be completely still. Through some unexplainable conjunction of what is and what is not, Hopi's spirit floated upward. At first he hovered above his body and watched in amazement. Soon, he followed Hoodee, hunting the canyon bottoms or soaring high above the mesatops. Sometimes, Hopi played with the Wind God, Yaponcha, diving into the center of his dust devils until Hoodee feared he could not pull out, then he would soar straight up into the heavens.

Hopi spent days searching for his home at Grand Gulch, sometimes flying the entire day only to return disappointed. As time passed Hopi tired of flying, preferring to walk or sit and observe. Flying takes great energy, he told Hoodee, and he was homesick and wanted to go home.

One afternoon, after a nap on a mound of green moss hidden from the sun, Hopi wandered the broken rock and happened back into the chaparral where he had been lost. Realizing his good luck, he happily walked home.

His family was astonished. He had been gone three complete moons. They had searched everywhere without finding a trace, not even his footprints. They reluctantly concluded an eagle had swooped down and carried him off. His family was happy for his return, but others treated him with a combination of reverence and suspicion. Hopi had disappeared a child, but he returned with a spiritual clarity and charisma few attain in a lifetime. His eyes reflected light from the sun into dark places, especially into the hearts of men. Good men offered him gifts, while those with evil intent were frightened and even plotted his demise.

One man, Jule, known for selling the children of his wives, took a particular dislike to Hopi. One day as Hopi played near the edge of a deep canyon, Jule suddenly leapt out from behind a bush intending to throw Hopi over the edge, but instead he tripped and plunged over the edge to the rocks far below. His wives and children were overjoyed. They were free from his cruelty. They prayed at Hopi's feet, and sang out loud that he had delivered them from Nedder.

Hopi's posture had also changed, he seemed both old and young, wise and childlike, confident yet willing to yield at the same time. Soon, people from surrounding villages came to sit in his presence. Word of this special person spread from one village to another until it was reported to the abbott's secret council meeting at Chaco. The Kokopilau astronomers, who normally took their eyes from the stars only long enough to work calculations, were very excited indeed. They had predicted two very special individuals would appear one day soon, and they were excited by the prediction's complexity and about its eventual manifestation, not in the fact of Hopi's existence. But, when Allander, the Kokopilau's head astronomer, learned of Hopi he quickly left the safety of Fajada Butte and traveled alone at night, hiding in the cloak of darkness, to witness this cosmic soul for himself.

Soya

Hopi sensed Amarna approach from behind, but he sat quietly on the sandstone outcropping. He did not move or open his eyes, but when Amarna knelt behind him and placed her hands on his shoulders he was greatly surprised. He did not expect this simple gesture of affection and he flinched away. Amarna, too, was amazed at her act of familiarity. In the tradition of Anaa it was unheardof for a wuti to touch a man she was not betrothed or married to. Amarna took Hopi's reaction as a rejection, but Hopi had flinched away only in surprise. He knew her caress had come from the heart and was nothing more than a thoughtful greeting.

Has my new life suddenly given me the right to make my own rules, Amarna asked herself? Is my greeting proof of my innate dirtiness, of the sinfulness born into my mother and destined to control me, too? Amarna felt humiliated and retracted her hands quickly, first, pulling them to her stomach, then raising them to cover her face. She felt defiant but began to cry.

"I came to make you happy," Hopi said turning to face her. "Do not be sad."

Amarna was embarrassed, but not speechless. "I only want to make you happy, Hopi my friend." Amarna's tears made Hopi uneasy.

"Please," he pleaded, "cry no more. I am confused. I feel the spring flood rushing through my veins," Hopi stammered, trying to put his feeling into words but he could not. After an uncomfortable silence he finally said, "I have come to speak to your mother."

Lowering her head, Amarna got to her feet and raced off.

Hopi stood and walked after her. He was tall, not as tall as Zuni, but tall for an Anaa and very muscular. His thick long hair was braided into one braid and hung to his mid-back. Hopi was often seen only as a mighty warrior, but when he spoke his elegance and command of the language of Anaa belied his physical strength. Halfway to the shack, Soya greeted him with an extravagant bow.

"You wish to speak with me?" she said.

"I have made arrangements for Amarna and by the new moon she will be gone."

"What right have you, or anyone from your cherished Chaco, to take my only daughter from me?"

"You will not break our agreement. I will care for you as I said and Amarna will have freedom."

"It is too late for that!" Soya shrieked, "It is too late now for you also. Everyone knows what happened this morning. Tell me," she said placing her hands on her hips, "how will you care for me?"

"You will receive what you need. I will see to it. Amarna must leave, we both know that."

"It is too late."

"Perhaps for you and me, but not for her. It can be cleansed."

"It cannot be cleansed," she answered angrily, her face was red and her hands clinched in fists, "You lie. It cannot be cleansed. What is done is done."

"What she has done is not by her own will." Hopi said defiantly, "If she is shamed it is your shame—you who forced her—and it is you who will pay not only for your sins, but for what you have done to your daughter. Amarna will leave and you will not get in my way."

"But, it is too late!"

"Silence!" Hopi demanded, and with outstretched arm, pointed at her accusingly. "You will not deny her the life you have forsaken." His voice resonated in the air as though amplified by a deep canyon.

Soya lowered her head, fell silent and was overcome by Hopi's power.

"You will be lonely and I am sorry for that," Hopi went on, now gently, "but the wrong you have done can be made right for Amarna. You will have what you need, I promise."

CHAPTER FOUR

Father, Amhose and Wonder

Instead of returning to the city down the steep trail, Hopi hiked to the top of the plateau, through the dying fields of desert rice and Chochmingwu and into the desert.

Back in Chaco, after he finished his meditation at Bonito, Zuni decided to visit his old room there. Zuni believed it was important to hold the thread of one's life. Without this continuity and the knowledge of one's beginning, the weave of life unravels, and if one denies his past he will surely forfeit his future.

Zuni's room at Bonito held special significance. It was the place he was awakened. His very first recollection was of Abbott Amhose smiling down at him as he lay in bed. Many moons earlier, Zuni was brought to Bonito near death. His father carried him in one afternoon and asked for help, saying Zuni had fallen ill. Zuni had a high fever and was delirious. When his fever finally broke and he awoke, his father was gone leaving behind only a leather sack filled with turquoise and gold. The sack was embroidered with a family emblem from Mexico and it was the only possession Zuni had of his previous life. Today, Zuni could remember nothing of his father or his mother or his life before Abbott Amhose's smiling face. Bonito and Chaco were all he knew and all he desired to know. For Zuni the world stretched the length of the canyon and no further.

When Zuni reached the doorway to his old room, he was startled to see Abbott Amhose, the most beloved and powerful man in all Chaco, on his hands and knees scrubbing the floor inside. Zuni fixed his dark eyes on the abbott who had not noticed him.

"I wish above all things not to worry you, gentle father, and it may well be that I am arrogant and if so, I beg you to punish me. But the Abbott of Bonito must not clean floors, what will others think?"

Without stopping or turning, Amhose laughed heartily. "But my dear young son Zuni, although you are eminently gifted in speech and thought you were taught the importance of not losing touch with your god given talents, is that not so?"

"Yes, eminent teacher, that is why you must forgive me for not assisting, for I have not the talent you possess. But is this not wasting your greater skills that you spend your time on lowly chores? I find this somewhat perplexing. Is this your wish?"

"My only wish is to keep the tradition. I have scrubbed this floor and many others for an epoch and do not see the wisdom in changing now."

"Forgive me, father, I am not certain as yet what my own wishes are. But from this day forth I shall take pleasure in scrubbing my own floor. For me, my greatest pleasure comes from my studies. But, a man's wishes are another matter. Wishes may not always determine a man's mission. Perhaps destiny shapes a man's future?"

The lighthearted banter, a hallmark of Zuni's and Abbott Amhose's relationship, had changed. The abbott stopped scrubbing and slowly got to his feet. Though his eyes sparkled as raindrops on a colorful flower petal, his face was now gravely serious.

"As I have come to know people, we all tend to confuse our wishes with predestination." The abbott said in a low voice. "Tell me, my son, if you could wish your pre-destiny, what would it be?"

They were silent for a long time.

"Speak, my son," the abbott ordered.

"I believe," Zuni said hesitantly, "I would stay in Chaco. That I would serve witness to many great and worrisome changes, but that I would be with you, kind father. Perhaps I might be the Abbott one day. I do not wish this, but I believe it so ordained."

"Are not the Kokopilau astronomers filling your head with manipulations and deceit against our gods?"

"Yes, father they make feeble attempts, but did you not trust my faith when you sent me to apprentice?"

The abbott paused before responding, "Do the astronomers know right from wrong? God from man? Manipulation from faith?"

"Yes." Zuni replied smiling again, "And one other thing, my father."

"Yes? Speak."

"They know that I am but a spy, the simpleminded servant to The gods of Anaa who have assembled us all, even the astronomers, to this place to enjoy this day and all our tomorrows."

"This is good, my son," the abbott said. "perhaps, then, since you see so clearly into our tomorrows, might you not tell me of the destiny of another, your brother, Hopi?"

With this question, Zuni felt the veneer become transparent. He could not speak for a very long time. He stood erect, and his tall, lean frame did not fit in the doorway. The abbott, who only moments earlier had been his friend, his brother and the only father he had ever known, was now the voice of God.

"I find it difficult to speak, father."

"And I, my brother, I find it difficult also, yet I do—so speak."

It was not like the abbott to set a trap like this. His way was to look a person in the eye and ask the question.

"How strange and inconceivable everything is," Zuni started, "the sun, the river, the wind, and even one's true being. It is my belief, good father, that Hopi's unique qualities will bring both tremendous joy and great unhappiness . . . . The sun will bring us good crops but will evaporate our water. The river will quench our thirst, but will flood our land. The wind will cool our brow, but will wash away our writings. And, Hopi will ask many questions, but will have answers to but a few."

The abbott smiled widely. "We have taught you well, my son. You speak convincing arguments, and one day—much sooner than you may think—perhaps even today," he said raising his eyebrows, "you might address the entire kiva cleric and tell us all about your friend and our brother, Hopi."

Zuni did not know what to think of this, but before he could enquire, the Abbott spoke to him as he never had before.

"My son, I fear we are in a time of great change. I believe destiny touches our face. I am not certain what will become of all of this, our beloved Chaco, the sun above us, the earth below; but I am convinced that a new day in history has dawned this morning. I have waited many solstices for a crisis of faith and I am afraid it is here." The Abbott looked deep into Zuni's eyes and into his heart. He then clucked his tongue in the way of Anaa.

"Dearest father," Zuni said choking down his tears, "Tomorrow, I will be here with you, father. With all my strength I will be Anaa, I will hold our traditions high against the wings of change. I will stand strong and no man shall pass."

The two men fell silent.

From Zuni's old room they walked out onto a terrace and into the sunlight. They gazed down at the streets below where thousands of pilgrims gathered. The festivities would begin tonight at Tasupi and there would be feasting, music and dance. The Anaa had suffered the great hardship of a drought, yet they would celebrate and give thanks. The two men watched the crowd without talking for a long time. Before Zuni left to return to his quarters, Amhose took him into his arms and embraced him the way a father embraces a son. Zuni held tightly, the way a son holds his aging father.

Despite the impending crisis, Zuni enjoyed his walk home through the streets and marketplaces. Everywhere the gloom of yet another poor Hohoya gave way to the celebration. It was not yet night, but sacramental wine was already being offered. All day long fresh Mother Chochmingwu, was gathered into baskets on the plateaus above then slung in the middle of a pole and carried into Chaco to be roasted over open fires. Pilgrims ate as much as they desired, but unlike the celebrations in years of bounty, the pilgrims could not fill their packs with corn to take home.

In the city's many plazas young wuti gleaned and winnowed grain as they danced—to the amusement of the men. The wuti stood in large circles, facing inward, scooping up the trodden grain into shallow bowls and tossing it into the air. The light chaff in the air mixed with the smell of the roasting corn and the frying concha. The wuti laughed, swayed their behinds in a circular motion and stepped to the left with the beat of a drum. This ceremony was for the unmarried wuti, some so fresh they had not menstruated. Students from the pueblos gathered and skirmished with students from other pueblos. These young braves drank, strutted, cavorted and fought mock battles. But the real warriors, the defenders of Chaco who fought only for principle and occasionally for glory, watched the young bucks and unmarried wuti from the perimeter. They would have their celebration later in the darkest part of the night.

The hardships of the drought which had been endured in silence—the way of Anaa—now had voice and it sang out, not in complaint but in praise of today's bounty and brotherhood. Nearby, farmers who had defaulted on their cultivator taxes were stripped, bound and humiliated. All lands, seeds, water and air was owned by The gods and administered by the seven pueblos. The pueblos divided all crops, made allotments to outlying communities and served as storehouses. Some pueblos had hundreds of storage rooms. Among the farmers, some were caught withholding a percentage of their Hohoya—a serious offense. These men stood tethered near the public toilets where passersby urinated on them. These farmers would be freed ultimately, but in all likelihood, a few would be whipped by the warriors late tonight.

These were difficult times and the Hohoya was the worst in years. This

Hohoya was the tenth in a row that failed to meet minimum quotas. It was rumored that in the far-off outlying communities such as Verda and Grand Gulch, community leaders were putting to death citizens who had again taken up the practice of cannibalism. Zuni's heart went out to the victims and the perpetrators. When men of God were hungry and their children bloated and died, the laws of Anaa were sometimes forgotten.

Zuni walked through the crowd and met old classmates from Bonito. He was not easy to miss; he was much taller than his former classmates, his flowing hair and his elegant face with its serene smile, high cheek bones and arching eyebrows made him stand out. After their schooling many of his classmates had gone out into the world. Zuni embraced them but did not partake in wine. He had no desire to go out into the world, for he was chosen by God to lead the monastic life. Yet he wondered what these men experienced and what the world meant to them. Some were great warriors, conquering the tribes of the outback. Others were farmers, jewelers or traders who traveled far south to obtain their share of the great bounty in Mexico. They wore robes of braided gold imbedded with turquoise and jewels. With them came exotic wuti whose lips were narrow, painted, and whose eyes were of the most provocative bird-like nature. These wuti batted their eyes at Zuni and had they been alone would have shown themselves to him, as did the wuti of Chaco. It was difficult for them not to seduce this tall, exquisitely handsome young man wearing the robes of the Kokopilau.

When Zuni arrived at his room, four warriors awaited. He did not speak nor did they. He knew to go with them.

CHAPTER

FIVE

Tar and the Many Clans

Among the throng on the roadway into Chaco, a young runner, Tar, known as Tar the Rabbit, sprinted away from his extended family. They had been on the road for four days and would reach the city before Tasupi. Tar ran to a point on the horizon and back again. It was his first visit to Chaco, and he was anxious to see the famed city. Tar also felt great apprehension because he was to run in the great foot race of Chaco. He and his family were members of the Blue Flute Clan which had won many great races over the generations. The signature of the Blue Flute Clan, a smaller branch of the city's larger Flute Clan which built Pueblo Chettro Ketl, was listed with the champions on Chaco's shrine wall. The Flutes had even won more races than the Antelope Clan. At the upcoming race, Tar had been chosen to uphold the honor of his clansmen.

From the furthest reaches of the empire the clansmen journeyed to the crossroads of Chaco for the races. The Snake, Sun, Bear, Sand, Coyote, Lizard, Eagle, Water, Parrot, Spider and Bow clans would all be represented. The runners were the clans' strongest, bravest and fastest.

This equinox there would only be one race, a grueling long distance course that began at Chaco on the morning of the second day of festivities and traveled north to the outlying community of Verda and back again. Runners ran day and night for six days, only stopping when they could go no further. On arrival at Verda, each was given a clay pot of water, symbolizing the rain that nourishes crops. From Verda they carried the jar of water back to Chaco trying not to spill a drop. The winner of the race and his clan was guaranteed ample rain by The gods for the next year's crops.

For many the great race was the high point of the celebration. Runners began by striding through the city and then up along the cliff line to the delight of everyone in the city. If there was one thing Chacoans loved it was betting. Great treasures of turquoise and baskets of trade beads would change hands on completion of the race.

Tar's father, Dol, a squat man with powerful arms and legs, watched as his son raced to the horizon, turned and made his way back. He, too, was anxious about this trip to Chaco. He had refused to let any of his seven sons attend school at Chaco, and as he approached the city he became fearful. Dol was convinced that Chaco was an instrument of evil. Dol knew his sons could learn much in Chaco, but he had witnessed many young men return home after schooling in the great city with the hole on top of their heads closed and exhibiting the ways of the two hearts. As an elder of the Blue Flute, one of Anaa's most fundamental clans, Dol would teach his sons at home. In his way of thinking, they had far more to lose by going to Chaco than by staying home.

The delights of the city were sure to test the faith of every member of his family, and this gave Dol great concern. He consented to bring his family to the celebration lest people think he snubbed the greatness of Chaco and Anaa, and also because his son was the fastest of the Blue Flute Clan. To run in the great races of Chaco was an honor as much to a father as to the runner, his son.

Tar came back to his slow moving family, turned and ran back out again. His family consisted of his parents, seven brothers, their wives and children—more than forty souls. I will run to the edge of the city, he said to himself, not even knowing where the edge of the city was. The idea of actually seeing Chaco excited him immensely, and the closer he got the more energy he possessed. He had heard the stories of how the flat and endless land suddenly dropped away to reveal the deep canyon where the world's greatest city was found.

Once, Tar's three elder brothers had tried to convince their father to allow them to attend school at Pueblo Chettro Ketl. They were not only rebuked but humiliated, so no one mentioned it again. From their home on the edge of White Mesa, where the cedar trees gave way to sage brush flats, the idea of Chaco took on a dream-like quality. And now, Tar was finally at its doorstep. He filled his lungs with air, felt the strength in his legs and quickened his pace until he ran full out.

For the last day-and-a-half he and his family had walked past small pueblos where tiny fields of corn and grain and melons checkered the land. Every bit of useable space was cultivated. There were still many workers in the fields harvesting the last of the crops. The closer they got to the city the more crowded the roadway became until the line snaked to the horizon. Wuti carried enormous loads of blankets, dresses and jewelry inside finely woven reed baskets atop their heads. Farmers carried chochmingwu, squash, maize and wild rice collected from the few remaining marshlands at the foothills of the mountains. Hunters watched over pelts of beaver carried by slaves. The solstices and equinoxes were the times to buy, sell, and trade goods. Troops of warriors, naked pilgrims, wanderers, merchants, clerics and even tribesman from the far north whose tribes had made war on the Anaa filled the roadway with more people than the combined number of souls Tar had seen in his life.

By dusk Chaco was filled and pilgrims kept arriving. From the south, men and wuti wearing fine clothing and jewelry of Toltec design rode in wagons pulled by slaves. From the west naked pilgrims straggled along carrying only water and medicine bags. Many had walked from the far reaches of Anaa influence without stopping; they honored The gods by pushing themselves to their limits and in doing so proved their devotion. All along the pathway, reaching east into the land of tall grass, were newly dug graves of the elderly and handicapped who had hoped to pass into the next life at Chaco. To the Anaa, dying in Chaco meant starting the new life on the pathway to heaven.

Every room at the pueblos was filled. Light from campfires and thousands of candles mixed with the smoke trapped in the narrow canyon and created an eerie glow which hung over the city. From the plateaus above, the view was spectacular, bonfires burned in the plazas and hundreds of colorfully dressed dancers, called Ankti, circled, swaying and jumping up and down. Campfires dotted the length of Galo Creek and hundreds of torches illuminated the seven grand pueblos. Only Fajada Butte was dark.

Allander, Gods and Judgement

Returning from his walk, Hopi reached the steep pathway into the city at the same time as a group of pilgrims. The pilgrims stopped at the cliff edge, awestruck by the fantastic sight below. Some were overcome and dropped to their knees and cried. Others raised their arms above their heads and prayed. Hopi was overcome too, but not for the same reasons as the pilgrims. He was overcome by their display of love and devotion to Anaa. These people are the heart of mankind and the soul of the land, he thought. They are the ones whose soft spots on the tops of their heads had not hardened. They listened for Tawa and when he spoke, they heard him.

Back in the city, Hopi quickly made his way to Fajada. Its imposing black outline stood against the celebration. It remained unlighted because the Kokopilau believed that darkness brought the moon and stars—the sources of mathematics and theory and logic—and from these came knowledge and light. To most of the simple and devoted Anaa the power of knowledge was a marvel beyond their understanding. They expected Tawa, the Creator, and the other Gods of Anaa to have all the answers, and the smartest thing they could do was to have faith.

Hopi paused at the base of the butte and cast his eye along its silhouette from bottom to top. At the crest, standing on the Cha'tima Rock, Allander peering down at him. A feeling of nakedness rushed over Hopi. Allander's silhouette melted into Fajada's and together became the blade of a knife.

Dutifully, Hopi climbed the well-worn foot stones. It was not a good omen that Allander stood on the Cha'tima Rock. Hopi had contemplated what punishment might befall him as he walked aimlessly in the desert. Death could not be ruled out and might well be forthcoming, but Hopi had not considered running away. If he had disgraced Anaa he was ready to pay. All afternoon he thought about the significance of the special treatment he had received since childhood. He was keenly aware that even superiors treated him with deference. He had been afforded the best of everything, tutors, food, clothing, and access to the most powerful and important men of all Anaa. Everything I have learned sits on the table, he thought, and will remain there if I am killed. Everything I have learned is nothing compared to what I'm destined to learn if I live.

As he climbed the steps, Hopi's Kaa spirit separated from his body as Hoodee had taught him years earlier. It floated a few feet above and looked down at him. The Kaa spirit marveled at Hopi's oxen-like beauty and strength. His wide shoulders and thin waist created a triangle of power, and his sinuous legs effortlessly propelled him up the steps to what—in all probability—would be his demise.

After Hoodee had taught him to separate his Kaa spirit, Hopi could perform the task at will. But sometimes, like right now, it happened without his knowledge or consent. He never told anyone about his ability to separate—at first assuming everyone possessed this gift—and then he realized that those who talked about it openly ended up as residents of Galo. The passing equinoxes told him that most abbotts and all Kokopilau could separate, but they referred to it rarely and then, in cryptic terms only with those who also possessed its power.

Hopi had trouble understanding why separating should be punished in one case and rewarded in another. In his way of thinking, separating did not necessarily better the world, an important criteria he used in evaluating worth of things. For him, this power sometimes complicated matters. Just two nights earlier while his body slept, his Kaa spirit floated over the rooftops where it spotted Amarna sneaking out of Galo and slipping into Chaco. She walked directly to his sleeping quarters but then mysteriously stopped, stood for a short time, and then hurriedly returned to Galo. Hopi was perplexed; what did this mean? What brought her here, and why had she turned back?

Hopi reached the first level of Fajada where records were stored and mathematicians hunched over equations. He realized his Kaa floated above him when it informed him that a man was hiding behind a rock in the shadows. Hopi stopped at the top of the stairway. He would not let on that he knew someone waited, but neither would he move forward. He would wait until the person came forth and showed himself. He did not have to wait long, the man quickly stepped into the starlight. It was Zuni.

"Greetings, brother. I've been waiting for you," Zuni said. He did not move to embrace Hopi as was his usual manner. "I thought it best to see you now before what will be, will be."

"Greetings to you my cherished brother, Zuni. I am very glad you are here. Thank you." Hopi replied.

The two men stood face to face but did not speak. Instead, they tweaked their heads from side to side and clucked in the way of Anaa.

"I have come from a secret council of the abbott leaders," Zuni finally said. "I was not invited but commanded to participate." he paused, overcome by tears and momentarily unable to continue. "It is known to all," he said finally. "They asked questions, but refused to accept my answers. I begged for forgiveness. Yours was not an act of heresy but of forgetfulness I told them."

"Thank you, my friend. There is no one I would rather have defend me than you. To have you speak on my behalf humbles me. But, my dear friend, it was not a mistake," Hopi admitted.

Zuni could not believe what he had heard. He swayed and then caught himself. "It was on purpose?"

"Yes, my friend. Not with ill intent, but I am responsible."

"But why?" Zuni cried out in anger.

Hopi was surprized by Zuni's response. They had disagreed about many things, but seldom had anger been expressed. For the first time, the difference between the two friends became a wall, and they stood on opposite sides looking at the other.

Just as Hopi was about to answer, Allander descended the stairway from above. He was cloaked in the ceremonial Gown of Darkness. Hopi and Zuni stood at attention, bowed, and greeted him in unison. Allander seemed small standing on the stairs above them, the oversized ceremonial gown was made many dynasties ago for a larger man, and it hung limply on the stairway above and behind him.

Allander turned and went back up the stairway without uttering a word. Hopi stepped forward, embraced Zuni, and followed. Hopi's Kaa spirit was no longer separate, it was time to stand together. When they reached the second level, Allander led Hopi through a simple stone doorway that opened into a giant circular room carved from the sandstone epochs ago. Few were allowed in this chamber and for Hopi to be admitted signified the importance of his transgression. Hopi hardly noticed the great works of art sculpted and chiseled into the walls: scenes of great battles, serpent-headed wuti swallowing men, and a long mural comprised of wisemen looking out into the room as though they anxiously awaited an overdue leader.

The Kokopilau Scrolls of Time were etched in strips along the length of the ceiling, starting with the first dynasty of Narmer and progressing to the present day. The floor was checkerboarded with exquisite black and red stone tiles. Sitting atop the black tiles were large, free-standing pyramid shaped stones, some the height of a man. Many of the pyramids had star charts and predictions sculpted into them, while others had faces of people looking out at the room from within many-faceted portals. These faces spoke of torment, like the images from Nedder.

Allander and Hopi walked around the perimeter of the room where Allander stopped at a table next to large fresco. The table held two challises filled with wine. Allander took the challises and offered one to Hopi. His posture was that of a general in the presence of his king. He offered a toast, "May the darkness surround you and lead you into the light of knowledge."

Allander watched Hopi drink before drinking himself. He then moved to a large fresco depicting Tell praying over the body of Mitanna and placed one hand on Tell's anguished face and the other on the forehead of Mitanna. The fresco slowly rose upward, revealing a hallway behind it. Allander beckoned Hopi to follow.

From the hallway they entered a simple round kiva not unlike those at the pueblos. Each seat around the kiva was occupied, and shouting, laughing and the cries of coyote filled the room. Allander and Hopi made their way down to the center of the kiva and the commotion died down. Hopi tried to avert his eyes but he wanted to see who was in this audience. He stole several quick glances and was surprised to see that the audience was comprised of life-sized sculptures of men and wuti. Each was painted in exquisite and minute detail and attired in the rich and beautiful robes of The gods. Some had heads of animals and all possessed an air of impeccability.

Standing next to Allander at the center of the kiva, Hopi did not dare look at the audience but instead unfocused his gaze. He could feel eyes rushing over him and he felt nauseated and dizzy. His head swam and everything seemed flat, without proportion.

"Oh wise leaders who have come to honor us in the last days of the Fourth World and our modern time," Allander began, "I bring forth one whose name is Hopi. He is humbled by your presence. Although his arrival was predicted by the Kokopilau, he stands before you tonight accused of a most grievous transgression. He awaits your consideration. He awaits you. Oh mighty ones, for he is your servant." Allander bowed and glanced at Hopi whose eyes were cast downward.

"Look at them! Each one of them." Allander ordered, his voice filled with scorn and mock anger. "These are your judges, the leaders of Anaa, the family of Anaa, a representative from every dynasty has assembled here. Hopi looked up and tried to focus but could not. The room and all its occupants were a blur, he felt himself gag and a great sickness exploded within him. He was very embarrassed and tried to regain his compose but could not.

The next thing Hopi knew was that Allander was standing over him, holding both of the challices that they drank from. A look of amazement masked Allander's face. They were not in the kiva but in the first great room next to the table where they had toasted. Hopi was laying on the checkerboard floor and Allander was no longer angry at him, instead he seemed strangely reverent. Allander placed the challices on the table and helped Hopi to his feet. Allander brushed red sand from Hopi's robe, then quickly went to a pyramid shaped obelisk nearby, where he knelt and prayed. Where did this sand come from, Hopi wondered? What has happened here? Why can I not remember?

"You must leave Chaco!" Allander stood and rushed to Hopi's side. "The gods have spoken, you must leave quickly before it's too late."

CHAPTER

SIX

Ramu

The equinox celebration began at dusk with the Promenade of the Maidens. All the unmarried, unspoiled wuti looking for husbands chugged single file, like a many legged insect, hands on the shoulders of the wuti in front, through the streets. At the same time, pueblo warriors painted in war-paint and displaying the black feathers of the raven and the white feathers of the swan danced in circles to the beat of drums. Young boys watched the braves, formed circles of their own and practiced in the side streets. Older boys followed the procession of the maidens, standing in one place until the parade passed, then running ahead and take up a new position.

At the pueblo courtyards jugglers, acrobats, magicians, singers and poets performed. The ceremonial wine ran freely and the fragrance of dried wild flowers and roasting antelope, deer and fowl filled the city. At the marketplace boisterous clansmen and gamblers gathered around bonfires to preview the runners of the race. They were a raucous group, they shouted, argued, exchanged insults, embraced, and made wagers.

After Tar and his family made an offering at Pueblo Chettro Ketl, he and his father made their way through the crowded streets to the marketplace where many of the Flute Clan awaited their arrival. Tar was quickly set upon by a group of drunken elders and dragged to the center of the circle where he was poked, appraised, and joked about by members of his own clan as well as anyone else who cared to join in. Tar was greatly insulted and looked to his father for a sign of how to respond, but Dol stood flat-footed, himself at a total loss. Dol felt embarrassment for his son, and angry at himself; how could he let such a foolish spectacle render him impotent against it?

Warriors from many clans were already in the circle. Winners of past races strutted like cocks, howled like wild animals, and occasionally kicked high into the air. These warriors stood face to face with the newcomers and made the grotesque faces of war, sometimes bellowing war whoops. This attempt at intimidation entertained and humored the crowd tremendously.

One large and very strong looking warrior, obviously a favorite of the crowd, decided he did not like the looks of Tar so he stood in his face, eyeball to eyeball, nose touching his nose. Tar did not like this at all, but felt that breaking off his gaze as hundreds of elders watched would be humiliating, so he stood his ground and glared back at his pompous opponent. When Tar could stand this torture no longer he took a half step back, planted his foot and shoved the warrior with all his might. The warrior reeled back, nearly losing his balance but he was not knocked from his feet. The crowd went wild. Tar had come to Chaco to run the great race, but it seemed inevitable now, he quickly concluded, that he would be forced to fight.

Instead of attacking, the warrior cracked a smile and it grew until it covered his handsome face. He strutted around the circle, hands raised above his head, and the crowd howled its approval. Was this a Chaco trick, Tar wondered? Would the warrior perform this kind of act before attacking him? The warrior milked the audience for all the praise it would give, then he walked to Tar and extended a hand of greeting. Tar stood ready to fight and did not grasp it. The crowd cheered again and the warrior looked into Tar's eyes and nodded as if to say, I was only playing, I will not attack, welcome to Chaco. Slowly, Tar reached out and took the warrior's hand. Another cheer exploded from the gathering. Tar would learn later that this warrior was the strongest and most respected brave in all of Chaco. He had won many races for the Antelope clan, and he was considered the only real contender for tomorrow's race. The warrior, Ramu, embraced Tar again and again as a true brother and member of the family of Anaa.

Tar and his father left the squabbling group and made their way back through the streets to the family encampment at the back of Pueblo Chettro Ketl. When Dol told the family of Tar's courage at the marketplace he was congratulated heartily by everyone for defending the honor of the Blue Flute clan. For the first time in Tar's short life the swell of pride enveloped him.

Later, when everyone slept, he laid on his back and listened to the music, the laughter, and the hum of conversation in the city. It reminded him of termites eating at the heart of a fallen tree. This place was so different, so exciting, so full of life. He was certain the simplicity of the forest and desert would be somehow lesser now. He relived cresting the top of a small ridge and the view of Chaco. His first sight was Galo, then the entire city unfolded below and he saw the giant pueblos rising from the valley floor, and the sprawling neighborhoods, and the marketplaces, and Fajada Butte. He could hardly believe his eyes. Thousands of people filled the street and at the center of it all was the jewel of Bonito. Tar would never forget this sight.

As he lay there, Tar also felt the press of responsibility. His self respect, that of his family, and that of the entire clan weighed upon him. The Bringer of Rain, was what the Flute Clan leaders called him at the marketplace. He would run for the clan, he would run with his heart and his victory or defeat —if it were destined to be—would be shared by all.

Ranal the Ruminator

Instead of watching the procession of men climbing the steep path into Galo to visit their favorite prostitute, Ranal sat sentry at the base of a large flat-topped boulder and watched Fajada Butte. Nothing escaped his observation. He saw Hopi and Zuni meet on the stairway, and saw Hopi and Allander disappear through a doorway on the second level.

Who will pass judgement on Hopi? Ranal asked himself again and again. He chanted, "Judgement! Judgement! Judgement!" Occasionally, his eyes darted the length of the canyon, stopping for an instant at each pueblo to assess the size of the crowd. "Who would have the honor of judgement,' he wondered? Would it be the Kokopilau astronomers, whose edicts were seldom challenged, or the clerics whose power had atrophied since the drought, or would it be the clan pueblos? Earlier in the day, he had observed the abbott leaders moving through the crowd and then one by one, disappearing into Pueblo Casa Rinconada. He also saw Pueblo del Arroyo warriors delivering Zuni to Rinconada.

Ranal was excited to have witnessed the abbotts gathering for a clandestine meeting. History was being made, he said to himself, therefore I must compose music for this history. This music will be so grand, he thought, they will honor my genius and end my exile. It had always been Ranal's practice to compose with his eyes closed, but Galo hoodlums had taken advantage of him during these creative periods. They had set him alight, and once, rolled him off an embankment. After that incident, Ranal swore he would get revenge, and when one of his tormentors suddenly fell ill and died, all were convinced Ranal had poisoned him with datura root. He had not been bothered since.

Ranal soon tired of thinking about his new composition and thought of Hopi instead. Hopi's crime not just warranted, but demanded a public spectacle, he thought to himself. A decree, he thought, a decree from The gods. Yes. But, whose Gods? He tilted his head back and stroked his hairless chin. Will it be Tawa, the Creator, the animal Gods of the clan pueblos, or will it be Narmer and Bask, The gods of the Kokopilau astronomers?

Talking aloud, Ranal continued. "Everyone banished to Galo was sent there to be held accountable for their crimes."

"Yes, that is right," he answered himself, "Therefore, there is no reason to think Hopi would be treated any differently."

"Right." He paused and a pained expression came over him. "But, when was the last time you saw anyone of Hopi's rank punished for anything?"

"Never! I have never heard of such a thing. Perhaps Special Ones do not make mistakes or they could not be Special Ones?" he wondered.

"Correct." Ranal was now angry and gesticulated wildly. "If that is correct, then, how could Hopi have made a mistake in the first place?"

"I do not know, why ask me?" he replied to himself. Another solution to his riddle came to him.

"Perhaps, it was not a mistake. Perhaps Hopi did not make the Cha'tima on purpose?"

Ranal was getting nowhere and became disgusted with his dialogue. He placed one hand on his hip and with the other he wagged a finger at the air and scolded Hopi, "You are such a fool!"

Ranal's reasoning tired him out. He decided to think about what torments Hopi might have to endure—public humiliation, stoning, or being thrown from the top of Fajada—a fitting climax to an equinox celebration! Or, perhaps an idea flowering so evil that even he could not imagine its gruesomeness until its devastating petals opened before his very eyes. Ranal had always been impressed with the inventiveness of Anaa punishment.

Though he loved Hopi, for Hopi had treated him with compassion, the law was the law! And, if Hopi is to be punished, why then, should I not enjoy it, he thought? In any case, Hopi certainly would not escape his due.

Escape

Ranal was surprised and angered when Hopi reappeared alone outside of Fajada's second level entryway. He never expected to see Hopi alive again. "You cannot escape justice!" he said out loud. When Hopi and Zuni bolted down the stairway together, Ranal jumped to his feet and shouted, "Stop them! Stop them! They are trying to escape!" No one listened to his plaintive call. Who listens to a talker of rubbish anyway? he asked himself. The only ones to take note were Hopi and Zuni who looked, but did not stop.

At the bottom of Fajada, Hopi and Zuni disappeared into the crowd. When they were safely hidden by the throng, Zuni grabbed Hopi and pulled him into an alleyway.

"What happened with Allander?" Zuni asked.

"I do not remember much right now," Hopi answered, disoriented.

"What do you mean you don't remember what happened?" Zuni asked incredulously.

"All I know is that I am confused. I am not certain what happened."

"Yes," Zuni agreed, "but think, try to remember. Try!"

As best he could, Hopi recounted everything that had happened. Had Zuni not known Hopi, he would not have believed the story he was told.

"But what of your punishment?" Zuni asked.

"I do not know."

"How will The gods and the people be paid?"

"This is for others to contemplate. All I know is that I must leave Chaco and leave now."

Zuni was quiet for a long time. None of this made sense to him. If Hopi was to go without punishment, the order of Anaa would be in jeopardy.

"I shall think of you often," Zuni finally said, "I will miss you." His words were hollow—sepulchers without bones. "Is there anything I can do for you?" As Zuni spoke he realized how empty his life would be without Hopi. They were opposites, yet Zuni had grown to respect and love the differences between them. Zuni found serenity in the knowledge that his life path was honorable and followed the great tradition of Anaa. At the same time, he respected Hopi for his questioning. Zuni wondered if Hopi was his counter-self. If day and night were reversed, he questioned, would I be as Hopi is? If I had come from the north as Hopi did, would I know exactly what is in his heart? Zuni did not fault Hopi for seeking his own answers where Zuni was guided by faith. He knew that Hopi was confused, as are all people who follow the Nanapala, the quest to Purify Oneself From Within.

"Yes." Hopi answered, "Pray for me from time to time." He paused, and then added, "Thank you."

"Thank you? For what?"

"For your friendship, and your kindness. I love you, dear friend."

Zuni could not speak. Hopi's words of love had unmasked a source of shame and he lowered his head. Just hours earlier, at the cleric council, Zuni reluctantly agreed that Hopi must be put to death for his crime. How is it possible that I can love Hopi and agree to his death at the same time?

"Where will you go?" he finally blurted out.

"I have no destination, but I must go."

"It is written?"

"I do not know." Hopi leaned hard against his friend and together they stood as one, the confused quester and the righteous servant of Anaa.

"I go because Allander said my judges have ordered it. I must take my leave." Hopi worried about Zuni, "Hours of prayer and repentance will be yours when the abbotts learn that you were with me."

"I will never forget you," Zuni said emotionally, "I hope one day we can be together again. I know in my heart that it will be." He paused and looked up and down the alley, "The abbotts have decided that you must join our ancestors on the other side."

Hopi did not speak. By warning him, Zuni had just violated the oath of silence sworn to the order of the clerics. Zuni was near the center of this crisis and Hopi worried that, in some way, he might be blamed for it.

"I expect you to call out for me," Zuni said very slowly.

"And you for me."

They clucked in the way of Anaa and embraced.

Zuni watched as Hopi disappeared into the darkness. He suddenly darted after Hopi but then stopped—Hopi was on his own now.

Instead of returning to his sleeping quarters and certain ambush, Hopi worked his way along the cliff line, past Fajada Butte and into some bushes. Dressed in the garments of the Kokopilau, he could be easily identified, so he stripped down, quickly making a loincloth from his garment's lining. When a group of drunken pilgrims staggered by, making their way to visit the prostitutes of Galo, he quietly joined their group. He could still be recognized, but the new moon had faded and the night was now full into itself. With luck he might be able to slip up the trail without being noticed.

He could not contemplate all that had happened now. All that mattered was that he escape. The clerics' decision to execute him made him angry. Hopi knew the heat of battle and had fought with other boys while a student. Once, when a great warrior saw him defeat several classmates at wrestling, he told Hopi, "If you had not been marked for leadership you would have been a great warrior." As Hopi moved slowly up the trail, his survival spirit surfaced. I will not surrender my life to anyone! I will fight!

The tortoiselike pace of the drunkards soon made him impatient, "Brothers," he said, "We have great need, can we not find haste?"

The group stopped, turned and looked at the new member of their party.

"Who might you be?" A large man asked, "We do not know you, naked pilgrim."

"You are lucky," another added, "that we do not tie and mount you." The group laughed and held their sides.

"Please, gentlemen," Hopi pleaded, "I apologize, it was not my motive to anger such honorable men, but just hurry us along." Hopi did not know it but these were not pilgrims, but seasoned warriors from the Eagle clan.

"I'll show you what anger is," the large warrior said, lunging forward and punching out at him. Hopi side-stepped and unleashed a kick, striking the man in the chest and sending him off the trail and down the steep hillside. Another warrior grabbed him from behind and two others stepped up to batter his face and body. Surprisingly, the punches had little effect, except to unleash a fury locked inside of Hopi that he had never known before. Dropping to his knees, he pulled the man behind him over his back and into the two men in front. All three went sprawling off the narrow pathway. He quickly got to his feet and dispatched the remaining foes with lightning punches and kicks delivered with the authority of a great warrior.

As he turned to escape he glanced up and saw a line of silhouettes standing on the ledge above. The last thing he wanted was to bring attention to himself, and now he had. I will not be taken prisoner, nor will I allow myself to be killed! Hopi ran up the trail but did not feel the ground below him. His muscles were tense and readied. A strange feeling of well-being rushed over him. The gods are with me, he thought. Nothing will stop me from going forth. When he reached the crest of the last hill, prepared to do battle, he was surprised to find himself alone. The onlookers had gone back to whatever they were doing, to them the altercation was just another festival fight. Hopi was disappointed, he would rather have faced his pursuers now. He scanned the path into Galo and the surrounding rock formations. He was alone and he gazed down on his beloved Chaco for one last time.

The city floated in soft light and smoke. Songs and laughter of the celebration echoed up to where he stood. Tears rose in his eyes, and he sensed he would never again see the city as it was now. Allander stood atop Fajada Butte and the Cha'tima. Hopi squared his shoulders, raising his left arm in the salute of the astronomers. Allander responded in kind. Hopi's nearly naked figure glowed in the eerie light, tall and strong, his head held high.

As Hopi stood with his back to the trail, a man who had been hiding behind a rock crept toward him. His movements were catlike and sure. He was cloaked in a black shroud and his eyes shone from under its hood. He moved in rounded leaps from one rock to another.

When the man came within striking distance, Hopi sensed danger and turned just as the man leapt forward, quickly raising something over his head that glinted in the starlight. Hopi stepped forward and with one lightning blow knocked the intruder head over heels backwards.

"It's me!" the man shouted, "It's me, your friend. Please! I mean you no harm."

Hopi kicked the figure lying in the dirt.

"Please. Please," the man pleaded, "I did not mean to harm you. It's me, Ranal, your friend."

Hopi paused, then reached down and grabbed the offender by the front of his gown and effortlessly lifted him up close to his face.

"If you value your life ruminator, never do that again," Hopi hissed. his eyes wild. Hopi held Ranal for a moment, then, lifted him over his head and turned to the cliff as though to throw him into the darkness. Allander watched from Fajada, Ranal pleaded for his life, and Hopi hesitated.

From behind him a wuti called out, "Please, please, do not do it!"

"Please, Hopi, please!" It was Amarna. She rushed toward him.

Hopi looked to Allander, but he did not move. He turned away from the cliff face to Amarna and then dropped Ranal to the path in front of him. Ranal cried out in pain as he landed, "I did not mean to hurt you," he said between gasps, "please spare my life."

Amarna and Hopi faced one another; Ranal sobbed in a heap between them. Without a word, Hopi stepped over Ranal and took Amarna into his arms. He picked her up and pressed his nakedness against her. Her feet hung in the air and she surrendered herself against his body, her face against his, her hands searched his back. She kissed his shoulder and ear.

Her kisses brought him out of his trance-like state and angered him, but instead of rebuking her, he gently placed her on the ground and stepped back. He was not embarrassed by his near-nakedness though men of his rank never let themselves be seen unadorned. He stood before her, proud and defiant. Amarna though humiliated by his rebuff, could not bring herself to look away; his beauty overwhelmed her embarrassment.

"Are you real, or an omen of the last days?" Hopi finally asked her. He was filled with confusion. "Are you here to deliver me to The gods or was I just dreaming?"

Amarna was puzzled and did not speak.

"Was I in your dream too, Hopi?" Ranal interrupted, still lying in a heap on the ground.

"Yes, Hopi answered, "but you were dead. I threw you off the cliff to join the rest of the garbage below."

Ranal feigned laughter, but Hopi was not to be trifled with, and his anger could not be hidden.

"I did not really want them to catch you," Ranal said, referring to his attempt to arouse someone when Hopi and Zuni left Fajada. "I really didn't . . . .No, it's true, I didn't."

"Shut up," Hopi demanded.

"But, I didn't. I really didn't." Getting to his feet Ranal pushed sand over the knife lying next to the path.

"May I go with you, Hopi?" Ranal enquired. "I will be your eyes and ears; no one will harm you if I go along. Where do you plan to go?"

"Be still," Amarna warned.

"I must be far into the desert by daybreak," Hopi said to Amarna, ignoring Ranal, "but please tell me now, are you from The gods?"

Again, Amarna did not know what to say. Hopi, too, was surprised by his words.

He could see Amarna was truly perplexed and went on, "I will not break my promise to you. I will return for you, and I will take you from this place and from what you've become. I promise I will return one day."

Amarna dropped her head and began to cry.

"She can't be saved," Ranal blurted out, "she's nothing more than a worthless whore."

"Enough!" Hopi demanded, taking Ranal by the nape of the neck and slapping him across the face. Ranal fell back to the pathway and his hand quickly found the hilt of the knife, but he did not move.

"Please take me with you," Amarna said bursting into tears and throwing her arms around him. "I will die without you. I love you."

"You are a child," Hopi said embracing her again. "I will return. The gods will keep you safe, I assure you. Please know that I too love you," he paused, "as a little sister." Amarna pulled away and slapped his face. "What kind of brother holds his sister the way you hold me?" She asked scornfully

"I am sorry."

"Please, please, forgive me," she said dropping to her knees and wrapping her arms around his legs. "I love you, Hopi. Please, take me with you."

"I must go," he said lifting her to her feet. He led her to a nearby rock where Ranal could not hear.

"Listen to what I say. If you are ever in need, seek out my friend, Zuni. He can be trusted and he will help you until I return." He took her into his arms again and he kissed her in a way he had never known before. Amarna pressed her bosoms into his chest and he was reminded of the judgement from The gods.

From the pathway a sound startled them, and they turned quickly to see what it was. Vanga dragged himself toward them.

"Go quickly," Vanga implored, "but do not leave by way of the trail, an assassin awaits you there."

"Thank you, my friend."

"Don't worry about Amarna," Vanga said, "no one will harm her. If they try, they will deal with me." Vanga looked at Ranal, his eyes flashed in the starlight. Ranal's hand wrapped around the hilt of the knife.

Brothers

Many hours later, Zuni stood in the doorway of his quarters smoking his ceremonial pipe. Above the serrated cliff horizon a giant wispy cloud turned pink and blue with morning. The air was clean and cool and a flock of cedar waxwings crossed the canyon above. How extraordinary, how infinitely puzzling everything was, he thought. Had his friend Hopi made the Cha'tima the outpouring of love he experienced from Hopi and Abbott Amhose might never have been manifested.

Zuni remembered the long walks he and Hopi made after doing their chores as boys living at Pueblo Bonito. They would amble aimlessly through the city or across the plateaus above, sometimes plunging into the desert. They talked about teachers and quizzed each other on their lessons. Zuni was amazed at how Hopi had the answers to the questions of faith, but how he did not seem to take any of it seriously. There had been times Zuni openly accused Hopi of lacking in belief, but Hopi would only laugh and they would end up wrestling. "If I truly lack faith," Hopi would say, "then you surely will win. The gods are with you." He joked if Zuni got the best of him, or in the midst of the struggle he would say, "your faith is failing you Zuni, for I will pin you to the ground." This infuriated Zuni who would grit his teeth and howl, but Hopi laughed all the harder.

At night, they lay awake in their beds and talked. Zuni tried to remember the face of his father and he cried for the mother he did not know. Hopi comforted him, sometimes leaving his bed to sit next to his friend and stroke his forehead. Hopi seldom spoke when Zuni talked of the time before he arrived at Bonito, and somehow his silence was a great comfort to Zuni. One night, when the winter brought snow, and water froze in their drinking bowls, Hopi sat up in bed and told his friend that he had had a vision. "One day," he said, "you will know the truth of your birth and this knowledge will unburden you." Zuni never forgot Hopi's words, and when he was tired or confused, they came back to give him strength and comfort.

Zuni would not sleep tonight. He stood in his doorway and faced the dawning of the new day.

CHAPTER SEVEN

The Race

Thousands of people were in the streets for the start of the Great Race. Tar's extended clan family including the Silver Flutes from the South, the Red Flutes from the West, and the Horizon Flutes from far-off Island Mountains lined the route. Before the race, runners paraded for the crowd, dashing from Bonito's entrance toward Fajada Butte and back again. Tar's clansman called out, "Tar the Rain-Bringer," or "Tar High Feet," as he raced by. They made the call of the clan, a high pitched nasal Hooowwwt. Tar heard these cheers but there was so much confusion that it was not until later, as he ran the lonely pathway, that the shouts of support came back to him. He recalled the exact words of his clansmen, the intonations, the resonance, and the hidden desperation.

The moment the Morning Cha'tima rang out through the city, the runners shot away from the starting line. The crowd went wild. From Bonito they sprinted to the base of Fajada, up the steep trail to Galo, and then north following a line of red colored cairns.

It was all Tar could do just to keep up with the pack. Tar hoped that once they were out of the city and on the expansive sagebrush plateau the pace would slacken, but it did not. The pack sprinted all morning and by late afternoon the race was still a demanding test of speed and endurance. Every time the lead changed, which was often, the pace quickened until the new leader tired and the next came forward.

Tar was not aware of the tradition that every runner would hold possession of the lead, even if only for a few steps so that each was guaranteed bragging rights to having led the race. If there could be only one winner, it was only fair that each participant be able to say that at one point he had held the lead. When old runners told of their youthful prowess, few left out the fact that long ago, when men were men, they had led the pack. The best storytellers always added some twist of fate or piece of bad luck which robbed them of their victory, and almost without exception they would tell of how they lost the race in the last few steps, after leading the entire way.

The sun greeted them on the second day, a string of runners stretching to the horizon. The powerful warrior Ramu and the long legged Tar ran one and two. Tar dogged Ramu all day keeping a few feet back. He was gaining confidence and believed he could match Ramu stride for stride. But Ramu was smart, he slowed to a crawl on the hills, ran hard on the straights and he did not stop for rest until he and Tar were a full half day ahead of the pack. Tar rested only as long as Ramu.

On the morning of the third day, when the sun was at the eastern horizon and the path turned into it, Ramu ducked into the shadow of an ancient cedar tree and quietly sat down. Seconds later, Tar ran by without noticing him sitting there in the blackness of the shade. Tar was transfixed on the path in front of him, he looked neither to the right nor the left. His eyes burned from lack of sleep and the harsh sunlight blinded him.

Tar reached the end of the long valley and suddenly realized Ramu's footprints no longer marked the path ahead of him. Oh God, I've taken the wrong trail, he said to himself. He stopped and searched the horizon behind him. "I've taken a wrong turn!" he shouted out loud. He quickly doubled back, following his own footprints. By the time he worked his way back across the long valley, Ramu was rested and waved to him as he approached. Ramu patted the ground next to him, an invitation for Tar to sit in the shade. Ramu knew Tar could not be outrun, but he could be out-maneuvered. The wily warrior had sent him on ahead knowing Tar's strategy was to stick close to him. Tar dropped heavily onto his back in the shade and did not say a word. Ramu turned away and smiled as though he was embarrassed. He laid back against the trunk of the tree, folded his arms and closed his eyes.

When the tree's shadow moved and the sun warmed him, Tar finally awakened. Ramu was gone, his footprints the only thing left behind to mock the inexperienced runner, as if to say, you are a fool if you think you can compete with the greatest of all Chaco warriors. The tree's shadow was now long and narrow. Tar had slept half the afternoon. His only hope was to run like Hedder and if he were lucky he would catch sight of Ramu before dark. If night fell with no sign of Ramu, his chance at winning was gone.

Ramu's pigeon toed footprints went back down the same path Tar had run earlier. Tar's humiliation was now doubled, he had been on the right path all along. Had I just waited at the far end of the valley instead of doubling back, Ramu would have arrived sooner or later, he scolded himself. "Damn!" There was nothing left to do but run for all his worth. He prayed. He visualized his father, his grandfather and his great grandfather running along side him. He was not alone, he told himself. The powerful family of the Flute are with me. The family's heart beats within my chest. The family's legs churn the ground beneath my feet. The family's lungs gasp for air. And, the family's honor hangs in the balance.

At the end of the valley Tar spotted Ramu just as he disappeared over a ridge into an ominous-looking group of white petrified sand dunes stretching northward. Again and again Tar caught sight of Ramu cresting a dune, rounding the base of another, or worming his way across the white sandstone expanse. By dusk, Tar had cut the distance to five hundred paces. They climbed a high ridge and ran along its crest, on either side were deep canyons where one misstep meant certain death. They went down into a canyon so narrow only one person could fit at a time. As darkness called the night hunters out of their hiding places, Tar was only twenty five paces back. He focused on the blue glow coming from Ramu's wide, sweaty back. For some reason Ramu's back glowed with an eerie light. This is strange, Tar thought, why does Ramu's back illuminate the rock walls as he runs past? Is this a sign that The gods favor Ramu and therefore make him glow, or do they smile on me, making Ramu glow so he can be followed? Tar prayed that each footfall would find a righteous place on the face of the earth.

Ramu was surprized when he spotted Tar behind him. He picked up his pace and hunkered to make himself more difficult to follow. When the opportunity arose he left the trail, running down dead-end canyons where he nimbly climbed the sandstone and then cut back to the main trail. Tar was right behind him. He would not be fooled again. He would not take his eyes off Ramu until the race was finished. Through the moonless night, in and out of canyons and under the pulsating black of the shadows; they ran. It was an honorable and graceful dance, up hills, through rivers, around and over ridges, and then up the foothills of the Grande Mountain to Verda.

At dawn they were only a few steps apart and in the midst of a beautiful cedar forest. It was cool and both runners were thankful for the mountain energy. From a plateau they descended the winding trail into Verda where the crowds waited for them. Nestled under a grand overhang in the canyon wall, Verda was a tight clump of well cared for pueblos stacked atop one another in a most unusual and unique way. The outpost's residents built their pueblos against the stone canyon wall because for ten dynasties the northern tribes of Chene and Crow had attacked them, stealing wuti, children and enslaving men. In the seventeenth dynasty, a wide faced wandering tribe known as the Utta, massacred the settlement and occupied Verda until the pueblo leaders of Chaco sent an army of warriors to rout them.

For the most part Verda's residents were members of the Eagle Clan and were not farmers. They hunted deer, lions, and black bear in the mountains. Verda produced great artists whose rugs and pottery possessed exquisite design and sold for many trade beads in Chaco.

Verda had remained quiet and peaceful until recently when the drought brought the return of roving bands of warriors—usually unsuccessful hunters from the north, too ashamed to return home empty handed so they raided Verda at night and carried off young wuti. Elders traveled to Chaco to plead for protection, but their requests fell like the stones from the cliffs at night. Chaco had its own problems and Verda had plenty of water and relied on the plentiful mountain game for food.

Cheers echoed up out of the canyon and Ramu and Tar hastened their pace. Down the steep trail, one foot disappearing below the other. Ramu and Tar did not stop to rest, except to drink greedily from jugs of water handed them by maidens. They were part of the equinox celebration of Verda and it was their responsibility to put on a good show by running for all they were worth. Down the trail, along a creek bed, up a steep embankment, under the protection of Verda's great overhang, and onto the steps of Pueblo Verda they ran. Standing on the steps, the Abbott of Verda, Hous, handed them each a bowl of water, and they started back up the trail. It was over as quickly as it had begun.

By mid-day the two began passing runners making their way to Verda. They now ran side by side and many times the good natured Ramu patted his new found brother on the back. The older warrior greatly admired his young counterpart. Tar was suspicious, he would not be tricked by Ramu's handsome smile and winning way. As they passed other runners, Ramu called out to them, saying, "We will greet you at the finish line." It was not dishonorable to finish the great race last, but humiliating to not finish at all. Once a follower of Anaa set out to reach a goal, he pursued it to completion. It was the way of Anaa.

CHAPTER EIGHT

Waxwings and a Coyote

By nightfall Hopi was far from Chaco. He ran along the trail all day, stopping only for a moment when an elderly couple asked directions to the city. His only destination was escape. He traveled north over the route that brought him to Chaco years ago. This path would lead him back, to his childhood home, to Grand Gulch.

Hopi's feet were cut and swollen, his stomach was empty, and his legs burned with pain. He was exhausted and cared little about what might happen to him alone in the desert. He did not think about the circumstances that brought him there, instead his mind was awash in images rippling from the center of his being—Amarna's face and the feeling of her body next to his—the pain of separation in Zuni's eyes—Allander standing like a ghost atop Fajada—and bits and pieces of his dreams: a funeral procession, the Goddess Amarna, his desire to touch her, an owl and a boy.

The trail north was wide, but the further he went the narrower it became, until it was nothing but a foot trail. His feet fell one after another in front of him. His arms swung mechanically. The fragrance of sagebrush and the open country filled his head. The further he went the more he noticed things around him—yellow and green moss on pebbles lying in the sand near the path, shooting star grass trembling in the soft breeze, great colonies of prickly pear cactus, and large barrel cactus whose once delicate red blooms were now blackened and impaled on its spines.

Hopi was entranced by everything he saw—the cedar trees far across the hills at the horizon, the sun burning a hole in the sky as the crows circled his progress. Tracks in the sand, mice, lizards, deer, coyotes and ringtailed cats—the natural world is woven together by all these footprints, he thought to himself.

Hopi did not stop at sunset, in fact, he did not notice the night had come and gone. The morning brought a new day. When he realized it was morning, he stopped and sang the Cha'tima. He left the path and disappeared into the land lying to the west. He traversed a wide sagebrush chaparral, cutting a circuitous path until the night again passed to morning. A flock of cedar waxwings paralleled his advance from the direction of Chaco, landing in waves on the tops of the sage. They argued, fought mock battles, and sang continuously. He followed their lead, his head bowed, occasionally glancing to the right or left. In the afternoon the waxwings departed, flying westward, leaving him to struggle over a high ridge on his own. Sorrow filled his soul when they disappeared.

By early evening Hopi stood on a table top of orange sandstone for the first time since his childhood. The sandstone's domes and spires, the hollowness underfoot, brought memories he had long forgotten. Bats appeared from their hiding places, swarming and darting playfully around his head. Coyotes called out from the distance, and replies came from nearby. An owl swooped down in front of him, taking a good long look, and showing Hopi its razor sharp talons.

At dawn of the third morning, Hopi wept. His tears were not just born from exhaustion or his current situation, but originated from a primal desire to survive. He had been taught to withhold his tears but now, with his new life surrounding him and even encouraging him, he had no reason to withhold any longer. The tears he had saved up for so many equinoxes came rushing forth. He did not stop to cry, but continued onward, mopping up tears with the back of his hands as he went.

He was home again. The redrocks, the blue-pink cliffs, the coral sand, the doorways possessed by shadow, and the rock out-croppings that looked like The gods as he approached, but evolved into animals as he hiked beyond them. He was alive.

Hopi stopped differentiating between his self, his path and his surroundings—everything became part of the whole. His vision was unfocused, myopic and transfixed. He found himself lying in the rocks, staring up at the sky. He heard the sound of his voice and saw his arms drawing circles in the air. He descended into canyons and climbed towering pinnacles. He crossed sand dunes so old they had become stone. He laughed aloud when he found a hidden spring where he bathed and drank. He slept without even knowing it and in a dream delirium, he hiked onward.

There he laid, tired unto death, extenuated, his pale face and bony hands corpse-like, and yet he listened to his friends, the land and the sky, the plants and the animals.

Nearby, the skeleton of a coyote lay scattered on the tabletop rock. The wind, rain and sun dried and polished its bones. The spirit of this coyote visited Hopi as he slept. It told him stories of the desert and sniffed around its skeleton, rearranging it. The coyote held no ill-feeling for the rabbit who led him to his demise. He told Hopi that his death had been a matter of playing out the cycle, but in this case, he had been the one to die, and offered his flesh to the world instead of to the rabbit.

Before the coyote left he told Hopi the real reason for his visit. "When a man shoots an arrow into the body of his prey but then cannot find the flesh, the prey is really a spirit and therefore cannot be found," he explained. After sniffing the air he added a warning, "Beware, a great power surrounds you. It might be a man, it could be an evil spirit, it may be a great coyote, but I believe it is God."

CHAPTER NINE

Istaqa

Hopi awoke to the sound of a flute. He sat up and turned to the left and then right. The music came from many directions at the same time, echoing through the surrounding canyons. Hopi could not tell where the music originated or how far it traveled to reach him. The flute sang a haunting melody.

Hopi laid back against the contoured stone and the music washed over him. This is very unusual music, he thought, I have never heard anything like it before. It possessed the integrity of an unbroken path and the truth of a child. The music echoed up and down the canyons and returning to the same hypnotic refrain. It evolved into a mantra, and Hopi was filled with both sorrow and joy. The music had so many hearts it was of other worlds. Suddenly, the music stopped and Hopi turned around quickly.

Behind him, on a large flat stone, sat a tall, gaunt man with a flute pressed to his full lips. He wore only a dirty loincloth and a coyote skin bonnet, the coyote's head peering out above his own. The face behind the flute came alive with goodwill when it realized Hopi had awakened.

"Good. You are awake," the man said. His voice was neither young nor old.

"Awake? Yes, am I?" Hopi asked.

The man laughed, propped his hands on the sandstone, did a somersault and came up sitting in the same spot. "Yes. You are awake. You have been very ill," the man told him. "I have been with you from the time of the crescent night until now, nearly half moon." He gestured to the sky, pointing his flute. The man lowered his head, and his bonnet made him look like a coyote with a man's body.

"Sick? How many days?" Hopi asked.

"You drank bad water." The man pointed with his flute to the spring nearby. "You nearly died. You had bad, bad fever. You had many demons, they entered your head and possessed you." The man leapt from the rock, danced in a circle and chanted in a language Hopi did not know.

"I fought with your demons," the man finally said rushing toward Hopi, and acting out a great battle. He threw himself to the ground as if wrestling an imaginary demon, then he leaped to his feet, raising the demon over his head and rushed to the edge of the sandstone where he cast the demon into the void.

"I drove them from you. It was a tremendous battle, and I was nearly killed." He strutted back and forth in front of Hopi, his chest thrown out and elbows pulled back. "I am a powerful medicine man and have defeated many foes" He then came very close to Hopi's face, thrust his jaw forward and and tilted his head back. He glared down past his flat nose and looked directly into Hopi's eyes and slowly said, "I saved your life, little boy."

Hopi bowed his head. "Thank you. I am grateful," he said, "but tell me, what was that music you played?"

"What . . . ?"

"I have never heard anything like it."

Without further encouragement the stranger played again. Hopi felt a kinship with this canyonman who reminded him of Narmer except for his wide face and flattened features. His skin was dark and the whites of his eyes were splotched red and yellow. It appeared as though he had been ill himself. When he finished playing, the man asked, "You be . . . ?"

"I am Hopi. And you?"

"Istaqa," the man answered. Bobbing his head back and forth, he threw Hopi a piece of dried meat from a leather pouch. "You must eat now or you will die."

Hopi ate the meat, its flavor sweet and savory like none he had ever tasted. Afterwards he fell back to sleep. When he awoke it was dark, and he was alone. Next to him he found a bowl of water and the pouch of meat. He consumed them before falling asleep again. In the morning, Hopi felt well enough to stand and walk. Istaqa had vanished.

When the sun stretched the shadows across the land toward the eastward hills, music from Istaqa's flute again floated through the canyons and across the redrock sandstone. Hopi climbed a ridge and spotted Istaqa at the horizon playing his flute, an antelope or small deer draped over his shoulder. Though Istaqa was thin he was very strong. He carried his kill effortlessly, and his gait was rhythmic and dancelike.

"It is very good to see you moving around," Istaqa said, arriving at the camp. He smiled widely and paused in front of Hopi to show off his kill. He was proud to bring back meat, but embarrassed by his own display of pride. Istaqa threw the carcass onto the sandstone. To Hopi's astonishment and horror, he recognized the gutted corpse to be human, without hands, feet or head. He leapt back, reeled and nearly threw up.

"She ain't too big," Istaqa said, ignoring Hopi and admiring his prey. Hopi could not speak, his gut wrenched, anger rising up inside.

"What is wrong?" Istaqa quickly asked, "You act like you have never eaten human flesh? She was full grown, not a child."

"Murderer!" Hopi blurted out.

Istaqa was confused. "The coyote is not a murderer. He kills to live, to survive. It is honorable."

"You call that honorable?" Hopi said, pointing to the carcass.

"My family does not murder when it kills to feed or protect the pride. No one murders when he kills to save his own skin." Istaqa pulled at the skin of his waist. "I am alone. I take only what I need.

"The gods of Anaa—I suspect your Gods—did not bring rain, the soil does not produce chochmingwu." Istaqa strutted back and forth with his hands on his hips. "You blame me because I eat. Should I lie down before your Gods and die?" He turned to Hopi, "You are a fool to come into the desert with nothing except your beliefs and your intolerance. You must be very strong. The creator of my world is honorable and accepts that what is, is. Besides," Istaqa said mockingly, "you are a hypocrite."

"I cannot condone what you have done! Do not expect it. Have you and your people stooped so low as to eat one of your own kind?" Hopi snapped back.

"She was not my kind. She was Anaa. I am the last of my tribe, I am one of a kind. She and her people would have eaten me if they'd had the chance."

"Anaa does not teach its people to eat the flesh of others. You cannot justify your actions as easily as that."

"I justify nothing. Only when man has food in his belly does justice have meaning. I leave justice to you and to the civilized Chaco." Istaqa paused, mumbled, shook his head, then continued, "We will see justice when your great city learns the lesson of starvation."

"Even if Chacoans suffer from starvation, I would not expect them to save themselves by eating the flesh of others. Starvation and torture cannot persuade one to compromise certain principles, even if they are threatened with death."

"Principles stronger than life! You are a fool. If there is no life there can be no principles." Istaqa replied. Addressing the carcass, he said, "Hopi here will not eat you, because of his principles. You have offered your life, and now he rejects you. He will not honor you by partaking of your flesh, you, who have given all." Istaqa stood with his hand raised to the heavens, "Like the rabbit who gives to the coyote; like day relinquishing itself to the night; or like the dream that rolls over and offers its soft underbelly to the skeptic, Hopi will sacrifice his own survival, so that he can die abiding the principles of Anaa." Istaqa dropped his arms and let his head hang, his coyote bonnet peering at Hopi, "It is a shame!"

"So," Hopi enquired, "would you kill and eat your mother to sate your hunger?"

"No. She is dead."

"If she were alive."

"No. I would kill you, and she and I would eat you."

"If it were just you and your mother and there was no food."

Talking again to the corpse, Istaqa said laughing, "Hopi is trying to catch me, he thinks he has set a trap for me. But he is wrong. It is I who have set the trap for him." Turning back to Hopi, he continued, "What you say is true. I could not eat my mother, and she could not eat me. And you, my self-righteous friend, believe you cannot eat anyone, friend or foe. You would die rather than eat human flesh, is that so?"

"Yes. It is so. It is a great sin."

"Too bad," Istaqa said petting his bonnet and acting as though he was speaking to it, "Poor Hopi has sinned. Dear Gods of Anaa, please forgive this unworthy wretch. He did not know what he was doing."

"What do you mean?"

"Oh nothing," Istaqa said pulling his stone knife and scraper from his loincloth and kneeling down to begin the chore of skinning and quartering the meat. "Oh nothing," he sang out again as he looked directly at the pouch of meat sitting at Hopi's side.

Hopi looked at the pouch and then to Istaqa who was holding both hands over his mouth to keep from laughing out loud.

"You mean . . . " Hopi cried out.

"Yes, my friend. It has been done."

Hopi could not speak, he felt anger and revulsion simultaneously. His legs and arms shook, his skin itched, and he felt sick to his stomach. He dropped to the ground, laid on his back, and stared up at the sky. Hopi heard Istaqa's sharp stone blade saw heavily through bone, and in his peripheral vision he could see Istaqa skinning the carcass with such skill that the skin came off in one large piece. Istaqa fastidiously laid the skin on the rock and straightened it out like it was a prized dressing gown.

"I wanted to bring her back alive," Istaqa said as though it was an afterthought, "but she fought too hard." He smiled, "It's too bad she fought so hard."

If I were not so weak, Hopi said to himself, I would kill you.

Istaqa hung his head and continued his gruesome task. "I know what you're thinking, no need to say it. I know," Istaqa said. "You think I am uncivilized, but what do you know anyway? I saved your life, risked being defeated by evil spirits so you could sit here in judgement of me."

Hopi did not speak.

Istaqa worked quickly and methodically deboning the meat from the legs, buttocks, chest and arms, and then cutting it all into thin long slices which he laid on the sandstone. He nibbled as he worked. He pulled out a large rock of salt from his pouch and rubbed it across each strip of meat. He gathered the bones and other waste and disappeared over a ridge. When he returned he busied himself slicing the skin into thin, long strips; some he used to fasten a wood frame dryer, on which he hung the meat.

After his revulsion subsided, Hopi watched Istaqa work. Istaqa was neither Anazasi nor Anaa. His wide features and flat face were of another race, one Hopi did not know. Twice a year, Mexican traders came to Chaco to barter for Chacoan turquoise. They brought silver, jewelry, dried fish and exotic birds to exchange. They were accompanied by slaves whom they treated inhumanely and to whom the Abbotts refused entry into the canyon. Thus, the slaves were left collared and tethered in Galo. Istaqa reminded Hopi of these slaves. Once, Hopi overheard a wealthy trader say that these men were a mixed-breed, a cross between humans and animals. He said they were hated by the rulers of Mexico and all would be annihilated.

When Istaqa finished, he built a fire under his meat drier and placed fresh sage on the coals. A blinding smoke snaked around the flesh while Istaqa bathed in the contaminated spring, meticulously cleansing his hands, face and hair. Afterwards he sat on a flat stone tending the fire and combing through his hair until it dried. He spoke to his coyote bonnet in low tones before firmly planting it on his head, securing it with a strap under his chin. He smoked his pipe. The deliberation of his movements was entertaining. Hopi concluded that Istaqa's agility belied his age.

Late that night when the owls returned to their roosts and Yaponcha roamed the canyon bottoms searching out the dawn, Hopi awakened to find Istaqa's face inches from his own. He was so startled he let out a scream, which, in turn, frightened Istaqa so badly he screamed and jumped backward, falling over himself as he went. Hopi leapt up and Istaqa ran off into what was left of the night.

Hopi remained awake. He imagined himself being skinned, cut up and dried, and he vowed not to sleep again, at least not until he was far away from this place and this strange man.

In the morning, Hopi noticed Istaqa watching from the nearby rocks. Istaqa made no attempt to hide, but when Hopi spotted him he quickly hunkered down or dove behind a rock. Hopi did not know what to make of these theatrics, but could not help but laugh. When Istaqa mimed an assailant strangling him, Hopi laughed so hard he doubled over holding his sides.

When Istaqa strolled nonchalantly back into the camp, Hopi's amusement had evaporated his anger.

"You scared the holy hell out of me last night," Istaqa said, checking the drying meat. He rushed toward Hopi, put his thumbs in his ears and waved his fingers back and forth.

"You are not only a murderer, but also a thief," Hopi said dryly.

"I am a thief?" Istaqa asked, shaking his head. "What did I steal?"

"Well," Hopi said, "I don't know what you were doing last night but you must have wanted to steal something from me."

"Control yourself," Istaqa said kindly. "I was not going to steal from you, since you have nothing to take. All of my people steal," he went on, "you cannot be from my family without stealing something occasionally. It is part of us. We will not deny it as you Anaa do. God made us thieves as he made you thieves. At least we admit it. We have honor, we do not lie. If I really wanted anything from you, I could have taken it when you were sick."

"That is true," Hopi said, confused. "But tell me, what other acts of savagery do your people honor with the truth?"

"Before the rest of my people disappeared, we copulated with animals." Istaqa raised his eyebrows, placed his hands on his hips and thrust his pelvis forward. "My father was a coyote. One day my father was hunting on the high desert when he came on the hogan of my mother. She was asleep, so he snuck in and put it to her. When my mother woke, my father was gone. He never came to her again, except in dreams and at first darkness— sometimes he and his clan would howl at the moon close to her encampment. That is how I know who my father is. My mother told me when she heard him howl. She also told me he would come to her in dreams. Coyotes come to people in their sleep." he said grinning, "I bet you already know that, don't you?"

CHAPTER

T E N

Faster, to the Finish Line

Ramu and Tar ran without thought of pain. Occasionally, each glanced down at the sacramental water in their bowls. Tar's legs had their own will, like the current of a fast moving stream. They flowed over the rocks and the sandy bottoms, snaking around the terrain and picking the path of least resistance. His eyes were the stream's surface, reflecting the clouds, the sky and the surrounding cliff tops.

Ramu had given up hope of outrunning his young competitor, but he was comforted knowing the race was not won until the first runner crossed the finish line. All he could do was to keep pace, his joints like those of a puppet, stiff, and mechanical. He could no longer stand straight, the dressing gown of old age descended about him. Ramu had known for a long time that this was his last race. He had earned the right to be the favorite of Anaa. He had honored his clan and had proven the Antelope's power, grace and integrity. Ramu was one of Anaa's greatest runners, and so this last race was the most important of all. This race was about impeccability, about the pursuit of knowledge, and about dancing with the spirit of the land.

When the sun caressed the world of Anaa on the sixth day, Tar delighted to see that he and Ramu were much closer to Chaco than he thought. They would enter the city by mid-day. A strange delirium enveloped him. He had run so long without sleep or food that his thoughts were muddled, and he had difficulty thinking. His vision blurred and at times he could see no further than Ramu running beside him.

The Great Race would end and Tar would have a new life. A warrior acquired a new life with every great struggle and every time he overcame impossible odds. Each new life wrapped the warrior and might be expended in battle or to survive arrows, wounds and illness. At the time of death, these acquired lives served as a carpet for the dance of knowledge. Tar felt himself being wrapped in new life for the first time. Now he had won the most important of all, the new life given when the boy becomes a man.

In just six days, Tar resolved the issue of his manhood and proved his worth to the Flute Clan. "All you have to do is place yourself at the point of action," his father had told him, "and you will accomplish great things." Tar now understood these words. He set out to race because he was fast and because of the clan. He never considered that the boy inside him might disappear during the ordeal, that he would be born into his manhood.

Tar's new eyes saw Ramu looking old this morning, the smooth stride and grace of this warrior, replaced by paralysis. Ramu did not bend his legs or knees. His feet were rounded like bows, taking up ground with his heels and displacing dirt with his toes. Ramu reminded him of an old water wuti at the outpost near his home. Tar felt sorry for Ramu and hoped when the race was completed, they might be friends.

As they neared Chaco, gamblers, warriors, and clansmen lined the pathway. Youngsters ran alongside the two leaders, matching step for step until they tired and dropped back. Ramu slowed down, and Tar was happy because of it. They would match step for step to the finish line. The race would end as it should, in an all out sprint between two great runners.

Near the city, warriors darted ahead of the runners to alert the population. From the cliff edge they sang out the war whoops of the Antelope and the Flute clans so the city would know who led the race. Their songs were echoed by warriors throughout the city and hundreds of voices rose up and shook the heavens. The song was the song of Anaa itself; the struggle for goodness, the search for spirit; it reached the place where the ancestor's bones vibrated Kaa.

The ancestors sang:

"As long as the summer wind rolls down the canyons
the song of Anaa will be there.
When the diamond stars explode into the blackness,
the song of Anaa will be there.
When the cool rain touches the back of the neck
the song of Anaa will be there."

Just as the runners reached the trail into the canyon, Ramu suddenly darted off. Tar could not believe his eyes, Ramu had tricked him again. His posture was erect and awesome, his legs were no longer stiff but ran smoothly, rhythmically. When Ramu reached the top of the trail, he raised his arms above his head and sang out the war whoop of the Antelope Clan.

From every neighborhood and every pueblo, the city responded. Cheers greeted the favorite son of the Anaa as he stood in the doorway of the champions once again.

Down the steep trail he flew, Tar right behind him. They ran fast in the straightaways and slowed at the switchbacks. Below them, the entire population of the city waited anxiously. The cheers deafened Tar and once again he felt out of his element. Why did I not take the lead when I had the chance, he asked himself? It will be impossible to pass Ramu on this narrow trail, I will have to keep close, and at the bottom, sprint ahead to the finish line. Ramu ran as though his life depended upon it. He tempted disaster, again and again. A misstep meant death. Back and forth across the cliffs they ran, and at every switchback, Ramu risked losing control and plummeting over the cliff's edge. Ramu ran on the carpet of lives he had won as a great warrior.

Tar fell far behind. He did not possess the courage of the greatest warrior of Anaa. Tar could not focus his on the honor of his family, his clan, or even on the promise of the rain. It was all he could do to keep his mind on the trail in front of him. Back and forth across the hillside they went. If Tar could not shorten Ramu's lead before they reached the bottom of the switchback, he would not be able to catch him on the straightaway to the finish line at Pueblo Bonito. For the last six days Tar's only goal was to keep pace with Ramu and to somehow overtake him near the end. It was too late now to strategize, and he knew it. His ability to run and his stamina were proven, but he had much to learn about projecting his thoughts to a victory.

Suddenly, Ramu stumbled, took several uneven steps, appeared to regain his balance and then went head over heels down the path and into some boulders. Tar could not believe this opportunity. "The gods are with me!" he shouted out loud. In an instant, Tar passed Ramu, who was bleeding from his forehead but who had already climbed back onto the path. At the moment Tar passed Ramu, their eyes met. Tar could not hide his joy, opportunity filled his face. To see the great Ramu, bloodied and in pain, was not pleasant, but Tar had a chance to win, and he was going to use it. Ramu struggled to clear his head. When he saw the look in Tar's eyes, the power of the pure light rushed through him and his strength was renewed. Run, rabbit run, he said to himself, for this warrior will skin your hide. Down they went, Tar, running for all he was worth and Ramu biting at his heels.

For the first time, Tar had the lead. Now it was his turn to pick the path and set the pace. He quickly counted the switchbacks between him and the bottom of the trail—there were four left. He could hear Ramu's feet slapping the stone pathway behind him. Ramu's breath made the hair on his neck stand straight up. Suddenly, Ramu tried to pass, first faking to the inside next to the hill, and then darting outside, testing the trail's edge. Instinctively, Tar moved to the inside before he saw Ramu on the outside. Had the trail been six inches wider, Ramu would have made it. In his peripheral vision, all Tar could see was Ramu's shoulders, his bloodied face and his long hair dripping with blood.

At the next switchback, Ramu touched Tar's back with his chest, as if to say, go faster or get out of the way. Tar opened his stride on the straightaway and counted three more hairpin turns below. The last part of the trail was the most dangerous, cut into the face of the white sandstone long ago, the ladder-like steps were now narrow and rounded. There would be no room for Ramu to pass here, Tar calculated. If Ramu did not pass him on the trail, Tar knew he would win the race. Ramu would have no chance on the straightaway. Six days of running proved that Tar was the faster sprinter. There was no telling what Ramu might try before they reached the bottom of the trail.

At the next switchback, Ramu bumped him again, almost tying up his legs. "Run, rabbit, Run!" Ramu shouted loudly. "Give the people what they want! Run! Run! Run!" Tar quickened his pace on the straightaway but as he slowed for the third turn he was unable to hold back and nearly lost control, only his youthful agility kept him from plunging off the trail. Ramu goads me, Tar thought frantically, but I must not make a mistake.

As they approached the last hairpin turn, Tar began to slow down. Ramu let out a blood curdling war whoop and leaped down the twenty-five-foot ledge to the trail below. A gasp went up in the crowd as thousands of onlookers watched. All Tar saw was Ramu's arms as they disappeared over the edge. By the time Tar made the final turn, a roar went up from the crowd and he knew Ramu had successfully made the jump. Ramu was in the lead again. It had been a spectacular jump, and Ramu had gauged it perfectly, landing on the trail below so that his momentum set him off in a dead run for the bottom.

From the bottom of the trail, the route to Bonito was a long, straight sprint with people lined up more than ten deep. The cheers were deafening and the spectators' faces were a mix of excitement, fear, hope and pain. The gamblers, who had bet on Ramu, looked stricken. They anxiously urged him on, some dropping to their knees and praying. Members of the Flute Clan called out Tar's name, and his father, Dol, screamed encouragement from the finish line.

When Tar reached the canyon bottom, Ramu was well ahead of him on the straightaway, but there was still a chance to catch him, so he summoned up the last of his energy and gave chase. Tar did not see or hear the spectators. It was as though he ran alone on the wide cedar plateau of his home. The ground was hard and level and his feet glided over its surface with ease. Ramu looked over his shoulder and staggered forward, blood gushing from his head. Tar gained quickly, but with each step the weight of responsibility grew. His arms were like winter corn stalks weighed down by the cold.

The faster Tar wanted to run, the slower it seemed he went. The finish line was in sight, and Ramu still weaved forward. He was no longer running but staggering. Tar was now only twenty steps behind. Then fifteen. Ten. He would catch Ramu and become the favorite of Chaco and of The gods. When he was only one step behind Ramu, Tar caught sight of his father. The look on Dol's face was anything but joyous and foretold what was to happen.

A cheer went out and both runners crossed the finish line. At the very last moment, Ramu thrust his chest forward and crossed the line first.

CHAPTER

ELEVEN

Keeping of History and the Massacre

Nearly a Sukop had passed since the last day of the equinox celebration and the streets of Chaco were still deserted. The pilgrims were home now, only those from Mexico or the far north would be on the path. Few people braved the streets—maintenance workers and those in need of food ventured out—and then with great trepidation. The appearance of tranquility belied the reality, just below the surface, anxiety and fear ran deep.

In the pueblo workshops, artisan-scribes worked at large tables, hunched over long, slabs of sandstone. At the direction of the Abbott himself, they etched with hammers and stone awls this dark chapter of Anaa history.

At Pueblo del Arroyo a section of sandstone—more than twenty feet— had been carved in the last week alone. But this was rejected by Abbott Ammett and destroyed. The discarded account told about an inventory of grain conducted during the equinox celebration, and about the decision to punish farmers for withholding crops. It recorded the crowd being incited to riot and of many people being killed.

At Pueblo Bonito a temporary scroll was being carved on thin soft sandstone. Abbott Amhose knew the events of the last quarter moon had importance that would not be recognized for many moons, and he kept Bonito's artisans busy with the framework while he thought about how to interpretate the final carving. Amhose had already decided that it would depict a tragedy stemming from the dubious judgement of Abbott Ammett, who, without consulting the Abbotts' Council, executed farmers found to have withheld corn and grain.

The Kokopilau astronomers, cross-referencing all events with their Book of Predictions, correlated the results with star charts, and accredited the tragedy and violent events of the equinox to an important decision made by Tawa. They would write no more of this dark episode.

The most revered of the independent historians, Bonar, had been in the city when the massacre took place and witnessed what had transpired. Bonar was neither of Anaa or Kokopilau descent, and this made him and his writings of special interest to intellectuals in the city. Bonar had been the city's most sought after artist until he suddenly gave up art and moved one day's trek from the city. He situated himself under an enormous cliff over-hang and began writing history.

Bonar would tell a story in pictures of the equinox tragedy as pro-phetic allegory. He told one of his apprentices, "It is important when dealing with such a sensitive subject as this, that your voice speak in poetic or even abstract terms, because if your history contradicts the Anaa's you may be imprisoned or even put to death."

Bonar gathered his apprentices around a waning campfire and told them what happened. "At dawn on the last day of equinox, a group of fifty warriors from del Arroyo marched to where the farmers were tethered. The city was quickly aroused to the thump of war drums and citizens and pilgrims alike flooded the streets to witness the warriors on their way to the stockade.

"The warriors from Arroyo marched in fighting gait, wearing yellow and red warpaint and crow feathers hanging from straps around their knees and elbows. They sang a fighting song, their voices low and hissing like a snake. Some possessed spears or axes, others carried the heavy wood-framed Impaler, lifting it from one shoulder, up over their heads, and back down to the other to the rhythm of the drums. They were impassive in the way of warriors, but their feathers and penises swayed back and forth like the pendulums of law and obedience. Thump, thump, thump." Bonar swayed from side to side.

"At first, the tethered farmers stood unconcerned, like summer pine-cones standing along the line of a bough. Like everyone else, the farmers were eager to see what was going to happen. But, as the scene unfolded and their fate became clear, a few farmers made desperate, and in some cases, nearly successful attempts to flee. But each man faced death alone." Bonar paused to wipe tears from his face, then continued.

"Their only crime was withholding food. The knowledge of this injus-tice was just too much for the farmers to confront, so they stumbled, trance-like to their deaths. At first, even the onlookers were paralyzed, unable or unwilling to believe what was happening.

"Many believed the warriors were only trying to frighten the farmers before releasing them. But as the first farmer was drawn onto the Impaler, strapped to its frame, legs spread wide apart, and then whoosh! It was done, a numbing sense of disbelief enveloped the crowd."

Bonar stood for a long time, unable to speak, overcome by emotion. "It was a gruesome and bloody spectacle," he finally began. "Again and again the Impaler pushed a sharpened ten foot pole, six inches in diameter, in the anus and out the top of the head of the farmers. Most of the time, the shank exited here," Bonar pointed to his neck, "because invariably the victim would throw his head from side to side or front to back as the shaft pushed through his body. The poles were then driven down into the soft sand where the victims hung like puppets.

"Within minutes of the first execution, the entire city and all its visitors had gathered. Most were still half drunk from the night before, and all were dumbfounded at what they witnessed. Devotees from the outlying communities hardest hit by the drought enjoyed the spectacle. It was the highlight of their visit." Bonar lowered his head in disgust and slowly shook it back and forth.

"Representatives from the pueblos and Fajada who witnessed the proceedings were horrified. Many of the victims were not followers of del Arroyo at all, but from the other pueblos, and Abbott Ammett had no authority to smite them down, no matter what their offense. There would be protests!" Bonar stood upright, raised his hand and showed his palm.

"I found out later that before the warriors had been sent to carry out Ammett's order, accountants from del Arroyo counted and recounted the grain and corn delivered from the outlying communities. When the final tally was recorded, less than half the storerooms were filled. Abbott Ammett was furious and, convinced of widespread theft, ordered his guard to take action. He decided to teach the thieving farmers a lesson with all the pilgrims of Anaa present. No one would forget what they witnessed.

"Without consulting the Council of pueblo Abbotts, Ammett ordered the death of all the farmers, even those whose infractions were minor. Chaco ended its bloodthirsty history long ago and has since been a bastion of civility and humanity. Seldom has Chaco used its might to such ends, choosing instead to obtain its objectives by diplomacy, negotiation and accommodation."

Bonar leaned forward, his face illuminated by the soft white coals in the firepit. He whispered, "Ammett was also infuriated by Hopi's escape from the edict of the pueblo Abbotts' Council. Ammett told his advisors he was convinced that retribution must follow Hopi's unforgivable sin, and, if he, Ammett, were forced to be party to a terrible situation, so be it! Ammett had another reason for wanting Hopi dead. He knew that one day Hopi would wield the power of Allander or the Abbott of Bonito or even worse, both. This concentration of power frightened Ammett, unless, of course, he himself controled it. Actually my children, Ammett was pleased that Hopi had missed the Cha'tima. Hopi cut his own throat, ahhhh yes. It was most satisfying to Ammett. The only problem was Hopi's escape and that he still lived. Ammett vowed to silence Hopi, one way or another.

"As to the bloody massacre, while the farmers were being executed, the families of the doomed men became hostile and attacked the warriors. The warriors' reaction was swift and bloody. They lunged into the center of the crowd and beat, stabbed and speared anyone in the way. They would not be stopped from fulfilling their orders. Again and again they thrust into the crowd, until the ground turned red with innocent blood.

"Out of nowhere tall, handsome Zuni appeared. He quickly worked his way to front of the melee and jumped between the warriors and the angry crowd. He tried to restore order, but a del Arroyo warrior came up behind him and struck him on the head with a battle axe. As Zuni fell to the ground, the crowd went wild. Pandemonium broke out, and the people rushed the del Arroyos. Among the crowd were warriors from Bonito and the other pueblos. They viciously attacked their del Arroyo brothers. Never have members of the warrior caste fought against one another other. Even some of del Arroyos could no longer tolerate the injustice and joined the crowd to quickly overpower and subdue their own clan brothers.

"Of all the events that morning," Bonar said quietly, "perhaps the most troubling was the fury of violence reaching from one end of the canyon to the other. Neighbors traded blows, long-standing feuds fired to action. A trader who had been duped into buying worthless turquoise cut the throat of the offender. A group of Outcasts seized the opportunity to run down the trail from Galo and loot the marketplace in the city. Husbands and wives escalated family arguments to mayhem, killing each other and their children. Supporters of Pueblo Tsin Kletsin stoned a group of Kokopilau. People were doused with cooking oil and set alight. Attempting to bring order in the city streets, the warriors of Tsin Kletsin and those of del Arroyo found themselves in a deadly confrontation. Wuti were raped and tortured, and for days after the incident, their bodies could be found—some, bound and gagged in the city's alley ways.

"The equinox massacre lasted less time than it takes to cook my evening meal of cornbread and desert rice." Bonar said sadly, "When the last axe felled its victim, the death count reached the hundreds. Most of the farmers had been executed, the warriors from del Arroyo were beaten, many beaten to death by the rioting crowd, and hundreds of people were injured. Pilgrims rushed to escape the city, and by nightfall had disappeared into the darkness of the desert.

"This is the first of many sad days in Chaco." Bonar concluded. "And inside the protected walls of the clan pueblos one person is being blamed. Who do you think that one person is?" he asked his students. No one uttered a word until an apprentice, meekly offered, "Ammett, my teacher?"

"No. It is Hopi who carries blame. He caused the tragedy by missing the sacred morning Cha'tima. It was written in stone long ago that when the Cha'tima was missed, the end had begun."

Bonar dismissed his students and retired to his work.

CHAPTER TWELVE

Kaa

In the days following the massacre, pueblo emissaries scurried about the canyon accompanied by contingents of warriors. Within the walls of the kivas, arguments raged for hours and negotiators had difficulty getting all the abbotts to agree on a time for a special meeting of the council to be held at the Grand Kiva at Bonito, by request of Abbott Amhose.

Chaco became an armed encampment, dignitaries required warrior escort where just days ago abbotts walked unprotected among the people. Guards were posted at every pueblo entrance—their placid demeanor belying the anger felt by many in the warrior caste. Never had they been ordered to attack their own people nor had they felt the sting of retribution at the peoples' own hands. Every day the warriors assembled in front of their pueblos, smoking, posturing and dancing to the beat of the drums. They formed lines and paraded off thump, thump, thump, through the city streets. Residents watched from doorsteps, fearing what might happen if the warrior groups again met face to face on the city's narrow streets.

For three days funeral processions snaked their way up the narrow paths from the city, across the fields, and into the desert where burial mounds had been prepared in advance. Trailing behind the deceased, mourners walked single file in descending order of importance and bewailed their loss. Wrapped in white muslin, the deceased went to the next world equipped with an assortment of goods—jars of food and drink, weapons, and treasured items of personal adornment.

For the Anaa the next world was one in a sequence of stops on the voyage of immortality, and would resemble the good life which they had experienced in this world. But, it would be better. An outcast who had lived without sin would become a citizen of good standing; a cleric might become an abbott—an abbott a demigod. A proper burial was a fitting capstone to a successful life and the burial mound, not merely its occupant, became the vital center of the being.

Anaa believed in a force given them by Tawa called Kaa—the mysterious cosmic double created alongside the living person at birth—living side by side throughout life, and surviving after death. Kaa was the spirit, and though no one could return from death, the Kaa lived at the burial mound making it the center and the home of the deceased and thusly, a magical spot for one's memory.

Confusion in the Warrior Caste

In one of the many alcoves along the canyon walls a temporary stockade was built to hold those accused of committing crimes during the massacre. Normally, each pueblo sat in judgement of members of its own clan, but since it was Abbott Ammett's unilateral decision to execute the farmers, the matter of jurisdiction was obscured. A special panel had to be chosen to dispense justice for all of the accused.

A cadre of warriors representing all seven pueblos marched through the city searching for those who took part in the riot and the crime spree that followed. It was very difficult for these warriors to carry out their orders. Many were forced to arrest their own brothers. The honor of the warrior caste was in jeopardy, and confusion reigned. Representatives from Pueblo Chetro Ketl insisted that all the warriors of Pueblo del Arroyo who took part in the executions and the attacks on the crowd, be arrested and punished. However, Pueblo del Arroyo wanted all the warriors from the other pueblos, those who intervened, detained and tried as criminals.

When the cadre started up the trail to Galo, Ranal took off running as fast as his feet would carry him. He could not bear the idea of being caught in the ugly cycle of retribution. Haven't I been punished enough? he asked himself. He made his way to the edge of the desert, hiding behind a large colony of briar bushes where he could quickly move into the desert if need be. From his vantage point he could see the warriors rounding up many people in Galo. Most of them were hiding in their huts and Ranal watched as the warriors pulled them out and tethered them together.

"Oh, oh, no, no!" he sang out as two warriors disappeared into his hut and reappeared with a bag containing rings and trade beads he had hidden there. When the massacre began, Ranal watched from Galo. While the commotion below turned bloody, he noticed the marketplace vendors had raced off to see what was happening, leaving their goods unattended. That was when the idea came to him. "If I had enough turquoise and trade beads," he muttered to himself, "I could buy my way to Mexico and live a life befitting a man of my talent."

Ranal now stood accused of inciting the outcasts to loot the market-place, but that was not entirely correct. He only had the idea first, and when he started down the path into Chaco, the others followed. He headed straight for the jewelry stands, pushing as many rings on his fingers as he could manage. He clasped bracelets around his wrists, heaped necklaces around his neck, and filled his pockets with trade beads. Nearby, farmers were being executed for nothing more than withholding a few handfuls of corn, but Ranal did not think of the consequences of his acts. The excitement and greed overwhelmed him. He burst into a cold sweat and yelled at imaginary conspirators. He frothed at the mouth. Had the authorities witnessed his outburst, they surely would have throttled him on the spot.

As Ranal watched the warriors searching Galo, he did not notice another group circle around behind Galo to catch anyone trying to escape. When he finally saw them, it was too late. Without thinking, he leapt into the briar patch and quickly wormed his way into the bushes. The warriors were amazed by this. Given the choice of being impaled or facing the briar patch, none would choose the latter. Only a great warrior or a crazy man would choose the slow and painful death that awaits there.

By the time the warriors got to the briar, Ranal had somehow snaked deep into the heart of the dense bushes with their long, sharp tines. The warriors were excited by Ranal's bid for sanctuary. The unpredictable and wily opponent challenged them and made them come alive. They stood in a half circle around the bushes and marveled at his predicament. They half-heartedly demanded he come out, thrusting their spears into the bramble at his silhouette. They knew Ranal was not going anywhere. Ranal's many wounds oozed blood and mixed with perspiration creating a viscous layer of gleaming fluid on the surface of his skin. His feet hung off the ground, his weight supported by hundreds of thorns. He could see the warriors' smiling faces, and they could see his torment. I have evaded you, he said to himself, there is no way to capture me here.

The warriors walked back and forth in front of the briar and talked loudly among themselves. They were in agreement that there was no way Ranal could survive. Some sat cross-legged and smoked pipes. They discussed ways to retrieve his body, or at least his head, as proof of his death. Ranal listened and smiled. Somehow, the tremendous pain of his wounds gave way to a numbness that spread slowly throughout his body until he could not feel a thing. Although he had not escaped, in his own mind he believed he had. In the tradition of Anaa it was far better to admit to a crime than be accused of one. The same thing was true for punishment. It was far better to throw yourself from the cliffs than to be thrown by others. Thusly, Ranal had robbed Anaa of the satisfaction of punishing him by doing it himself.

The warriors concluded there was no easy way to retrieve Ranal, and that if anyone wanted proof of his death they could be brought to the briar to see his rotting carcass. Just as they were preparing to leave, the leader of the group had an idea. Kneeling down he quickly made a fire; his fellow warriors raised their eyebrows and smiled approvingly. The drought had nearly killed the briar and it exploded in flame when the first spark lit. A wall of thick white-blue smoke hung in the limbs, slowly working its way to where Ranal lay on his bed of thorns. When he smelled the smoke and realized what was happening, he screamed out, "I have done your work. I have impaled myself, I promise I will die."

The warriors burst out in laughter, some held their sides.

When the heat grew near, Ranal remembered what he thought after looting the marketplace. Now that I am a rich man, he told himself then, I could very easily fall prey to scoundrels. The wisdom of his self admonishment had proven accurate. This group of scoundrels has forced me to impale myself and now will finish the job with fire. This is what happens to you when you are rich, he said to himself, shaking his head.

After looting the marketplace, Ranal buried one half of his booty near Galo, and kept the other half hidden in his room. He knew he would have to leave Chaco or face justice, but he languished, intoxicated by his new riches and sick with ruminations. He walked through Galo gloating over his good fortune and called out accusations to unseen conspirators. He tried to buy Amarna but she rebuffed him, so he offered her a beautiful butterfly necklace as a show of his good intentions. Amarna was struck by its colorful beads and amber stones, but refused, knowing where it had come from.

When the flames were nearly upon him, Ranal found himself twisting and squirming to get away from the heat. He attempted to retrace his path into the bushes, but the route had closed behind him. He pulled and squirmed and twisted and pushed and pulled himself until he was within the grasp of the warriors who watched, paralyzed by the grotesque sight of the fool's attempt to free himself. They hoped the flames would catch him, so they could witness his death by fire. But more importantly, they would experience the smell of death by burning. It was important for all warriors to know the smell of death, so they could avoided it themselves.

When the flames grew very near, Ranal collapsed and the leader of the warriors ordered two men to reach in and pull him to safety. The leader did not act to save Ranal because of compassion, but because if Ranal burned beyond recognition the question of his identity might be challenged—it was important to act with forethought. The warriors were disappointed at not seeing Ranal burn, but they offered him the respect of a fallen brother. They tied his hands and feet together and carried him back to the city slung below a long pole. His head fell toward the ground and repeatedly smacked against rocks along the trail into Chaco.

Dreams

While the warriors brought Ranal down the steep trail, Zuni lay unconscious in the room he shared with Hopi as a child at Pueblo Bonito. Every day before dawn, Abbott Amhose and the Ya Ya Witches kneeled beside his bed and prayed. They burned sage, painted with sand and offered chants, but still Zuni stood at the threshold of the next world. When Amhose and Allander heard the story of Zuni's bravery and the injustice that befell him, they protested directly to Abbott Ammett of del Arroyo. Ammett was unmoved, saying, "Zuni was injured because he interfered with the carrying out of my order."

CHAPTER

THIRTEEN

Warrior Way of Life

During the day people were back on the streets, but the city was unusually subdued. No one languished in the morning sun. Trips to Galo Creek for water or to the marketplace were done with dispatch and children were noticeably absent. Clansmen talked only among themselves. Devotees of Anaa gathered in their pueblo courtyards and prayed. The voice of the city had become a whisper. People waited to hear from the clerics, but their patience was rewarded with long suffering.

For the Kokopilau the weeks after the massacre were extremely difficult. For the first time in dynasties, the Kokopilau felt the hand of hatred and discrimination leveled against them. Many Kokopilau wives and young wuti had been raped, kidnapped and murdered. A group from Pueblo Kin Klizhen stoned its Kokopilau neighbors without provocation.

It was suspected by the Kokopilau and the pueblo leaders that a few warriors were responsible for the crime spree. This was particularly troubling because warriors were a proud and honorable caste. Even though they fought and died for Anaa without question, it was known that they lacked civility and did not abide by all the laws of Anaa. But the warriors had sacrificed much for Chaco. They protected the clans, defended Chaco against enemies, and each warrior had spent long, difficult separations away from his home. It was the warrior's solitude, which kept him strong and wild. In the warriors' mind, men were the highest order of life. Wuti fell in the group with bears, antelope, rabbits and other game animals. A warrior believed a man had the right to take any wuti, even if she was unwilling.

Grief was great within the warrior caste after the massacre. Most of the pueblo warriors had spent their youth together and to be pitted against one another or even their own clan was difficult to accept. The warriors' greatest strength was the friendship forged and galvanized in the heat of battle. They had always recognized the enemy, but now everything was turned upside down and they were confused. They were fearful of what the future might bring.

Ramu witnessed the massacre from afar. Afterwards, he retrieved his bedpack and bow and disappeared into the expansive wasteland east of the city. He traveled for days until he reached a deserted place he had found many equinoxes before. From his camp, the land dropped off in all directions and he was alone. He built a large fire and gazed into the flames. He danced with the wind and cried to the darkness. He prayed to all The gods he could name. At dawn, he slept under a rock outcropping until dusk, and then he began again.

Days and nights passed, but still it was impossible for him to escape the memory of what he had seen. He decided to starve the memory out, so he did not eat. When that did not work, he tried bleeding it out. He dug a deep hole, cut his wrist and let his blood flow into the hole. Bleeding helps, he told himself, but only for a short time. He bled himself again and again. If bleeding proves unsuccessful, he thought, I will force the memory from my head with a rock, or even burn my eyes out. Surely, he thought, that will do the trick.

After the conclusion of the Great Race, Ramu decided to give up the warrior life and become an Initiator. He wanted to spend the remainder of his days instructing young warriors. But now, all that had changed. He was a disgraced man. Ramu was of the Antelope clan and the Antelopes had precipitated the massacre. The crime of a warrior is the crime of the entire caste, and so Ramu carried the burden of those unspeakable acts. Something unexplainable happened during the equinox celebration, Ramu thought. I must understand all of this, but I am only a servant and cannot see it. It was inconceivable to Ramu that the integrity and honor of his caste and his clan could be soiled and subverted to such a low level.

CHAPTER FOURTEEN

Rain

Zuni leaned against the doorway in his small adobe hut. He listened to Yaponcha moving through the branches of the old cottonwood. Ever since regaining consciousness, he suffered painful headaches which robbed him of sleep. When he heard the first rustling of the leaves, he sat up on the edge of his bed, leaned heavily on the corner of his writing table and pulled himself up. His legs bowed, but he quickly steadied himself.

When Zuni left Bonito he had been cautioned by the Ya Ya Witches not to get up or move around, but earlier in the day he had ignored their advice and walked up the trail near Galo. Now he paid the price. His head swam and the sullenness and brooding which had consumed his waking hours gave way to a gut wrenching dizziness. Abbott Amhose wanted him to stay at Bonito and convalesce, but Zuni needed to be alone.

He stood in the middle of his room for a long time gathering strength to move to the doorway. He would not always have noticed the wind in the cottonwood tree at midday, he thought to himself. Yaponcha brushed his face with a cool breeze that carried the scent of rain. The whistling of the wind through the tree's branches rose and fell again and again, each time growing louder. It had been a long time since he listened to the leaves of the tree clacking like the laughter of many wuti.

From his doorway Zuni could see over the tops of the single story houses to the outline of Pueblo Bonito and the old cottonwood standing at its entrance. The street in front of his room was narrow, the houses were small and had doors that opened onto the street. In front of the houses sat benches, stools, cooking pots and empty water bowls. Before the massacre, families spent their days outside sitting on the benches, observing the activities of the neighborhood. Wuti wove beautiful fabrics on their looms, and they tended small children. Tradesman built furniture, and wash wuti carried heavy loads to and from nearby Galo creek. It was a clean and friendly neighborhood, and the people were proud of their families and especially of being the chosen citizens of Anaa.

Zuni often stood at his door when the city was silent and tried to imagined the streets in the far-off cities of the Toltec. Deep within, Zuni longed to travel, and sometimes, he gazed at the stars and wondered how they might appear in Mexico. He wondered if someone there was looking at the stars, right now. Do the Toltec have thoughts similar to mine? Do they think about the universe? Or, are their thoughts so impenetrable that I would not be able to pierce them with my simplicity?

Zuni also thought of Hopi. Could he be watching the sky this very instant? They had spent so many nights atop Fajada Butte counting the stars and drinking from the bowl of kinship that the night seemed incomplete without Hopi here, beside him. It would do no good to worry about Hopi, Zuni thought, he is in the hands of the fates.

To the north, a large dark cloud rolled over the head of the canyon and consumed the moonlight. It swallowed the heavenly bodies and took control of the sky. A tempest rumbled through the city. The cottonwood dipped and rolled, its clacking leaves bringing a smile to Zuni's face. He stepped into the street, turned into the wind and let it rush over him. It pulled his robe against his body, and his long hair danced. Cooking pots and wash buckets rolled end over end and chairs propped next to the doorstep overturned. The wind rushed through the streets and alleyways.

People peered out to see what the commotion was. They ran from their doorways and into the street. No one spoke, and the eeriness of the moment reminded Zuni of the gathering of clans outside the house of a wuti giving birth. Suddenly, a drop of rain landed on the back of Zuni's hand. Slowly, he brought his hand to his mouth and touched his tongue to the place. Rain! He glanced around. People stood in the street looking up. Men lifted their chests. Wuti and children let their blankets drop and faced the storm. The gods had not forsaken them. They were thankful and humbled.

The entire city was awakened by the storm's arrival. At first the rain mixed with the wind, then a curtain of water descend upon them. Many people retreated into doorways, but most stood in the street and let the rain wash over them. It was a joyous moment in Chaco. The gods had answered their prayers. Some laughed and sang and locked arms with their neighbors and danced, others stood quietly and sobbed, still others placed bowls and buckets in the street to catch the sweet liquid. Their patience had been rewarded and their faith restored. The waiting was over, and a wave of goodwill swept over the city.

Illusion

Earlier that day, when Zuni refused to stay in bed, he went up a trail near Galo to a rock outcropping where, as children, he and Hopi retreated to watch the city below. Zuni was very weak and sat motionless for a long time. Had he been well enough, he would have been invited to the Abbott's Council meeting at Bonito, but alas, he remained burdened with headaches and confusion. He did not have control of his equilibrium, and for the first time he suffered bouts of unhappiness.

Zuni was plagued by memories that came and went. Sometimes he retained these memories for an instant or two, but mostly, they came and then vanished. This unhappiness and these memories brought him to the plateau this day. Perhaps, he thought, this place will help me discover the source of these confounding mysteries. But it was no use—no matter how hard he tried or how much he wanted it.

At dusk, the sky turned gold and met the black horizon in magnificent contrast, and Zuni felt so much love for this place called Chaco that his heart swelled, and he thought he would burst.

"May I sit with you?" a voiced asked.

"Yes, yes you may," Zuni responded. He spoke without forethought, his mind had been far away.

Amarna stood before him and her companion, Vanga, pulled himself toward them. Amarna quickly sat down and followed Zuni's gaze toward the horizon. Although she did not know Zuni, she knew Hopi loved him, and she remembered what Hopi said to her when he left. She had watched Zuni for a long time and was unsure whether she should approach, but when the sky turned gold, she took it as a sign.

"I wonder if Hopi knows the beauty of this sunset?" Zuni said after a studied silence.

"Everyday we watch for him," Vanga said in a deep gravelly voice from the sagebrush a few feet away.

"He has promised to return," Amarna added.

"I hope for his return, too," Zuni remarked. "but I am fearful that if he returned, harm would befall him."

"He can take care of himself," Vanga said proudly.

"He has promised to return for me," Amarna said nonchalantly, without taking her eyes from the horizon. "Hopi is an honorable man. He is the most honorable man of Chaco. One day, people say, he will lead the Anaa, because his heart is pure and will never be corrupted by the illusion and the hypocrisy that plague us now."

"Illusion?" Zuni asked.

"Illusion!" she repeated emphatically, "It is a good life here in Chaco—for you, and for the others." Amarna nodded toward Chaco. "But you do not know the life of an outcast. We breathe the same air, we see the same sunset. But you," she said stiffly, "you and your precious religion do not understand our life in Galo, or the hardship you impose upon us. You are blinded by your self-righteousness. Your so-called generosity is an illusion and nothing more."

Amarna continued, "You hide truth behind the gown of religion. I know the faces of your honorable men. They visit me and then return to the city to kiss their children and to beat their wives. All of us here," she lifted an arm and gracefully motioned to Galo behind her, "are forced to beg for handouts and to listen to your contemptible lies. We see your greed, corruption and faithlessness. There are many two-hearts in Chaco."

"Everyday we sit here and await Hopi's return." Vanga said changing the subject and smiling at Amarna. He did not trust Zuni, and he worried that Amarna's words could make trouble. No one asked him to do it, but Vanga vowed to protect Amarna until Hopi's return, or until the death wagon came for him. He felt worthy for the first time since his accident. Amarna welcomed his concern, but she doubted what a cripple could really do if she needed help. Every night Vanga sat at her door, watchful that no one should beat or humiliate her. Amarna accepted the futile and sometimes embarrassing efforts of her bodyguard.

Zuni was not surprised by Amarna's opinion, but it was his nature to see the redeeming aspect of the exchange between Chaco and the outcasts. They had food, clothing and shelter. They could receive visitors, they could move about freely, going south to Mexico or north into the canyons; and, most importantly, many among them were lucky to still be alive. The abbotts could just as easily sentenced the hardened criminals to death, and, in fact, many in the city had been victimized by residents of Galo. He did not attempt to justify himself to Amarna. But he was surprised by Amarna's feelings about Hopi and wanted to learn more, "Do the people blame Hopi for missing the Cha'tima?" he enquired.

"The blind see more than the pueblo leaders," Amarna scoffed, "even here in Galo."

"They respect his courage," Vanga added, his voice so raspy as to be nearly undiscernible, "Many people listen to the leaders, and some blame Hopi, but people love Hopi, too. He is the spirit of us all, the best of us. If Tawa were alive, he would be Hopi." Vanga looked at the ground, to Zuni, and turned his gaze to the sunset, "When you and Hopi walk the streets we cannot but help see the power you share. When we see you together, we know The gods exist. The magic is strong."

Vanga quickly changed the subject. "We learn to question one who accuses, for accusation sometimes serves the thief." Vanga paused, eyebrows raised. He continued, "If a thief steals your robe while you sleep, the first thing he will do when he is caught is blame someone else."

"We know the word of God is sometimes only the word of a man," Amarna added angrily, "and I know the word of men to be worthless."

Zuni was taken aback. He was not aware that people saw in his friendship with Hopi such preposterous import; or that they thought of Hopi as being Tawa; or that the people looked upon the pueblo leaders as thieves! It was almost too much for him, and he struggled to contain his anger. Lamely, he asked, "Though you do not trust the leaders of Anaa, you trust Hopi?"

"Yes," Amarna said sitting up quickly, unable to hide her excitement. "He will come for me, and until he does, I will wait." She took a long look at Zuni who was watching a group of geese threading a path between the gold and black of the sunset. Inwardly Zuni was troubled, but outwardly, his handsome goodness, did not go unnoticed. "You ask if I trust Hopi," she said inquisitively, "Are you not his friend?"

Zuni, startled, sat up straight, his thoughts flashed, "Hopi constantly intrigues me. For the life of me I cannot figure him out. He and I are like opposite stars, each revolving around the other by some unexplainable power." Zuni took a long breath and for the first time looked directly at Amarna and Vanga, "Yes," he said emotionally, "I love Hopi. He is my brother."

Amarna fell into Zuni's arms and began to sob. Vanga pulled his massive hulk close and stroked her back gently.

"He will return for you." Vanga whispered over and over.

Zuni was surprised by Amarna's embrace, but did not question it further. Hopi had never told him about the young and beautiful Amarna, but then Hopi treated all the outcasts with dignity and helped everyone. Hopi, he concluded, was truly loved in Galo.

"I'm sorry," Amarna said through her sobs, "I am so afraid that he will not return, that something terrible will happen to him out there."

"He is much safer in the wilderness than he is here." Zuni said reassuring her, "If Hopi said he would return for you, he will return."

Amarna felt safe in Zuni's arms, the way she felt when Hopi held her before his departure. If Zuni was Hopi's friend then he would be hers, too. Soon, she would return to her shanty and the string of men who awaited her, but for now she would linger in the arms of her new friend until the golden sunset vanished.

Every night more men came for Amarna, and no matter how much her mother demanded, they paid willingly. In all of Chaco there was not a more beautiful and soughtafter child than Amarna. As her child-beauty blossomed, so did a cynicism which began to strangle her spirit from within. For her, Hopi was the essence of goodness and she hung tightly to the thought of him. If he does not return for me and soon, she told herself, I will set out by myself to find him.

CHAPTER FIFTEEN

The Last Cottonwood

Angry lightning marched toward Pueblo Bonito, cracking off pieces of sky and scorching the ground. The canyon trembled as shock waves bounced off the canyon walls. The rain came in waves, and Galo creek filled and overflowed its banks. On the plateaus, rain flooded over the sandstone cliffs, filling and clogging the drainage canyons with debris and creating waterfalls that spilled into the canyon below.

Lightning leaped across the sky and bolted into the city, sending even the bravest warriors running for cover. Zuni stood his ground. He marveled as the lightning touched down behind Bonito and silhouetted the structure in an intense ball of white. A tremendous explosion of thunder followed, and its concussion knocked Zuni off his feet. Another bolt followed, striking with pin-point accuracy atop the old cottonwood tree. Flames shot into the sky and the lightning lingered, tracing the great branches and searing the soul of the tree. The cottonwood shuddered, and one great appendage broke away. The branch tore slowly at first, but gained momentum and crashed down, collapsing Pueblo Bonito's outer wall. The cottonwood's trunk tore open exposing its core all the way to the ground.

The lightning spider-webbed again, sending short bursts of energy across the face of the sky. Zuni lay in the street looking up. Suddenly, a white bolt came straight at him. For a moment, time stood still. Memories washed over him, an unknown face, the shadows of his mother and his father, the massacre, the deserted city of Chaco. Then it was over. The images lingered only long enough to be acknowledged. The blade of lightning etched across the rain-soaked canyon walls illuminating hidden ghosts. Zuni had no time to fear the lightning's caress, nor did he experience it. Instead of touching him, it struck the Cha'tima Rock atop Fajada Butte. The Cha'tima stone exploded, bulleting hundreds of pieces of stone into the surrounding neighborhood. Its foundation collapsed and an entire section of the butte crashed down to the valley below.

Zuni struggled to his feet and began walking toward Bonito. Flames leaped skyward from the burning cottonwood. When he finally arrived, a large crowd had already congregated. Most stood holding themselves, while a group frantically searched for victims in the debris of Bonito's collapsed wall.

Inside Pueblo Bonito's grand kiva, Abbott Amhose knelt and prayed. The circular subterranean room was dark except for his candle which burned nearby. Amhose's candle could not hold back the darkness. He offered a prayer and bent over a small silver plate where he placed sage, dried datura root, ground badger, bear, mountain lion tooth, and the tail feather of an eagle. He danced in a large circle and chanted a song that echoed in the cavernous room. Tawa had not spoken to him for many days. This was not unusual, but recent events puzzled him. Amhose needed guidance, and he needed it now! If Tawa does not answer my prayer soon, he thought to himself, I will take his silence as his answer.

Amhose had been chosen Abbott of Bonito in part because of his patience. He would not be rushed into making decisions or forced into action without forethought—and never without a sign from The gods. Unlike other Abbotts of Bonito whose leadership had been inspirational—some had even been great warriors—Amhose's appeal was in the quiet wisdom and humanity with which he ruled. He was stalwart. He would not be moved when he knew he was correct, but he would not hesitate to change course in the pure light of truth and reason.

Amhose's rise to power was accomplished with little of his own energy expended. Very early in his life, he was earmarked by the leaders for the mantle of leadership. They saw the bliss and serenity that accompanied him and knew that he was the one. The invisible Kaa spirit of Amhose was intense, often his mere presence had a calming effect on those around him. It was widely believed that Amhose's aura could be seen by the naked eye. As to matters of religious doctrine and interpreting puzzling predictions, no one was his equal. While other pueblo leaders mixed and mingled, building alliances through good deeds, reciprocities, politics and business, Amhose spent his time studying and praying.

Amhose could hear the thunder outside, even within the thick walls of Bonito's ceremonial kiva. Since the drought began, he had sent many prayers to Tawa asking for rain. As the drought worsened, people flocked to Chaco for food and protection. At first, the drought gave the people a sense of unity in face of their crisis, but some were slowly losing heart. When people asked,

"What have we done to deserve this drought?" Amhose had no answer.

Outside, the rain fell in earnest, but Amhose continued praying. Since the massacre and the Abbott's Council, Amhose spent all his waking hours praying, desperately trying to make sense of the situation. The leadership council was in disarray. In the wake of the massacre the finger of blame pointed in many directions. There was tremendous anger against the warrior caste and distrust between pueblo clansmen. Pueblos closely aligned to Bonito and Anaa, Kin Kletso, Kin Klizhen and Chetro Ketl urged Amhose to force Amment to step down. They wanted to try him as a common criminal.

On the other hand, Amment at del Arroyo and his allies, the clan pueblos of Casa Rinconada and Tsin Kletsin, were very powerful. They refused to participate in a leadership kiva until the time was right for them. They were the largest and richest of all the pueblos. They controlled most of the storerooms of corn left in the city. And, they possessed the largest contingents of warriors.

Amhose lit another candle against the darkness and as he did, a soft but persistent knock came at the kiva's entryway. Amhose slowly got to his feet and went to the door. "I beg your forgiveness master," Juxz, Amhose's personal servant and old friend, pleaded, "Please come master, the rain has come! The rain is here! We are saved; our prayers have been answered."

C H A P T E R
S I X T E E N

Fear in the Outback

Dol and his family were among the last of the equinox visitors to make it home. On the evening of the fifth day they approached their homestead. It was nearly dark and everyone was very tired and wanted to rest, but instead of going straight to the house, Dol ordered the family into the nearby cedar forest while he investigated the pueblo and outlying storage huts. He sent Tar and his older brother, Sagg, onto the plateau to see if they could spot any sign of raiders who might have visited while the family was away.

Armed with bow and arrow, a war-ax tucked under his waist band, Dol crept across an open field to the house and went from one hut to the next searching every hiding place. When he was convinced that no one was lying in wait, he returned to where his family waited. Soon, Tar and Sagg found them and also reported finding no evidence of visitors. Only then, did Dol allow his family to enter their home.

They had planned to stop and visit with the family of Dol's wife, members of the Beaver clan, after the celebration. But Dol decided it was not a good time to stop, and instead the family walked without rest from before sunrise until long after dark. Dol seemed unusually distant and anxious. He had spoken very little since witnessing the massacre, except to organize his family so they could leave without delay. Dol drove them as though they were pack animals. He walked quickly and looked back over his shoulder constantly. When the others became tired, he became angry and beat them with a stick. "Pick up your pace or be left behind!" he warned.

Long after Tar's family was fast asleep—so far away from the grand city of Chaco—he lay awake, unable to sleep. He wondered what his father's peculiar behavior meant, but then his thoughts drifted back to the Great Race and to everything he experienced in Chaco. He, too, had seen the violence which tragically marred the celebration, but he would not let the bloodshed detract from his excitement and his love for the city. He could hear the city sounds in his ears, the music, the conversations, and the hum that was created by so many sounds mixed together. Closing his eyes he could see the clerics draped in pink, red and orange; the beautiful wuti adorned in feathers; the white washed pueblos; and the bonfires that set the cliffs alight.

Sooner or later all of Tar's recollections took him to the finish line of the Great Race. Though he learned much about will power and endurance from Ramu as they ran, it was Ramu's demeanor at the finish line which struck at his heart. When the cheer went out and Ramu had crossed the finish line first, Tar fell to the ground and sobbed. His tears were not so much for his loss, but for the disappointment he witnessed in the eyes of his clansmen. But, what happened next would forever live in his heart.

From where he lay at the finish line, forgotten by the joyous crowd, he was suddenly aware of a pair of bloody feet standing in front of him. At that moment, the crowd fell silent. When he looked up, Ramu looked deep into Tar's eyes and held out the container of ceremonial water he had carried from Verda. He slowly upturned it. It was empty. Leaning down, Ramu brushed the hair from Tar's face, then took Tar's water container from his hand. Ramu stood up and held it over his head. He turned in a complete circle so the crowd could see it and then he turned Tar's bowl upside down. A stream of water rushed out and spilled to the ground.

Tar was immediately set upon by the crowd who lifted him onto their shoulders and carried him off through the streets. When the call of the Flute Clan rang out, a tremendous groan was heard, especially from the gamblers, but it was quickly muted in the deafening cheer for Tar and the Flute Clan. Tar had won the Great Race of Chaco.

Having won the race again in his mind, Tar fell into a deep sleep. Sometime later he was awakened by a strange sound. He got to his feet and listened. It was the sound of someone struggling against a heavy load. He crept to his door and looked out. He saw a man, his father, carrying a heavy load away from the compound and in the direction of the forest. Tar could see candlelight coming from the corn storehouse. After a short time, his father reappeared, went back into the storehouse and came out carrying another load over his shoulder. Again, he disappeared into the darkness. Tar was confounded by his father's actions, but went back to bed and fell asleep again.

A Return to the Past

The morning after the storm, while the rest of the city slept, a group of

Kokopilau set out into the desert. They were returning to the honorable life of their ancestors. Walking single file, wearing long leather packs and carrying colorfully decorated staffs, the group made its way out of the canyon onto the southwestern trail. Their destination was the unending pathway known as Kuskuska: *to arrive and to depart simultaneously*. At the start of the Fourth World, Tawa's nephew, Sotnang, had given the Kokopilau a special calling, to be the teachers of all men. It was their duty to journey to the far corners of the land and seek out all who had the heart to learn.

After the violence had befallen them, a group of Kokopilau elders, led by Lama, the oldest and most venerable, decided it was time to leave Chaco. Their mission in the city had long since been accomplished, and they were obliged to move on. Lama told his followers that the study of the stars kept them in Chaco for this long and now it was time to leave.

"The passing of time has secured the relationship between the Anaa and the Kokopilau," Lama told all who would listen. "It has been good for all, but now, it is time for us to join our ancestors on the road to eternity."

The Kokopilau had not practiced the wandering life of their ancestors since the time of Bask, and many refused to leave. Allander would stay at Chaco. He decided there was little wisdom in walking away from the legacy of observations and knowledge of twenty-one dynasties. Besides, Allander knew only a few of his tribesman would follow Lama. His own work was at Fajada; it was his duty to offer leadership and protection for the people.

As the group of mostly elderly Kokopilau crested the last ridge above the city, they anxiously looked to the western horizon. Their destiny awaited there. Unfortunately, they could see little, the morning haze had obscured the land, and it appeared that parts of the horizon had fallen out, disappearing into a void. They stood on the ridgetop with their backs to the city when the Morning Cha'tima echoed up to them.

The Kokopilau turned for one last look at Chaco before disappearing into the sea of desert and broken rock. It pained them to leave, and it was painful for those who stayed behind. The Kokopilau of Chaco were the last of a great tribe, and many worried that the legacy of the Kokopilau would soon pass forever from existence.

CHAPTER

SEVENTEEN

Istaqa's Preposterous Tales

Hopi had stayed too long with Istaqa, and now it was time to leave. He said farewell, and set out northward. He had regained his strength and was anxious to see the redrock canyon of Grand Gulch once again. He carried a knapsack filled with dried corn, pine nuts and a small gourd of water given to him by Istaqa.

Hopi sang aloud as he started off, his spirits were high, bolstered by the great rain of a few nights earlier. He knew what the rain meant to his beloved Chaco. He and Istaqa spent the evening of the storm huddled next to a fire under the protection of an enormous sandstone cliff. The overhang extended so far that not a single drop of rain touched them. When Istaqa wasn't feeding the fire, he made whistles from snake grass, or soothed his feet with moss that he peeled away from the rocks at a dry water hole nearby. When Istaqa tired of making whistles, he wove shooting star grass into figurines of birds, coyotes and animals so outrageous Hopi doubted they ever existed. One thing Istaqa never tired of was telling stories.

Istaqa's stories were preposterous, but Hopi did not reject them. Istaqa told them with such conviction and child-like enthusiasm that Hopi became infected with the hope that they were true. As Istaqa spoke, his hands moved quickly, segmenting the long reeds of snake grass, pinching each segment near the center and lowering it to the fire to squint a look down its shaft. Some, he discarded immediately, others he blew through until they sang with a sweet wooden pitch. He then stacked them in a pile next to him.

According to Istaqa, he had once been chief of a tribe whose name he could not recall. He had ridden woolly buffalo and hunted giant bear with the Chene on a land so beautiful no one from Chaco would believe it existed. "That land was alive," he told Hopi, "the ground smoked and rumbled, hot water shot high into the sky from small holes in the ground, and the rivers ran red hot."

Istaqa once had several bitches and hundreds of whelps; he counted his fingers and toes again and again naming all of them. Some of his children, he explained, were dead, and others had disappeared while he was away hunting. "I am looking for them now," he told Hopi, "and I've heard they are looking for me." One of his wives and ten of his children were killed by a marauding wolfpack as he and his family walked the tall prairie grass east of the great mountains, at the foot of a river so wide it could not be crossed. Istaqa had spotted the wolves lurking behind a hill at sunset.

"The wolves," he said seriously, "were very thin, they had not eaten in weeks. They suffered from the slobbering fits. The pack was large," Istaqa said again counting on his fingers and toes, "maybe fifty males and twice the number of bitches and whelps." He shot a glance at Hopi whose face in the firelight was a plaster of belief. 'Ah, yes' he said to himself. "At nightfall, they wailed at the moon and circled up around us. I knew they would attack because their heads and tails hung low to the ground. They tightened their circle making it smaller and smaller until I could reach out and touch their yellow teeth."

Istaqa jumped to his feet and struck a defensive pose, feet wide apart, torso bent forward, arms and hands at shoulder height. His face was awash with a great horror. His eyes danced in the reflection of the campfire, his brow beaded with sweat. "I screamed, 'LEAVE US!'" he looked directly at Hopi as though he were one of the wolves.

Istaqa suddenly looked skyward, thrust his hands above his head and howled a perfect coyote cry. The veins in his neck, arms and chest pulsed to the surface. His howl went into the stormy night and rolled up the canyon. He howled again and again, each time attempting to muster the energy of the last, but each time becoming weaker until he could howl no more. He then collapsed in the sand next to Hopi and sobbed. Hopi had never witnessed such a scene.

Finally, Istaqa stopped crying. He sat up and began making snake grass whistles again.

Hopi patiently waited to hear end of the story, "He finally said, "what happened?"

"When?" Istaqa replied, screwing his hat back firmly on his head.

"To your family! The wolves!"

"Oh, that," Istaqa said, feigning nonchalance, "Oh, they closed in on us until I could smell death in their mouths. Have you ever smelled death in the mouth of a wolf?" Without waiting for an answer, he continued, "It is a horrible dank smell, but it gave me an idea. I filled my mouth with skunk oil I carried in a pouch on my belt," Istaqa now got to his knees and his hands went to an imaginary belt at his waist. His face contorted and he turned a grimace to Hopi, "and then I filled my mouth with the skunk oil and spit it at them, and I attacked them with my knife and drove them off."

Istaqa was proud of himself and his story.

"But, I thought you told me your family was killed?"

"Yes, yes, that's right. Yes, that's right. After driving the devils away I fell asleep because I was tired, and when I awoke the next morning I found that the curs had kidnapped my wife and all my children. I can't honestly say that they were killed, but I never saw them again."

Without hesitation, Istaqa launched into a story about how—after stubbing his toe on a stone while hunting on a high cliff—he tumbled down an embankment and over the edge of the cliff where he hung by one hand until he could hold on no longer.

"There was only one thing to do," he paused and bobbed his head at Hopi as if to invite the question. But Hopi failed to take the bait, and Istaqa answered anyway, "I let go and dropped to the bottom."

"And you weren't hurt?" Hopi asked, disinterested, but prodding Istaqa to the end of his story.

"No, not a bit. Imagine if it were you?" Istaqa shook his head back and forth as if to say, it's so unbelievable I don't blame you if you don't believe it. When Hopi did not respond, choosing rather to gaze out at the storm, Istaqa picked up another snake grass reed and lost himself making another whistle.

For days before departing Istaqa's camp, Hopi spent his time sitting on a worn sandstone pedestal whose slow disintegration made it appear to be melting. He looked across a long, wide valley to a high escarpment of vermillion cliffs running the length of the northern horizon. His family and his childhood home were somewhere atop that massive barrier. It would take at least a half moon to cross the valley, another several days to find a footpath to the cliff top, and then who knows how long to locate his home in Grand Gulch. Not once had his parents or his sister visited him in Chaco. Occasionally, visitors from the gulch sought him out with news of his family, but many equinoxes and solstices had passed since he had seen them. He he had been very young when he left, and he wondered if his family would even recognize him.

Many Paths and the Sand Dunes

Setting out at sunrise Hopi walked along a white sandstone tabletop which pointed straight to the escarpment. He was in particularly good spirits and enjoyed the early morning light. He liked the hollow sound of the rock under his feet and the sight of the beautiful Valley of The gods that lay before him. The valley could easily accommodate a thousand Chacos and was home to many gold and brown buttresses, spectacular pinnacles, a colony of migrating pink coral sand dunes, and a vast sagebrush chaparral.

This exotic world changed its face as Hopi moved through it, fascinating him and at the same time, giving him enormous comfort. There is no wrong path across this valley to the escarpment, he told himself. There are only different paths, all of which lead to the same place. Of course, he thought, there are paths that lead to dead ends or drop offs, but I will simply turn around and find another path. It seemed so simple to him.

By the time Hopi reached the place where the tabletop sandstone gave way to the valley of pink sand dunes, the afternoon sun made everything appear naked and hard. The lighthearted banter which eased his morning had abandoned him to this landscape of mazes.

From his vantage point the rounded tops of the fleshy pink dunes looked like young wuti's breasts. They created the illusion that one could step from nipple to nipple all the way to the other side. He started around the perimeter of the first dune, and before disappearing behind it he turned back to get a fix on his location. For an instant he thought he caught sight of someone far back on the sandstone. Shading his eyes he looked again, but no one was there.

Each footfall became more difficult than the one before it. The hot sand swallowed his feet to his knees. He worked around one dune, then another and another. His pace was torturously slow and difficult. He must keep heart, he told himself. He marched on further and further, hour after hour. The dunes were enormous, the smallest was twice the size of Bonito and impossible to climb. He felt small and was unable to see out of the dunes to gauge his progress. They all looked alike, and only the sun gave him direction.

When Hopi saw footprints in the sand ahead of him he first thought he had found a trail. His happiness was shortlived when he realized that the footprints were his own and he had been going in a circle. He drank what was left of his water and steeled himself against the will of the dunes. I will master you, he swore to himself. He set off again, this time trudging one hundred steps, resting, taking one hundred more steps, and resting again. He lifted his feet high as if to say to the dunes, try as you may I will not submit. Hopi continued this tedious pace until, to his astonishment, his own footprints lay ahead of him again. He laughed out loud and turned in a circle, screwing himself deeper into the sand as he turned.

Hopi missed Zuni, Amarna, Allander, Amhose and his life in the city. He wondered if this new land would offer new friends to replace those he left behind. He doubted it, though he had already met Istaqa, a man the likes of which he never knew existed. Strangely enough, he missed Istaqa, too. It was not easy for Hopi to brush aside Istaqa's ruminations. Somewhere within the paradox of his ridiculous stories, beyond the exaggerations and outlandish lies, was a solid wisdom. Such wisdom was the foundation of The Fourth World. But, Hopi could not deny Istaqa's criticism of Anaa. Istaqa had a way of attacking the contradictions of Anaa so that Hopi could not discount or defend them.

Hopi worried about the trouble he created for those he left behind. Zuni, he thought, could be blamed for helping me; Allander is left to support the Kokopilau against an angry pueblo council; Amhose will be blamed for encouraging me to seek the place of equanimity; and, Amarna lives in humiliation, waiting for my return. By missing the Cha'tima, I let them all down. Somehow, I must redeem myself and banish this mistake into the void.

The sun lay near the western horizon and every grain of sand glistened and sparkled with light. Hopi squinted and rubbed his eyes, wiping sand into them. Desperation swept over him, but he would not allow the dunes to see his weakness. His mouth was dry and his thirst consuming. He tried climbing a dune to get his bearings, but it was impossible. Darkness brought a cool wind and he shivered. The temperature dropped quickly and it became so cold, he buried himself in the sand for soothing warmth. The dunes would not fight him if he did not struggle. His desperation turned to resignation and he slept. In the middle of the night he awoke and started off again. To his surprise, the surface of the sand had hardened in the cold, and he could walk across it without sinking.

At dawn, Hopi left the dunes at the same place he had entered them. The dawn mingled with the pink dunes as Hopi reclined against a large boulder and admired their hypnotic beauty. Perhaps, he considered, I was mistaken to believe that all paths crossed the valley. This land is alive and the spirit of the dunes is strong. I am a fool to force my will upon it.

Because of my arrogance, he thought, I missed the Cha'tima, and I have created great hardship for many. I then drank from a spring knowing it might be poisoned, and I nearly died. Without Istaqa's help I would surely be dead. Now, I challenge the dunes without even considering their own will. Should I have obeyed the tenets of Anaa? Hopi was humbled and fell soundly asleep.

When he awoke Hopi thought he heard the sound of a flute carrying on the wind. It came to him through the hole on top of his head. He sat up but heard only the hungry cry of a pair of crows and nothing more. The sun had started its descent, but Hopi fought his inclination to get up and leave quickly, rather he sat quietly and meditated. His thoughts were of the land and of his insignificance. He would learn to be part of the land, not separate from it. He prayed to the greatness of the world and its power and then he got to his feet and looked at the valley with new eyes. "I will go north, around the dunes," he said aloud.

By nightfall, he reached a massive bronze sandstone buttress that climbed far into the sky. The dunes lay peacefully behind him. Hiking northward, Hopi discovered the dunes in that direction to be solid rock. Long ago they had given up their migration and had petrified into stone. He ran across their surface, climbed their crests, sang in their cleavages. He bid them a happy farewell from the other side. The lonely dunes seemed to welcome Hopi's caress. He would not discount the living earth beneath his feet again, and when the spirit of the buttress entered his body, and shook him to his core, Hopi acknowledged it. He tendered his introduction with respect and asked permission to stay the night.

For the next three days, Hopi methodically worked his way across countless small ridges—from buttress, to tower, to pinnacle—and across vast expanses of sagebrush and tablerock. Hidden within the valley were cottonwood oases where he replenished his water supply. The green of the cottonwood leaves contrasted the pink, gold, and copper of the valley, a pleasant invitation to rest. Many of these oases had once been occupied, and some had broken-down, burned-out houses. Although the oases were welcome sights along the way, some possessed evil and Hopi did not linger.

After twelve days, Hopi camped in the shadow of the massive vermillion cliffs. Tomorrow, he thought, I will camp at the foot of the escarpment, and I will look back on my journey and smile. Hopi spent the last light of day collecting desert rice and building a snare for rabbits. He had not eaten for days and was famished. As he grazed on rice and cactus blooms, he heard laughter and the sound of a flute.

CHACO

PART
TWO

CHAPTER

EIGHTEEN

Pow-wow

They were naked and painted white. The Owl, Antelope and Snake priests; the Flute Clan chiefs; the Horn leaders; the Fire, Eagle and Badger elders; the Ya-Ya witches; the pueblo abbotts; Allander, the Kokopilau Master; the Matriarchs; the virgin maidens; and lastly, the male servants. The Grand Kiva of Bonito hosted the most important pow-wow to be held in many generations.

The Abbott's Council pow-wow would begin when the spirit of each participant separated and co-mingled with the others—like waters of many rivers into an ocean. They fasted and meditated. They smoked the pipe, danced, prayed and shouted incantations. Two days. Three days. Four days. Many quietly left, unable to cleanse the hole on top of the head. Only the wisest sat upright, legs folded underneath, arms crossed and eyes closed.

After five days, Abbott Amhose stood slowly, and walked to the center of the kiva where he placed the headdress of the abbott leader on his head. The head-piece, of leather, turquoise, silver and hundreds of eagle feathers creating a peacock crown, flowed down Amhose's back to the ground. It was the chieftain's headdress, made in the First Dynasty for Narmer, the first abbott of Bonito. Amhose danced in a circle, stopping in front of each person long enough to hand them an eagle feather plucked from the headdress. When he finished he moved to the center of the room, bowed and spoke.

"It is told that after the Anaa arrived at the Fourth World and their migrations brought them to the canyon called Chaco, two scouts met a beautiful and brave eagle to which one asked, 'Have you lived here long, Great One?'

'Yes,' replied the Eagle, 'since the creation of this, the Fourth World.'

'We have traveled a long way to reach this new land,' said the Anaa spokesman, 'Will you permit us to live here with you?'

'Perhaps,' answered the Eagle, 'But I must test you first.' Drawing one of the arrows he was clasping in his claws, he ordered the two Anaa to step closer. To one he said, 'I am going to poke this arrow into your eyes. If you do not close them, you and all the people who follow may remain here.'

The eagle thrust the point of the arrow so close to the Anaa's eye it almost touched, but the Anaa did not blink. 'You show great strength,' he said. 'But the second test is much harder and I do not believe you will pass it.'

'We are ready for the second test,' said the Anaa.

The eagle pulled out a bow, cocked an arrow, and shot the first Anaa through the body. The Anaa, with the arrow sticking out one side of him, lifted his flute and began to play a sweet and tender melody.

'Well!' said theEagle, 'You have more power than I thought!' So he shot the other Anaa with a second arrow.

The two Anaas, both pierced with arrows, played their flutes still more tenderly and sweetly, making a soothing vibration and lifting up a spirit which healed their pierced bodies.'"

Amhose walked around the kiva, his gait lithe and unburdened.

"The eagle, of course, then gave the people permission to occupy the canyon, saying, 'As you have stood both tests you may use my feather any time you want to talk to our Mother Sun, the Creator Tawa, and the Star Gods, and I will deliver them to you because I am the conqueror of air and master of the heights. I am the only one, except the sacred Owl, who has the power of the heavens, for I represent the loftiness of the truth spirit and can deliver your prayers to The gods.'"

Amhose took a feather from the headdress for himself and placed it on the floor at the center of the kiva. The elders got up and one by one placed their eagle feathers with Amhose's. When they were finished, the circle of feathers created a vibrant wheel. Amhose summoned the virgin maidens to bring a bowl containing the spiritual flesh of Mother Earth—the fig shaped buttons of the Onowe plants. The virgins doused the torches and candles and sealed the door behind them.

In darkness, the bowl passed from one hand to the next. They chewed the bitter fruit and focused on the hole on the top of their heads. They sought the place of emergence. The kiva began to rotate gently around the axis of eagle feathers at the center of the room, at first imperceptibly, but accelerating until the elders vomited and were forced to protect their wills by placing their hands over the spot below the navel.

When the rotating stopped they were no longer in the kiva. They sat around a small campfire high atop an unfamiliar white and yellow sandstone mesa. The ground dropped off in all directions. The sky was filled with gray, orange and black smoke. Two towers, higher than any structure at Chaco, billowed white, oily smoke at the northern horizon. The smoke snakes rose into the sky where they married and became one. Together, they spread across the sky in the shape of a fat serpent. The elders did not move, they sat silently and looked on in wonder. Above the smoke, tiny silver insects crossed the sky, accompanied by a booming noise like the river of the canyons. From the tail of the insects came a thin trail of desert cotton which hung in the smokey air after the silver insects had disappeared.

The land below the mesa was barren and dead. The elders sat quietly, astounded at what they witnessed. Suddenly, at the center of the fire an eagle appeared in the flames. "I come to you with a heavy heart," the firey eagle said, "Tawa has sent me. I want you to look around. One day, a few of your people will find their way here. This will be their land—the land of the devoted. Your people will be surrounded here. Men with white faces will be will trap them here. The sky will poison them. The waters will be impure. Great putrefied wounds will cover Earth Mother. She will be laid open and will cry out loud. Your people will be slaves. They will be forced to beg for what is rightfully theirs."

The eagle continued, "Look deep into the Legend of the Creation, and find out what is there." It fanned its wings until it suddenly disappeared into the flames.

After a long silence, Amhose spoke, "Once we traveled, and for many generations we migrated over the land taking what we needed and leaving the rest. We shared the gifts of Mother Earth. We hunted the antelope, gathered the seeds and nuts, fished and followed the curve of the mountains' breasts and the desert's flat stomach—our home was everywhere and our journey was honorable. That was at the beginning of the Fourth World, the time of Nuptu, the purple dawn of Anaa and Chaco. Our life was simple then, we did not count the grain, or the days, or the stars above. We did not build; we did not covet, cheat or kill. We were of one flesh and wanted only to run and play, to celebrate our families and to copulate.

"Then, we came to Chaco. It was magic. The forest grew from the Blue Mountains to our doorstep. The game was plentiful and offered its flesh in friendship. The seed and nut bearers were rich and profuse, and Galo Creek ran deep with colorful fish. At Chaco, we learned to plant Chochmingwu, the flesh of the Mother, and Narmer and Bask built Bonito. We wearied of traveling and Chaco and Anaa showed us how to live in one place.

"We were God-makers.

"Ours has been a history of riches and plenty. We have grown large, our families reach to the far corners of our mother's womb. We have been joined by our brothers, the Kokopilau, who landed on the Fourth World in reed boats and who follow their own search. But others came in the Back Door over the ice, and they sometimes frustrate and castrate us. The tribes of the North follow the buffalo and make its journey their life. To the south, our brothers, the Toltec, found their place and have built a great civilization. And, in Chaco the spiritual line—from Tawa, The Creator, to Narmer and to us, who sit here today—has not been broken.

"We have had many leaders, and as the sun passes to the underworld and returns to us each morning, we have obeyed. It is the way of Tawa and of Anaa. From this place, where the future resides, we will sing to the hearts of our children as our ancestors sang to us." Amhose paused for a long time before continuing.

"We have come here to discuss the taking of life on the morning of the last day of the solstice celebration . . . ."

"There are many here who share the burden of blame!" Ammett interrupted loudly, jumping to his feet, "I, for one, look around and see everywhere the faces of the implicated. Everyone gathered here is responsible for what happened."

"How is this so?" Allander asked rocking back on his haunches. He was the only Kokopilau present.

"You!" Ammett hissed, "You and your astronomers and predictions should not even be here. It was a bad day for Anaa when the Kokopilau came to Chaco. If anyone is to blame, it is you!"

"But, my brother," Amhose interrupted, "How can you say this? The Kokopilau have given us much. Tawa sent them. Together the Anaa and Kokopilau have traveled far and the rewards have been great."

"Yes," Ammett sneered, "They have given us much—predictions of rain which never came true. For this, we give them corn and grain. We waited for the rain, but they now say it is out of their control. They are shameless curs groveling at our feet and sucking from us the Alo and the Chochmingwu."

"So," Allander said coolly, "you blame the Kokopilau, and Amhose and others. Is there anyone else you should mention?"

"Indeed!" Ammett said, "There are the lying, cheating farmers who eat when we at del Arroyo starve. There are the outcasts who we support and who occupy our most valuable lands. There are students who better themselves at our expense and who end up looking down on us. There are the old, the lazy, the wicked, and all who eat while we go without."

Allander responded, "You stand on knowledge of many things, Ammett, including where to place blame. But, I wonder, is it on the stone of truth and knowledge you stand, or, as I suspect, on the pile of dung your mouth spews forth. The flatulence of your empty heart and mind covers the truth with its self-serving stench." The gathering erupted in laughter, even the clan leaders allied with Ammett rocked back and forth, grasping their sides and slapping their knees in hilarity.

Ammett jumped from where he stood and glanced involuntarily at his feet as though he might have stepped in a pile of dung. This brought an even greater round of laughter.

"It would be easier," Allander continued, "if we all had your wisdom and foresight, Ammett. We could stand knee deep in our understanding and blame one another in an unbroken circle. Unfortunately, my honorable brothers, not even wise Ammett can summon Tawa's rain." Allander stroked his chin, "Or, can it be that Ammett knows something we do not? Perhaps he believes he speaks for Tawa? Ammett delivers a death sentence for the unspeakable crime of hunger. He passes judgement without even consulting the Abbott's coun ... "

"No!" Amhose interrupted, his voice filled with sorrow, "Ammett cannot be blamed for our own greed or hatred, not even for spilling the blood of the innocent. He cannot bring back the forest—our axes are too sharp. I am sad because," Amhose looked at Ammett, "because today we use our axes to fell one another—without benefit of reason, justice, or belief."

Ammett smirked, "I see the smoke of a great and glorious fire, but I see no flame, only old wuti fanning a would-be fire with their skirts."

Turning in place, Ammett fanned an imaginary fire and clucked, "It takes little courage to send smoke signals, but it takes great leadership to feed the Sacred Fire of Life. We abdicate our responsibility. If we do not teach, we cannot punish those who do not learn. If we do not enforce the law, who is to blame when the law is broken?"

Ammett bowed, hands clasped. "Our forefathers understood the Sacred Fire of Life. An animal dies in the desert, and plants grow from its body. Rodents eat the plants. Predators eat the rodents. The people consume the flesh of the predators. The circle is complete. But, the forefathers' saw that the Sacred Fire of Life was all consuming, the fire of life must be fed. They understood the price of sacrifice. All living creatures sacrifice themselves to the consuming fire of life. Tawa created us, the people of the Fourth World, and he created the eternal fire. We honor the spirits of those we consume. We pray for them.

"Today, the flame of the people grows dim. There are too many mouths, and too little sacrifice. We feed the outcasts, we allow our wuti to marry non-Anaa. We are satisfied with trinkets and with bird-feathers. We allow our students to dictate to the pueblos. And how do these so-called, Special Ones, thank us? They question our judgement and wisdom."

Ammett continued, "There is one from Bonito who neglected to make the sacred Morning Cha'tima and brought all the wrath of Tawa and The gods down upon us." A grumble of acknowledgement rattled through the kiva. "It is written that if a sacred law is broken, all will suffer, not just the offender. So, when the sacred Morning Cha'tima was forgotten, it cost the lives of many citizens. To make matters worse, the offender, a Special One from Bonito and Fajada, goes unpunished. Today, he walks free in the desert! He walks free because he was encouraged to leave Chaco before he could be punished. And we cower at every utterance of the astronomers atop Fajada but, I, for one, believe they have their heads buried . . . " he paused and smiled at the circle of faces, "buried deep within the blackness of the stars. But, worse, the astronomers themselves helped the guilty one to escape."

Allander waited for Ammett to finish before responding, courteously observing the custom of Anaa before he spoke, "Our honorable Ammett speaks of justice. But does a man of justice order warriors to execute farmers for simple crimes? Does he allow the murder of innocent bystanders by his own guard to go unpunished? There has been no punishment for Ammett's warriors because this bloodshed was no accident. It was Ammett, not The gods who punished the citizens of Chaco." Again a murmur swept through the gathering. "My fellow council members would agree that a man of justice tempers his anger with prudence. A man of justice does not blame another for his own mistakes, but stands and accepts responsibility. A man of justice, prays for guidance and does not force his will upon others. A man of justice seeks the council of his peers and of his betters—and in Ammett's case, there are many. No, my honorable council," Allander implored, "a man of justice does not fight for justice by raining injustice upon the innocent.

"I would not presume," Allander continued, "to counsel the Abbott of del Arroyo in meting out justice to the Anaa. The abbotts confer with The gods and with their fellow counsel members on matters of justice. Allander of Fajada confers with the Book of Predictions and the configuration of The gods in the palette of the night sky. For the Abbott of del Arroyo to suggest that Allander of Fajada would take action on any important issue without first consulting these greater powers, suggests that perhaps the Abbott, himself, acts upon such whim."

"So," Amhose enquired of Allander, "You consulted the Book of

Predictions before sending Hopi into the desert?"

"Yes. I also summoned Hopi to stand before The gods. I sought guidance in the Chamber of Stars within the walls of Fajada."

The council of elders gasped. If this were true, the implications were monumental. Even Ammett, who hated the Kokopilau, knew that Allander would not lie about this.

"You solicited The gods," Amhose asked wringing his hands together, "And they came?"

"They did."

"When?" Amhose enquired.

"At dusk—the day Hopi missed the Cha'tima—the same day he was sentenced to die by the council." A murmur rose up from the council.

"We sentenced him to death," Amhose said, "but The gods spared him?"

"Yes." Allander confirmed, "Tawa, Narmer, Bask, Amarna, Sotnang, Spider Wuti, all the others."

Again, the elders gasped. Ammett sat down quietly.

"Why do The gods not come to *us* or answer *our* prayers?" Amhose asked his fellow council members rhetorically. "Have we strayed so far from the true teachings that we no longer merit the attention of our gods?'

Around the kiva, heads were lowered.

"Let us pray for guidance." Amhose concluded.

CHAPTER NINETEEN

Burning Images

The massacre did not leave Ramu's thoughts. He fasted and prayed for relief, yet he could not drive the memories away. They remained—vivid, lurid. He let blood flow from his arms, to no avail. The gods must have retribution. Only retribution would relieve him of the guilt he shared with his Antelope brothers. A sacrifice is needed, he concluded. Someone must pay for our crimes with his life.

Take me!

Ramu demanded to the sun and sky, Take me! He begged the moon and the stars. Please, take me, I am a great warrior. I am Ramu. I offer myself to you. He lay on the sandstone and waited, but death did not come. Crows circled. Coyotes approached cautiously, hiding behind sage and sandstone to watch.

Waiting to die is tiring, he thought to himself, so he got up and began building a crucifix from strong cedar branches. He buried its base in the ground and stacked wood around it. Dizzy and disoriented from loss of blood, he shook his head violently, trying to clear it. He fell to the ground again and again, delirious with fever.

Propping himself against a tree, he called out, "If you will not come to me, I will come to you myself. Retribution! Please . . . Retribution." On his knees, he arched his back and offered his chest to the sky. He raised his powerful arms to heaven. Sweat beaded his brow and rolled off his torso. Still, he waited, but nothing happened.

Finally, he took flint from his waist band and lit the stack of wood at the base of the crucifix. The fire grew quickly, Ramu struggled to his feet and heaped more wood onto the fire. He sang the song of warriors as he worked. The flames soon leaped high onto the cross.

When the fire raged he stepped back four or five steps, hopping one foot to the other, in the way of a warrior preparing to fight, then—leapt forward onto the crucifix's cross-beam. Ramu shouted the war cry of the Antelope Clan. Fire burned into his feet, and he struggled to keep balance. From the desert, the coyotes and nocturnes watched intently while Ramu danced atop the great flame. Suddenly, the crucifix collapsed, and Ramu fell into the flames, his momentum rolling him out and into the desert.

I will surely die soon, he thought. "This is my redemption," he muttered aloud, and fell unconscious. When Ramu awoke, nothing was left of the fire except white coals smoldering under layers of ash. A single smoke snake wafted into the sky from the base of the burned crucifix.

Ramu was very much alive. He lay on the cool sand, his skin on fire. He tried to move but the pain was too great. Have I crossed to the other side, he wondered? No, this cannot be, he said to himself, I am not dead! The fire still burns, and I am still here in the desert. Why am I not dead?

Ramu had offered his life willingly, yet his body would not give up so easily. He passed in and out of consciousness many times. He still remembered the massacre in Chaco. "I will endure this death," he shouted out, "but I can not endure seeing this crime again!" Ramu tried to stand but could not. He crawled on his hands and knees to the ring of fire. Each movement was excruciating, and he cried out in pain. At the fire he grasped a shard of white hot coal in his hand, and with remarkable speed, drove it first into his left eye and then into his right. He screamed, and his body convulsed, twisting in agony again and again. His cries were lost in the vast expanse of desert.

Faith

Zuni did what he could to help bring order in the aftermath of the storm. He was very weak and his head ached severly. He was forced to sit and cradle his head in his hands. The sight of the destroyed cottonwood tree made his heart pound. Zuni could not bring himself to say his thoughts out loud. But to him and to many other devout Anaa, a part of Bonito was dead.

The people filed past the cottonwood all day. They stared in disbelief. They had waited patiently for rain, and when it came, it carried both a blessing and a curse. Should they rejoice or grieve? The life of the cottonwood intertwined with the greatness of Bonito. It was impossible to separate the two. Every resident of the city had experienced some part of their life under its great branches. The tree was a part of the sky itself.

By mid-morning, Zuni had tired, but before returning to his room, he went to an ornately painted prayer room within the walls of Bonito. Zuni knelt and bowed his head. The room was filled with the chants and prayers of the devoted Anaa. The prayers mingled like the fragrance of flowers.

Amhose entered the prayer room and knelt next to Zuni. His clarity of spirit warmed Zuni's heart. Tears streamed down Zuni's cheeks. Amhose whispered, "Time is no longer a line but a circle; a circle like the calendar of the Kokopilau; or the circle of the coyote's territory; or the invisible circle of the crows. Time is the water circle, the wind circle, the circle of caring and the circle of family. Time is the circle from beginning to beginning."

When Amhose finished speaking, Zuni left his body through his own mouth and floated upward. Prayers, smoke and spirits hovered over the Anaa devotees. Zuni's spirit joined them swimming through the circular kiva like a school of fish. Zuni's spirit was long, blue and had no extremities—only energy. His spirit family swam together, faster, faster until it had no beginning, no end, only now.

Distribution of the Chochmingwu

The Abbott's Council pow-wow ended in disharmony. After much discussion the elders were forced to vote on a plan put forth by Abbott Amhose. They would collect all the Chochmingwu remaining in Chaco and distribute it equally to all subjects of Anaa.

"This way," Amhose told them, "no one among us will starve. Everyone receives an equal share."

The shortage of food was so critical in the outlying communities that every day new refugees arrived, swarming into the already crowded city. Plazas once reserved for recreation became makeshift tent neighborhoods. Every empty storehouse became an apartment for a new family. Those not lucky enough to find room inside the pueblos pitched tents along the outer walls.

Amhose's distribution plan was not without precedent. During the Seventh Dynasty, many hundreds of Anaa starved to death while their brothers ate well. The Time Scrolls confirm that when the rain finally returned and some storehouses were found to be filled with Chochmingwu, The gods were infuriated and decreed that hoarding, in time of great need, was a sin.

But Abbott Ammett and the leaders of the clan pueblos were adamantly opposed to Amhose's plan. The clans had worked hard and del Arroyo alone possessed more Chochmingwu than all the other pueblos combined. Del Arroyo had always been generous and helped its clansmen without question. In its long history, the clan Arroyo had been so generous that now it rivaled Pueblo Bonito in importance and power. It had always given its full share to Anaa so its subjects, including the outcasts and the

Kokopilau, did not go without. But, Ammett had not become leader of the richest pueblo in Chaco by giving away their wealth.

Ammett informed the council that such practices must end. It was unthinkable to open del Arroyo's storehouses to parcel out their contents. Ammett argued that the situation did not yet warrant such a drastic move. He told the gathering, "The plan of life given to us by Tawa tells us that we should study the Ant People and emulate their ways. This is why we built vast rooms for storage. The Ant people work hard, store food and survive hardship. Should we not learn by their example?"

Ammett went on, "We at del Arroyo have sacrificed much for Anaa.We have worked hard. We have been frugal, and now we have scarcely enough for our own people. We should not be obliged to feed the lazy, the outcasts, the thieves, the interlopers and the fools." Ammett's voice became shrill. "It is enough that we give a fair share to Bonito. It can do what it wants with that!" Ammett was finished and sat down.

"Ammett speaks the truth," Amhose said standing, "but we do not ask Arroyo to share its vast treasures of turquoise and silver. We do not ask for its property or its labor. We ask only for what belongs to all the people of Anaa. Del Arroyo will feed its family, and it will feed the family of Anaa as well. It must be so. The Chochmingwu belongs to all, equally. I say that all of our hardship," Amhose spoke with conviction, "is a test of our honor and our worthiness. When the gods see that we are just, they will reward us with rain and prosperity once again."

Turning to Ammett, Amhose said, "When the rains return, the great family of Arroyo, with its proud and honorable history, will once again be able to fill its storehouses." Amhose addressed the entire gathering, "The Ant People worked together as one. We must not forget how the Ant People took in the Anaa when Tawa destroyed the first three worlds. The Legend of Creation tells us that the Ant People opened their storehouses without reservation and welcomed the Anaa.

"Together," Amhose continued, "we fought the wandering tribes when they coveted our wuti and children. Together, we have grown and prospered. No one of us would have survived without the others. Our power lies in the strength of our whole people, and only together will we continue." Amhose lowered his head and took his seat.

Ammett stood and spoke. He and the other clan pueblos would start a new order, he warned. He threatened that Arroyo would break away from Anaa. Amhose leapt up from his seat. His demeanor was that of a young warrior, not an old man. He invoked the Word of The gods, which was his right as Abbott of Bonito,

"The gods do not care how much Chochmingwu you have in your pockets Ammett. The gods care little of your pettiness. The gods care about the people and the welfare of Anaa. The love and peace we share is Tchvala (liquid from the mouth of Spider Wuti). Without it the world and all of Pueblo del Arroyo will fall into the void and be lost. I implore you," Amhose said facing Ammett, "mend your ways or you shall certainly be punished. Your hands are covered with blood."

Amhose prevailed but with the provision that del Arroyo and the other clan pueblos would keep their storehouses of Chochmingwu only until the North Star again appeared in the heavens. If the drought continued when the North Star came in view, the pueblos would release their Chochmingwu to be distributed by Bonito.

But in a matter of days, Ammett laughed in Amhose's face, a great insult. Ammett was convinced that Amhose planned to strip del Arroyo of its wealth and at the same time prevent Ammett from leading Chaco and Anaa. Now the drought had ended, and the agreement made by the Abbott's Council no longer mattered, or so concluded Ammett.

Before workers completed repairing the damage done by the storm, Ammett's representatives spread word that the lightning which struck the cottonwood tree and destroyed the Cha'tima Rock was sent as punishment from The gods. According to the rumors, Ammett believed The gods were angry at Bonito and the Kokopilau. Why would The gods send rain to the people while at the same time striking out against Bonito and Fajada, Ammett's emissaries asked.

In the grand hall of del Arroyo, Ammett told his clansmen, "The rain is evidence that the Abbott of Bonito's plan was a ploy to exert control over del Arroyo and Anaa. Through misuse of leadership, the Abbott of Bonito has diminished the fortunes of his pueblo."

Over the following days and nights, Ammett spoke to all Anaa though he was neither the Abbott of Bonito nor Allander of Fajada. He claimed that del Arroyo was more powerful than Bonito. "Amhose is old," Ammett declared, "he does not have the will to guide us through these hard times. He is a philosopher, not a leader." We need strength and discipliner. Punish the fools. Reward the strong and worthy," Ammett preached to all who would listen.

CHAPTER TWENTY

Huhuwa

When Zuni returned from his duties on Fajada, a messenger awaited him. He was summoned to Bonito, yet another unusual event on a night filled with the unexpected. He walked in silence, anticipating calamity.

Zuni went to Fajada at dusk the night before and watched the full moon on the horizon spreading soft light across the city. He looked into the face of the moon and saw that the lower part of it had disappeared. He alerted his superiors, the black-robed Kokopilau astronomers, who already observed the night sky with concern. In a short while, the full moon had been devoured, and only the glow of its outline remained. The Kokopilau whispered excitedly as the world of Anaa fell into darkness.

"Huhuwa!" Zuni heard one of the astronomers. Huhuwa, Zuni thought, the eclipse of the Moon. An astronomer might wait a life time to witness this rare astral event. Allander sent runners to tell his people. The Kokopilau would not sleep tonight. They climbed onto their roofs to watch. Huhuwa energy instilled hope, but also engendered a homesickness in the Kokopilau. They began their long journey in darkness, and this dark sky echoed their homeland. Many children would be conceived tonight.

The Kokopilau historians rushed indoors to search the Book of Predictions. They were they not aware of this Huhuwa. Had they overlooked it? The records of each dynasty of Anaa would have to be checked. Unfortunately, each dynasty compiled a complex record of astrological predictions and charts, plotting the course of thousands of stars. They would have to re-examine The Time Scrolls as well—symbol by symbol—for every nuance of meaning.

Some Kokopilau believed the Huhuwa was a message from their recently departed brothers and sisters, substantiating their decision to leave. Furthermore, some Kokopilau believed that they, too, should have joined their departed clansmen.

No one knew what had become of their tribesmen, though it was widely discussed in the Kokopilau community. Of the many travelers passing through Chaco, not one had encountered the wandering Kokopilau. No one in the outlying communities had seen them either, save one. The historian, Bonar, told Allander that one day at sunset, when the sun was submerged in an orange sky, he had seen a line of humpback flute players crossing the horizon from south to north. He believed the group to be Kokopilau because of their distinctive backpacks, long staffs and flutes.

Of the Kokopilau, Allander was most excited about the Huhuwa. He paced nervously, embraced his colleagues and remarked repeatedly on the magnificence of the black moon. As the Huhuwa grew, so did Allander's agitation. He rushed into Fajada, gazed into the murals, and ran out again. He waved him arms wildly. He was feverish and covered in sweat. He dropped his ceremonial gown in a heap and ran to what was left of the Cha'tima Rock. He stood there naked and reached upward and crying out, "It is time!"

Secret apprenticeship

Amhose knew about the Huhuwa, but it was not the reason he summoned Zuni to Bonito.

"Let us walk," Amhose said. From Bonito they climbed out of the canyon and meandered along the cliff edge for a long time. Neither spoke. Each was comforted by the quiet companionship of the other. The small plants growing in and among the rocks caught Zuni's fancy, and he stopped many times to examine them while Amhose walked ahead.

Amhose stopped and sat on the ground, visibly shaken. Tears streamed down his face. They had come to a place where they could look across the canyon to the City of the outcasts.

"Galo. Look at this place. Imprint it upon your mind. You must remember it well. Remember everything, remember the spirit of this great city." Amhose gestured to embrace the panorama of Galo. "One day you will be called upon to remember this place. Its days are short."

"This is not true," Zuni implored, "Galo and Chaco will always exist. All who live here today and tomorrow will know Galo and Chaco, too." Zuni had never refuted his mentor in such a manner, but Amhose's words overwhelmed him. "As long as I breathe, I am Anaa, I will fight and spill my blood onto the soil of this sacred place. I . . . ."

"Enough!" Amhose interrupted, "I did not ask you here to listen to you. I, Amhose, the Abbott of Bonito, speaks to you." He paused. "You must not speak, but listen, and do as I instruct."

"Yes, father. I am sorry."

"You must begin a special apprenticeship. I will instruct you. I will teach and you will learn. Do you understand?"

Zuni knelt, "Yes, father I am honored, but, why have you chosen me?"

"Be assured. *You* have been chosen."

"But . . . ."

"Silence!" Amhose demanded. "Your name and the name of another are chosen."

There was a long silence, then Zuni asked, "When I finish this apprenticeship, will you and I be together?"

"Be at peace, my son. What happens to me is of little consequence." Amhose paused and gestured toward his body, "One day my soul will be free of this burden." He lifted his face to the horizon, "It is all very simple."

"But, father . . . ." Amhose placed a finger to Zuni's lips.

"Remember what I have said and do not speak to others of our conversation. There is danger for you. You should not draw attention to yourself. No matter what happens, you must hold your tongue."

Zuni was confused by Amhose and the need for secrecy. For the first time in his life, he questioned Amhose and all he said. This doubt was like rain changing the color of sandstone. But he was resolved. It is my duty to be obedient and faithful. I must not question.

CHAPTER

TWENTY-ONE

Disgraced Warriors

Vanga tired quickly of the del Arroyo warriors. Every day they swept through Galo, cracking down on the outcasts. "Leave us alone!" Vanga demanded of the warriors. "We have done nothing to you."

"What kind of warriors are you, anyway?" he hollered out, "Cowards! Server of Cowards! Slaves of Cowards! I spit on you! I spit on what you stand for! I spit on your meaningless life! You are nothing!" he shouted.

The warriors were equally tired of Vanga. Their beatings had not silenced him. Four warriors wasted themselves hitting and kicking him until their arms and legs could throw no more punches. Vanga's thick, muscular torso absorbed the abuse, and through it all he shouted insults. By the time they finished, most of his teeth had been kicked out; through his own blood he swore, "Yellow dogs, Eaters of deer droppings."

"Kill me!" he shouted, "Kill me now where everyone can see. Kill me the way you killed the starving farmers. Kill me now in the sunlight," Vanga pointed at them, "You have raped and slaughtered the Kokopilau wuti! Killers! Criminals! We see your crimes, you cannot escape us. You are hypocrites and Tawa sees your crimes! You will pay!"

The warriors—masters of masks—were dispassionate, but they heard every word Vanga uttered. They closed the circle around him again. His words hit them deep. "Punish those among you who disgraced the warrior caste, or I will not be silent." The warriors could not silence Vanga with their hands, but they could use a stone club or an arrow. They stood over him, undecided. They did not move.

"What are you bastards waiting for?" he shouted, "Kill me!"

Amarna rushed to Vanga's side and begged the warriors to have mercy on him.

The leader of the warriors grasped Amarna by the arms and pulled her close to him, "I will take you, whore, instead of this half man," he turned to

Vanga, "We will all have this whore, and maybe we will kill her. I will spare you, and we will take her instead. She will receive your punishment!"

"NO!" Vanga cried out pulling himself up on his hands, "Kill me! Leave her alone!" A warrior kicked Vanga's arms out from under him and he fell back to the dirt. "I swear I will kill you!" Vanga shouted.

"Ahhhh," the leader said, "So, I see now Vanga, you are in love with this whore. Aww, Yes, now perhaps you will be silent . . . ." The other warriors nodded. It was important to learn a man's weakness and apply pressure there. The leader puffed out his chest and stuck out his chin, "We have our orders, they do not include this whore," he pushed Amarna to the dirt, "But, Vanga, if you do not be quiet, I promise you we will take her away and kill her."

Vanga turned his face to the dirt and was silent.

The warriors moved off, they were ordered by Ammett to search and intimidate the residents of Galo. They did not question their orders. It was easy for them to be cruel to the outcasts. The warriors resented the unconcealed satisfaction the outcasts felt at the turmoil in the city, below. The outcasts, having been under the thumb of the city for so long, could not suppress their glee at Chaco's troubles.

But these were dangerous times, and the outcasts feared for their safety. If chaos swept through the canyon, the outcasts would be punished. It mattered little whether they were responsible. They would feel the whip.

In the moons since the rainstorm, the various warrior groups had nearly come to battle on several occasions. Once, when warriors of del Arroyo beat boys from Pueblo Chetro Ketl for throwing stones, a much larger contingent of warriors from Ketl appeared and challenged the attackers. Out-numbered, the del Arroyos took arrows from their quivers and placed them in their bows. The warriors from Ketl did the same. Each group eyed the other, and the standoff continued for some time. It was a frightening scene: Chaco warriors facing battle in the center of the city. These men had lived together, fought common enemies as one army and, now, they faced each other. Their masks of death stared vacantly into the faces of their enemies. Finally, the leader of the Ketl warriors ordered the Arroyos to withdraw. It was a sullen departure, leaving a pall of distrust in the air.

Vanga, Amarna and others witnessed this scene. Amarna pleaded with Vanga to be quiet, but after the two groups disengaged, Vanga let out a hearty laugh at the retreating del Arroyo warriors.

"This will do us no good!" Amarna chided him. "These warriors will be back. You must be quiet," she pleaded.

"It is written," Vanga cried, looking up at his beloved Amarna. "It is all written, we are doomed. We all are doomed!"

After the warriors were gone, Vanga and Amarna sat quietly for a long time. They did not speak, but their thoughts were the same. Every day, since Hopi missed the Cha'tima, another piece of Chaco's mosaic fell away. When would Hopi return to save them?

Yalo

Near the vermillion cliffs in the deep canyons, a colony of rebels, outlaws and outcasts prepared to raid an Anaa farming village two days march away. Sitting on their haunches, they chipped arrowheads out of obsidian and flint. They faced the south and watched the sunset climb a massive cliff face in the distance. The cliffs faded blue and purple. The men did not speak.

"We will be gone before the moon crests," Yalo told them.

No one spoke, some shook their heads or shifted from side to side. Yalo was a thin man with sinuous muscles. His long black hair often obscured his piercing, narrow eyes which squinted and darted at everything and everyone. Few were brave enough to look straight at him. One direct look from Yalo's eyes could mean death. For the most part, Yalo's rebels were the grown children of the outcasts of Galo and thieves, robbers and lunatics Chaco had disowned.

Death on the Impaler awaited Yalo if he ever returned to Chaco. He had beaten a man to death and was sentenced to die, but Abbott Amhose pardoned him from execution and instead banished him from the city. Since then, Yalo had gone mad, raiding farms and robbing traders and pilgrims. He was trained as a warrior but grew unpredictable and brutal, so the caste disowned him. Yalo hated all Chaco warriors for betraying him, and he vowed revenge.

As the sunlight disappeared from the cliffs, the light of the full moon illuminated the opposite canyon walls. It would be time to leave soon. The canyon glowed a dull, iridescent pink. The moonlight acted as a powerful aphrodisiac on the desert landscape and turned cracks, cliffs, rocks and towers into penises, vaginas and lips. The rebels linked arms and danced slowly in a circle.

When the moon tipped the horizon, its light streamed into the canyon. The war party turned toward the light and stood motionless. The light reflected off their chests and they breathed in great gulps of night air. They shouted, shrieking war whoops crashed into the cliffs and echoed loudly back at them. They danced round and round, lifting their feet high, and the more they danced the faster they went, and the faster they went the louder they shouted.

By the time the moon rose above the horizon, the raiding party had started down the canyon to the valley below. They ran fast, shouting and cavorting, but soon they slowed and ran single file. Yalo had taught them the gait of battle—a slow, mesmerizing, forward pitch. They ran up hills and down, over flats and in the bottoms of stream beds. Nothing could stop this human coil from its forward track, and at the viper's head was a mad man. Yalo would be the first to reach the battle, the first to fight, and the first to spill blood—be it his or his enemy's.

By the second night they reached the small valley. The full moon shone directly above them. It would not be wise to attack by this revealing light but the men were desperate, and bold action had to be taken.

The farmers of this outlying community tilled the wide canyon bottom and lived in one great house protected by a sandstone overhang. The farmers worked hard, loved the land and abided by the traditions of Anaa. Even during good times they did not produce enough food to carry to far-off Chaco, but since the drought they could no longer trade with nearby communities for staples such as salt and dried antelope. Their storage bins, perched on dangerous cliffs to discourage theft, were long empty. Every day, from morning to night, the wuti walked far up the canyon to a spring where they filled jugs with water, carrying them back to the fields to water new Chochmingwu sprouts.

Yalo and his men neared the farmer's cliff dwelling. Yalo had predicted his party would arrive while the men of the household were away in the mountains hunting, and he was right. When the moonlight was at zenith, the raiding party overwhelmed two guards left behind and raped and killed all the wuti and the children.

CHAPTER TWENTY-TWO

Deceit

It would do no good for Ranal to lie to the tribunal about his involvement in the looting of the marketplace, so he decided to tell the truth.

"I swear on the black feathers of my ancient ancestors' spirit of Kaa, I am unjustly accused. It was not me that they saw in the marketplace . . . It must have been someone who looked like me . . . I know nothing of the trade beads and jewelry found in my hut . . . Yes, I am telling the truth, I swear. I admit, I did spend many trade beads in the days after the looting, but I found them. Yes, I know it is hard to believe, but I found a leather sack on the trail and it was filled with beads. Tawa smiles on me, I said to myself. It is my destiny, I said to myself . . . Yes, I am aware of that . . . somewhere within me I knew it was wrong, that some honest trader had dropped them there. But what was I to do? I am only an outcast. I am foolish. I punished myself in the briar, didn't I? I was nearly burned. I have suffered much, look, my wounds fester still. I am nothing, but a ball of pus. See, I ooze. It is likely I will die a slow painful death . . . Have mercy, please."

The temporary tribunal—to try those accused of crimes during the massacre—had been assembled in haste. Its very existence attested to the power and respect given the Abbott of Bonito. The tribunal was made up of leaders among the pueblo warriors. The absence of clerics, citizens, and clansmen among the tribunal members was not coincidence. This tribunal would be responsible to mete out punishment to warriors accused of killing innocent citizens and Kokopilau wuti, and it was imperative that warriors be punished by their peers.

The tribunal dealt quickly with the marketplace looters. Most of the outcasts accused of crimes were banished or sentenced to the Impaler.

"I have enemies!" Ranal told the chiefs seated before him. They sat on colorful, thickly-woven rugs and smoked their smoked pipes and were not interested in Ranal and his story.

"I am not one of them," he pointed in the direction of Galo, "I have stopped talking rubbish, I swear to it."

The tribunal heard enough. The guards were summoned to lead Ranal away.

"Wait!" Ranal shouted as two warriors took him by the arms. "I have to tell Ammett! . . . about the Cha'tima, the Morning Prayer . . . Hopi! Please!"

The white haired men looked up, puffing on their pipes. "Tell us more," one of the elders demanded.

Ranal quickly told them that he had been duped by the evil Hopi into becoming his friend.

"More," another demanded.

"I . . . I believe I should give this important information to Ammett himself . . . I think, Yes?"

The tribunal agreed, but they told Ranal the punishment for perjury was the Impaler.

"I can catch Hopi. I swear it. I know where he is, right now. He told me where he was going. He will be back, I know this . . . ."

The Abbott of del Arroyo seldom went to where the prostitues, slaves and prisoners were kept. But, when he was told that Ranal spoke about Hopi, he canceled his appointments and walked quickly across del Arroyo's grand plaza to an entryway guarded by four warriors. It would better for him to meet Ranal there.

Ammett blocked the door, his silhouette darkening the room. "Speak," a guard demanded of Ranal. "Tell Ammett what you have to say. Speak now or die."

Ranal, tethered to the wall, pleaded to be released. "I am sick and my wounds bleed. Please, honorable Ammett, have them untie me. I will not try to escape."

Ammett motioned to the guards, and they untied him.

"Speak now!" the guard demanded.

"Yes, yes, I will, gladly. Oh honorable Ammett, you are the true leader of Chaco. I . . . ."

Ammett said impatiently, "What information do you have?"

"Oh honorable Ammett, I am your faithful servant and I know you desire to see Hopi brought to justice . . . ."

"Yes," Ammett said.

"His crime is great, look what has happened since he missed the Cha'tima. Great harm will come to the city of Chaco if he is not . . . ."

"Yes, I know this," Ammett said, "But tell me what *you* know."

"It is my wish to be of assistance to you, both now and in the future. I know much about this city and what the people think. I could be of great service to you."

"If what you tell me pleases me, your life will be spared, I promise. So, speak."

"Your graciousness, I know where Hopi is. I can lead your men there if it pleases you."

"How do you know where Hopi is?"

"When he escaped from the city, I was the last person he spoke to, and he told me where he was going." Ranal bowed his head, shameful of his betrayal, but Ammett was excited, and sensing his interest, Ranal began making up the story as he went. "Hopi is hiding in the Blue Mountains. I swear it. He plans to raise an army and come back to kill everyone. Hopi is evil and . . . ."

"Silence," Ammett shouted, "If this is all you have to say, then you shall die slowly and painfully."

"But, it is the truth," Ranal pleaded.

Ammett motioned to the guards who began viciously whipping Ranal with braided leathers straps. They ripped open his festering wounds and Ranal screamed out, crying for mercy.

"Tell me more, ruminator, tell me all of what you know. Hopi did not go to the Blue Mountains, we know this."

Ranal could not think, the pain was unbearable.

"Take him to the salt bin," Ammett said. "He gives me no information."

Ammett turned to his men, "You see this wretched, stinking feces, he and his kind will be eliminated. They eat at our stomachs like worms. We must scourge them from our system. We must restore truth and order . . . ."

"Wait," Ranal cried out. "Hopi has a wuti."

Ammett turned back to Ranal.

"He is in love. He is in love with a whore and has promised to return for her. I swear it! It is the truth. You must believe me."

Bonito's Sacred Storehouses

Every day, from morning until night, the Chochmingwu arrived at Bonito as mandated by the Abbott's council. It came in large woven baskets carried on the heads of workers in lines stretched, unbroken, like a caterpillar. The workers came from the three spiritual pueblos to the great storage bins of Bonito. Their work song came from the Ant People, "Work as one," step, step, step. "Pour into one," step, step, step. "Be as one," step, step, step.

"All are one," step, step, step. Basket by basket, the workers poured Chochmingwu into the empty storage rooms.

Since the storage rooms had been consecrated, countless hohoyas had been brought to them, and the storage bins were held in great reverence. These very rooms held the food that had nourished their ancestors.

One by one, the great storage rooms of Boniti were filled and then sealed with great wooden barricades. A hohoya prayer was offered, and the filling of the next bin began. The Chochmingwu came from the three spiritual houses: Pueblo Chetro Ketl, Pueblo Kin Kletso and Pueblo Kin Klizhin. The spiritual houses had supported Amhose at the Abbott's Council and had voted to move all the Chochmingwu to Bonito for distribution among the population. But, all the Chochmingwu from the spiritual pueblos combined would not fill Bonito's great bins. Only with the full harvest of the clan pueblos of Tsin Kletsin, Casa Rinconada and del Arroyo, could they hope to accomplish that task.

At del Arroyo, Ammett watched the workers transfer Chochmingwu from the spirit houses. The North Star had not yet appeared on the horizon and, until it did, Ammett would not even consider sharing Arroyo's harvest with anyone. Besides, he thought, it had rained—albeit only once—and the council's vote to collect and distribute the Chochmingwu would hold only if the drought continued. If the drought ended, the distribution plan would be cancelled.

To Ammett, the gods had sent a very clear message with the storm. The destruction of the old cottonwood and the Cha'tima rock meant The gods were angry with Bonito and with the Kokopilau. "I have received much criticism for my part in the massacre," he told his clerics, "but when the gods brought rain, I was vindicated. The gods did not punish me, or the great pueblo of del Arroyo, instead The gods struck at Bonito and the Kokopilau."

Seeds and the Beautiful Amarna

Amarna and the other prostitutes of Galo slept during the day and worked long nights. The drought brought much unhappiness to Chaco and the fleeting comfort of a concubine was in demand. Amarna's mother, Soya, stopped selling herself—no one wanted her once they had been greeted by Amarna. There was no reason for Soya to continue, even if she could find customers, she and her daughter were becoming rich with what Amarna made alone.

Each passing day, Amarna grew more beautiful. Even though she was an outcast and a whore, every man in Chaco knew of her. Clerics walked the steep trail into Galo to admire her beauty. Warriors secretly dedicated themselves to her. Young men and students from the pueblos dreamed of making her his wife. Even the wuti were struck by her poise and grace. What a shame that she was an outcast, they said to one another.

Every passing moon, more men wanted to be with Amarna. Soya doubled the price and when no one complained, she tripled, then quadrupled it with no loss of business. Slave traders from the south offered much silver to buy her daughter, but Soya was too smart for that. She knew Amarna was worth far more in Galo than anywhere in Mexico—besides, Amarna was no longer a child and would never allow herself to be sold. In fact, Amarna possessed a fortune in trade beads, turquoise and even silver jewelry. She could buy slaves herself and lead a life of luxury in Mexico if she chose to, but she stayed in Galo. She was not aware of her power, and she waited for Hopi to return.

"Come, it is time," Vanga said, pushing his head through Amarna's beaded entryway.

"Yes, my friend, I am coming." Amarna answered, moving past Vanga and into the evening light. The sun neared the western horizon, and they walked the short distance to the rock where, every day, they prayed for Hopi's return.

"I am worried about you, Amarna," Vanga said as he pulled himself along behind her.

"About me, Vanga? This is new." Amarna's voice was sweetly mocking.

"I fear that Soya conspires to run your life."

"I am her daughter."

"You are a queen. She buys much with your earnings."

"As well she should, my friend,"

"She takes in more than you know, but tells you she has much less."

"So what, Vanga? Is this your business?" Amarna tried to sound angry.

"Hopi would say these things to you."

"You are not Hopi."

"I am not Hopi, but he chose me to watch over you. I promised to look after you until his return."

"This gives you the right to accuse my mother?"

"It gives me the right to look after your interests."

Amarna stopped, leaned down to Vanga and hugged his head. "I do love you. I do appreciate your concern. I see Hopi when I see you. I know you would never desert me."

"Of course not, I would never . . . " Vanga broke off as Amarna started to cry.

"Oh Vanga, where can he be? Why has he not returned? Perhaps he dead. Oh, why does he not return?"

For the very first time, Vanga was angry with Hopi. He, too, had been patient and had waited for Hopi's return. But he suppressed his anger and said, "There must be a reason Hopi has not come back yet. We must not lose hope. He will return."

"One more thing, Amarna, may I ask you a question?"

"Yes, what is it?"

"Why do you not become pregnant from the seeds of the men you are with?" Vanga was embarrassed and looked away as he spoke.

"You are a fool, my friend, a foolish man." Amarna reached down and cradled Vanga's head in her hands. "You do not know, really?"

"Know what?" Vanga responded, quizzically.

"Among the prostitutes there is a ceremony. Initiates are made barren by putting the root of the Datura plant into the womb. You did not know this?"

"I . . . I . . . No, I did not know this.?"

Amarna paused and tears filled her eyes, "It happened when I was very young. It was the decision of my mother."

"Soya, your mother, chose this for you when you were a small child?"

"Yes."

There was a long silence before Vanga spoke, "Does Hopi know of this?"

Vanga's question was too much for Amarna to endure and she broke down and sobbed. "No, my friend, he does not."

CHAPTER

TWENTY-THREE

Apprenticeship and the Abbott's Robe

The Chochmingwu poured into Bonito's storage rooms, but Amhose, who normally supervised most undertakings of the pueblo, was conspicuous by his absence. He had not been tending to his other duties either. Amhose had retired to a special prayer kiva to pray. Even when his fellow abbotts came to discuss the drought or other important issues he would not meet with them. They were turned away by Juxz, with the explanation, "Amhose wishes your patience. Amhose instructs you to return to your pueblos, pray for your people and study the Legend of Creation."

At first, Amhose's refusals were accepted, but as time passed, the abbotts became concerned and even frightened. The people needed their leader, and Prayer and contemplation were important, but there was a very important matter at stake. Ammett of del Arroyo was making accusations against Amhose and the Kokopilau. These falsehoods had to be addressed, and Ammett had to be put in his place.

The only person admitted to see Amhose was Zuni. Every morning at dawn, Amhose met Zuni as he left Fajada Butte, and they walked the nearly deserted streets of the city. Sometimes they went to the City of Outcasts and prayed. Other times they meandered through the neighborhoods and marveled at the beauty and simplicity of the Chacoan streets. Still other times, they walked the cliff edge above Chaco.

Dressed in the hooded, ceremonial gown of Bonito, Amhose moved slowly and had much to say. Zuni walked with his arms folded or clasped behind his back. Occasionally, Amhose raised an arm above his head and turned to Zuni excitedly explaining something. When they were alone and away from the many eyes in the city, Amhose dropped the Abbott's ceremonial gown and taught Zuni songs and dances. Wearing only a loin cloth, Amhose looked naked. His body looked like the elderly warriors who played Senat in the city's plazas.

Every time Amhose dropped his gown, Zuni could not take his eyes from it, something about the gown lying there on the sandstone hypnotized him. Only when Amhose stood in front of the gown or made Zuni learn a song or a dance was Zuni able to look away.

"The gown has much power." Amhose said as he lithely danced around it. "Please, my son, the gods will not strike you down. Place it over your shoulders," Amhose said, holding the gown out for Zuni to slip on.

"No, my father, I cannot—I mean, I do not wish to disobey you, father, but it is not right for me to do this . . . is it?"

Amhose laughed, "If it pleases you, I shall give it to you."

"Oh no, father. I cannot. It is the gown of the Abbott of Bonito. It is sacred and I cannot . . . ."

Amhose laughed again, then effortlessly flung the gown high into the air. The gown opened, flattened like a carpet, and descended over Zuni's head, covering him completely. "Do not move," Amhose teased, "If you move you will certainly disappear." He cackled.

Zuni cowered, the gown draped over him. It was heavy and smelled of sage and musk and dust and age.

"Are you in there?" Amhose asked.

"Yes, my father," Zuni answered.

"Are there no Abbotts in there with you?"

"No, my father."

"Good. I am glad of it."

Messenger

Zuni arrived at Fajada before dusk and requested an audience with Allander. Allander's assistant informed Zuni that he could not be interrupted.

"Please tell him I carry a message from the Abbott of Bonito," Zuni said.

The assistant quickly left and when he returned, he motioned Zuni to follow him up the stairway to the second level and into the sacred Kokopilau room where Hopi had been tried. The assistant disappeared, leaving Zuni alone. He marveled at the frescoes and reliefs, at the polished floor and at the obelisks which sat upon it. He turned in a circle and gazed at the fabulous Time Scrolls etched into the ceiling.

"Yes, my son?" Allander said appearing in front of the fresco of Tell and his daughter, Mitanna. Zuni was very surprised. Just moments before he looked directly at the fresco and no one was there.

"Yes, most honorable Allander, my teacher, I bring a message from

Amhose. May I approach?"

"Yes, my son." Allander said smiling," but do not cross the center of the room. Come this way, around the edge." Allander motioned with his eyes and Zuni followed, walking slowly and methodically around the room's perimeter to Allander's side.

He asked, "Whisper?"

"Yes."

Zuni drew close, cupped both hands around his mouth and whispered into Allander's ear.

When he finished, Allander drew close to Zuni's face and looked into his heart. What do you know? How much of this do you understand? Allander drew back slowly, cupped his hands and then whispered into Zuni's ear.

From that day forward Zuni carried messages between Amhose and Allander. Most of these messages related to predictions and the weather and the niceties exchanged between the two leaders of stature. But occasionally, these exchanges were confusing and made little sense. At first, Zuni did not understand these messages, much later though, their meaning would descend upon him.

It was not long before Allander relieved Zuni of his duties at Fajada and Zuni spent his time listening, remembering and recalling what was said to him by the two leaders. He became adept at remembering long messages without making a single mistake in retelling them. When Zuni was not being a courier, he was allowed to read the secret Time Scrolls of Bonito. These histories were for high clerics, and it was an honor to be allowed to read them. Amhose visited Zuni often in the chamber and quizzed him about what he had learned. "You must remember all that you read, my son," Amhose admonished.

Zuni moved from his quiet neighborhood to his old room at Bonito. It was the same room that he and Hopi had shared as students. He often went to Bonito's roof at night and observed the sky as he had done at Fajada. He missed the fellowship of his Kokopilau friends, with their intellectual banter about writings and songs and their jokes about the simple Anaa. But most of all, Zuni missed Hopi. Now that he had returned to Bonito, the memories of their childhood washed over him. He heard Hopi's laughter echoing down the long hallways. Sometimes he stood in the empty passageways or secret corners, his mind filled with all that had happened in Chaco since Hopi missed the Cha'tima. Hopi would be proud of me, he thought, I have been chosen as emissary from Bonito and Fajada! But, when will you return to me,

Hopi, he wondered? What grand lessons are you learning my beloved friend?

Standing in the hallways Zuni often thought he heard the voices of the ancient ones. One day I will return to dust, Zuni thought, and then I shall mingle with Amhose and Allander and Tawa and my brother, Hopi within these very walls.

Hopi

From the top of the narrow trail that led to the crest of the high vermillion cliffs, Hopi turned and looked back at the vast expanse of the world of the Anaa. No wonder the gods chose the heavens to look down upon the Fourth World, he thought. In the far south he could see the tops of the Blue Mountains and to the southeast the flat, featureless plateau where the city of Chaco with its history, grandeur and power was hidden.

I have never experienced such a sight. The world is so magnificent and so large, he thought. He could see mountain ranges and forests and the purple and blue tops of domes and high spires. To the west were countless canyons and rolling sandstone waves that appeared to wash up against the vermillion cliffs. Among the canyons and domes was a great snaking river, with water as radiant as silver, and whose width was so great he had never imagined rivers of its size.

Hopi was humbled, the way he imagined the Ant People must feel in the presence of humans. He found a large flat rock and sat for the entire day looking out over this new world. Was all of this for the people of Anaa? he wondered. Or, is there another plan, one which no individual or collective can comprehend? The greatest city in the entire world, Chaco, cannot compare to this vista, he thought. When the sun finally set, he looked down at the blackness and it became a void, a negative space which softly called to him. Though I cannot see this world which lies below me, I can feel its pulse, he said to himself.

When the darkness descended and stars filled the sky, Hopi sensed the power of the forest behind him. He turned and gazed into its green depth. I will experience its wonders tomorrow or the next day, he thought. Tonight I will stay at this place and soak up all that it is and all that it makes me feel. Hopi did not sleep that night, and morning found him sitting on the rock, still enchanted by the world below him.

Many days passed, and Hopi could not bring himself to leave this place. In the early mornings and late afternoons he ventured into the forest to find food and water, and by sunset he was back again.

I needn't ever return to Chaco, he concluded. This land, this place, is home to me now. The longing which has lived within me is satisfied now. My heart is at peace, and for the first time, nothing seems impossible. The night cleansed his memories of Chaco and of all its people. The dawn told him he was free again. The cycle of night and day melted into one and even in the darkness Hopi could see every feature of the new world below.

After many days, he did not know how many, Hopi left his rock and wandered far along the cliff edge. He found animal tracks leading to the edge and disappearing. He watched crows gliding in the air currents. He saw the forest not as individual trees but as one organism—a family of life so attuned to living it was indeed sacred.

One evening he entered the forest to forage for food when he noticed a soft, glowing light illuminating the trees and ground in the distance. It is a campfire, he told himself, but when he approached there were no people and no campfire, only cedar trees growing in a family circle. The glowing light had moved deeper into the woods as he had approached it. He followed the light all night as it moved ahead of him, first going left and then going right. In the morning Hopi slept under an ancient cedar tree. At dusk the light appeared again, moving slowly through the trees. Again, he followed it, trying to catch sight of its source. Sometimes, he could see the light caught in the eyes of antelope, deer and coyotes who shared this forest. At first sunlight, he slept under the protection of the cedars.

I must learn the secret of this forest light, he told himself. The bronze soil of the high desert's forest floor was soft and welcomed him to walk over it. The forest provided seeds and cactus pulp. If he was thirsty, the forest led him to springs where clean water quenched his parched throat. If he was tired, it offered him soft pine needles or green-blue moss to sleep upon. Every evening when dusk filled the air the pulsating glow appeared and Hopi followed it.

CHAPTER
TWENTY-FOUR

The Slave

Yalo and his band grew larger and stronger. Every day brought new fighters from the ranks of the outcasts and from smaller raiding parties, primarily bandit clans, who for generations had made their living by stealing from the prosperous Anaa. As their numbers swelled, Yalo became brazen, raiding outlying farm communities only five days from the city.

Word of Yalo and his vicious marauders moved quickly through the empire, and entire communities deserted their homes and rushed to the city for protection. They took with them only what they could carry. Yalo was surprised at how little resistance he encountered and how little Chochmingwu remained in the storage bins of the communities he raided.

He became even more brutal. He captured men, forcing them to carry the skinned, cleaned, beheaded carcasses of their wuti back to his stronghold where the men were forced to watch as their wives were roasted and eaten.

"Chaco is weak," Yalo told his men, walking along a line of tethered slaves. He squinted, appraising of each of the slaves as he passed. "One by one, I will pick off their warriors, and my fame will grow and grow."

Yalo looked for two slaves of equal size and strength to entertain his men in a fight to the death. Suddenly, he spotted someone different from the rest. He swaggered in the direction of the man who possessed a powerful body, his legs and arms well muscled, his back sinuous and his hands like great handles of the red bear. All the same, something was wrong with him. The man had been burned severely and his wounds were still healing.

The slave sat with his head bowed and his thick, long hair obscured his face.

"What is your name, slave?" Yalo demanded. The man neither raised his head nor acknowledged Yalo's voice.

"You!" Yalo pointed, "Do you not hear me? What is your name?"

Again, the man did not move, so Yalo stepped forward angrily and grasped him by the hair and pulled his head back to look at his face.

"Augh!" Yalo bellowed and quickly pushed him away in disgust.

"What has happened to this slave?" Yalo shouted to a guard standing nearby.

"He was found wandering the desert," the frightened guard answered, "He was like this when he was found."

Yalo stood motionless surveying the man for a short time, then asked, "Do you not hear me, man? If you value what is left of your life, tell me your name?"

The man rocked back on the ground and faced Yalo "I am called Ramu."

"You are Ramu, the great warrior of Chaco and Anaa?"

"I was, once," Ramu answered.

"What happened to your eyes?"

"I am blinded," Ramu said.

"I can see that, but who blinded you?" Yalo laughed.

"I did."

"You? You did this to yourself?"

"I did."

Yalo could not hold back his excitement. "Everyone," he shouted, "Look what I have found. It is Ramu, the greatest of all Chaco warriors!" Yalo grasped Ramu by his hair and held his face so everyone could see the black holes where his eyes once were. "I witnessed this pathetic louse when he won the great race of Chaco. He has killed more men than any other warrior alive." Yalo gloated, kicking the tethered man repeatedly. "Ramu is famous as no other warrior has ever been. But look at him now. This is what our enemy does to himself. They have become so afraid of me, they cannot bear tthe sight of my strength." Yalo laughed.

Ramu knocked Yalo's hand away with his arm and tried to stand, but Yalo tripped him.

"You are nothing," Ramu shouted, "I can crush you and all these cowards you call men. I can take you on without my eyes. Come! Come if you dare. I will take your life away." Ramu rolled to one side and stood in a crouched position. He waited to fight or to be killed.

Yalo took a spear from the guard, raised it over his head and brought it down, cracking it on top of Ramu's head. Ramu fell to the ground stunned, and Yalo walked around him in a circle beating him until his own arms were tired. When Ramu no longer struggled, Yalo turned to his men and laughed again. They all laughed.

Turmoil in the City

In the city, turquoise and trade beads were fast becoming worthless. A large sack of beads would not buy an equal sack of Chochmingwu. Rugs and peacock feathers were traded for small baskets of Chochmingwu. The people did not complain but remained quiet, and all were very worried. The most devout of the Anaa fasted, giving their portion of Chochmingwu to the refugees, or saving it for another day. It would do them good to fast; and the Legend of Creation instructed them to do this. The Ant People welcomed, housed and fed the Anaa twice while Tawa created new worlds, and now the Anaa welcomed the needy as the Ant people had done. This hardship would pass too, they believed, and again the bounty of Chaco would return.

For the first time the spiritual pueblos opened their doors to the non-Anaa. Everyone was welcomed equally and each was treated with respect. They were given blankets and clothes and were fed Chochmingwu twice a day. It did not take long before the great pueblo plazas were filled with the needy. The cries of hungry children and sick old people echoed from the walls where before only prayers, chants and songs had been heard. A great feeling of brotherhood bolstered the refugees, and they worked hard keeping the streets and pueblos clean and free of refuse. Together, they would face the peril of tomorrow. It was the way of Anaa. They constructed great open toilets, and worked night and day building underground reservoirs to capture every drop of water—in case it rained.

Refugees begged for food to pay healers who promised to save family members who fell sick. Many of the Anaa were desperate. If a person lingered too long without care, it could mean death. The Anaa were known to be compassionate, but also ascribed to the basic need to survive. They extended help to all they believed would benefit, leaving those deemed too ill, to die. Every few days, the spiritual Abbotts, excluding the elder, Amhose, walked among the very sick, offering a final blessing to those individuals they could not help further.

From the Morning Cha'tima until dusk, the city echoed with songs of farewell celebration for the dying. The memories of many lifetimes mingled with tears and spilled into the already heavy air. Sometimes, these celebrations included visits to the sacred prayer rooms of the pueblos. Mourners carried the dying through the city to the south end of the canyon, where they wrapped them in rugs, made them comfortable and left them to die. Others were taken to a nearby canyon and thrown from a high cliff. Later, their bodies were buried in the manner of Anaa and their spirit Kaa separated and protected their burial mounds.

Kalo and the Cougar

The slave trade, outlawed in the city many dynasties ago, flourished at the perimeters of the empire. Toltec traders, men who never dared show their faces in Chaco, brought birds, monkeys and songs from the south. They traded these for slaves at makeshift bartering camps. Caravans of slaves, mostly criminals who had toiled in the turquoise mines of the Blue Mountains, were tethered by strong rope and walked single file to new miseries in Mexico. Each slave carried a heavy bag of turquoise on his back.

It took Yalo two days to decide what to do with Ramu. He would not sell Ramu to the slave traders. A blind man would bring a low price and Ramu's reputation threatened to bring the wrath of Chaco upon anyone who tried to keep him as a slave. Yalo decided to behead the great warrior and carry his head on a pole, but then decided—in spite of the risk—to keep Ramu alive and make him his personal slave. The powerful warriors of Anaa were after him anyway, he concluded, so what would it matter? Yalo was shrewd and his act of reckless defiance would engender the respect and even fear of his enemies.

Ramu will be for me, Yalo thought, what the cougar was to the great bandit Kalo. When I was young, it was told that Kalo hunted the cougar and fought with him bare-handed before defeating the magnificent animal. Instead of killing the beast, Kalo tethered and paraded him. With the cougar at his side, Kalo proved his power and benevolence. Before the bandit, Kalo, was finally tracked down and killed by warriors from Pueblo del Arroyo, his courageous fight against the Anaa drew admiration from all who suffered injustice at the hands of the pious men of Chaco.

Yalo fancied himself another Kalo, and Ramu was to be his cougar. When his men paced round and round the fires, anxiously awaiting word to prepare a war party, he dragged the helpless Ramu by a strong rope attached around his neck.

"I am the protector of truth, friend to the poor, champion of the weaklings!" he sang out.

His men laughed under their breath, but nodded their heads in agreement to his face. The price of disagreeing with Yalo was death.

"I am the shadow behind the cedar, the moss that grows on the bottom of the lake. I am the pain of the knife. I am the greatest of all heros. Yalo's name will echo through the canyons, across the plateaus and in the skull of anyone who stands in my way!" he shouted. As his excitement grew so did that of his men. They moved faster around the flames and fired war whoops, like arrows, up and down the canyon.

"You see my power, don't you?" he demanded, pointing to the pitiful Ramu struggling to keep on his feet at the end of his leash. "This is our enemy, big, strong, and stupid! He is so stupid, he blinded himself. Yalo pointed in the direction of Chaco. This," he screamed, "is what I will do to them all!" He reached down quickly and picked up a long piece of cedar from the edge of the fire ring. He turned to Ramu and struck him over the head with the red hot log. Ramu screamed out in pain, dropped to his knees, and struggled while Yalo poked and jousted at his torso and groin. Yalo's men cheered and shouted. They danced wildly around the fire.

A Wanderer's Voice

Hopi roamed across the land. He followed endless riverbeds, pink, grey and bronze pebbles encrusted in the hardened sand. He meandered along sandstone mesas and around the foot of chocolate-colored hills embedded with crystals that reflected the sun. Just to satisfy his curiosity, he worked his way into dead-end canyons choked with clumps of red river birch. The land called out to him, "Come touch my face and walk along my body." So Hopi did, and at the end of many days he was no more than a shout from where he began. Sometimes, far-off buttresses and towers, domes and spires called out. "You know me," or, "I am the world. You must come this way!"

The earth loved Hopi, its son. He was so fresh and beautiful. His hair gleamed like spring, his broad and mischievous smile danced for them. His feet tickled and titillated the earth.

After many days Hopi wondered if the land was really calling out to him or if he only heard a voice within him. The voice of the land did not enter through his ears but vibrated in the fibers of his stomach. Maybe the land does not speak, he thought. Perhaps my soul gives it a voice which is not its own!

CHAPTER

TWENTY-FIVE

Amarna's Admirers

One afternoon a young man appeared, sitting alone on a flat rock on a hill above Amarna's shack. He was from one of Chaco's large neighborhoods and was the son of a humble mason. He did not attempt to talk to Amarna nor did he approach her, but his eyes followed her. A few days later, another young man appeared, and then another. They too, sat or stood on the ridge and watched. Before long, scores of men, even elders and some Kokopilau came to sit in the company of this mysterious wuti.

Amarna had no idea why the men came or what they wanted. She did not know any of them. Some laid gifts in the path before her, but she politely walked around them. Amarna was embarrassed, but she held her head high and acted like these admirers did not exist.

Every evening since Hopi's departure, Amarna and Vanga sat on a high rock near Galo and prayed for his return. The Talamuyaw moons came with the summer, but still there was no sign of her beloved Hopi. He will return, she told herself, and I will wait. Not even death will keep me from him. Please, carry my love to him, she pleaded to the crescent moon as it cradled the night at the western horizon. "I can feel the warmth of Hopi's love," she often told Vanga, "its caresses my bosom."

With every sunset more men came to share the hillside with Amarna and Vanga in their silent vigil. From the city below, people watched the men gathering where Amarna sat. When Amarna emerged from her shanty and slowly made her way through the crowd, they bowed, and some even wept.

Among Amarna's admirers were four warriors from del Arroyo. They did not mix with the others. They had another reason for being there. They were seasoned fighters, masters of the art of war and self discipline, not be swayed by Amarna's grace or magic. She would not entrance them or make them burn with desire. These men were possessed of great clarity and purpose. They could fire arrows quickly and always hit their target. They could endure fire and not flinch away. They could even stand in the presence of a goddess and not forget their mission.

When the sun disappeared in the city, Amarna and her admirers were still bathed in sunlight on the plateau above. From the city they looked like a stand of pine trees viewed from a distance. Even the abbotts noted this forest of silhouettes around Amarna.

The Tribunal's Decision

The warrior tribunal had concluded its work. Fellow warriors were sent to their deaths for the rape and murder of Kokopilau wuti. Others were remanded into slavery for their ruthless attack on innocent citizens during the equinox celebration. Yet, the uneasiness within the warrior caste, which the clans hoped would dissipate, had grown. The warriors were mixed in their feelings that the punishments meted out by the tribunal were either too harsh or too lenient.

Clan warriors, especially those of del Arroyo, were furious at seeing their brothers sold into slavery and at seeing warriors who had rushed to help the people, found innocent of wrongdoing and freed. Del Arroyo warriors painted their faces, carried axes and knives and paraded through the city several times a day. They trotted shoulder to shoulder, several abreast, and any pilgrim or refugee who happened to be in their path was trampled or pushed out of the way.

Abbott Ammett did nothing to stop his angry warriors. He too, had been rebuffed and humiliated by the tribunal's decisions. Although his authority had not been openly challenged, the tribunal's punishment of his guard for carrying out his orders sent a clear message: Ammett had acted hastily in executing the farmers without consulting the Abbotts' Council.

One of the tribunal chiefs, a proud old master named Una, commanded the del Arroyo warriors. He sat stone-faced on the tribunal court and, without flinching, found his men guilty and ordered them put to death. Una had been reluctant to carry out Ammett's orders, but he did so out of duty. Now, Una carried the guilt and disgrace of the massacre as his own.

After the tribunal concluded its work, Una and his top commanders gathered at their headquarters at del Arroyo. They toasted their conquests and the brotherhood of the warrior caste with deadly datura root mixed in ceremonial wine. When word reached Ammett of their deaths, he laughed, content to be rid of the smug and impassive Una.

Ranal the Citizen

Having told Ammett of Hopi's promise to return for Amarna, Ranal languished in del Arroyo's dungeon. Once a day he was given food, water and salve made of sage, frankincense and cactus pulp to spread on his open wounds. He suffered high fevers, and sweat pooled on the floor beneath his trembling body. Nothing he did could relieve the agony of the hundreds of briar needles festering under his skin. One by one, needles worked their way to the surface where Ranal picked them out, or they worked deeper into his flesh and became more and more painful.

Many of the warriors held Ranal in awe. Suffrance of pain was greatly respected by the warriors. They believed that to become a leader, one must endure great hardship and pain. When Ranal slept the guards jabbed spears into his pus-filled boils. He screamed out and writhed in agony. The warriors laughed and showed no mercy. Still, they respected Ranal's decision to live rather than choosing the freedom of death.

After many days Ranal's fever broke, and he began to heal. When the warriors reported his progress to Ammett, he smiled and ordered Ranal freed. "Bring him to me before you release him," Ammett told them.

Ranal, hands bound, was led to Ammett's quarters.

"Untie him, and leave us." Ammett ordered.

"Do you know why I have sent for you?" Ammett asked.

"I do not," Ranal said.

"I am setting you free. Because you have given me important information, I pardon you."

"I am free?"

"Yes. But, in return for your life and your freedom, you shall bring to me any word of your friend Hopi, or any other news I might find interesting." Ammett took a small sack from his table and threw it across the room at Ranal who leapt back and let it fall to the floor. The sack broke open and beads spilled out across the floor.

"These were found in your hut before you were arrested. Are they yours?"

Ranal did not know what to say. He looked at the bag on the floor for a long time.

"Well, are they yours?"

Ranal's eyes went from the bag to Ammett and back again.

"They were found in my hut?" Ranal asked slowly.

"Yes. Are they yours?" Ammett smiled.

"I . . . I do not recognize the bag, but if you say they were found in my hut, then I guess they are mine. Right?"

"Ah, I see," Ammett said, "You are not as crazy as some may think."

"Yes," Ranal answered, then, "No, I am not."

"If they are yours, take them now."

Ranal leaned down and slowly reached out his hand and snatched the bag from where it had landed.

"Do you understand our agreement?" Ammett asked.

"Yes . . . I mean, yes your grace. I am free to return to Galo?"

"You are free to do as you wish. You are no longer an outcast. You are pardoned. You will remain free as long as I am happy with you and with the information you bring me."

"Yes, master. I am honored that you . . . ."

"Quiet!" Ammett commanded, "You are to mingle with the people, and tell me what they say. Seek out Zuni, and Hopi's wuti, Amarna, and bring word of their goings on to me."

"Yes!" Ranal said. He hurriedly gathered up as many beads as he could, "I am in your debt. . . . I am your servant, I . . . ."

"Silence, ruminator," Ammett interrupted. "and keep silent about our arrangement, or I shall personally watch you die."

"Yes, your grace . . . I am your servant. I will . . . .."

"Go now!" Ammett said waving Ranal from the chamber.

Mission

Hopi lost all sense of time. At night he followed the mysterious light, and by day he slept or lazily traced the lay of the land. Surely, he thought, if I honor Mother Earth she will not betray me. He followed dry creek beds until they delivered him onto ridges. He ambled between hills and changed course whenever he crossed the beaten down path of a fox or coyote. The animal trails wound through sagebrush to waterholes and secret hiding places.

The further Hopi walked, the more the land spoke to him. Side canyons whispered his name inviting him to touch their walls. Large tilting plateaus begged his attention. Hilltops reflected light to catch in his eyes. Distant buttresses touched the sky at the horizon and beckoned him forward.

One night the light moved very quickly and Hopi was forced to run to keep up with it. At dawn, he found himself looking up at a family of sandstone towers. They cut high into the sky, dwarfing the forest and slicing into the wind. They were sharp and twisted, and Hopi could feel their power.

Beyond the towers, Hopi made a remarkable discovery. There, lying in the sand, were skeletons of animals so enormous he could not believe his eyes. He retreated a few steps but then stopped and silently studied these massive remains. "These creatures are not of the Fourth World," he said aloud. He moved closer and touched one. It was stone! Stone? Hopi walked amongst the skeletons for a long time. One skull was the size of a whole antelope and another, sitting on a table of sandstone, had a backbone the length of fallen tree. The Legend of Creation says nothing of beasts like this, Hopi thought.

The bones kept Hopi at the towers for many days, and only when their spirit released him was he able to continue. While he camped among the remains of the mysterious animals, Hopi brooded about the nature of life. How can stone have life, he wondered? Hopi was amused with this strange, deep current of thought moving through his head. I am not stone, his inner voice said, or if I am, I am not aware of it.

Leaving the towers Hopi entered a valley where the wind sang through the mighty trunks of a forest of stone trees. The forest was so perfect he did not know the trees were stone until their lilting song, carried on the wind, whispering to him,

> "Greetings, oh man of the world. Greetings to you from all of us. Many sand storms have visited us since we have shared the beauty of the animal called, Man. Greetings to the man-animal of the World, we are the stone forest of all times."

The stone trees played the wind with such elegance and virtuosity that Hopi laughed and then cried.

> "Do not cry. We have waited so long for you. We are happy to see you. We all envy you—for your journey is so very short and then you become dust."

"I will become dust?" Hopi said turning in a circle. "Yes," he answered himself, "I will become dust, and Yaponcha will carry me to the far corners of the Fourth World." Hopi's words greatly excited the trees.

> "We love you Man, and what you say is sweet. Tomorrow you will be dust, and if you return this way we will hold you and make you part of us. We love you Man, but go now. Your time is almost up and your mission is very important."

"My mission?" Hopi asked confounded. "I am on a mission? I am not aware of such a mission."

The forest was giddy,

> "We never know our mission! We have told you a sweet secret. Please don't betray us."

Reluctantly, Hopi followed his feet out of the valley and onto a ridge.

From his vantage point he saw what appeared to be a village perched on the edge of a high butte on the far-off horizon. He shaded his eyes with his hands to get a better look. The village faded then came back again. He thought he could make out buildings with windows, towers and turrets. Then he saw it transformed into a jumble of slabs and broken sandstone, eclipsed in its own shadows. Something about the butte made him want to go there and to escape from it at the same time.

He plunged back into the forest at sunset. Tonight, he told himself, if I am indeed on a mission as the stone trees have told me, I must find what lies at the heart of the light. Sure enough, as soon as it became dark, the light appeared in a stand of cedar across a small canyon. Until now, Hopi had been content just following the light from dusk until dawn. But tonight he said to himself, I will use stealth and speed to make the knowledge of the light mine. Dropping to his stomach he crawled in the direction of the glow. From one tree to the next he worked his way closer. As he neared, the light became brighter, casting sharp black shadows opposite anything it touched.

The light started to ebb and flow rhythmically, but it did not move away as he approached. He slid down an embankment into a dry creek bed where he hid. He stood and ran down the creek bed to where he could climb the embankment. He slowly worked his way up the rim of the creek bed and quickly looked to the place where the light originated. To his utter amazement at the center of the light was Hoodee, the owl who had befriended him in the forest when he had been lost as a child.

"Hoodee!" Hopi yelled out, losing his balance and falling backward down the embankment. From where he landed he could see the light at the top of the trees fade and then disappear. He scrambled back up the embankment and sprinted after the light as it moved away from him. Hopi ran quickly through the blackened forest as though his feet knew every footfall of the way.

CHAPTER

TWENTY-SIX

Songs and Stories

By day Zuni carried messages between Amhose and Allander through the misery-filled streets of Chaco. Children pulled at his robe and begged for food. From the houses, alleyways and plazas people followed him. He could not escape their questions. Where is Amhose? When will he come to us? Why has he forsaken us? Zuni averted his eyes and walked with his head lowered. He did not have the answer. The despair in the voices of the people burned inside, and he struggled not to let their suffering overwhelm him.

When he passed the trail leading to Galo he often looked up and caught sight of Amarna and Vanga waiting for Hopi's return. He waved, and Amarna waved back. Zuni was strangely attracted to Amarna but did not understand why. Since becoming Amhose's apprentice he did not have time to visit her, though he often thought of her. Like the others, Zuni noticed her beauty and saw the boys and men gathered around her.

When Zuni spoke of these admirers, Amhose was very interested and asked many questions. Who is Amarna's mother. Was Amarna from an unknown seed? She is very beautiful? Zuni was perplexed by Amhose's interest, but concluded the abbott's interests were many, and it was not his business to question.

By night, Zuni learned dances and songs in Amhose's private kiva. Before Amhose instructed Zuni to disrobe, they prayed and smoked from the abbott's pipe. Amhose too, disrobed, and when he did, Zuni was always strangely disappointed. The robe created an illusion of strength and virility, but beneath the great robe of Bonito, Zuni thought, lives a small, old man.

"You must learn well, my son," Amhose said to him, "you must remember everything I say and do."

Amhose recited long poems and sang songs. The sound came through his nose. Zuni felt a sense of urgency hidden within his voice. "You must be precise when reciting the Ya Ya Witches' instructions," Amhose told him.

"Never let anyone see the great sacrifice of the snake dance. It is sacred, not for the eyes of outsiders or visitors," he admonished.

Amhose said to Zuni about the Palmalma ceremony, "Do not be concerned about the measure of sand you pour onto the stone, or you will forget the incantation and you must speak the words with deep conviction."

One night Amhose told Zuni about the importance of architecture as taught to the Anaa while they lived with the Ant People. Still another night, he taught Zuni the Prayer which Stops the World. Zuni knew that learning these prayers and histories were preparation for becoming an abbott. He also knew that this was not the traditional course of ascendancy to abbotthood. Only after many years of faithful prayer and study, were men much older than Zuni taught these rituals, and seldom by the Abbott of Bonito himself.

"Father, may I ask you a question " Zuni requested.

"Yes, my son."

"The people . . . father. There is much hunger and fear in the city. The people need you. They need to hear from you. The Abbott of del Arroyo, Ammett, says many provocative and untrue things . . . . Slavetraders are camped nearby . . . . There is much more, my father. Please tell me. Why have you not spoken to the people?"

"My son, there is much I could tell you. But you would not be able to live with the answer. Not yet. You must first learn many things."

"But there is so much suffering and chaos."

"I am aware of it." Amhose lowered his head, tears glistening in his eyes. "Do not be afraid of what you do not know. You must learn the dances and songs I teach. It is enough that you know there is a plan—few are able to grasp the immensity of the whole."

"But, father . . . ."

"My son," Amhose interrupted, "I have a beautiful dance I must teach you. You will like this dance, and when you have learned it well I assure you, it will bring you joy and clarity of vision."

Amhose moved to the center of the kiva where he stretched his arms outward and turned in circles. Tears filled his eyes and dropped to the stone floor. As he rotated many, many tears fell there. Amhose smiled, and it lifted Zuni's spirit. With a gesture Amhose instructed Zuni to follow his movements. Round and round they danced until the candles were all blown out, and laughter filled the blackened kiva.

Hunger and Chaos

At dawn, from atop Fajada Butte, the city appeared placid, but the once great cottonwood tree was gone. Refugee campsites filled the flood plain from one end of the canyon to the other surrounding the great pueblos. By mid-morning the city transformed into something akin to chaos. Desperate people filled the streets searching for food. They shoved, pushed, argued and fought their way from one place to the next. From Fajada Butte the Kokopilau were very frightened at what they saw.

Many farmers stayed home from their fields. There was no point in planting their sowing seed. Nothing could grow in the dry and dusty soil. Every day, many of the Anaa refrained from eating, saving what they had for the next day. But each day they became weaker and less able to withstand the numbing hunger. Farmers secretly dipped into their sowing seed, one handful at a time, to feed their children. It was a sin to eat the Chochmingwu seed, and a betrayal of Anaa, but what could they do? Every kernel of seed taken, diminished the outlook for the future. When the drought was over, there would be no Chochmingwu to plant and feed the people.

The number of funeral processions grew daily. The abbotts of the pueblos, except for Bonito, walked through the crowds and decided who should received the final blessing of Anaa. The Abbotts' faces were long and they felt the pain and sorrow of their people. Mothers begged for food to feed their children. Fathers stood stoically at the perimeter and said nothing. Flies swarmed the open toilets and filled the city as never before.

A new illness swept through the city. At first, its victims were the old, the young and the very weak, but then, even the strongest warriors were stricken. Without warning they fell sick, throwing up violently and writhing from diarrea. Within two days they had been drained of fluids and were so weak they could no longer withstand the hunger. Ya Ya witches and healers burned sage, fended off evil spirits and danced day and night. Even so, more and more people fell ill and died.

For many, the stench of death, the fear of this new scourge and the numbing and unceasing hunger drove them away from Chaco. Some went south, hoping to make it to Mexico. Others went north to Verda where it was said there was plenty of food and much game in the mountains. Many of these poor souls fell prey to the hot sun and long march, or to bands of outlaws who took their belongings. The bandits enslaved the men and slaughtered all but the youngest and most beautiful wuti. Word of these attacks spread quickly, discouraging some from leaving the city.

And while some still risked leaving, many more arrived from the outlying communities. At Pueblo del Arroyo and the clan pueblos, the refugees were viewed with distrust. They were not welcome. Del Arroyo's storage rooms were filled with Chochmingwu because they had defied the mandate of the Abbott's Council. Every day hundreds of starving people, tired of waiting in line at Bonito, crowded around Arroyo's front gates begging for food, only to be turned away by the Antelope warriors.

Ammett Moves to Consolidate Power

Ammett assembled all his non-Antelope clan warriors and sent them out of the city in search of bandits and thieves. "Yours is an honorable but difficult chore," he told them, "Take many arrows and do not return while even a single enemy lives."

To his Antelope clansmen, Ammett said, "It is time for Chaco to lash out at its enemies. They will kneel to the power of the city or they will die!" Privately, Ammett told his advisors, "Amhose, of Bonito, has no stomach for this work, so I will do it."

By sending a select group of warriors to deal with bandits, Ammett purged his remaining guard of all but the Antelope clan. To bolster his pueblo's army, Ammett sent word to all Antelope warriors to return to del Arroyo to protect its family. Overnight, Antelope warriors deserted their posts at other spiritual pueblos and returned to del Arroyo.

The warrior caste was unhappy with this order, but they were in disarray since the massacre and tribunal that followed. Not even the strongest and bravest elder would speak out against Ammett's order. The warrior elders also worried about the Ammett's growing army. Del Arroyo was already the largest of all the families, and their numbers grew by fivefold.

In another attempt to consolidate power, Ammett invited Larkin, the Abbott of Kin Klizhin, and Shola, the Abbott of Casa Rinaconada, to discuss ways the clan pueblos could help each other in this time of crisis. Ammett suggested they form a secret alliance to defend one another. "The family clans have worked hard, and when the Chochmingwu of Bonito is gone, the lazy and undeserving will come knocking at our doors. We must protect the Chochmingwu for our families." he told them. When Larkin and Shola left del Arroyo they had sealed an agreement.

At the spiritual pueblos the clerics viewed Ammett's behavior suspiciously but had little time to spend countering his manipulations. If they could not bring about the end of the drought, all would likely be lost anyway. The prayer kivas echoed day and night. Why has Tawa and Amhose forsaken us? they asked. Everyone questioned Amhose's mysterious disappearance, but tried to accept that he must have a good reason to remain hidden.

CHAPTER
TWENTY-SEVEN

Lakon

Rabbits were plentiful, but Hopi had neither the taste nor an interest in the hunt. He was content to choose from whatever lay at his feet, usually wild desert rice, cactus pulp, pine nuts, and lichen. When he was thirsty, he followed the well-worn paths of the coyote to potholes and springs. With each footfall Hopi's previous life slipped further away.

Hoodee had not returned, so Hopi hiked during the mornings and cool evenings. He slept on beds of pine needles under ancient trees. One day as he moved along the edge of a stand of junipers, he discovered a small plot of Chochmingwu. He had neither seen nor talked to anyone for a long time, and the idea of meeting people now disturbed him. He turned and took refuge in the trees. This is my forest, he said to himself, I have had my fill of people. I am not certain whether I even like people anymore. All the same, he was relieved, yet he did not know why.

Hopi no sooner disappeared from sight when several wuti balancing large containers of water on their heads came up a trail. They talked and laughed as they meticulously poured water at the base of each Chochmingwu plant. They bragged about the stockiness of the plants and turned and left, all except for one tall, handsome wuti whose beautiful, beetle-black hair glinted in the morning light. She kneeled and pulled out young velvetgrass growing near the Chochmingwu's stalks.

Hopi watched as the wuti worked. She was neither young nor old and sang to herself as she cultivated. Hopi was entranced by this creature as he was by all the creatures he had seen in the forest. He enjoyed watching her go about her work, but he felt it was impolite to spy and was about to leave when she suddenly stood up and whirled around.

"Who is there?" she asked, frightened.

Hopi was very surprised and before thinking he stood up and said, "Do not be afraid, I mean you no harm. Please forgive me."

For a moment both stood quietly, unable to speak.

"I mean you no harm, I am a wanderer and just happened this way. Please, my only sin is watching you."

The look of fear vanished from the wuti's face and without a word she leaned down and continued working.

"You should be ashamed," she finally said looking up and pulling her hair back away from her face, "It is not polite to spy like that. Who are you?"

Hopi did not know what to say. "I . . . I am sorry. I have no name. I am nobody, I live here in the forest with the animals."

"Nobody?" the wuti repeated several times, laughing. "Come closer Nobody, let me get a look at you."

Hopi approached and the wuti was immediately taken by his beauty and his aura. She pulled her hair back and looked at his wide shoulders and muscular legs.

"What is your name?"

"I am Lakon," she said, then pointed over the hill behind her. "My people live there on the mesa. It is called Kowawa, the Village that is Always There. I am the daughter of Nanu, the leader of the village."

"The Village that is Always There?" Hopi asked.

"Yes! You have heard of it?" she asked excitedly.

"No, I have not," Hopi answered slowly. "I have never heard of Kowawa."

Lakon's smiled disappeared, "No one has ever heard of us," she said lowly, "Few people come this way and none of them has ever heard of this place."

"It may be a blessing," Hopi said.

Lakon looked beyond him into the forest. "This is the land of the magic, no one wanders here. How is it you have come to this sacred land?"

"I have traveled far," Hopi began, turning in the direction of Chaco, "I began my journey in the city of Chaco and I have followed the pathways of the land."

"You are from Chaco?"

"I was, but no more. My home, now, is the land. My father is the day and my mother is the night. They are my masters, and I am their servant." Hopi was surprised at his own words. He had never thought of himself this way before.

"I have never met anyone from Chaco, but I have heard of fabled city from others. Is it beautiful?"

"Oh yes, it is very beautiful."

"But, why then did you leave?"

For the first time in several moons Hopi was forced to think about the home he left behind.

"Please forgive me, but I choose not to speak of it. It is not important. Today, the sun shines, and I am fulfilled in the quiet of this place. This is where I belong now."

"I have always wanted to visit Chaco, but I did not know if it really existed or was just a story told by the elders and wanderers."

"Oh yes, it exists."

"Are all the men of Chaco as beautiful as you?" Lakon asked without embarrassment.

"I cannot say."

"Your voice is strong and you possess the circle of magic around you. Are you real?"

Hopi laughed, "I am real. I have traveled far."

"May I touch you—to make certain?"

"Yes, if you wish, but I promise you, I am only a simple man."

"Simple men do not follow the paths of the forest. Its magic is awesome and only special men venture within."

With the palms of her hands, Lakon touched Hopi's chest. She ran her hands from his shoulders to below his navel and back again. She looked at every detail of his face and then deep into his black eyes.

"Do you have a wuti, Nobody?"

"A wuti? No, I am alone."

From a distance the voices of the other wuti returning told of their arrival.

"I do not have a man anymore," Lakon replied quickly, "My man left to hunt great Red Bear and never returned. It has been a very long time now that I am alone."

The voices grew closer.

"Go now, Nobody. You must hide. If the others know that you are here they might harm you." Lakon turned and walked quickly away. Turning back she said, "Go now, but come back in the afternoon. I will bring you food. Promise me, yes."

"Yes. I promise."

"Go quickly!"

Hopi spent the day sleeping in the shade and awoke to find Lakon lying naked, beside him.

"What are you doing?" he asked as he pulled away.

"Do you not want me?" Lakon asked, confident of his answer.

"I . . . I have not . . . . "

"You have not been with a wuti before?"

"It is not that but I . . . ."

"I see. You have never been with a wuti before. Let me teach you."

"This is not right."

"It is right. I do not have a man, and you are so young and beautiful."

"But,"

"In your forest do not the animals mate and make love? In your Chaco do not the men and wuti copulate?"

"Yes, but . . . ."

"Please, Nobody. I will not hurt you." Lakon's hands moved across Hopi's body and his groin was set afire.

"If you are a true wanderer, you must explore the passion that is a wuti." Lakon climbed astride Hopi and gently touched his chest with her ample bosom. Hopi surrendered, pulling her down on top of him.

Eyes that Cannot See

Yalo often tied Ramu to a tree and left him there for days without food or water. He wanted to see how much this so-called great warrior of Chaco could endure. Ramu sat without uttering a word. Though he could not see this Yalo, but he could sense his presence.

Ramu's other senses told him what his eyes could not. His ears counted the men in Yalo's raiding party and listened to their plans. His nose recognized the stench of his captors, and with only a whiff he could tell the difference between them. His sense of touch could feel the earth move if someone approached or the air being displaced by the wings of birds overhead.

Ramu was forced to make long marches with other slaves, trailing behind raiding parties, and then carrying the carcasses of the wuti back to camp where they were butchered and devoured. At first, Ramu had great difficulty keeping his feet beneath him during these marches. He fell again and again, and his captors whipped him unmercifully, but over time he found his balance. Using his other senses he could walk or even run without falling, but Ramu did not let his captors know the extent of his agility. When he sensed they were watching, he tripped or stumbled.

One night when clouds covered the half-moon and Yaponcha did not sing across the land, Ramu was awakened by a sound of something moving in the bushes behind him. He lay very still as the sound moved gently from one group of weeds to another. When it came within his grasp, Ramu quickly rolled over and snatched at the darkness. He sat up and smiled, "This is a good omen," he said aloud. In one lightning quick move Ramu had captured a rabbit. He quickly broke the rabbit's neck and ate it. "I am sorry sweet rabbit," he apologized, "but the gods brought you to me, and I need your meat to strengthen my body." From then on every night Ramu listened for the nocturnals and when they ventured too closely, he quickly made a meal of them. Most of the time he caught insects and spiders, occasionally a lizard or mouse, and if he was really lucky, a rabbit or a sage grouse.

Ranal returns to Galo

As soon as Ranal was set free by Ammett, he hurried back to Galo. Amarna was surprised to see him coming up the trail. After the warriors pulled him from the briar everyone believed they had seen Ranal for the last time.

"Amarna, Amarna! It is I, Ranal. I have come to visit you," Ranal called out and ran to her side.

"Welcome home," Amarna replied, though not entirely pleased to see him.

"Oh, I no longer live here," Ranal boasted loudly. "This is no longer home for me. I am now an honored citizen of the city." Ranal gestured to the city below, "I am no longer one of you. I have received my rightful pardon, as I always knew I would, and now I come and go as I please."

"This is good," Amarna said, "but how can it be?"

Ranal ignored her question and from his waist band pulled the sack of trade beads. "You see," he said, "I am no longer an outcast, and I am no longer poor man. I am a rich and important man now. I can even buy you if I want." Ranal marched back and forth in front of her.

"You are still the same ruminator you have always been," Vanga said loudly as he pulled himself to Amarna's side. "Certainly, there must be a mistake, they would never let a worm like you go free."

"I should have you flogged, legless man," Ranal said, "I would do it myself, but you stink so . . . ."

Vanga eyed the bag of beads, "With that paltry bag of beads you think you could buy Amarna, Haaa! That measly bag could not buy Amarna a bracelet. Your bag might buy a flute so you can compose music but nothing more, especially not Amarna. You are a fool and will be a fool until you die."

Ranal was outraged, "And you are a liar Vanga! You are nothing, you are not even half a man. How dare you insult me, a citizen of the city? Why, you are lucky I do not have you killed for your insolence."

"Come to me now," Vanga begged, "I will squeeze the air out of you!"

"But he is right," Amarna interrupted, "Vanga is right, Ranal. I am sorry, but you have been away for a long time and your trade beads are now nearly worthless."

Ranal could no longer tolerates these lies and insults. He turned his anger on Amarna. "With this bag of beads I can buy one hundred whores like you. You and this half-man are trash. I have heard the guards of del Arroyo talking and we, in the city, are tired of you outcasts. We will soon destroy you and this place, too." Ranal frothed and a long strand of saliva hung from his chin. "I am now a powerful man, working with the great Ammett, and I will laugh when I watch you die."

Ranal had overstepped himself, and he flinched. "Besides," he said lowering his voice, "I ... I ... knowww you are just jealousss because I, Ranal, am now richhh . . . rich . . . and I am no longer an outcast."

"Then I am happy for you, Ranal," Amarna said angrily. "Since you are a free man I suggest you go to the marketplace and see what your beads will buy. But before you go, I would like to know . . .how did all of this happen? Why were you pardoned?"

"This fool was not pardoned," Vanga said, "he probably escaped and the warriors are searching for him right now."

"This is not true," Ranal said quickly, "I . . . I received my pardon because . . . .." Ranal did not know what to say.

"Yes? Tell us fool, if indeed you were pardoned, why so?" Vanga insisted. "Even you could not have forgotten already!"

"Well, you see . . . ." Ranal began then broke off, paused, and then changed the subject, "Who are all these men sitting on the ridge? What are they doing here?"

"You see, Amarna, I was right, he did escape!" Vanga looked to Amarna and then down the trail, expecting to see the warriors in pursuit.

"Who are these men?" Ranal repeated, confused.

"I do not know." Amarna mused. "They come at the same time each day."

"But why?"

"Why do the geese fly south after Hohoya, fool? Why does the bear slumber all winter? Why does . . . ."

Amarna interrupted, "Perhaps, since you are such a powerful and rich man, Ranal, you should ask them yourself. We here in Galo know nothing."

"Perhaps I will ask them. Perhaps I will . . . ." Ranal's voice tapered off.

"Why do they stare at us that way? What do they want?"

"They are not staring at you. They come every day to be near Amarna." Vanga explained.

"Amarna? They come to buy you?"

"No." she answered, "I do not know why they come."

"So, tell us why were you freed?" Vanga asked again.

"There is only one reason I was pardoned," Ranal said bouncing his head from side to side. "While I waited for the tribunal I composed a powerful song . . . and it just so happened that as I sang it aloud Ammett heard the composition . . . and he was so impressed he pardoned me, and he gave me this bag of beads." Ranal looked down at his bag.

"Really?" Amarna asked.

"Yes, it is true. I swear it. It is quite true."

Vanga did not fall for Ranal's lie. "If that is so, then let us hear this music. You say that the great Ammett, killer of the innocent and betrayer of the Anaa, was so pleased with your music that he gave you your freedom, made you an honored citizen and at the same time gave you a bag filled with worthless trade beads. Hmmmm . . . Yes . . . I see clearly."

"Quiet, Vanga," Amarna pleaded, "someone might hear you."

"I refuse to stand here and be insulted any longer," Ranal said. "I came here to visit my friends and share my beads and nothing more. I just wanted to see that all my outcast friends were alright."

"Yes, as you can see, we are alright. Thank you." Amarna said sincerely.

"Thank you, Amarna. At least I have one friend in Galo." Ranal cast an evil look at Vanga. "By the way," he asked, "have you heard any news of Hopi? I do pray he is alright. I love him so. He was good to me. In the stockade I prayed for his safety. Will he return for you soon?"

Amarna looked down and tried to hold back her tears. "You were there when he promised to return to me, Ranal, do you remember?"

"Yes, I do indeed remember. He has not sent word to you?"

"No. I wait and wait, but still I have no word. I am so afraid."

"Hopi is an honorable man," Ranal said moving closer to Amarna, "Let me be your friend until he returns."

"Thank you, my friend. Hopi was your friend, and I know how much you love him." Amarna broke down in tears, and Ranal rushed to her and held her in his arms. Vanga's neck turned red and he longed to throttle the ruminator.

CHAPTER TWENTY-EIGHT

Lust and Betrayal

Hopi stayed in the forest near the plot of Chochmingwu. Not far away was a small meadow circled by tall rounded boulders. At its center was an oasis of cottonwoods and dogwood growing around a small spring. Hopi spent much of his time there sleeping on the wheatgrass, watching the plateau creatures sipping water, and waiting for Lakon. He longed for her. It was a longing Hopi had never experienced.

Mornings and afternoons Lakon came to water the Chochmingwu and to nurture her young man. She had never known a man like Hopi. He was a child, yet he radiated the confidence of a wiseman. Hopi now learned the wonder and pleasure of a wuti's body. When the wuti of Chaco had shown themselves to him, he had no idea what power they possessed.

When Lakon appeared over a small knoll and saw Hopi waiting there for her, she ran to him, and they fell onto the velvet grass as one. Afterwards they lay together and watched the clouds. Lakon had many questions about Chaco and pestered Hopi to tell her of its glory. "I am of the forest and of this island in the sky now," he told her, "I wish to forget the life I left behind." Sometimes they walked silently through the deep grass and flowers by the spring. Hopi picked Lakon bouquets of paintbrush and yarrow and scarlet bugler.

"Tell me of your family," Hopi asked once.

Lakon seemed troubled, "I have told you, Nobody. I am a widow and I work in the fields." She then pulled him down onto the lush greenery.

One afternoon when the Yaponcha played with the cottonwoods in the meadow, making the leaves spin and sending shards of light spiriting away, Lakon appeared on the knoll. There was no smile on her face and instead of falling to the ground where her lover lay waiting, she stood above him.

"I can no longer come to you."

"Lakon, what is this? I cannot believe it, why?"

"Please, please listen to me. I must tell you something and I do not want you to hate me."

"I could never hate you Lakon. Please, tell me now, what is it?"

"I have not been truthful with you, sweet Chaco man."

"What do you mean?"

"When I first saw you standing in the forest I fell in love with you—you are so special and so beautiful. And then after you told me you were from Chaco, I had to have you."

"Yes, go on!"

"I am sorry, but I have deceived you. I know you will be hurt and have every right to beat me and turn your back on me, but I must tell you now and then you must go."

"I will not!" Hopi said stridently, "I am in love with you, I want to be with you."

"You foolish child," Lakon said sarcastically, "You know nothing of the world. I thought you were worldly because you came from Chaco, yet you are only a love-sick boy."

Hopi was hurt. He got to his feet. "You are right. I may be a boy, but I do love you. Don't you understand that?"

"Yes, Yes." Lakon said half laughing and stroking Hopi's hair away from his face, "I know you love me, and I love you in my own way. But, I can no longer come to you. You must leave now before it is found out that I have been coming to you."

"But, Lakon, I do not understand."

"I lied to you. I am not a widow. I am married, and my husband heard me call out your name last night as I lay dreaming."

"Husband? But . . . I thought . . . ."

"I did not want to lose you. I thought we could have time together. Now, it must end. I must go before my husband comes looking for me."

"I will not leave. I love you and . . . ."

"You still do not understand, do you?" Lakon interrupted. "I wanted you for your beauty and nothing else. Don't you see? Is that not enough?"

"But, Lakon, you can't mean that."

"Leave now before it is too late."

Just then a man's voice called out Lakon's name from the path below.

"It is him. Go." Lakon turned without saying goodbye and ran back to the Chochmingwu field.

"Wait!" Hopi called out, running after her and stopping her. "I cannot let you go . . . ."

"Leave me alone, boy. I have a husband, and I do not want you anymore. Can't you see that I deceived you? You mean nothing to me. Let me go!" Lakon laughed and darted a look into Hopi's eyes, "You deceived yourself as much as I deceived you. Do all the pretty boys of Chaco deceive themselves?"

The Missing Time Scrolls

When Zuni arrived at the second level of Fajada with another message from Amhose, he was surprised to see that the Time Scrolls, which covered the entire ceiling, were missing. In their place was the raw sandstone which had been chiseled out to create the room many dynasties ago. Allander could see the surprise in Zuni's face and instructed him to mind his own business and recite the message he had brought.

Zuni lowered his eyes and drew close to Allander.

Afterward Allander pulled back and asked, "How are your lessons going? Are you learning many songs?"

"Yes, master. I have the honor of Amhose's undivided attention. My head and heart are filled with new songs and stories."

"This is good. Very good." Allander stroked his chin. Zuni had never seen this expression on Allander's face before. It was as if Allander was both sad and frightened. "Do you remember all that we, the Kokopilau astronomers, taught you while you apprenticed here?"

"Yes, master. "

"Please do not forget these things, take them with you on your passage. Promise me that."

"Why, yes master. I will always look to the stars and remember what I have learned."

"Good!"

There was a long silence and both men glanced to where the scrolls had once been.

"Shall I take Amhose a message from you, master?" Zuni finally asked.

"Yes, Zuni. Tell Amhose what you have seen here." Allander's eyes moved again to the ceiling.

"Is that all?"

"Yes, my son."

Worming for Confidence

Ranal not only kept his eye on Amarna, but he took it upon himself to patrol the streets and neighborhoods of Chaco, alert for traitors and those he suspected of hoarding food. He then reported back to Ammett. Ranal noticed that Zuni made many trips between Bonito and Fajada and told Ammett. Ammett instructed Ranal to find out what was so compelling that Zuni made the trip to Fajada so many times.

When Ranal was not spying on Amarna, Zuni and other unsuspecting citizens, he spent his time gambling and playing Senat with the traders and merchants who frequented the marketplace. Ranal won sacks of trade beads and jewelry, and he even bragged of having a storehouse filled with Chochmingwu. "You may all starve,' he boasted to his companions, "I will eat well."

While the city slumped further into despair, Ranal prospered. He found this notion amusing and concluded that justice had finally been bestowed upon him. I can see why, he mused to himself, the prosperous often look upon themselves with such favor. Encouraged, Ranal bought a new set of clothes and wore rings and necklaces. He frequented the prostitutes of Galo and tried to seduce Amarna, but she would have none of it. He was generous to all and made certain that they acknowledged it.

One day when Zuni raced down the steps of Fajada on his way to Bonito, he saw Amarna and waved, and she waved back. Ranal, who was sitting with Amarna, took notice.

"Oh, why will Zuni not come visit me?" Amarna said aloud. "Do you think he has word of Hopi? I wish he would come to me, or I could go to him."

"Shall I run to him?" Ranal piped up quickly, "If I tell him you want to see him, he will surely come!"

"Do you think so? You would do this for me?"

"Of course, Amarna. I shall return." With that Ranal ran down the trail into the city after Zuni. Amarna and Vanga watched as Zuni disappeared into the crowded streets, Ranal close behind him.

Later, Ranal returned to Galo, but Amarna could not speak to him. He had not caught up with Zuni before Zuni disappeared into the sanctuary of Bonito, and even though Ranal could have gone inside to find him, he stopped at Bonito's entrance and did not go any further. I cannot fool the gods of Bonito, he thought, and if I enter, some punishment may well befall me. Outside the walls, Ranal stood in the pueblo's shadow and smiled as he thought of how simply he would work his way into Zuni's confidence.

Grand Gulch

Hopi did not follow Lakon. He watched her disappear into the forest and stood alone in his meadow and cried. The wind blew his long hair around his face and the cottonwood trees cried with him. When the moonless night descended over the world, it found Hopi sitting against a cedar tree at the edge of the meadow. He had cried until no more tears would come, but his grief and disbelief had not abated.

Hoodee returned that evening and was brighter than ever. He moved back and forth just over the crest of the hill, and though Hopi was not in possession of his heart and wanted nothing more than to sit and mourn, he reluctantly got to his feet and followed. By dawn the light had led him far from the Chochmingwu field and Lakon. For days Hopi slept when he could. At night, he pursued Hoodee away from the place known as Kowawa, The Village that is Always There.

One afternoon after he had bathed in a deep koritvi and was sunning himself on a wide, flat rock, Hopi looked around and had a strong sense he had been here before. This cannot be true, he told himself. He got to his feet and walked northward toward an enormous network of canyons. Every step took him further into a strange land he somehow knew.

I have dreamed of this place, he told himself. Yes, I have come to where my dreams live, he thought. "There is a white hilltop to my left," he said aloud, climbing out of a drainage canyon in the broken land. At the top of the drainage, he found a white hilltop to his left. I will find a sagebrush flat near here, he told himself, and again he was right. And then suddenly it dawned on him, "I am in the forest where I was lost as a child! Grand Gulch is very near! My family is here! This is the land of my birth!"

Hopi was very frightened. When he left Chaco, Grand Gulch had not been a destination but a direction in which to travel. Since scaling the great vermillion escarpment and seeing the vastness of the world, he had thought little of Grand Gulch.

The faces of his mother and father appeared in his mind. He had not seen them with such clarity for many equinoxes. The expression on their faces was sad and mournful. He turned and walked quickly away. I will wait until dark and let the light show me the way, he decided. He found a large rock, sat down and waited, but when darkness fell, the light did not come. Perhaps, he thought, it is time I make a decision on my own.

After much contemplation, Hopi still did not know what to do or where to turn, so he waited. Be patient, he told himself, and it will come. In Chaco, the elders and clerics always told him what to do. No one was allowed to think for himself. The Anaa predetermined the outcome of all things. Hopi had resented the Anaa for this, but now he was free and there was no one to tell him what to do. He was free to choose, so what now?

When I left Chaco, he mused, I wandered without a thought in my head except to survive. Fear was my master. I allowed Mother Earth with her sand dunes, buttresses and escarpments to dictate my footsteps. She taught me much about nature and humility. I abdicated my will to her power. Then the Hoodee appeared, and I found the stone animals, the stone forest and the beautiful wuti, Lakon. Hopi suddenly realized that he had really made very few decisions for himself. Someone or something had directed his journey.

I participated little in making the decisions on this journey. Life has its own destination, like a falling leaf from the cottonwood tree. I am like a leaf. I am happy to be free of the branch and float in the wind, and for now I am truly on my own quest. But I am at the mercy of Yaponcha, and I cannot see my destination and am powerless to change it.

Hopi's new-found freedom was no freedom at all. I have traveled the pathway thinking I decided my own fate, but it is not true! He looked at the sky above and shook his head. From now on I will make my own decisions! He considered his options: I can go into the canyon of Grand Gulch and open the door to my past. Another, deeper voice, added, You cannot be complete and true to yourself and ignore this part of your life. On the other hand, he thought, I can stay here and move into the future the natural course of events has shown me exists. Again, the deeper voice spoke, Life moves forward, not backward whether one knows his past or not. Or, he thought, I can leave and come back another time. Yes, the deeper voice said sympathetically, Come back when you have heard the voices within you.

Hopi could reach no decision. A day passed and then another. Decisions are hard work and I am not as good at it as I thought I was, he said to himself. He decided he would not think about it anymore. I will let the earth, the animals or even the gods decide for me. Nothing happened. Again, he considered his options. He was in a void of indecisiveness. It is a trap, the deep voice told him. If you have the power to make decisions, make them quickly before the quicksand of deliberation sucks them away.

He walked back and forth from the rock to the cliff, and he looked into the canyon. Every time he neared the cliff, the wind wafted a deep, penetrating smell of death up to him. "Ahhh," he said aloud, "the smell of death has told me what to do!"

Hopi crept to the edge of the canyon, there he could see many stone houses and storage bins built on the steep cliff faces below. What will they say? And what will I say when I see my mother and my father? Hopi could see his father's strong features and the smile his mother so generously bestowed upon him. He could not hold back the tears.

For the first time in many days Hopi thought of his friend Zuni and of Chaco. Zuni, my friend, I am so sorry that you do not have a father or a mother that you can return to, he thought. The passage of time had somehow washed Hopi's memories clean of his family, and he now realized that his wandering had washed his memories of Chaco and Amhose and Amarna and all that he had loved away. How can this be? he wondered. Why do I not remember those I have loved so deeply? Can this be the way of life? Does the wanderer remember those he has passed along the pathway? Does every day and every new horizon cleanse the mind and the soul of its past? Is this what life is made of, new people and ever new experiences until the last sunset takes us away?

By mid-morning Hopi had not seen anyone below. There were many houses, but the canyon seemed deserted and empty. He moved cautiously along the ridge line, hiding behind trees and rocks and peering into the canyon. He could see scores of small plots of land where Chochmingwu was to be planted next to a nearly dry creek, but still he saw no one. Everyone must be gathered for a celebration, he thought. Yes, all of the people of Grand Gulch must be gathered to celebrate.

Hopi walked down a trail into the canyon. He felt conspicuous because he had not combed his hair and he wore only the loin cloth that Istaqa had given him. I will be taken as a worthless wanderer and will be told to leave the canyon, he thought. Then, a horrible realization sickened him. What if I am arrested and taken back to Chaco? He stopped on the trail and considered this. If I leave now they will never catch me, and if I proceed, I must face the chance of being arrested. This infuriated him. I have already made my decision, I will take my chances, and if they try to arrest me it will take many of them to make me a prisoner. If I must die, then I will die fighting!

Once in the canyon Hopi walked the main pathway. He heard voices ahead of him, around the corners of the winding canyon, but when he made his way to their source, no one was there. He went from house to house, but all were deserted and appeared to be ransacked. In some of the houses, it seemed the owners had left quickly, leaving everything behind. Hopi called out, but no one answered.

By sunset Hopi had walked a great distance and had seen hundreds of houses and not a single soul. He hiked back up to the gulches' rim, deciding to sleep on the plateau. He looked further down the canyon. It, too, appeared deserted except for the silhouettes of many large birds circling above. As Hopi looked for a suitable cedar tree to bed down under, he found several fresh burial mounds. A few steps away, in an opening in the trees, there were hundreds of mounds, each constructed within the last equinox.

The next morning he walked back into the canyon and continued his search. As the sun crossed the sky above the canyon, it brought with it recollections of Hopi's childhood. The shadows told him much. Soon, they said, you will reach a place where two large canyons meet the main gulch. It is only a stones throw away from your house and the large wide place in the canyon where gatherings take place. If there is anyone left in this place, he told himself, they will certainly be there.

Soon, the cliff tops where the canyons meet in the main gulch came into sight. He broke in a trot. He could see vultures circling above, and their cries filled his ears. Suddenly, to his right, Hopi saw someone, or he thought he saw someone. He called out, but no one answered. He cautiously made his way to the place, and as he approached, a head-swelling stench greeted him. He reeled back, gagged and covered his face with his hands. He proceeded slowly. A warrior lay dead, spread-eagle over a large rock with his battle ax still gripped in his hand. He had been dead for sometime and his stomach had exploded with maggots. On the far side of the rock lay another dead man. This man was not Anaa but from one of the wandering tribes of the north.

Hopi backed away slowly, turned and retreated to the pathway. He walked on, finding other bodies in the dry creek bed, on the hill sides and even in the houses next to the path. He picked up an ax laying on the pathway and moved cautiously forward. At the place where three canyons met stood the main village of Grand Gulch, he stopped in his tracks. Bodies were everywhere, the ground was covered with them from one side of the canyon to the other. In some places they were stacked many deep. Warriors, old men, wuti and even children all intertwined and reeking. Among them were the bodies of men of the same wandering tribe he had seen earlier.

There had been a tremendous battle—to the very last person. Vultures were the only victors, delighting in their feast and picking at the carcasses with vigor. Hopi worked his way through the battlefield. He looked at each face, hoping for he knew not what, perhaps a familiar face or the story of what had happened here, or maybe even the face of his mother or father. The faces of the children were expressionless. The wuti's faces held terror and the warriors' faces grimaced with pain, anger and hatred. The stink made Hopi's head swim. Still, he moved from body to body, praying over them. For the first time, Hopi felt a seething hatred, but his hatred was not directed at those who had attacked Grand Gulch, but toward the gods who gave birth to man and then led him to this destiny.

"What have we done to deserve this?" he yelled out. "Why do you treat us in such a despicable way? What have we done?" Hopi was overwhelmed and for a long time he cried out, or casually talked out loud to the souls he stepped over as he picked his way up a side canyon to the house where he was born.

Nearby, he spotted a rock carved with histories and stories in the soft stone. This rock told Hopi of the drought and the black sickness that killed many old and young. It told of repeated attacks by an unknown tribe who numbered many and who raided the smaller Anaa camps away from the main gulch. They carried away the wuti and children.

When Hopi arrived at the place where he remembered his house had been, it was gone. All that remained were its broken-down walls and nothing more. He sat and cried and a great emptiness came over him. He was alone and the connection to his family, which he had long neglected, was finally severed.

CHAPTER
TWENTY-NINE

Ranal's Ruminations

As long as Vanga protected Amarna, Ranal would never gain her confidence, and he knew it. What would a citizen of Chaco do, a citizen of good standing, faced with such a dilemma, he wondered. If I were a cleric, I would pray. Yes, but it would take so long. Ranal tried to think for a long time. What would I do if I were a Kokopilau? Ranal's eyes were a blank and after a few moments he hit himself on the side of his head with a clenched fist. I am not Kokopilau, I cannot think as they do. What would Ammett of del Arroyo do? Ahhhh, yes. What he would do?

All of this thinking was too much for Ranal. He walked though the miserable streets of Chaco babbling, his arms making circles in the air. In other times, his behavior would not have been tolerated in the streets, but now it was barely noticed. The pueblo warriors, whose job it was to police the streets, were paralyzed by the recent events. Behind their warrior masks they were confused and wondered where to place their allegiance—with the clan, the spiritual pueblos, or with the warrior caste?

"I will cut his throat," Ranal mused aloud, "I will watch the sand soak with his oily, red blood." Ranal bobbed his head from side to side . . . No, this will not due, Ammett's voice told him. He will easily crush you if he gets his hands on you. "Yes, of course, master, perhaps then I could wait until he passes close by the cliffs and then push him." Ranal smiled at his own ingenuity. "I will wait until Vanga pulls himself to the rock at sunset and just as he passes the place where the trail nears the cliff I will push him." Ranal, my son, Ammett's voice said, how many admirers watch Amarna daily? "Oh, yes, I forgot. Yes, you are right. If one of her admirers saw me, it would not look good."

Ranal spoke loudly as he passed a group of refugees standing on the street. They turned to face him. Realizing they were watching, Ranal said, without stopping, "Perhaps this is not the best idea and I should rethink it."

At the Mercy of Chaos

Word reached Chaco that a great disaster had befallen Grand Gulch, and everyone there was dead. Survivors told stories of cannibalism, disease, warring among the clans, and a siege by many braves from an unknown wandering tribe. Many who escaped the gulch were caught and enslaved by bandits.

As the story spread through the city, the idea of being trapped in Chaco burned in the imagination of the Anaa. Those who planned to escape to Mexico or to the north were devastated by the news. The prospect of the grand city of Chaco coming under siege was openly discussed. Wuti whispered about preparations for battle as they waited to fill their bowls at nearly dry Galo creek. Men tested their archery, repaired axes, limbered their muscles and smoked many pipes.

Nothing had been done about the drought and many Anaa had already suffered immensely. Nothing had been done about Hopi missing the Cha'tima or the equinox massacre that followed. Nothing had been done about del Arroyo's refusal to relinquish its Chochmingwu to Bonito or about the thousands of refugees who brought disease and hardship to the clogged city streets. The people felt that Amhose, leader of the Anaa, had deserted his people. With the news of the disaster at Grand Gulch, the people of the city were angry and frightened. Will this, too, go unchallenged? Is Chaco dead? Are we now at the mercy of chaos?

Zuni was besieged for word from Amhose. "Do not forget what Tawa has said about keeping the spot on top of your head open," Zuni told them. "Amhose has not forgotten you. Listen to his words, Pray, listen and wait, the time of true believers will arrive, but only for those who are pure." Zuni's attempts to soothe the people were not entirely successful, and his words spelled doom to those who listened. To confuse the matter, Zuni did not have a directive from Amhose to use his name or to pass on this message. The message had been given to Zuni in personal conversation and was not meant for the general populace. But, Zuni could not help himself. He loved his people and felt responsible to them for Amhose's absence.

Descent into Darkness

Hopi sat at the ruins of his childhood home and wept. I am nothing but a shadow, a wisp of smoke in the night. Hopi was truly alone and felt he could not stand. With the passing of sun to sun, moon to moon, season to season—everything changes, nothing stays the same. Yesterday, I was a boy within these walls, today I am a man crying over memories that just a few days ago were not important to me. Tomorrow? Where will I find myself and what will I become? I will surely be dust, he thought.

Hopi looked down at his arms and hands. The power in these arms will disappear quickly, and I, too, shall become weak. To think that I am invincible was folly, and I am a fool. A heaviness descended over Hopi and the idea of man's foolishness made him laugh aloud. The good people of Grand Gulch believed, and look how their devotion has been rewarded. Hopi looked down the canyon. "There is nothing but pain and dishonor in this life," he hollered out to the lifeless forms below him. "Life is a curse! We are fools! We believe we can endure against time, but our essence will not live forever. Nothing can withstand this descent into darkness." Hopi cupped his hands over his face and sobbed uncontrollably.

"I shall leave this sham of man's existence and live what days I have remaining in the cedar and juniper forest," he said aloud. "The pretense of man and of wuti cannot subvert me there."

Though Hopi attempted to separate himself from his humanness, he could not entirely break free. He was a man with a man's nature. As the trees are of the trees, the water is of the water, and the paintbrush blossom is of the flowering paint brush plant. I am a man, he anguished. I cannot escape. I am a party to all of this.

Thoughts of his childhood overwhelmed him. The backdrop of the canyon brought them before him and one by one the images stepped up and introduced themselves. Every person who had lived in the canyon passed before his eyes. His father's voice came from beneath the rubble of the house. His mother's tears floated down from the sky. Hopi craned his neck and looked as far up the canyon as he could. This is my life. I was born here. This voyage began within these canyon walls.

What shall I do? Where shall I go from here?

Istaqa and the Dance of the New Hopi Man

Above, on the canyon rim, the sound of a flute drifted down to where he sat. Its song was joyous and brought him alive again. It was Istaqa's flute. No one plays as Istaqa does, he thought. The grip of despair which engulfed Hopi's chest released it grip, and he leapt to his feet and danced. Round and round he went. His joy surprised himself, and he felt his body acted without his consent. His movements were wild and elegant. He leapt high and kicked, his arms left streamers in the air, his body hardly touched the ground.

Hopi's dance was not Anaa, it came from a place deep within the innermost canyon of his soul—a tributary not yet explored. It was his dance, fed by this tributary and dedicated to the honor of his family. It was the dance of a new Hopi, one who had been released from the abyss. Much later his dance would be known as the Hopi-Man Dance of Renewal. Hopi's dance was for his family, to release their souls to wander. Hopi's dance would free them to live in the canyon with the cottonwoods, and in the creek, and within the cracks of the sandstone walls rising to the sky above.

On Yalo's Trail

At Yalo's stronghold in the foothills of the Blue Mountains one of his men arrived after a long run.

"They have sent an army to wipe us away," he reported to Yalo. "They caught us by surprise as we decimated the last of the farms to the south. The warriors were fierce and fought as the cougar who has been cornered."

"How many?" Yalo asked, his voice, high-pitched and nasal. His chest rose and fell quickly.

"I do not know. Many hundreds or more."

"Hmmm," Yalo stroked his forehead and paced back and forth. He knew that sooner or later the empire would deal with him. He questioned the man about the direction from which the army arrived, and if they took prisoners. He wanted to know if they were well equipped and well fed, Yalo asked, "Are you the only one to escape?"

"I do not know."

"Of my one hundred men, no one survived?"

"They quickly overwhelmed us. I fought hard and escaped. I returned as quickly as possible."

"You have done well," Yalo told the man and then ordered him beheaded for not fighting to the death.

Yalo was not easily frightened, but neither was he foolish. Nearly one third of his men had been lost, and he immediately ordered his camp disbanded, moved further into mountainous country. One thing the messenger said stuck in his mind. "They fought as the cougar who has been cornered." Chaco is a cornered animal, but it has teeth and claws, he considered. The idea of toying with the wily and professional warriors of Chaco excited him. His plan was simple and its success would mean his ascent to greatness. If he failed, it would mean his demise. Yalo knew that once the Chaco warriors began their search, they would not stop until they found him, and they would fight to the death to kill him.

Duty is Truth

Zuni marvelled at the growing number of men in waiting near Amarna. Just a half-moon ago there were only a handful, now there are hundreds. He reported this to Amhose.

"Tell Allander," Amhose told Zuni.

"Allander?" Zuni responded queerly.

"Yes, my son. He will find this of great interest and importance."

"Importance?" Zuni asked incredulously.

"Yes. You must always remember to observe everything around you. Everything is a message, even events concerning a prostitute, who for some reason unknown to you, has gained a large following."

Amhose went on, "I find meaning in the death of the last Cottonwood, in the Cedar Wax Wings who for countless springtimes arrived in Chaco to eat sweet sage berries, and in the movements of the insects and ants. Did you know the ants of the pueblos have disappeared?"

"No, my father. I do not watch the ants and the birds. I have been upset about the drought, about Ammett, about the starving people and about . ..."

"Enough, my son. I will worry, I will worry for both of us. It is your duty to observe everything, especially the small things. They tell much about truth, for they do not lie or fall prey to jealousies, or lust or become greedy.

"What happens in Chaco will happen with or without your concern. I have not forgotten all that has occurred, and I see more than you know."

"Yes, my father, your wisdom is great and it is an honor to be chosen by you, but I am concerned about the people. They try so hard to do good, but the world collapses around them, and they are hungry and you do not offered them comfort."

"Quiet, my son, this is not your concern. The people who are pure will continue." Amhose's words comforted Zuni and he dropped his shoulders in relief.

"Go now, my son. Tell Allander about Amarna and her admirers. It is my message to him."

"Yes, my father."

The silver Cottonwood Leaf

Observe the small things, Zuni said to himself as he walked to Fajada. He listened for the sound of the birds, but only heard the din of the dirty city. He watched for insects, but all he saw were the tired feet of refugees. Then on a side street, something lying on the ground caught his eye. It is just a piece of garbage, he said to himself, but picked it up. As he leaned over a deep sadness filled his heart. It was a leaf from the ancient cottonwood tree.

Zuni had not thought of the cottonwood since it had been destroyed by the lightning. He had been far too busy with Amhose. The magnificent tree was gone now, and the only trace of its existence was the leaf he held in his hand. The green waxiness was replaced by a silver web. The veins of the leaf were intact, and its intricate detail reminded Zuni of the many roads leading to the city and of the complexity of the world of Anaa. Zuni was struck by its beauty, though its life had ceased more than two moons ago. His stomach ached, he was dizzy and his head swam. Thoughts rushed so quickly through his head his mind could not keep up.

Zuni's reverie was ended by the sound of a man and wuti arguing inside an adobe house. He dropped the leaf and turned to leave but then he stopped, leaned down and retrieved the leaf again.

When he reached Fajada he gently placed the leaf on a nearby rock and climbed the many stairs to deliver his message. Allander stood at the center of the now empty ceremonial room as though he were waiting for Zuni. After Zuni delivered his message, Allander put his hands on the small of his back and arched. His eyes scanned the rock face of the ceiling where once were the Great Time Scrolls of Kokopilau.

"The sky has not yet fallen," he started, "but the stars are all gone."

Zuni did not know if he should respond or listen. He dutifully stood and waited.

"The sky has not yet fallen, but the only stars that remain shine within the hearts and souls of a few Anaa. You, Zuni, possess the luminosity of a heavenly body. The gods have picked you as a leader, and your light will grow as time passes. Amarna's glow cannot be judged. It could be a meteor whose light will brighten then disappear, or it could even be a falling star, the embodiment of an empty tomorrow. Time will tell.

"I find myself questioning the predictions and the manifestations of the gods," Allander said in the familiar voice of an old friend. "I know that this is not the role of Allander. My role is to observe and to acknowledge the universe which is created for the Kokopilau." Allander's voice cracked with emotion and Zuni trembled.

"You and I have served well, my son. We have obeyed and studied. We have questions, but have not doubted. We will be rewarded, though my reward has already been given me. I am joyous at all the nights and all the darkness I have experienced. I am joyous to speak now, for I hold council with only the gods and within myself. It is good that I give my joy the wings of words.

"Take my hands, Zuni," Allander moved in front of Zuni and lifted Zuni's hands into his. "I will teach you a song and a dance that no Anaa has ever known. It is the luminosity of the Kokopilau and it will burn into your heart."

Around and around the room Allander danced, pulling Zuni along with him. Zuni felt the dance in his feet, and the two of them moved effortlessly around the large and empty room. Zuni heard the sound of crickets singing. At first, it was low and barely audible, but the sound became louder and seemed to originate from many places at once. Then the sound of midnight frogs croaking, joined the sound of the crickets. The keening of night birds wings and the howling of coyotes in the distance joined as well. Zuni looked at Allander's face and realized the songs of the wild were coming from his lips. He closed his eyes and Allander turned him faster and faster.

Then, Zuni was aware of standing at the base of Fajada and his hand reached out to pick up the silver cottonwood leaf—but it was gone.

The next morning, Allander, himself, stood atop Fajada Butte and sang out the Morning Cha'tima. For three days Allander greeted the new day but on the fourth day, the Cha'tima did not come. The sun moved the shadow of Fajada to its appointed place, the Tawtoma. But Cha'tima did not come. A group of devoted Anaa gathered in the streets and walked to the base of the butte, but the Cha'tima did not come. They could see no one on the butte. There were no Kokopilau on the street or anywhere else.

CHACO

PART

THREE

CHAPTER THIRTY

Vanga

When Vanga did not come to Amarna's shack at sunset she went looking for him, but he was not to be found. While her admirers waited patiently for her arrival, Amarna searched desperately, asking everyone she met if they had seen him, but no one had. Finally, an old wuti told her that she had seen Vanga late the night before. He was sick and pulling himself toward her house. "No," another wuti interrupted, and pointed to the cliff where outcasts were thrown after they died, "I saw him before dawn crawling in that direction."

Amarna rushed to the cliff and peered over the edge. The sun-washed bones of outcasts were stacked deep in the small ravine. Lying on the top were the decaying remains of the recent dead. Unlike the Anaa, who were laid to rest in mounds, the outcasts' journey to the other side was began on this bed of their ancestors' bones.

Amarna searched for her devoted servant and friend. He was her link to Hopi, and like Hopi he had made a promise to her. Vanga vowed to be by her side and to protect her until Hopi's return. Vanga was not among the stacks of white bones in the arroyo. But her relief was swept away when she turned and saw Vanga's bloated form sitting upright against a boulder nearby.

One of Vanga's hands clutched at his neck, and his bulging eyes stared flatly into the day. His waxen face was dark blue, almost black, and his swollen tongue protruded from his mouth. Amarna dropped to her knees at his side but could not bring herself to embrace his grotesque figure.

"Oh Vanga, my friend," she cried out, "what has happened to you? Amarna covered her face and sobbed. "Oh, what will I do without you? Why have you gone from me? We are both alone now. What will I do without you? I am alone again!"

From behind, Amarna suddenly felt the hand of someone on her shoulder, "I am here, Amarna. It is I, your friend and servant, Ranal. You are not alone. I am here with you."

Amarna turned and grasped Ranal around his legs and clung to him. She sobbed uncontrollably. He stood above her, looking down at her beautiful, long flowing hair. He felt excited and powerful at the same time.

"Ranal, Ranal, what has happened? What has happened to Vanga?"

"Va . . . Van . . . Vang . . . Vanga was very sick, my lovely Am . . . Ama . . . Amarannaa," Ranal stuttered, "We all knew he was sick. Not many men could have lasted the way he did after his accident. Van . . . Vanga was a gooood man and loved you very much, but I want you to know that there are others who love you, too."

Amarna cried for a long while next to Vanga's body, then Ranal helped her up and went with her to sit on the wide flat rock to pray for Hopi's return. Ranal's proximity to Amarna was noted by the four warriors from del Arroyo who waited for Hopi's return. Many of Amarna's admirers were jealous of Ranal, but tried not show it. Instead, each man sat quietly and wished that he alone could comfort her.

Later that night, while Amarna entertained the rich men who now came to her, Ranal rolled Vanga's stiff body to the cliff edge and, with one foot, pushed it into the ravine.

"Good bye you fool—you stupid, stinking, half-man," he said aloud. "You will never stand in my way again." He laughed hysterically.

Wait for Me

"Amhose! Amhose!" Zuni hollered down the hallway to Amhose's room. "Where are you, my teacher? Where are you?"

"Yes, yes my son—what is it?"

"The Morning Cha'tima—it was not offered!"

"Oh, that. Yes, Zuni, I am aware of it." Amhose appeared at the doorway of his room. His voice did not reflect the response Zuni expected.

"What does it mean?" Zuni asked.

"My son, no storm can shake my devotion, my love for Chaco and our way of life. No storm can stop my singing," he said as though speaking to the gods. "How can I stop singing?" Amhose turned and went back into his sparsely furnished room, motioning Zuni to follow him. He sat on the edge of his cot and instructed Zuni to sit on the floor in front of him.

"Let us sing together," he smiled at Zuni. "If you do not know the words, sing anyway, when you can."

Wait for me, and I will return
But you must wait very hard.
Wait when you are filled with sorrow,
as you watch the yellow rain and
when wind sweeps over the snow drifts.
Wait for me when the heat of summer
brings sweat to your brow, and
wait for me when others stop waiting and
forget the glory of their yesterdays.
Please wait for me when, from afar,
I have not spoken to you and when
the others tire of waiting,
and when you sit at the campfire
honoring my memory, please
WAIT.
For I will return to you defying every death,
every distance, and even time itself—
For by your waiting you have saved me.
And only you and I will know that I have survived,
because you have waited as no one else did.

Amhose sang in such a beautiful voice and with such feeling that Zuni bowed his head and cried. He could not help himself, and his tears flowed freely and without embarrassment. Amhose leaned down, lifted Zuni's chin with his hand and told him, "Sing with me, my son. It is the Anaa Song of Life, and to say the words will make you stronger. I promise you these words will give you strength. Hold them in your heart, and share the song when your heart moves you."

Then, Amhose instructed Zuni to go to Fajada and see what he could find.

Zuni climbed the steps to Fajada but found no sign that the Kokopilau or anyone had ever been there. He rushed down the steps and into the Kokopilau village. Every house was abandoned as though its occupants simply walked out the door and had disappeared into the black veil of night.

The Kokopilau were gone.

The life force within Zuni flickered, and the energy left his feet. He fell exhausted against the wall of a Kokopilau house. His breath came fast, and his head swam. What happened? Where have you all gone?

The Plan of Life

Hopi climbed quickly out of Grand Gulch and followed the music of the flute. He carried a sense of loss, but he was excited to see Istaqa and smiled at the prospect. He often thought of Istaqa who was so different from the Anaa, yet whose code of ethics and action were, in their own right, honorable. On the plateau, he plunged into the hilly forest. The music moved away from him so he quickened his pace. He soon came to a place where deep footprints covered the bronze sand. Istaqa was not alone! Advancing from one tree to the next Hopi moved toward the music. Without his consent, Hopi separated, and his Other rose up above the squat desert trees and moved quickly forward to see what was ahead.

On low ridge, his Other spotted Istaqa and three men marching north. Istaqa was not a willing traveler. A rope was knotted around his neck, and he was being lead by one of the men. The Other could not tell who the men were except that they appeared to belong to the same tribe who had attacked the gulch. A fist of anger filled Hopi's stomach as his Other returned inside of him. He moved quickly forward, carrying the war axe he had found in the Gulch.

Hopi cut the distance between the group then moved ahead of them. As they rounded a large rock, Hopi jumped out and struck the last man on the head with his ax. The man's head made a loud cracking sound under the powerful blow, and the stone ax head sunk into his head. The man fell forward with the ax secured deep in his skull. Hopi looked up in time to dodge a spear thrust at him by another brave. He grasped the spear by its shaft and pulled the man in a half circle to the ground. Hopi raised the spear above his head and plunged it into the man's chest. The third brave came up behind Hopi and grabbed his neck with one hand, and was about to sink his long knife into the small of Hopi's back when Istaqa lunged out and knocked the man and Hopi to the ground. The three men struggled, rolling back and forth across the sand, each trying to find the knife which had been knocked loose in the fall. Hopi found the knife first, and he buried it to the hilt in the man's chest. The brave screamed out, looked directly into Hopi's eyes and fell limp in the sand. Hopi lay distended on top of the man's body. He could not move.

"Are you injured?" Istaqa asked.

There was no answer.

"There is no time to lose," Istaqa said frantically, "the forest is filled with these devils. Come, we must go!"

Istaqa pulled Hopi to his feet. Hopi turned in a tight circle. He had never taken the life of another, and he wanted to look into each man's face.

"Come!" Istaqa grabbed him by the arm and the two men slipped into a nearby maze of giant mushroom-shaped rock formations.

"There is a great warrior within you, my boy." Istaqa said when they were hidden some distance away. "You saved my life, as I saved your life. This is the way of my people. This is the natural way of events." Istaqa could see that Hopi was disturbed. "Do not fret my friend. Had you not killed them, they would surely have your scalp—and mine, too."

"Who are these people?" Hopi finally said.

"They are called Utta. They are from the mountains near the great sea of salt. The drought has spread, and now coyote eats coyote and man eats man—one tribe against the other. It is the cycle of life."

"The cycle of life?"

"Yes, my friend. It does no good to deny nature as do the Anaa. We are honorable until we are thirsty and hungry. We do what we must, or we die. Do not blame yourself for killing those men."

"I do not blame myself," Hopi interrupted, "I take pleasure in killing those who have killed my people. It is strange, but I enjoyed it."

Istaqa said sternly, "No! Take no pleasure in killing! We kill to survive and only for that. That is the plan of life."

CHAPTER THIRTY-ONE

The Green Mask Cave

"You must dance for the men you have killed." Istaqa told Hopi. "They are proud warriors, and you have taken away their future. You must dance for them as they would for you." Istaqa sensed that Hopi was in no mood to listen. "I know they killed your family, and they massacred your people in the gulch. But even if you find it difficult, you should dance for them. It is the honorable thing to do," Istaqa added.

"Honorable! How can you talk of such a thing?" Hopi was angry. "You are a cannibal! You kill wuti and children and eat them! Do not speak to me of honor. I have heard enough talk of honor."

"Ahhh," Istaqa said slowly, "Here is a man who will not talk of honor, but who risks his own life to save a man he says has none. Hmmmm." Istaqa raised his arms and spoke to the sky, "What have they done to Hopi's sorry little soul? He cannot see who he is and what he is doing. He wanders across the land, but he does not realize that his feet leave deep prints in the sand. His footprints start in Chaco, and they lead here." Istaqa pleaded, "God, help this confused man trace his footsteps back to the place his honor lies so he can reclaim it once again. God, let this man know who he is. Let him trust his own heart."

Hopi was unimpressed and pretended not to listen.

"You must dance for the dead." Istaqa demanded. "If you do not, their faces will haunt you. It is the way of battle, and the way of life."

Hopi did not move. "I will not!" Hopi finally declared. "I have already forgotten their faces. They have no faces. They walk the horizon. They steal in the dark. They kill behind the back! They destroy everything. Tomorrow I will take you there," Hopi gestured to the gulch, "and you can see for yourself."

"The men you killed have your face, right now, Hopi," Istaqa turned his back. "Oh God, little Hopi will dance for the men he has killed tomorrow," Istaqa told the sky. "He is angry now, but he is a good man."

The next morning, Hopi and Istaqa descended into the canyon. They walked among the dead. The people were at rest, and only their hollow eyes told of the pain they suffered. Coyotes, insects and swarms of birds devoured the souls of Grand Gulch. Everywhere along the pathway they found bodies. "If there is indeed a Nedder world," Istaqa said, "it must be this place."

The further they went, the narrower canyon became. The stream that ambled through the upper part of the canyon was now forced into the narrow gorge. The water carried pieces of clothing and rotting flesh; both Hopi and Istaqa were thirsty, yet could not bring themselves to drink.

Although the canyon narrowed, the pathway was wide and well traveled. After a length, the trail abruptly turned left and climbed over a steep sandstone embankment. From there, Hopi and Istaqa could see that the trail continued up a steep incline to the base of the cliffs and into the mouth of a cave. Above the cave entrance was an unusual, spectacular, oval-shaped painting.

As they approached they could see that the painting was of a mask, an ominous-looking face with hollow eyes and frowning smile. Running across the face was a swath of green paint. Neither Hopi nor his worldly companion, Istaqa, had ever seen anything like it. It was not Anaa nor any other of the tribes Istaqa knew. The glowing green paint was also unknown to them.

Istaqa turned and looked back up the canyon. "I have seen much today, more than I have seen in many seasons. But of everything thing I have seen today, I have never looked upon anything to compare with this green mask cave."

Hopi looked at Istaqa quizzically. Istaqa continued, "From here we can look back up the canyon. See, the path comes right to this place. It has been traveled much, yet this place is not Anaa, or not of an Anaa that I know!"

"Anaa," Hopi whispered, "is Anaa. It cannot be anything else."

"Yes, but this painting is not Anaa."

"I agree."

"We have a decision to make," Istaqa said. "We can go further on this path and into this cave, or we can turn back and go another way."

"There is no decision to make," Hopi said dumbfounded. "only one path lies before our feet. We cannot go back. We must continue on."

"That is not true, my friend. We can return the way we came. We can go back down the hill and go down the canyon walking in the creek."

"But, Istaqa," Hopi said excitedly. "We cannot go back into yesterday! We must go forward!"

"Yes, my friend you are right. We cannot trace our steps into yesterday, but we can return by the path we have come by. It is our choice."

Hopi could not understand his friend's logic. He wants me to dance for those who have killed my people, he thought, and retreat from this cave to the place where my family lies rotting.

"There are many paths from which to chose," Istaqa said softly, "You, my friend, believe there is only one. "Oh God," Istaqa asked again, "give my friend, Hopi, the knowledge that there are many paths beneath his feet."

"Enough!" Hopi said angrily. "You may follow whatever path you like, but I will go into this world and into this cave. I will not go back. I cannot go back. I have decided!"

The Kokopilau's Disappearance

In Chaco, the Kokopilau's disappearance sent a shock wave through the city. People swarmed the empty houses of the Kokopilau, searching for signs of what happened, taking whatever they could find and claiming property for themselves. Sacred Fajada Butte was defiled by trespassers. For a thousand solstices the punishment for setting foot on the butte was death, but with news of the Kokopilau's disappearance, thousands swarmed to the butte to see for themselves. Pueblo warriors, assigned to protect the butte, stepped aside and let the people search without impediment.

The end must surely be near, people whispered as they thronged the streets. The Kokopilau were gone, and the Cha'tima had not been made. Everyone was confused and fearful of what might happen next. At mid-morning a large contingent of del Arroyo warriors, painted black and wearing snowy-white owl feathers, marched in fighting cadence toward the butte. They pushed through the crowd and took up positions surrounding Fajada. While half the painted warriors stood guard, the other half stormed the stairways, attacking trespassers and throwing them into the crowd below. At the same time, another column left del Arroyo and moved forcefully to the butte. At its center, carried in a high-backed chair on the shoulders of his men, was Ammett.

When Ammett arrived he jumped down and hurriedly climbed the butte's many steps. He went from one room to the next searching for any clue to what happened. When he found nothing, he climbed the last staircase to the Cha'tima Rock and looked down at the mob. At first the people cheered when they saw him there, but they became silence as Ammett slowly raised his arms to the heavens and in a deep and beautiful voice sang out the morning Cha'tima. Each word hung in the air. The crowd cheered its approval and Ammett smiled down at the city of Chaco, the ancient empire of the Anaa. It sprawled in all directions as he had never imagined it. This was the first time Ammett had set foot on Fajada Butte, and the magic he beheld infected his mind with omnipresence.

A Meeting of Friends

The haste with which Yalo moved his camp told Ramu that warriors from Chaco were not far away. Ramu was forced to carry a great burden of treasure, mostly silver and turquoise, on his back for five days until they reached an easily defendable meadow high in the Blue Mountains.

When they arrived, many of Yalo's followers were already there. The mountain air was rich, and Ramu smelled the scent of pines and maidens. He was tied to a huge ponderosa tree and lay in the deep, cool grass at its base. He listened to the birds, squirrels, and the wind rushing through the trees. Ramu was very tired and slept until the sound of a familiar voice awoke him. Have I been dreaming, he asked himself, or do I know this voice? He sat up, cocked his head and listened. There it is again, Ramu whispered to himself, I am not dreaming.

Ramu laid down, feigning sleep. A group of bandits approached within a few feet and tied a newly-captured group of farmers to a tree. When their prisoners were safely tethered, the bandits left to find something to eat. Ramu sat up and spoke.

"Welcome Tar. It is I, Ramu."

"Ramu?" A voice muttered, "It cannot be!"

"Yes, my friend. I am Ramu."

"It cannot be," the voice said, "Your eyes! What have they done to you?"

"They did not take my eyesight, but they have taken what is left of my freedom."

"Ramu! It is you," Tar declared. "But, how is it so? How did they capture the greatest warrior of all Chaco?"

"The same way they captured the greatest runner of all Chaco," Ramu said flashing a broad and warm smile. "I will tell you my story later, but please tell me how you have come to this place."

Tar told Ramu that one morning when all the men had gone to the dry streambed to dig for water, a raiding party attacked them. "We had no chance," Tar told Ramu. "We were outnumbered and did not have our bows or hand weapons. Many of my Blue Flute brothers were killed, and the rest of us should have been killed too, but, like cowards, we surrendered, hoping to save our worthless skins." When Ramu asked what had become of his father, mother and sisters, Tar broke down and sobbed.

"I do not care about myself," Tar finally said, "If I get a chance to kill one of these murderers I will gladly lay down my life and be done with it all." Tar sobbed and his anger flared, "I will avenge the death of my family and I will gladly go to the next world to be with them for I have nothing to live for."

After a long time Ramu spoke, "Tar," he said, "tell me, is there a snow covered mountain peak to the south?"

"Yes, but how do you know?"

"Is there a great shelf of granite to the east and a pine-covered plateau across a narrow entry way to the west?"

"Yes, Ramu. You have been here before?"

"Yes, my brother. This is the place of many bears. I was here as a young warrior." Ramu grabbed Tar by the arm, "Tell me Tar, this is very important, did you see any sign of Chaco warriors on your march here?"

"No. I did not," Tar replied, but then added, "I did overhear Yalo's men talking about Chaco warriors and that it was important to get to this place as quickly as possible."

"Can you get to your feet?"

"Yes, Ramu I can, but why?"

"Can you see back down the trail?"

Tar stood and looked down the mountain trail. "Yes, I can see part of the trail."

"What else?"

Tar strained, "I can see the valley below and the great sandstone welt in the distance."

"Do you see smoke or dust in the air above the valley?"

"Tar shaded his eyes with his hand and squinted, "Yes! Yes, Ramu. I see dust! I see the dust!"

"Quiet!" Ramu said, pulling at Tar's leg. "Sit, sit down quickly."

"What is it my friend? Is it the warriors? Are warriors coming from Chaco"

"Yes."

"We will be saved!" Tar said enthusiastically.

"No," Ramu looked worried. "this place is a trap for anyone who comes here. The only way into this meadow is the trail which you came by. Yalo and only a few men can easily overwhelm a much larger company of fighters from this place. This is a trap!"

CHAPTER

THIRTY-TWO

The Family Kachinas

By the time Hopi and Istaqa arrived at the Green Mask cave, shadows had reclaimed the canyon below. Rather than continue arguing whether to proceed or not, they fell silent and rested for the night. Later, when the evening stars had fallen out of the sky and a faint, waxing moon appeared in the east, Hopi was awakened by voices coming from within the cave. He lay motionless, fearing any movement would alert the intruders of their presence. The voices were squabbling but Hopi could not make out what they were saying. Hopi rolled over very slowly and opened one eye.

"Hopi," a tiny voice said, "have you finally decided to join us?"

Hopi was dumbfounded and could not speak. Standing before him were ten or more very small people attired in elaborate dressing gowns and crowned with spectacular headdresses. Hopi opened his eyes very wide in a look of disbelief. The people were no taller than a coyote.

"We know you are watching us Hopi. There is no reason to pretend," one said.

Another added, "Perhaps, if you open the other eye your vision will improve."

They laughed, held their sides and rocked back and forth. Hopi sat up and rubbed his eyes with the back of his clenched fists.

"This is a dream!" Hopi exclaimed, turning to Istaqa. "Wake up Istaqa, please!"

Istaqa did not move.

"Do not try to wake your friend, Hopi. We have come for you."

"We have brought you here." another explained.

"You have been chosen."

"Chosen? I am only a wanderer. What do you want of me?"

"You know. You must stop pretending you do not know. We have been watching you."

One of the little people stepped forward. His headdress was made of the white wings of the owl. "Do you not remember me?" he asked.

"No. I do not." Hopi said, "Have we met before?"

"Does my voice not sound even a bit familiar?"

"I do not know, I cannot say."

"Remember, search for it."

"Yes, I will try . . .but it was so . . .so long ago."

"What was so long ago?"

"I was lost," Hopi said before even thinking. Surprise filled his face. "I remember crying and it was cold . . . "

"Yes. You were lost and crying, and in the night I came to you."

"Wait!" Hopi blurted out, surprised, "Hoodee! You were in the forest at the center of the light! You, you are the one who taught me!"

"Ahh, yes. Thank you. I am glad you have not forgotten. You have grown tall, Hopi man."

"Hoodee! But after I went to Chaco I did not know if you were real or if you were a dream. Am I dreaming now? What is happening to me?" Hopi quickly touched himself.

The group erupted in laughter again.

Hoodee said in a soothing voice, "We have been waiting for you."

"Waiting?" Hopi echoed.

"Yes, does that seem so strange? "

"Of course, it seems strange to him," another said. "This poor whelp believes that all he has done, everyone he meets, is only a whim of fate." He placed his hands on his hips, turned to his companions and shot a quick glance at each. "Hopi, do you remember following the light in the forest?"

"Yes!"

"Did you not wonder about the light or wonder that it might be leading you?"

"Yes, I mean, no . . . I don't know what I mean!"

"If you had stayed at the cliff's edge for one more day, you would certainly have leapt over its edge and fallen to the ground below." He went on, "In truth now, did the idea of leaping ever come to your mind?"

"Why, I guess it did, but . . . ." Hopi paused, then blinked his eyes, "but until this very moment, I did not know that I had even thought of it!"

"See, I told you." one said, disgusted, "This cannot be the human we have been looking for."

"I am a fool," Hopi hung his head, "I followed the light, and I did not contemplate its nature. I did not know it was leading me. Yes, I am a fool."

"See, I told you! He has no idea what is going on!"

"He is not quite awake yet," another added softly in his defense.

"He is awake, but his head is not yet empty," still another said.

"Hopi," Hoodee said gesturing with his hands, "These are my family. I will not introduce them to you now. There is too much for you to understand. You will know each of us as time passes. You may call us Kachinas.

"Kachinas?"

"Yes. We are the family Kachinas. We are here to teach you the dances and the songs of the future. It is time for the Second Half of the Fourth World to begin."

"Stand up," another demanded.

Hopi got to his feet, and as he did so, the family Kachinas grew until they were much taller than he. Hopi reeled back in amazement.

"Take my hand," Hoodee said, "follow the circle. Feel it in your feet. Feel it in your legs. Feel it in your groin. Feel it spread through your soul."

"This circle is the dance of the Lost Family. Remember, just days ago. You thought you created it yourself, that you taught yourself. You did well at your old house, but now must learn the right steps. Do as we say."

Hopi joined hands with the family Kachinas and they circled.

Teacher

Zuni watched the del Arroyo warriors take possession of Fajada butte and listened as Ammett offered the Cha'tima. He felt strangely satisfied that the trespassers were forcefully evicted, and that someone had taken control and restored order. Events were moving faster than Zuni or—for that matter—anyone could comprehend, and he desperately wanted everything to return to the way it was before Hopi missed the Cha'tima. Zuni felt lost. He did not know this world anymore. In less than two equinoxes, a civilization built by countless generations had been shaken to its foundation.

When Zuni discovered the Kokopilau were missing, he ran to tell Abbott Amhose, his mentor, who sat quietly and did not comment. Finally, after a long silence, the abbott rose and instructed Zuni to follow him to the plaza where an elderly stone mason awaited next to a large pile of uncut stones. "Teach this apprentice how to build dwellings—the planning, the gathering of materials, and stone-cutting," Amhose instructed the mason. Without a word the abbott left the surprised Zuni in the hands of this master.

For two days, Zuni worked with the man but did not hear or see a thing. Though the master mason spoke without hesitation and his articulation was that of a wise man, Zuni was too preoccupied to listen. He wondered about the Allander, the Kokopilau disappearance, and the strange behavior of Amhose. Everything we have worked for is falling to pieces, he thought, and now Amhose wants me to learn to build houses. What does this mean?

Zuni chided himself aloud for his faithlessness, "You are a fool, Zuni! Do not question Amhose's intent. Never!"

Zuni cut many stones and chiseled them into flat bricks. He knelt, placed each stone on its side on a hardened surface, and hits it squarely with a quick blow from a mallet to split open a flat workable surface. Zuni found he could work, listen to the master, and still consider the questions which flooded his mind. Somehow, he thought, this simple work and this man's simple chatter calms me. "Ahh," he said, finally figuring it out, "that is why that Amhose made me do this work."

"When one builds a pueblo," the mason told him, "it creates something new, a fiber inside the soul of the man. This new thing is a recreation of something very old."

Zuni nodded.

"The fibers we create within our souls cling to the stones we have shaped into bricks. When we place the bricks, one on top of the other to make a house or pueblo, our soul fibers bond them together. In a way, we are intertwined like the web of the red spider and the branches of the trees."

Zuni nodded again.

"These fibers within us originate here," The old man held both hands against the place right below his navel. "This is the place of our will. When we build a pueblo, it connects our will to our homes and strengthens both at the same time."

Zuni again nodded without looking up.

"When our pueblo is destroyed by wind, or rain, or the shaking of Mother Earth, or by the deeds of bad men, we must learn to disengage our soul fibers from our broken down pueblos. In order to survive we must gather new materials and begin again."

"What?" Zuni said, finally acknowledging the old man's words.

"We must disengage our soul fibers from our broken down pueblos and then gather materials and begin anew. This is not an easy process," the old man said raising an eyebrow as he chipped away at a brick, "There are people who lay down and die when their homes are destroyed." He again placed both hands on the spot below his navel, "Their soul fibers—connected here—have been severed, and their will to live and to rebuild has been destroyed."

"How does one protect oneself so that this does not happen?" Zuni asked anxiously.

"Why," the old man said smiling, "one learns by building a pueblo. It is not an easy task. One must first find a suitable location, where good stone can be found. Next, one must have a plan, he must know beforehand what his new pueblo will look like when it is finished. He also needs strong timbers for ceiling beams. All of these things and more are necessay to reconnect the soul fibers to stone so the will can grow and strengthen itself again."

"May I know your name, master?" Zuni asked.

"I am Adobe."

Ammett and the Circle of Power

Ammett worked feverishly to fill the vacuum created by Amhose's voluntary withdrawal from the circle of power. Ammett had dreamed of this opportunity, but never thought it would happen like this. It was too simple to think that he could become the leader by abdication, without struggle or bloodshed. The disorder in the city made his ascent so much easier. "The drought and all subsequent events, even the solstice massacre," he liked to say, "were arranged by the gods for the purpose of making me the leader of the empire."

There was much work to be done and Ammett invited the abbotts of the clan pueblos, Larkin from Tsin Kletsin and Shola from Casa Rinconada, to come to del Arroyo to continue discussing a plan of defense.

"As you can see," Ammett told the abbotts as they toured del Arroyo's storerooms of Chochmingwu, "the drought has not affected us in the least. We can survive any drought. The gods instructed del Arroyo to build and to store food, and we obeyed."

The leaders were very impressed. The storerooms of their pueblos were nearly empty, and they were very surprised at what their eyes beheld.

"The walls of del Arroyo are very thick, and you can be proud that you have the biggest and strongest pueblo in the city," Shola commented. "But I am afraid of what will happen when the people become hungry. If they find out that del Arroyo is full of Chochmingwu, your walls will not withstand the assault."

Shola's observation enraged Ammett. He spoke loudly, and his emotions flared, "The only thing they will find if they come snooping around del Arroyo is death. Only the strong will survive and del Arroyo is ready for any threat. I will not tolerate such action against del Arroyo. I will crush anyone who stands in my way."

Shola and Larkin took an involuntary step backward and lowered their eyes. Ammett acknowledged their response, lowered his voice and continued, "These concerns have brought us together today. It is in our interest— if we are to survive—to unite and take control of the situation now. We cannot let recent events continue out of control. We must unite and act forcefully now."

The clan abbotts listened intently to Ammett's plan, and before they departed, they smoked the pipe of agreement. Shola and Larkin did not agree with Ammett's violent approach, but they held their tongues in order to keep them. Besides, they had no better plan, del Arroyo's storehouses were impressive, and they were fearful of appearing to disagree with Ammett.

CHAPTER

THIRTY-THREE

Ambush

The warriors of Chaco marched in fighting cadence to the foothills of the Blue Mountains. In the two moons since Ammett ordered their departure they had located and destroyed many bandit camps killing all they found. They were now on Yalo's trail, and his retreat led to the base of the Blue Mountains. He could not outrun them, and soon his scalp would be theirs.

The contingent of two-hundred-and-fifty men were homesick and worried about their friends and brothers in the city, to no avail. Their duty was to locate and destroy Yalo and his band. Only then could they return to their homes. The normally obedient warriors were impatient with this chase and angry at this renegade, Yalo, who dared not only to stand against the empire of Chaco, but who killed many of their brothers and sisters.

They were anxious to finish Yalo and this anxiety made them forgetful. They should have sent scouts ahead, but instead they moved quickly up the trail. They were convinced that Yalo would only fight if he were cornered, and if they did not press forward he would run as fast as he could, forcing them to pursue over the mountainous terrain.

Two by two the warriors snaked up the mountain path in a slow but even trot. Their bodies were painted white, their faces black, and black feathers hung from their elbows and knees. They carried bows and arrows, shields and axes, spears and knives. These were Chaco's strongest men, trained in a tradition of discipline, hardship and bravery. In open battle they could overcome twice their number of any of the warriors of the northern plains or the mountain tribes. Their honor pulled them forward, and their proud lineage of fueled the muscles in their legs.

From debris left behind by the bandits, the warriors concluded they would catch up with this mad dog, Yalo, the day after tomorrow. They ran up the path until the light began to fade. They camped in a lush meadow and built great fires to prepare themselves for the battle sure to ensue in the coming days. They believed that Yalo was a coward and that he had no more than a hundred ragtag fighters.

Message from Amarna

Zuni worked almost every morning with Adobe. They walked to the base of a Kayenta sandstone outcropping east of the city where Adobe showed Zuni which stone was best suited for making a kiln, lining water culverts and building pueblos. They spent several mornings carrying heavy loads of stone to Chaco where Adobe taught Zuni how to sort them into piles.

"Making a pueblo is three parts preparation and one part building," Adobe told him. "One should begin a pueblo only if the materials are plentiful and prepared before the foundation is laid."

Wiping sweat from his brow Zuni asked, "Does not the hard work tire you and defeat the joy of the building?"

Adobe smiled widely, showing his blackened and broken teeth. "No. I have not felt the work for many solstices. That part of the job is called the Breath of Work. Our bodies lift, carry and strain, our chests rise and fall deeply, we sweat and sometimes stumble, but our spirit works ahead of us. We consider the tasks we have ahead of us, the tasks which will deliver us to the foundation of our next beginning."

"You do not feel the weight of the stones as you carry them?" Zuni mocked.

"No." Adobe answered as he worked, "I have not felt the weight of the stones since I was a young man. If you project your thoughts forward, to the tasks you will accomplish tomorrow, or to some other place, the work is done by the body and not by the spirit."

Zuni shot Adobe a look of total disbelief.

"It is true." Adobe said, "You have come to learn, and if you learn well, you will know that what I say is true."

Zuni enjoyed working with Adobe who possessed a strong and clear will and who seemed oblivious to the mounting problems in the city. Adobe's duty was to build for Anaa and to build for himself. While Zuni was consumed by the situation around him, Adobe saw only buildings. When they passed a house in bad need of repair, Adobe told Zuni, "The stones used to build this house have been used and reused for many dynasties. One day they may be used again."

Zuni often walked the streets trying to view the buildings as Adobe did. It was impossible. Zuni was a man of special education and had been a member of the elite his whole life. He could not think as Adobe or view the world as Adobe did.

The Anaa he met on his walks treated him with reverence. He was often called upon to settle disputes or to find assistance for the sick. In the absence of Amhose, the people needed someone to give them hope, and that task often fell on Zuni's shoulders. People asked, "Why has Amhose not come out among us?" or, "Do you believe the Kokopilau slipped away during the night or did their gods spirit them away?" People complained about the del Arroyo warriors and the way Ammett behaved as if he were their leader. "What will Bonito do about it?" they wanted to know. Zuni did not know how to respond. He promised Amhose to keep secrecy, so he governed his words well. "Have faith," Zuni counciled. "Do not let the hole on the top of your head close. Listen for the voice of Tawa, and you will be saved."

But at the same time, Zuni was very troubled. The disappearance of the Kokopilau and especially their leader, Allander, caused him great concern. Did the Kokopilau desert the city like cowards, as some people believed? Did they not know that their departure would turn the government of Chaco upside down? Zuni was consumed by questions, but he turned to his faith in Anaa. There is a plan, he said to himself, and though I cannot see its outline, I know it is there. I will not forget my duty.

One day after leaving Adobe, Zuni walked in a marketplace.

"My greetings to you," Ranal said, making an exaggerated bow and exposing the turquoise bracelets covering his arms from his wrists to his elbows.

"My greetings to you, Ranal."

"I wonder if I might have a word with you?"

"Yes. What is it?" Zuni asked.

Ranal seemed nervous. "Maybe we could speak in private?"

"We have the privacy of this crowd. What do you have to say?"

"But, Zuni," Ranal said, "All these people. They will see us talking."

"Yes. So? I have nothing to hide from these people."

"Oh, neither do I," Ranal said apologetically, "I only thought that because of the personal nature of what I have to say, you might want more privacy."

"I appreciate your concern, but speak, Ranal. What brings you to me?"

Ranal was taken aback by Zuni's directness. "There are many things that are similar between you and I," Ranal began, "I am composing a great piece of music for the abbott of del Arroyo, and you are said to be a very special apprentice to the abbott of Bonito, so in a way, we have been chosen for special treatment, and I was just thinking . . . ."

"Who has told you that I am apprenticed to the Abbott of Bonito?" Zuni asked sternly.

"Oh, I do not know. That is, I cannot say. You know, one hears things and one gets ideas. And, it is not difficult to place individuals together at certain times, and . . . ."

"I see," Zuni said. "what you refer to is no more than idle speculation of people whose vision is obscured by doubt and self-interest. If I were you I would listen to my prayers and not to what others say."

"Oh yes, I agree, Zuni." Ranal responded, "But I was thinking that you and I, because we have a very special mutual friend, we might be friends also."

"We share a mutual friend?" Zuni asked.

"Oh, yes! Did you not know that Hopi and I were close friends?"

"Ahh yes, Ranal, I remember. Hopi did speak kindly of you."

Ranal's mention of Hopi disarmed Zuni, and Ranal saw his chance. "I have worried a great deal about Hopi. I do hope that he is well and that he will return to us one day."

"I miss him very much too." Zuni admitted, gazing sharply into Ranal's eyes.

"It would be comforting to know that he is alive and well."

"I agree."

"Have you, his best friend, not had word from him?"

"No. I am sorry to say that I have not. Have you?"

"Oh no. He would definitely contact you or perhaps my friend, Amarna, before he would contact me. Really, I am nothing in comparison to you and to . . . ." Ranal stopped and swayed back and forth, "The real reason I have come to you, Zuni, is that Amarna has requested that I do so."

Zuni was surprised, "Amarna? What does she want?"

"As you know, Amarna, the sweet child, is in love with Hopi, and before he left, he promised he would return for her."

"Hmmm," Zuni muttered more to himself than to Ranal.

"Yes. I was there when he made the promise." Ranal continued, "Since he left, Amarna suffers waiting for him and she asked me to come to you to ask you to visit her. She is very sad and would find comfort in your presence."

"Have you told anyone else about their friendship?" Zuni enquired.

"Oh, no. I would never do that. I loovve Hopeee," Ranal stuttered, "I looove him, as you dooo."

"And Amarna has asked you to come to me?"

"Yes. I come in her name."

"It is in everyone's best interest, Ranal, if you do not mention Hopi to others, especially not to the Abbott of del Arroyo. Hopi is in danger and if you love him, you will keep quiet."

"Of course, I would nevvveerrr . . . ."

"Please tell Amarna that I will come to her tomorrow when the sun is high."

"But," Ranal said excitedly, "is that the best idea? Everyone will see. Everyone will know."

"I have nothing to hide. Please tell her of my visit. And, thank you Ranal. It is good to speak to you."

Zuni turned and disappeared into the crowd. Ranal turned and shrugged his shoulders at the two del Arroyo warriors who had been watching.

CHAPTER THIRTY-FOUR

Exodus

The disappearance of the Kokopilau confounded the Anaa and was an omen to others. While still afraid to leave the city for fear of being waylaid by bandits, the non-Anaa hastily packed their belongings and set out.

Chaco had always been a city of plurality, where Anaa, Kokopilau and all peace-loving peoples lived together, but now that was changing, and fear of the unknown hastened the exodus from the city.

The travelers' only protection against the desert was their number. Everyday hundreds departed—traders, merchants, craftsmen, men with their wuti and children. Entire families who lived in Chaco for generations reluctantly said farewell and climbed out of the canyon for the last time. They carried only their most precious possessions—turquoise, silver jewelry, feathers, and weavings. They left behind their houses, property and their lives. Most importantly, they left behind their ancestors. The spirit of their Kaa was now alone to watch over and protect the burial mounds.

Still, many people remained in Chaco. There was great pain and despair. No more would they break concha with friends and family. No more would the laughter and tears of their loved ones comfort them. They walked the streets without shadows, deprived of everything except the comfort of the canyon horizon, the smell of the city, and the memories they loved.

It was painful for the Anaa to see their neighbors depart. The fabric of life in the city had begun to unravel and, thread by thread, the color, fragrance and diversity was disappearing.

Among the Anaa were those who were glad to see the outsiders go. There would be more Chochmingwu for themselves. There were others who delighted that the long-resented influence of outsiders was leaving the empire. Yes, the Kokopilau brought education, cultivation, architecture and water systems which still quenched the thirst of the people, but the Kokopilau and the others were not Anaa and therefore impure.

None was more exhilarated than Ammett. The Kokopilau had long impeded Ammett's plan to become the next leader of Chaco. At the same time, the sudden disappearance of the Kokopilau greatly worried Ammett. He gathered his advisors and asked what this disappearance meant. He enquired whether anyone could shed light on Amhose's seclusion. "Do they know something we do not?" These were difficult questions, and knowing Ammett's intolerance for conjecture, the advisors declined to speculate, except to say that they, too, were equally confounded by developments.

Into the Cave

When Istaqa awoke, Hopi was gone. His footprints marked a path into the Green Mask cave. Istaqa would not enter, so he waited, sometimes playing his flute or sitting quietly in the shade of a nearby squat bush. In the late afternoon he foraged for food, and by nightfall he was tired and settled down to sleep. The next day he made his way leisurely back to the stream, gathered snake grass and returned to the cave's entrance. He made many grass flutes and grass animals. It was easy for Istaqa to wait and he did not consider what he might do if Hopi did not return. He was content.

On the third day, Istaqa stood at the entrance of the cave under the threatening Green Mask and peered into the darkness.

"Yoo hoo, are you there? Yoo hoo," he called out into the cool darkness, "Hopiiii!"

"Yes," Hopi's voice answered back. "I am here."

"Hopi! Are you alright?" Istaqa said excitedly, not really expecting an answer.

"Yes, I am safe." There was something strange about Hopi's voice.

"Come out here where I can see you." Istaqa said.

"Come in and you can see me here. There is no reason to be afraid," Hopi responded.

"I cannot," Istaqa said in a high, shrill voice, "this place is not for me."

"Do not be afraid, Istaqa. This is the place of the invisible spirits."

"I am not ready to die yet!" he said holding his head with both hands, "Are you dead, Hopi?"

"With the passing of each day something dies and something else is born within us."

A icy breeze blew from the cave.

"Does that mean you are dead now, or alive now?"

"Of course, I am alive now. Do not be foolish Istaqa, come and see what is here. I promise you will not lose your life."

Istaqa was not convinced, in fact, he was certain that the voice he heard was not Hopi's, at least not the Hopi he knew.

"If you are my friend, then show yourself."

From the darkness Istaqa watched the outline of an image moving toward him. He blinked quickly to make sure he would not be entranced. The outline moved closer, and Istaqa could see it was Hopi, but instead of wearing his loincloth he was draped in a beautiful white leather gown that reached to the ground and was adorned with beads and bones. On his head sat a tall, square headdress also made of white leather.

"Whoaaaa, You are DEAD!" Istaqa screamed, stumbled and fell backward over himself.

"Nonsense! I have not gone over to the other side."

"But why are you dressed so?" Istaqa asked, getting to his feet and planning his retreat down the trail at the same time.

"What are you talking about?" Hopi asked.

"The dressing gown!"

"Have you lost your mind, Istaqa? I am not wearing a dressing gown. But, look what I have." Hopi held something out in his hand and moved stiffly forward.

"Do not come any closer!" Istaqa demanded. "I am not afraid of you. I will fight and the spirits of the coyote are my companions." Istaqa's eyes gleamed madness.

"Istaqa, my friend, fear not, it is I, Hopi-man." Hopi rushed forward to calm Istaqa, and he passed out of the cave and stood beneath the Green Mask at the entryway. As he moved into the sunlight, Istaqa screamed and fell back in terror. This time he tumbled backward down the the steep trail.

"What is it?" Hopi yelled and ran to assist him.

"Your dressing gown! It is gone. It has disappeared."

"What dressing gown?" Hopi asked again. "I do not wear a dressing gown."

Istaqa squirmed closer to the ground, not wanting Hopi to touch him. "Back, get back. Do not touch me." From his waistband Istaqa drew his knife. "I will fight. I will not be easily taken!"

Hopi stopped in his tracks and stood silently over his tormented friend. It was obvious to Hopi that Istaqa believed in the existence of what he saw. His chest rose up and down quickly, sweat covered his face and his knife trembled in his hand.

"I will not harm you." Hopi finally said.

"But, but . . . Are you really Hopi? You are not something else?"

"No, my friend. It is I."

Istaqa did not take his eyes from Hopi. "What is it that you have with you?"

Hopi held out his hand, "It is one of the family Kachinas," Hopi said. "It is a Kachina doll. It is a good omen."

Istaqa squinted to focus on the doll and then let out a blood curdling scream, hiding his face in his hands.

"Istaqa, Istaqa, What is it? What is it?"

"Get away. Go away from me!" Istaqa begged. Hopi obligingly stepped back a few steps and waited. Finally, Istaqa looked up at him. Standing before him was his friend Hopi, dressed in his loincloth and holding a doll dressed in a white leather dressing gown with a tall, square white leather headdress. He looked at the doll and then at Hopi and then back to the doll again.

"Are you bewitched?"

"No. I am not, but the family Kachinas came to me last night and told me that you were right, that I must dance for the men I have slain. They taught me a powerful dance and told me many other things as well."

"Last night?" Istaqa said incredulously. "Why Hopi, you have been gone for three days."

"Three days? That cannot be."

"You have been bewitched by the spirits of the Green Mask," Istaqa said, "We must leave here now and then find a way to drive these evil spirits out of you."

"There are no evil spirits, Istaqa. I told you I have met the family Kachinas and they are here to help me along the path. They gave me this doll and told me to keep it safe."

Istaqa looked at the doll again. "You must destroy this thing. It is evil, it will control you. You will be its slave!"

"Nonsense. I will not destroy it. It gives me strength and helps me find the path of my destiny."

"Hopi, listen to me, when I saw you standing in the cave you were wearing the dressing gown that is now on this, what did you call it, Kachina."

"I was?"

"Yes, I swear it. I would not lie to you."

Hopi looked at the Kachina and then to Istaqa. "This is odd," he began slowly, "but I do remember wearing a dressing gown like this, but I don't remembe . . . ."

"See! We must leave this place, now!"

"Yes, I agree but not for the reasons you think. The Kachinas are my friends. They are not evil and have not come to harm me. They are my guides, and I will try to follow the path they set for me."

"You will travel alone then," Istaqa said emphatically. "I, for one, will go alone."

But Istaqa did not go alone. He and Hopi climbed out of the canyon and walked deep into the forest before they stopped for the night.

Faith

The next day, Zuni left Adobe to mix a dirt and water paste, and walked to meet Amarna in Galo. Instead of walking through the city filled with the hardship, flies and Anaa lined up awaiting the day's rations, Zuni climbed out of the city and meandered on the plateau above. The city below possessed a face he had never seen before. Dust and smoke, anger and suffering filled the canyon and rolled out onto the barren fields in every direction. At the center of the city, the base of Fajada Butte disappeared in the haze, but its crest floated like a new pinecone on putrid water.

Zuni could not breathe; his neck muscles constricted. This will not happen to me, he said to himself and drew in a large breath of poisoned air. He thought of something Amhose told him, "Look past what is in front of you, and do not lose sight of the horizon. When one looks at what is in front of him, he cannot tell what is true from what is false. Only when one turns to see where he has been, does truth and falsehood become evident."

He had been standing for a long time when he noticed someone waving to him from Galo. Sitting on the rock where she waited for Hopi, Amarna watched Zuni climb out of the canyon and make his way toward her. Zuni returned the wave and went to meet her.

"Were you thinking of Hopi when you stopped and looked into the city?" Amarna greeted Zuni.

"Why, no, I was not. "

"What was it then?" she asked boldly.

"The city is becoming a place I no longer know. It is difficult to know what will become of it."

Amarna was puzzled, "I would think that you, Zuni, would have knowledge of the future."

"Me?"

"Yes, you are close to Tawa the God. The rest of us are in the dark."

"Perhaps. But even those who listen, seldom hear. Tawa speaks so seldom, and he does not repeat himself."

"Has he spoken to you, personally?" she enquired.

"Yes, but not in the way of men. It is a feeling. Tawa surrounds you. It is how he speaks."

"I know," Amarna added excitedly, "I think I have the same feeling too, but," she paused and dropped her head, "perhaps it cannot be because I am unworthy." Amarna cast a hopeful look at Zuni, "Is it possible that I, too, can be looked upon by God?"

"Yes, of course, my child," Zuni said. "Tawa sees you." Amarna was heartened, "Tawa sees everyone. He watches all of us."

"If that is true, then why does he treat some with so much favor and others with disgust?" she asked angrily.

"I cannot answer that. It is a puzzle to me. Look," Zuni pointed to the city. "There are so many righteous people, people who have spent their entire lives dedicated to Anaa and its principles, and look how they suffer today."

"But, what about us, the residents of Galo? We exist in shame and suffering. Many of us are guilty of nothing more than being born. We have never had the chance of the Anaa . . . ." Amarna lowered her head, and gently swayed back and forth. She could not continue, tears dropped to her skirt.

"I cannot feel the injustice or pain you carry," Zuni began. "There are many questions that remain unanswered for all of us. As I stood on the cliff looking down at the suffering in this city, I found solace in knowing that what I see is not a true representation of what is really here."

Amarna did not understand, and Zuni saw it in her eyes, but he continued, "I remember once, Hopi and I found a fallen antelope that died in the barren sand. It was beautiful, and we mourned for it. It was a shame that something so pure should be taken. We returned to the place many times and watched its slow and ugly decay. Finally, only its bones remained. One day as we approached, we saw a young antelope standing where our antelope had fallen. It nibbled on the thick fresh grass that grew from the ground where the white bones of our antelope lay. When it saw us it darted off, and we were happy because it would survive. In part, it owed its life to the death of our antelope."

"Yes!" Amarna said with the conviction of a pupil to her mentor. "I know now why you have been chosen. You possess the greatness that surrounds Hopi."

Zuni was embarrassed and proud, but before he could say anything, a voice called to him.

"Zuni," Ranal said, "We are glad to see you." Ranal bowed and moved to sit next to Amarna on the rock. "I hope I am not interrupting."

"Oh no," Amarna assured him, "You are welcome. Zuni has just told me a story about himself and Hopi."

Zuni was uneasy but did not know exactly why. "Ah," Zuni realized, "I know what is missing now—Vanga. Where is your friend, Vanga?"

Amarna lowered her head.

"Vanga, poor soul, died a half-moon ago." Ranal piped up. "We all miss him so."

"I am sorry," Zuni said to Amarna. "I know he was a good friend."

"Oh, yes," Ranal answered, "Amarna loved him and he loved her."

"Tell me, Amarna, how did Vanga die?"

"We do not know," Ranal answered sarcastically, "The gods do not tell us their plans for us. All we know is that a sickness came over him suddenly, almost overnight, and he died. It is indeed a shame."

"I miss him," Amarna said without looking up, "But Ranal has helped me. He is a great comfort."

Ranal beamed. "Amarna has been so unhappy that she has refused to go to all the men who want her. She is the most beautiful of all the whores— and maybe the most beautiful wuti—in all of Chaco, especially since the blood sucking Kokopilau have disappeared."

Amarna was embarrassed at Ranal's outburst.

"I cannot agree with you Ranal," Zuni said, "but this is not why I have come." Turning to Amarna, he continued, "I come to you today because Ranal told me that you wished to speak with me."

"Yes, yes. That is true, Zuni. I . . . I . . . ." Amarna could not find words.

"Yes, my dear, what is it?"

Amarna was tongue tied.

"Amarna wants to hear news of Hopi." Ranal prompted.

Zuni unleashed his frustration. "How long has Ranal spoken for you?" Zuni impatiently asked Amarna. "Is it your place to speak for Amarna, Ranal?" Zuni asked sternly.

"Why, noooo," Ranal stuttered, "I just thought I couuuld beeee of assssisstence."

Zuni approached Amarna and raised her chin with his hand, "Come child, let us walk, alone. Perhaps then you can tell me what is on your mind."

Without a word, Amarna slipped off of the rock, took Zuni's arm and they walked away. Ranal attempted to hide his fury with a smile, but neither Zuni or Amarna even looked at him.

"I hope I did not embarrass you," Zuni said when they were far enough that Ranal could not overhear.

"No, Zuni. You did not embarrass me. It is I who have embarrassed you. I am what Ranal says, a whore. It is not what I want, but it is what I am. It is my fate."

"We are not so different," Zuni said, "though my path may cross the mountains and yours the valleys, neither you nor I know what lies ahead. I know it is difficult for you to believe, Amarna, but I am convinced that a grand plan exists and we must not question our destiny. We must make the best of the circumstance we have been given."

"I try, Zuni," she mourned. "It is strange and probably impossible, but sometimes I feel as though I play some part in this plan." Amarna was embarrassed. "I know it is selfishness to say this—I have been tainted by the men who admire my form. I sometimes believe their words of praise, and I cannot help myself, I am weak. But I feel The gods have a special task for me. I believe it is connected, in some way, to Hopi." Amarna stopped and shook her head, "It is preposterous, I know, but I feel it inside."

"I do not know, Amarna. But, for myself, all I have ever wanted is to serve Tawa and Amhose and the people of Anaa. In the last few days I have seen so much that I never imagined." Zuni shook his head and frowned. "I have also witnessed that men come to you every afternoon and sit on the hill. It is mysterious."

"Yes, I cannot explain it."

"I should not tell you this, but when I told Amhose about the men who come, he was surprised. In fact, he told me he already knew it."

"The Abbott of Bonito knows of me?" Amarna asked in a disbelieving tone, "He really said he knew about me?"

"Oh, yes. He also instructed me to tell Allander of the men who come to sit in your presence."

"Did you?"

"Why, of course. It was my duty."

Amarna was shocked and strangely honored that her simple, sinful existence was known to such important people.

"I do not know what to say," she blushed, "I am honored but I do not know if I should be." Amarna was suddenly frightened, "Do they think I am evil?"

"It is not for me to say, but I sensed no anger in their voices or in their behavior. It was as if they they this mystery was already known to them."

"All of this is too much for my simple mind, I cannot understand its meaning, Zuni."

"It is not for us to ponder, it is enough that we serve." Zuni then warned

Amarna, "Amhose has instructed me to hold my tongue, but I am worried about you and must follow my heart. I believe that you should have this information, but I warn you, it is for you and no one else."

"Yes, I will not tell a soul."

"There are many eyes and ears around us. I am worried about your friend, Ranal. I do not know why he was spared the Impaler. I know he was a friend of Hopi's, and I know he has helped you, but I do not trust him. He is dangerous and he has the ear of Ammett. This troubles me."

Ranal speaks with Ammett?"

"You did not know this?"

"I only know that he claims to be making music for Ammett. I did not know that he speaks to Ammett."

"It is true. Be wary of what you say to him about Hopi."

"You have my word, Zuni."

Zuni and Amarna walked quietly for a while, enjoying each other's company.

"I must confess to you," Zuni said, "without the faith in my heart, I would think that Hopi is either dead or has forgotten us."

"Oh, no Zuni! You are wrong. In this matter, I have great faith. Hopi will return. It is true. I believe that he, too, has a very important mission."

Amarna's comment gave Zuni great satisfaction. "I do hope you are right. It would be good to see him again."

CHAPTER
THIRTY-FIVE

The Hopis

Istaqa and Hopi traveled south, following cedar mesa in the direction of the Blue Mountains. Hopi walked quickly and resolutely, no longer in the manner of a wanderer changing paths on whim. When they stopped, Istaqa asked him questions about the Green Mask cave, but Hopi did not answer, instead he gazed at the Kachina's doll.

After three days they spotted Kowawa, the hilltop Village that is Always There, the place where Lakon lived. Istaqa wanted to skirt around Kowawa territory, telling Hopi that the people there had once driven him away, but Hopi was determined to visit the village. Nearby, they entered a clearing and were met by arrows shot close to their feet, but this did not dissuade Hopi. He held his Kachina over his head and without breaking stride, he hailed the village with a well known Anaa greeting, "It is the honor among us that gives us the will to continue."

Istaqa was convinced that the madness which possessed Hopi at the cave had not subsided, yet he went forward, hiding behind his friend. If Hopi is mad, he said to himself, his madness shows itself in a brave and righteous manner. Hopi's power shines, he thought, and it is my duty to follow him, for Hopi may be of God, and this is why I am here.

When they were within range of the village, and no more arrows greeted them, Istaqa breathed easier. Hopi strode up the path into the walled village. Several boys approached, void of expression and carrying the tools of war. Their movements were slow, ungainly and non-aggressive. He held out both arms and motioned the boys to come to his side. They quickly embraced him as though he was the father and they were his sons. Wuti approached cautiously and stopped many feet away. They looked worried and folded their arms tightly across their bosoms. Among them was the wuti, Lakon. She stood at the rear of the group and acted as though she did not know Hopi.

Hopi and Istaqa soon discovered that the army which destroyed the community of Grand Gulch had been here, too. The survivors had escaped by running into the surrounding forests. Only now, many days later, had they returned to the village. There were no men left alive, they had stayed to defend the village and were killed. Only a handful of boys, a few grand parents and about twenty wuti were left.

The eldest of the boys, now the village leader, had shot a deer earlier and invited Hopi and Istaqa to stay and eat.

"We are honored to share a meal with you." Hopi answered and bowed.

The children were entranced by Hopi and crowded around him.

"Where are you from?" one asked

"What brings you here?" another said.

"Who is the strange man, with the coyote headdress?"

"Tell us about the doll you hold in your hand."

Hopi was very happy and Istaqa, who crouched in the nearby shade, was surprised at Hopi's endearing way with children. Even the grief stricken wuti smiled and found comfort in Hopi's presence. All seemed glad this stranger had come, except for Lakon who quickly disappeared.

Late that night, after everyone had eaten and fallen asleep, Hopi was awakened by a pack of coyotes singing to the moon far-off in the distance. He rolled over, opened his eyes and saw Istaqa sitting upright in front of him, his flute to his lips.

"Istaqa?"

"Yes, my friend?"

"Did I hear coyotes singing?"

"No," Istaqa smiled, "I was playing the flute."

"Why do you not sleep?"

"I am worried about you, Hopi."

"About what?"

"You have acted very strangely since you entered the Green Mask Cave."

"Perhaps you are right, my friend."

"What is in your mind?"

"I am not sure," Hopi replied, "Since leaving Chaco I have believed in nothing. Although I was treated very well in Chaco, even made a Special Student of Bonito, I hated the hypocrisy and injustice I saw there. When I left, I wandered without thought of honor or responsibility. I felt free for the first time, as though I had been unburdened. My life, though without direction, was my own. But now, like my friend, Zuni, who devoutly believes in Anaa,

I realize that I, too, travel the road of apprenticeship. "

"Apprenticeship?" Istaqa asked excitedly.

"I believe so. But unlike the path of my friend Zuni, my apprenticeship does not follow a clearly defined path. The family Kachinas told me that all the wandering I have done, meeting you and finding the massacre at Grand Gulch, is part of this. The Kachinas told me my path goes south to the Blue Mountains."

"The Kachinas spoke of me?"

"Oh yes, my friend. They told me you were the last of a great tribe and had traveled far to be with me."

Istaqa did not speak. He slowly placed his flute into his waistband and looked into Hopi's eyes.

"I must ask you. The wuti who left when we arrived—does she mean something to you."

"You noticed her?"

Istaqa shook his head.

"Yes, my brother. I had never known a wuti until her."

"She is a danger to you, Hopi."

"A danger?"

"You must beware."

The next morning when Hopi and Istaqa prepared to leave they discovered that all the people of the village, including Lakon, had packed to accompany them. "It is not possible," Hopi said, "even we do not know where the land and gods will lead us, so you see, you must stay here." But the people of the village did not listen and followed anyway. Hopi insisted they return, but they did not obey.

Istaqa poked Hopi in the side and said, "They are supposed to come with us, Hopi-man. Now, you have started your own clan."

Hopi shot a piercing glance at Istaqa who laughed heartily.

Trapped

In the light of Nupta, the Chaco warriors worked their way up the difficult trail into the Blue Mountains. The path wound over rock slides, through dense underbrush and followed a loud stream whose icy white waters rushed down over boulders and fallen trees. The warriors appreciated the cool breezes near the stream, and its icy mist caressed them.

Yalo watched from above. He anticipated the ambush with a sense of excitement and fear. His men were prepared, but few men had ever challenged the power of Chaco. Those who did were not around long enough to boast of it. When the last of the Chaco warriors had passed the halfway mark on the trail, Yalo signaled a group of his men stationed in a side canyon to close off the trail behind the warriors. If they tried to make a retreat, they would be caught.

Ramu was keenly aware of the preparations being made for the ambush. For two days he listened to Yalo's men making arrowheads from flint, and he smelled the cooking of plants used to make war paint.

"Our brothers from Chaco have little chance in the mountain pass below," Ramu whispered to Tar. "We must warn them."

That night while everyone slept, Ramu summoned all his strength and tried to break the straps binding his hands. He strained and twisted.

"It is no use," Tar whispered to him, "no man can break these straps." But Ramu tugged and wrestled, until at last, the leather straps snapped, and his hands were freed. He quickly untied his feet and then freed Tar.

They crept to where the guards stood. Ramu listened for a moment then jumped up, smashed his elbow into the face of one guard and sent him reeling into a rocky embankment. Ramu grabbed the other by the hair and delivered a violent kick to his head. Without a whimper, the guard's knees buckled and he fell limp where Ramu gently lowered him to the ground.

"Go now, Tar! Run like the winner of the Great Race. GO!" Ramu whispered.

"What about you, my friend?"

"Forget me. Go!"

The two men embraced, and Ramu listened as Tar's footsteps led him away. Ramu heard a noise behind him and reeled around just in time to meet the attack of four men. During the fierce fight, one of the men landed a rounded stone ax on Ramu's head, and he collapsed to the ground. Realizing Tar was missing, they set off after him. Tar ran as fast as he could, but his legs were weak and the early light hindered his progress. It had been a long time since he had run, and his feet could not find solid footing.

As the last Chaco warrior passed into the trap, Yalo raised his arm to signal the attack, Tar appeared running out of the forest toward the mountain trail. Yalo's eyes flashed hatred; he quickly brought his arm down, and the attack began. At the same time, Tar reached the tip of the plateau, "Go back! It is a trap!" he yelled. No sooner had the words left his mouth than an arrow struck him from behind, pushing him forward, off the embankment into a rock pile below.

The Chaco warriors had no time to respond to Tar's warning. They reached for their weapons, but even as they armed themselves, the enemy was upon them. Yalo's men leaped from behind rocks and underbrush and attacked. From both sides of the canyon and from above, archers laid the warriors low with deadly accuracy. In the first few moments more than half of the Chaco warriors were cut down. Fighting hand-to-hand the warriors easily defeated their rivals, but the attack from the air made them easy targets for Yalo's bowmen.

The warriors first up the trail were surrounded and slain quickly, but those further down, turned and retreated. These warriors fought with great courage and ferocity. From his vantage point, Yalo smiled as he watched the retreating warriors run directly into the ambush. But, Yalo's grin soon faded when, after only a few moments of intense battle, the smaller group of Chaco warriors defeated his men and sent them scrambling.

CHAPTER THIRTY-SIX

Weight of Responsibility

Every morning a del Arroyo warrior sang out the Morning Cha'tima from Fajada Butte, and Zuni and Adobe began the day's work. In just one half moon they gathered the materials, chipped stones into bricks, and laid the foundation for their pueblo. Today they would begin to build its walls.

"I am amazed that the building goes so quickly," Zuni told Adobe.

"Hmmm, yes," Adobe answered, "once the materials are gathered the work proceeds quickly."

"We will be finished soon," Zuni ventured with a sense of satisfaction. "is that not so?"

"You are like all the rest," Adobe laughed. "The young and the inexperienced are afraid to begin the work. To you, building a pueblo is a complex task with many interwoven elements. But once the work has begun, and you can identify each step of the construction, the work is demystified. The fear disappears, and you can think past the work and past the complexity to the completion. You are just like all the rest." Adobe shook his head from side to side gently.

"Did you expect I would be different?"

"You have been chosen for leadership. Your life is full with teachings, and you have the presence of a god. I thought you would be different, but you are the same as every apprentice I have ever had."

"Is this so bad?" Zuni asked, disappointed.

"No," Adobe conceded, placing a layer of stones on the foundation of the pueblo. "It is the way of life. Some people treat me with great respect because I am a master builder, but I am only a man. I am sure that many people treat you with respect, too, but you are only a man. You are made of the same materials which build the rest of us."

Zuni and Adobe had laid stones waist high around three walls of their pueblo by the time Zuni left to return to Bonito and Amhose. As he departed,

Zuni turned back to the pueblo, placed his dirty hands on his waist and smiled at the building which was taking shape.

At Bonito, Amhose greeted Zuni in his traditional way but his voice was weak and he hunched over.

"Are you well, my father?"

"That depends on what you refer to, my son."

"You look tired and . . . ."

"It is nothing, my son."

"You and Adobe build a pueblo with mud and stone. The mortar that binds me is knowledge, faith and devotion, but the responsibility of completing my duty is indeed a burden that saddens me and presses me down."

"Can I be of assistance, my father?"

"Do you not realize Zuni, that everytime we meet, my burden lessens and yours grows heavier? But enough of this. I have something very important I want you to read." Amhose led Hopi to his private prayer kiva where on the floor rested three large pieces of sandstone covered with writing.

"Look, my son. I want you to read what is here."

"This is ancient Kokopilau script, my father!"

"Yes."

"They look like the sacred Time Scrolls from the ceiling of Fajada!"

"Yes, my son. You are correct."

"But father, where did they come from? How did they come to be in your possession?"

"You will learn very soon. But for now, read what is written."

Zuni bent down and slowly deciphered the three tablets. When he was finished, he sat on the floor of the kiva and sobbed. Amhose knelt behind him and placed his hands on his shoulders, "My son, it is not the end. It means a rebirth, and you and your friend, Hopi, have been chosen."

Zuni was inconsolable.

"Look here," Amhose said, moving to a stand where the original parchment of the Legend of Creation sat. "It is confirmed here, read this section."

Zuni had never seen the original Legend of Creation written by Bask as told to him by the eldest of the travelers who settled the canyon. He looked at the parchment, at Amhose and again at the parchment.

"It is alright, Zuni," Amhose assured him. "The mantle is being passed to you. You have the right to touch and to read."

Amhose pointed to a passage and told Zuni to read it. When he was finished Amhose said, "Please, read on."

It was difficult for Zuni to remain calm as he read and when he finished his legs trembled beneath him and he collapsed to the floor.

Yesterday's Pathway

On the trail toward the Blue Mountains everything Hopi put out of his mind since leaving Chaco came back to him—his promise to return for Amarna, the smile and righteous love of his friend Zuni, the smells and sights of the grand city of Chaco, the injustice which he could not ignore, and the guilt he owned for missing the Morning Cha'tima. It had been six moons since his departure but it seemed like many equinoxes. It was as if he had been gone from Chaco for as long as he had lived there.

He traced over all that happened since he took up the path of the wanderer, hoping to understand his circumstance. The cedar waxwings followed me on the second day I left Chaco. I drank bad water. I dreamed a coyote came to me. I met Istaqa—a new kind of man—despicable yet honorable and wise. I ate the flesh of another human being to save myself.

He remembered Istaqa's preposterous tales, the valley of migrating coral-pink dunes, and the power of the Vermillion Cliffs. He remembered the dreams, the light in the forest, days spent without thought, the lust of Lakon's body and the pain of her denial. He remembered vividly the families at Grand Gulch, the men he killed, the Green Mask Cave. The family Kachinas.

There was more but Hopi could not think of it all. Remembering did not help him to see the wisdom or to see his pathway. The Kachinas had told him none of it had been a whim, but he was unable to fit together the puzzle of his apprenticeship from any of it.

When Hopi, Istaqa and the people from Kowawa reached the great escarpment of the Vermillion Cliffs, the villagers were overwhelmed. They had never seen the world beyond the boundary of their forest and stood in awe of the enormity of what lie below.

Instead of making their way down the narrow trail and on to the Blue Mountains, they stopped and rested. They were still fresh and could go further, but Hopi told Istaqa, "I have a bad feeling about going forward."

Istaqa said, "There is something evil out there, but it will pass soon."

The next morning as Istaqa stood on the cliff edge, he spotted a column of men marching east.

"Hopi!" he called out. "Come. Look at this."

Hopi stood next to Istaqa and squinted. "Who they are?"

"They could be an army from Chaco, or it could be the bandit known as Yalo and his men. It is good we stayed here. Had we continued on the trail we would have easily been seen."

"Yes, my brother."

They watched the column snake in and out of the large sandstone welt that ran to the east like a festering wound. When the way was clear, Hopi and his troop descended the Vermillion Cliffs and moved south to the foothills of the Blue Mountains.

⁂

The Warriors Return

When only a handful of warriors returned to Chaco, the people were oddly sedate. Few spoke publicly. The starving citizens were numb. Were it not for the other calamities to befall them, the defeat of Chaco's army would have been regarded as a tremendous misfortune. But, as it stood, the defeat of two hundred men was just another sign that the world of Anaa was coming apart.

Only Ammett and the allies of del Arroyo were furious. Someone must pay and pay dearly for this disgraceful defeat. With his advisors by his side, Ammett stalked back and forth in his visiting room, asking the survivors the same questions again and again.

"Why did you not send an advance troop to scout the trail? How many were there? It happened so quickly you could not tell. Ahhh, yes. And all the rest are dead? Terrible! How can this be?"

When Ammett asked who the attackers were, several men stepped forward to explain that some of Yalo's men had come from the city of the outcasts.

"Galo . . . you say? Very interesting . . . . Yes, Galo has a long history of discontents and critics of Anaa . . . . Hmmm . . . . Now they have created an army . . . . Very interesting, very interesting indeed . . . ."

Ammett dismissed the survivors, praising them and sending them home to their pueblos. With Shola and Larkin, he discussed how the yellow dog, Yalo, would ultimately pay. But these discussions did not go well, and there was arguing. They smoked many pipes before Ammett convinced his fellow abbotts to follow his lead.

Toothless Warrior Elders

On a lonely plateau south of the city, unknown to the spiritual and clan leaders, the old warrior leaders and teacher-masters discussed the warriors' defeat and the slow dissolution of the mighty warrior caste. They worried that young, hot blooded braves could not be controlled much longer. The elders also wanted revenge, but their ire was not directed only at Yalo.

"We should remember," one said, "that none of the warriors from del Arroyo were slaughtered. Every pueblo but one lost many fine men."

Another added, "Yes, and it was Ammett who organized this army and who gave them their orders. We must not forget this."

Still another continued, "And it was Ammett who ordered his guard to kill the farmers during the solstice which started the warriors fighting against one another for the first time in our history."

Even the leader of del Arroyo's warriors agreed, "The tribunal has punished many, but still the shame of what happened infects all of the warriors, not just the warriors of del Arroyo. The young warriors harbor great resentment and even hatred against the leaders and their own brothers."

"What can be done?" one asked.

No one answered. They lowered their heads and gazed into the firepit. The youngest of the elders finally spoke.

"We can call all the men together, from every family and every pueblo and then," he paused for a long time, trying to find a fitting continuation, "and then, we can all leave the city and go to the mountains until we are one again—at which time we will return."

The elders roared with laughter, rocking back and forth, slapping each other on the back and holding their hands over their toothless mouths. The man who had commented laughed too, though he meant his idea in all seriousness.

Amarna's Suspicion

"Amarna, Amarna," Ranal called out as she was giving conchas to an old couple at the center of Galo's squalid housing. The food from the storerooms of Pueblo Bonito had not arrived and the outcasts, who had always depended on the kindness of gifts of food and clothing from the Anaa, were desperate. Over the objections of her mother, Soya, Amarna spent much of her treasure on concha to insure that the outcasts were fed.

"Amarna!" Ranal sang out again as he ran to her side. "Amarna, look what I have brought you." Excitedly, Ranal pulled an intricately woven and jeweled shawl from his dressing coat.

"Look! It is for you. It is a gift."

Amarna smiled widely and reached out, but pulled her hand back.

"It is very beautiful, but I cannot accept this gift."

"You do not like this fabric? Look, it is of the finest design."

Amarna did not look at the shawl. "Do you not see the great suffering around us?"

Ranal stopped and glanced around casually. "Yes. It makes me ill, it is hard to imagine how I survived this place. The smell is ghastly."

"The city is starving and you buy expensive gifts."

"I buy *you* expensive gifts!"

"Look at you," Amarna insisted sternly. "Everyday you grow fatter."

"What has gotten into you, Amarna? I bring you a gift, and you insult me. I could insult you if I wanted, but you are my friend and I . . . ."

"Are you my friend?" Amarna asked.

"Of course, I am. I am also Hopi's friend. Don't you remember?"

"No, I do not remember. You claim to be his friend, but I can neither confirm or deny this claim."

"What did Zuni tell you?" Ranal said angrily.

"What he said to me is not your concern."

"He must have said something to defame me. Whatever he said is a lie. He makes out to be such an important person, but you just wait, I suspect that he and his kind will not be so important one day."

"You talk as if you know something," Amarna said looking at Ranal with a wanton look. "What is it you know?"

"I do not tell what I know," Ranal said swaggering. "I know much, but I do not tell. I've become quite an important person."

"Come on, what do you know, Ranal? Tell me." Amarna fluttered her eyelashes at Ranal.

"I . . . I knowww that Zuni has been a messenger boy between Amhose and Allander, that is, of course, until the Kokopilau disappeared."

"How is it you know this?"

"It is impossible to hide one's movement in the canyon. From here we can see much of the city and I have made a practice of watching the movements of certain people, including Zuni. There's no secret to it."

"Yes, it is impossible to hide," Amarna agreed. "In fact, I saw you early this morning going to the far entrance of del Arroyo and going inside."

Ranal looked from side to side quickly.

"What were you doing there?"

"I had business there," Ranal claimed.

"But I thought no one but clansmen could enter there."

"I have special permission. As I said, I am now an important person."

"What kind of business?"

"I cannot say."

"If you cannot say, then tell me, with whom do you have business?"

"I . . . I am not supposed to tell."

"You want me to believe you are an important person, as you boast, but you refuse to tell me who your business is with? I suspect you went to del Arroyo to beg and that you do not know anything or anyone of real importance."

"That is not true! Not true at all! Why do you treat me this way?"

"You know my business, Ranal. I have nothing to hide from you. You know what I do, where I go, and what I think, but I know little of you—except that you say you are my friend."

"I am your friend, Amarna."

"Then tell me, who do you visit at del Arroyo and why?"

"I cannot."

"You say you are Hopi's friend, yet you have business with del Arroyo. It is well known that Ammett wants Hopi dead. Where are your allegiances?"

Ranal was silent

"Ranal?" Amarna finally asked.

"Yes?"

"I've often wondered, when you stood before the massacre tribunal, how did you *really* escape the Impaler?

"You know, I've wondered about that myself. Ah, I mean I told you, remember the music I composed . . .I honestly don't know."

"Did they find you innocent?"

"Why, ahh, no. They found me guilty."

"And they let you go?!"

"Mmmmm, yes."

"When the others were all executed, they let you go free?"

"Yes, I have The gods and my talent to thank."

"And, they pardoned you from Galo, and made you a free man?"

"Yes, isn't it amazing? I cannot tell you how surprised I was."

"Ranal?"

"Yes."

"One more thing . . . ."

"Yes, what is it?"

"Did you see or talk to Vanga the night he died?"

C H A P T E R
T H I R T Y - S E V E N

An Injured Man

By afternoon Hopi and the others made it to the cool foothills of the Blue Mountains. They stopped by the trail and camped in a large, open meadow surrounded by pine trees that climbed steep hills on three sides. At the meadow's center was a deep, meandering stream where the boys hunted for frogs. They swam and laughed and laid in the deep grass until sleep overtook them. The wuti collected firewood and pinenuts and took an accounting of this new place. For the first time the Kowawa's old lives seemed to fade and the possibilities of this new beginning filled the wuti's hearts. All the wuti, save one.

Lakon, the daughter of the chieftain, lost not only her husband and parents, but all the privleges due her position in the tribe. Lakon had always taken what she wanted and was known for being cruel. She did not speak now, and her eyes were vacant like the windows of the deserted ruins of her village. Since the massacre, the other wuti neither spoke to her nor did they attend to her sickness.

The people had been in the meadow for several days when Hopi informed Istaqa he was going into the mountains to meditate. "I will return on the first evening of the crescent moon. I hope then I shall know what we shall do next. You must watch over the people. Please make sure that nothing evil befalls them."

"Yes, master," Istaqa replied.

Time passed quickly at the meadow, and everything was quiet until a grandmother named Ol burst into camp and told Istaqa that she had found a man, near death, lying on the trail into the high mountains. When Istaqa reached the man, he appeared stiff and dead. He had been shot in the back days earlier, and had lost a lot of blood. Hopi made me promise not to eat the sweet meat of humans, Istaqa thought. This man would have made many meals for the people. Istaqa kicked at the man and to his surprise, the man cried out softly in pain.

Back at the camp, the wuti were angry when Istaqa appeared carrying the man slung over his shoulder. "What if he is an outlaw? What if he is one of the men who attacked our village?" they fretted. "No," Istaqa replied, "look at his loincloth and his cheek bones, this man is Anaa. He is a victim, like you." The wuti fell silent. One went to the stream and brought water to wash him, another placed her blanket over him, and a third dressed his wounds. "This is good," Istaqa told them, "but he will most likely die."

At twilight on the evening of the crescent moon everyone in camp was anxious for Hopi's return. Several times the boys thought they had spotted him—but it was nothing, a mountain shadow, a deer's behind. At the moment when it was neither day nor night, Hopi appeared striding across the meadow in their direction. The boys ran out to meet him, and the wuti, too. Hopi raised his arms and embraced the boys.

"What is it that Hopi wears on his head?" Istaqa said more to himself than to the wuti nearby.

"I cannot say," someone said. "The light plays with my eyes."

When Hopi was only a few lengths away, Istaqa could see that he had another Kachina, this one tied to his head by a leather strap around his chin.

"New hat?" Istaqa asked as Hopi embraced him.

"I have found the second Green Mask Cave, my friend," Hopi smiled widely. "I have much to tell you, but first take me to the man you have found."

Istaqa's mouth dropped open, "You know of our guest?"

"Yes, but please, do not ask how I know."

Istaqa led Hopi to the man who was still unconscious and Hopi kneeled at his side. "I must dance for him now, or he will surely die."

Hopi stood up, lifted his arms straight out from his shoulders and danced. His arms dipped and rolled like a bird riding the high winds. He sang in a language that Istaqa did not know. The people circled around their leader, joined hands and began swaying gently from side to side. As the crescent moon touched the horizon, the wind swirled the pines, and the sound of a great river filled the meadow.

Later, Hopi sat alone next to his campfire when Istaqa approached.

"May I sit with you?"

"Of course, my friend. I have missed you."

"You are a very strange and remarkable man, Hopi," Istaqa started, holding his flute in one hand, "magic follows you. It is within you. I can see its aura."

"This is not for me to say. But I believe you, Istaqa. I can feel it."

"Tell me Hopi, where did you get the Kachina you wear on your head?"

"What do you say?"

"The Kachina tied to your head?" Istaqa pointed with his flute.

"Nonsense," Hopi dismissed with a disbelieving smile.

"No, really. It is sitting right there," Istaqa sat forward, reached up to touch the Kachina but it disappeared. "Holy coyote crap!" Istaqa screamed and fell backward.

"What is wrong? There is nothing on my head. I swear it."

"But, but, Hopi-man, I saw it there. You had a Kachina tied to your head. Believe me!" Istaqa shook from head to toe.

"I should know if I have something tied to my head," Hopi said sarcastically. "You are seeing things, my friend. I assure . . . ."

"No. You must believe me," Istaqa interrupted. He then turned and called out for help. A wuti caring for the injured man came quickly.

"Yes, can I help?"

"Please, the truth," Istaqa enquired, "Did Hopi have a doll strapped to his head when he returned to us this evening?"

Hopi leaned back on his haunches.

"A doll on his head," the wuti repeated. "Yes, you did, Hopi."

"See! See what I say?"

Hopi was incredulous. He sat up straight and asked the wuti, "You saw a doll strapped to my head when I came into camp?"

"Yes. It was a beautiful doll wearing a long blue, leather gown. On its head was a headdress that looked like wings."

"Are you certain?"

"Yes, Hopi."

"Did the doll look like this?" Hopi pulled a doll from behind him.

"Yes. Yes, that is the doll," the wuti said.

"Yes. That is it." Istaqa added.

"But, I was not wearing it strapped to my head," Hopi said. "I carried it in one hand and my other Kachinas in the other!"

Both the wuti and Istaqa shook their heads from side to side.

"In one hand you carried the first doll, but the second doll, that one," Istaqa pointed again with his flute, "was strapped to your head. It only disappeared just moments ago when I tried to touch it!"

Hopi was truly puzzled. He did not speak for a long time. Finally, he said, "Somewhere in my mind I do remember wearing this Kachina on my head."

A Night Visitor

Zuni could not sleep, he lay in his bed and listened to the sounds of Bonito. The cries of a newborn baby and its jubilant father's laughter came from the makeshift camp in the plaza below. Ya Ya witches shuffled along single file down the long empty hallways, and chants from the subterranean kivas wafted into Zuni's room through his open window. The light of the fast sinking crescent moon settled like dust onto his writing table and wooden floor. Zuni had not slept for many days, and now he understood his teachers' warning that knowledge is responsibility.

He lay motionless, trying to visualize a new world—a place where Chaco and the Anaa did not exist—where people lived in peace in a city on the banks of the river Future. It was no use. All he could imagine was his beloved Chaco. I have never seen another city, he thought, and even though I know other cities exist, they are not real to me. They are only markings on the maps of the Kokopilau and words in the books of the Anaa. The only thing I have in common with the people who live in these places is that we share the same sun and stars and moon.

Zuni left his bed and stood in the soft moonlight of his window. "I have never wished to be anywhere else but here," he said aloud. "Please, oh God, Tawa, please give my people another chance to live. We are good people and we love you. For every sin and every deceit, there is an act of goodness. For every act of immorality, there is a measure of righteousness to level the scale. I know in my heart the people are good." Zuni cried out, "Oh please . . . ." Zuni's voice trailed off and vanished in the darkness. The light of the crescent moon faded from his face. Zuni stood in the dark, framed in his window.

There was a knock on the door.

"Yes, who is there?"

Who could this be, he wondered? It is late.

"It is I, Amhose."

Zuni quickly wiped the tears from his face and moved to the door. "Of course, my father, please come in."

"We have no time. Come with me."

Zuni followed Amhose without a word and noted the urgency in Amhose's voice. From Zuni's room they walked down several hallways, four flights of stairs and through a maze of rooms and kivas to the Abbott of Bonito's private prayer kiva.

"Light this candle from mine," Amhose told Zuni and handed him a candle.

"Open the door, my son."

Zuni opened the door, and he and Amhose entered the large, blackened room. Amhose secured the door behind them. At the far end of the room was a chair and sitting in the chair was a man in a long, black gown, a hood obscuring his face. The man did not move. Amhose stood behind Zuni who tried to discern who was there.

"Do you not have a greeting," Amhose said to Zuni, "for your mentor, teacher and friend?"

Zuni turned to Amhose with a puzzled look. Amhose's eyes were afire.

"Allander?" Zuni finally asked, "Is it you?"

The man stood, "Yes. Zuni. It is I, Allander."

Zuni rushed to Allander and shook his hand wildly.

"Do not hurt Allander,." Amhose said laughing.

"Oh, yes, father you are right," Zuni said excitedly, "I am sorry Allander I did not mean to . . . ."

"You do not hurt me, my son." Allander assured, smiling.

Zuni stepped back and looked into Allander's face and then turned to Amhose.

"I know you have questions," Amhose offered, "and there are answers. Tonight, my son, you will learn all that you need to know."

The Time has Arrived

After speaking with Amarna, Ranal waited for darkness then made his way to del Arroyo. He paced back and forth waiting for Ammett. A blush of fever rushed over him and sweat beaded his brow and the palms of his hands. "They have found me out. They have found me out," he said to himself, but out loud, "I could be killed at any moment! Indeed, any mommment indeed! Amarna's admirers will beat me or burn me to death!" Ranal pulled at his hair. "They will throw me into the briar! Noooo, I cannot stand the briar again. The needles, ohhhh the needles! I cannot stand that again!" Ranal grabbed at his sides and legs and back. "The briar needles—nooooo!"

Ranal suddenly saw Ammett standing before him.

"I did not hear you enter, Master."

Ammett stood with his fists on his hips and scowled, "Obviously, you pathetic fool. I witnessed your pitiful scene. You make me ill, were it not for the fact that I need you, I would have you put out of your misery." Ammett moved to his chair and sat down. He brought a hand to his chin, "What information have you brought me, ruminator?"

"They have found me out, master!"

"Who has found you out?"

"Zuni and Amhose and Amarna!"

"Amhose?" Ammett asked.

"Ahh, well, I do not know for sure about Amhose, but of Zuni, I am certain, and if Zuni knows, then Amhose must know too."

"You flatter yourself, what do you think they know?"

"That I am a swine—Ahh, what I mean to say is that I am a spy. A spy for you."

"So, what if they do know?"

"I could be killed. I could wake up dead. I could be poisoned in the same way that I poisoned Vanga. I could . . . ."

"I see," Ammett said with a slight smile. "Is this all you have to say?"

"No, I . . . ."

"What is it you have to tell me that is of importance to me? I hope you have not taken me from my important work to listen to the yammering of a ruminator's fears."

"Why, no. Of coursssse noottt." Ranal tried to think but nothing happened. "Ahhhh . . . it is Hopi, yes. Hopi."

Ammett sat up in his chair. "You have information of Hopi?"

"Ahhh, yes my master, I doooo . . . ." Ranal had to think fast, "Ahhh, Zuni has led Amarna to believe that . . . . Ahhh . . . ."

"Yes, yes, What?!" Ammett demanded.

"That ahhh, that he and Amhose know of Hopi's imminent return."

"Is that all?"

"I . . . I . . . can only tell you what I have heard from Amarna, master."

More to himself than to Ranal, Ammett mused, "So, the time has come to make my move. I must not let this opportunity be taken from me."

"May I be of assistance?" Ranal asked.

"What?"

"Making your move, master—may I be of assistance?"

Ammett thought for a moment. "First, do not tell Zuni or Amarna of our meeting. I do not want them to escape before I send my guard. Secondly, make certain that tomorrow night you are no where near Galo. That is, if you want to live. Go now. You have done well. Leave me."

"Yes, but master if I may?"

"What is it?"

"When all of this is finished, whatever it may be that you are planning, if I have been of assistance to you, and if it pleases your mastership, would you, perhaps, see your way to giving me the whore, Amarna?"

"We have no slaves in Chaco."

"Oh, yes. I know that but I was just thinking that . . . ."

"Leave me!"

"Yes, master."

Illumination

More than a hundred admirers were gathered to wait for Amarna that evening. Now some women who had heard of Amarna sat among the men. They came to see for themselves what drew their men, their husbands and brothers, to this beautiful woman. Some women came only out of curiosity and were surprised to find Amarna's beauty was as much spiritual as of the flesh.

Every evening Amarna's ritual was the same. She left her shanty and walked serenely to the rock to pray for Hopi's return. But this night was different. Instead of sitting on the rock, Amarna walked past it and up the hill to walk among the people gathered there, holding their hands and embracing them. They cried and bowed at her feet.

From that night forward, Amarna walked among her admirers every evening and spoke to them about matters of belief.

CHAPTER

THIRTY-EIGHT

Admitted Responsibility

"Come quickly!" Istaqa hollered to Hopi who played tag with the boys in the lush meadow.

"Come!" Istaqa waved with his arm. "He has regained consciousness."

When Hopi and Istaqa entered the lean-to, the man was sitting up and drinking water.

"I am glad to see that you are feeling better," Hopi declared.

"Where am I?" the man asked, looking around.

"You are in the foothills of the Blue Mountains."

"How did I get here?"

"We found you on the trail. You were shot by an arrow, and we did not believe you would survive," Hopi answered.

The man looked puzzled and slowly drank more water.

"Thank you for helping me. But, who are you?"

"We are wanderers." Hopi replied.

Istaqa was irritated at Hopi's response, "We are The New People, and this is our leader, Hopi. I am Istaqa, second in command."

"You are Hopi of Chaco?" he said.

"Yes, I once was."

"You are the Hopi who missed the Cha'tima?"

Hopi looked down and did not speak.

"You were the Anaa's Cha'tima?" Istaqa asked Hopi, astonished.

"I was," Hopi admitted raising his head.

"I knew from the moment I set eyes on you that you were important," Istaqa confirmed. Turning to the injured man, he asked, "How do you know of Hopi?"

"Everyone knows of Hopi, the special student. He was destined to be a leader, but he missed the Cha'tima and brought on the massacre of the equinox celebration."

"What is that you say?" Hopi asked, dread in his voice. "A massacre?"

"Oh yes. Only days after you left Chaco, at the equinox celebration. The Abbott of del Arroyo ordered his warriors to execute the farmers who withheld corn from the hohoya, and there was a great battle between the people and the warriors. Many were killed and injured."

"You said Hopi caused this?" Istaqa blurted out.

The stranger looked down, averting Hopi's anxious gaze, "Many, many people blamed Hopi. They said the massacre happened because he missed the Cha'tima. Many believe that missing the Cha'tima was the beginning of the end for Chaco."

"Haaaa!" Istaqa exclaimed, turning to Hopi, "No wonder you were on the run when I found you."

"But, but I did not know." Hopi answered, his voice filled with emotion. "I would never have missed the Cha'tima if I had known this would happen. I am responsible . . . I admit it, but I . . . ." Hopi had many questions and badgered the wounded man. He asked first about his friend, "Was Zuni a victim of this massacre?"

"I do not know of Zuni. My family and I left Chaco the same day. We were afraid of what might happen."

Hopi sat hard on the ground. He buried his face in his hands. He shook his head slowly. His breath slowed, his ears clicked.

"You are not to blame," Istaqa consoled him, patting him on the back.

"Tell us," Istaqa asked of the man, "Who are you?"

"I am Tar of the Blue Flute Clan of Cedar Mesa and a follower of Anaa."

"Cedar Mesa is far away. How did you come to the Blue Mountains?"

"My village was attacked and destroyed by the bandit Yalo, and my family was killed, except for me. I was enslaved and brought here. I escaped when an army of Chaco warriors came for Yalo . . . I tried to warn them but I . . . I did not make it. The Chaco warriors were ambushed and slaughtered. I tried to warn them, but I was shot and left for dead."

"An army of Anaa warriors defeated by a bandit?" Istaqa asked, amazed. Hopi did not look up, as if he hadn't heard a thing.

"It was an ambush."

"Where did this fight occur?"

Tar nodded toward the high mountains, "Up the trail, near the place where the high meadows begin."

"How did you get here?"

"I do not remember. I remember laying very still and hoping Yalo's men would think I was dead. I overheard them talking about attacking

Verda, so after they left I pulled myself onto the trail, hoping I might find someone who could warn the people there."

"Ahhh," Istaqa said to Hopi, "It was Yalo's army that we saw marching below the Vermillion Cliffs."

Hopi did not say a word.

Tar was still very weak, and Hopi and Istaqa left the lean-to. Istaqa had never seen Hopi so low. Hopi shuffled his feet, bent over like an old man, and his chin rested on his chest.

Later, Istaqa scouted up the trail to see what he could see. At the battlefield, the bodies of Chaco warriors greeted him. Many of them had been strung upside down from trees and hacked into pieces. On his return, he found Hopi alone, sitting cross-legged with his eyes closed. He gave Hopi a full accounting of what he witnessed. Hopi answered with a nod of his head.

The next morning Istaqa found Hopi preparing to leave.

"Where are you going?"

"I must stop this Yalo and his army," Hopi answered.

"Alone? What do you think you can do?"

"I am not sure. But I must try."

"You are talking foolishness, Hopi. You will be killed. There is nothing you can do."

"I am not alone," Hopi answered, lifting his two Kachinas and showing Istaqa. "I have the help of the family Kachinas."

Istaqa shook his head, "Let me come with you. Together . . . ."

"No," Hopi interrupted, grabbing Istaqa by the shoulder, "You must stay here and protect the people. We cannot leave them alone."

But, Hopi . . . ."

"I have spoken."

Hopi walked to where the people were canopied under lodge pole pines.

"I must bid you goodbye. I will return, but until I do, Istaqa will take care of you. Please do not be afraid. Be at peace in your hearts."

The people called out farewells, and as he turned to leave, Lakon ran to him, throwing her arms around his neck. She pleaded with him not to go. "I will return, I assure you," he told her. Lakon would not release him, she sobbed and cried wildly. Finally, Istaqa pulled her away and held her until Hopi was gone.

The Prophesy

Amhose placed a woven mat on the floor in front of Allander and instructed Zuni to sit. He then placed a chair next to Allander's and sat down.

"To ease your curiosity, you may ask one question of Allander." Amhose said smiling. "But, when he answers, you must listen and remember everything that is said to you."

"Yes, father. I will do as you ask." Turning to Allander he asked, "Where have you been, and why did you leave us?"

"Ahhh, no," Amhose wagged a finger, "that is not one question, but two."

"I apologize, but then, where *have* you been Allander?"

Allander smiled widely, pointed to the floor with his index finger and did not speak a word.

Zuni did not know what Allander was doing. He folded his arms, looked at Allander and waited. After a long silence Allander finally said, "I do not mean to be cruel Zuni, but I wanted to see your reaction." Turning to the abbott, Allander remarked, "You are right, Amhose. Zuni *does* have the face of an owl when he dislikes our answers." The two old men laughed.

"I told you he was most devoted," Amhose added. They laughed again.

Turning to Zuni, Allander said, "The answer to your question is that I now reside below the city in the catacombs of the Kokopilau. The rest of my people are there also."

Zuni was flabbergasted.

"You have been selected, and therefore this knowledge is passed to you. Only the Abbotts of Bonito have ever had knowledge of the catacombs. And now, my son, so do you.

"Many dynasties ago," Allander continued, "my ancestors decided to emulate the Ant people revered by the Anaa. In many ways, the Ant people are like the Kokopilau. The ancestors dug under the ground on Fajada Butte and as the consuming fire of time passed, the catacombs were finished. They remained empty, waiting for the Splitting of the Fourth World. That time is now upon us. Now the catacombs are the repositories for the knowledge we have gathered. The Time Scrolls, charts and predictions of the Kokopilau are there, as is the entire history of the canyon and the Anaa's Legend of Creation. They are all stored safely below. With my fellow Kokopilau, we guard these repositories."

Allander answered Zuni's next question without his asking.

"The catacombs are under us here," again he pointed down. "An entrance is on that wall." Allander pointed.

"May I father? Please?" Zuni asked Amhose.

"Oh yes, my son. But please hurry."

Zuni went to the wall and searched its surface. He ran his finger tips across its length and then from the floor to as high as he could reach.

"Ahhh," he finally said, standing back and scrutinizing the wall. "There is a passageway here!"

"Come. Sit now." Amhose said sternly. "It is time to listen. Many of your questions will be answered." He continued, "In recent moons you have developed great powers of memory. This is good and it is the way it should be. I implore you to listen well and to remember all that is said to you this night. It is your sacred duty, and it is as important as life. Do you understand?"

"Yes, my father."

"Now you must hear the story of the Splitting of the Fourth World. This knowledge is only for those leaders who have been selected. The splitting of the Fourth World is written in the Time Scroll Star Charts of the Kokopilau—part of which you saw here recently—and it has been passed from one Abbott of Bonito to another since the beginning of Anaa and Chaco.

"Remember the eclipse, the Huhuwa, that you observed several moons ago?" Allander asked. "That event was predicted many dynasties ago. Listen," Allander left his chair and read from sandstone tablets lying on the kiva floor not far away. "In the last days petty criminals will be executed and One will stand against the oppressor. This One comes with no father or mother but with great devotion to Anaa. He will be known by his discovery of a magnificent Huhuwa."

Amhose added, "There are many revelations and predictions which also serve as guides—the drought, the missed Cha'tima, the lightning that killed the cottonwood tree, and the wuti named Amarna. It is written that a wuti will come forth whose beauty and feminine energy will give hope to those who seek a new spirituality. She will be a contradiction. It is written."

"And, your friend Hopi is the counter to you, Zuni," Allander added.

"Counter?" Zuni asked.

"Yes, my son." Allander spoke. "Tawa understands the complexity of man's nature, for it was he who ordered Sotnang to create man. Tawa knew that some men learn through devotion and by listening to the words of wisemen. You, Zuni, are such a one.

"Tawa also knows that other men learn best by doing. This doing is like following a path blindfolded. It is a very difficult pathway, but it teaches, tests and strengthens at the same time. Hopi challenges the world and by this, gains strength and learns devotion. Hopi's path is called the Nanapala, 'The Purifying from Within Oneself.'"

"He is your counter, my son," Amhose said shaking his head up and down. "Your duty is to carry Anaa and its sacred blessings into the future. It is Hopi's duty to traverse the path of our ancestors. Hopi resides in the world of the unknown, but from that place he will emerge into a new light."

"To understand why Tawa has set in motion the splitting of the Fourth World, one must study the Legend of Creation." Amhose went on. "It is written that Tawa and his assistants, Sotnang, Spider Wuti and others created the First World for the people . . . ."

The candlelight flickered—wicks burning to nothing—while Amhose and Allander told Zuni of Tawa's creation and destruction of the first three worlds.

"When Tawa had destroyed the first three worlds," Amhose concluded, "there was only enough material left for him to make one more world, the Fourth World—the world of Anaa. But Tawa worried that if people again grew lazy and corrupt and forced him to destroy the Fourth World, the honorable people he wished to save would have nowhere to go.

"Therefore, Tawa decided to Split the Fourth World in two—a first and a second half. If he had to destroy the first half of the Fourth World, the good people would have a place to begin again." Amhose stopped and Allander continued, "Unlike the destruction of the first three worlds," Allander began, "Tawa decided that the destruction of the first half of the Fourth World would be accomplished by the people themselves. The only way men learn the value of righteousness is by seeing for themselves the evil which lives deep within each person. Tawa would put the blood of the people on their own hands.

"Tawa hopes the people will remember their guilt and shame, and that this knowledge of their innate evil will humble them and serve as a warning before it is altogether too late."

"And now, as you can see, these events have already begun." Allander told Zuni, "For many dynasties we have been preparing for this crisis. Tawa brought us the drought to begin unraveling the world and to separate the faithful from the selfish."

Amhose faced Zuni, "There are good people within the walls of Bonito and all the pueblos, but the city and empire has grown large and many are corrupt and driven by power and possessions. It is time for us to cleanse ourselves for tomorrow."

Chaco

With the passing of each sun, the situation in Chaco worsened. The exodus continued, the hunger increased, the mysterious disease spread. The devoted Anaa stayed indoors and prayed. Tawa had not forgotten them, and at some juncture the suffering would end and their patience and dedication would be rewarded.

But others had no strength. In order to feed their chldren, parents stole from their neighbors. Many people stood in line at Bonito for rations of Chochmingwu while their own shelves were not yet empty. Petty injustices turned violent, and old wounds festered. Wuti sold themselves for handfuls of rotting grain. Proud men walked south of the city to sell themselves and their families into slavery, hoping that once they were safe in Mexico they might purchase their freedom again. Each new dawn found the twisted bodies of those who transcended the trauma of this life by throwing themselves off the canyon cliffs.

At the clan pueblos, corn was still plentiful, but the mysterious disease was no respecter of the pueblos' strong walls, and struck down inhabitants with impunity. Fear, distrust and resentment also visited the clan pueblos. Clansmen who had married outside the family were told to leave. Many mixed-bloods were forced out.

Shola and Larkin, the Abbotts of Rinconada and Kletsin, distrusted Ammett. Though they had sworn alliance with del Arroyo, Ammett's ambition did not go unnoticed, and they worried about del Arroyo's quest for control of the Chaco empire.

The spiritual pueblos, Chetro Ketl, Kin Kletso, Kin Klizhin and Bonito were without their leader, Amhose. The onslaught of refugees brought hunger and sickness which quickly overwhelmed the pueblos ability to respond to the empire's needs. The houses of spirit were far too busy praying and tending their people to challenge del Arroyo's manipulations and tyrannical posturing. Dedicated Anaa did not complain, yet the situation etched itself in each stoic face.

CHAPTER

THIRTY-NINE

Del Arroyo Moves

Somewhere within the mighty walls of del Arroyo, a single warrior beat a drum. It boomed and echoed from the pueblo, reverberating off the canyon walls and throughout the city. The war drums of del Arroyo stopped people in their tracks; old men sweeping, mothers cooking, merchants counting beads. Young wuti spilled water from the jugs balanced on their heads. Not even the oldest of Chaco's citizens had ever heard war drums beat within the city.

Then came other drums, large and small, a few of them at first, until the tympany of del Arroyo's drums was palpable and hung in the stagnate air. People preparing to leave the city stopped preparing and hurriedly departed. The marketplace emptied, and the only people out of doors lined up to fill water jugs at nearly dry Galo Creek. The pueblos closed their massive doors and posted warriors at entrances.

Emissaries from the pueblos, trying to comprehend what was happening, rushed to del Arroyo and were told, "The Abbott of del Arroyo, the Supreme leader of the Anaa, will not see you."

Anyone at odds with del Arroyo or the Antelope clan left the city quickly. Some sought safety within other pueblo walls. The warriors of all the pueblos were greatly agitated. The sound of war drums was more than they could stand. At Pueblo Chetro Ketl, warriors were convinced they were the target of the coming attack. Since the equinox massacre, skirmishes between the two pueblos had escalated into violence. The Ketl warriors prepared to fight, bringing loads of stones and casings filled with animal fat to the ramparts. These warriors were not afraid. They had spent a lifetime preparing for battle. They were sanguine and at ease, the fulfillment of their destiny before them.

The only pueblo with its doors open was Bonito. The people of Bonito ignored the drums and offered sanctuary to all. Before the drums began,

Amhose retired to his private kiva leaving word he was not to be disturbed. He also instructed the clerics personally, "Do not close the doors of the pueblo. They must remain open, from dawn until dusk." The clerics were troubled by his orders, but hearing the war drums, wrung their hands and sensed that Amhose knew something of which they were yet unaware.

In late afternoon, the gate of del Arroyo swung open and fifty warriors came dancing out. They were painted white on one side and black on the other and ran three abreast. Each held a bow and a spear in his left hand. They marched in a Ceremonial High Step, a defiant strut witnessed only by important guests during pow-wows and by doomed enemies. The few people still in the streets ran for cover. The pueblo abbotts stood atop their walls and prayed.

The war party marched through the streets and up a trail to the plateau, occasionally stopping to dance and kick their feet. When the last warrior disappeared over the ridge, the population exhaled in relief.

Warning

Ranal ran to Galo as soon as the warriors disappeared.

"You must leave Galo now!" Ranal ordered Amarna.

"I will do nothing of the kind!" she retorted.

"I beg of you, Amarna." he pleaded, "Look at the sky. The sun has risen on the last morning the outcasts will ever see. This day is the last day."

"What do you mean?" Amarna asked, stamping one foot and putting her fists to her hips.

"Is it not clear?" Ranal frothed. "Look at the city, Amarna. See it for the last time. Remember its aroma. It is over. The music has ended. You outcasts are history. Good bye. Good bye, Good bye!"

Ranal turned and walked away shaking his head. "I tried to tell you, but you would not listen. You think I am a liar, a thief and even a murderer." Ranal turned and pointed at Amarna, "This is your last chance. Come now and you will live, stay and you are surely dead!"

"I would rather die than go with you. Fool. That you know something terrible is going to happen here is proof to me of your worming nature." Amarna stopped and stood straight. "You have been allied with Ammett since you were set free. I detest you. I will not honor you with my thoughts. You are not even worthy of my disgust. Go, ruminator! I, for one, shall stay where I belong, here in Galo. The sun is fine from here. This is my home. These are my people."

"Fool!" Ranal shouted angrily. "I shall mount your head on a pole and parade it through the city!"

Circle of Stones

It took many days for Hopi to overtake Yalo and his army. They had not been difficult to follow. Their path cut deep into the coral sand and their campsites were littered with the burnt bones of slaves they feasted upon. At one camp, he found the heads of two men resting on a tree branch where someone had placed them, and at another, he discovered what was left of a wuti tied to a tree and skinned alive.

Hopi followed Yalo's progress for a day then moved ahead to a likely camp area. They will not pass up the opportunity to camp in this magical place, Hopi assured himself. The site was a perfect circle of stone, surrounded by enormous wings of sandstone on two sides, a group of mushroom-shaped towers on another and a large overhang completing the circle.

Hopi said a prayer. He held his Kachina over his head, danced in a small circle and sang out,

> You have taught me,
> you have showed me,
> you have filled my soul,
> I am not alone.
> Your wings are with me,
> Your towers watch my back
> Your shelter will assist me
> In overcoming my obstacle
> and in bringing peace and order back.

Hopi moved gracefully, his arms and hands supplicant, his body undulating. His legs leaped wide, and his head followed his body's rhythm. His movements sanctified the stone circle where the reign of Yalo would end.

Yalo's scouts arrived at the campsite early, and by late afternoon the last column straggled in. Yalo was impatient with the pace of his men and slaves. He warned them to pick up their gait or he would make a meal of them, but they were spent and could go no faster. Few of his men were as bloodthirsty as he. Most were neither trained warriors nor brutal by nature. Most did not desire to conquer, yet many hated the Anaa.

From his hiding place Hopi watched the ragtag army arrive. He was not impressed by Yalo's contingent, but he was very surprised by how many men and boys he recognized from Galo. The hand of emotion squeezed his chest. If it were not for my "gifts," he thought, I might have been one of these forgotten souls.

As the last of the riff-raff arrived, Hopi was startled when he thought he recognized someone among the slaves. Hopi strained to get a clear look, and when the slaves were forced to squat in the harsh sunlight, he recognized Ramu! Hopi leapt to his feet and was about to call out, but stopped himself and ducked down. It is not yet time, he whispered to himself. Something was wrong. Ramu's face was drawn, and his eyes were dark and vacant.

After Ramu and Tar had failed in their attempt to warn Chaco's army, Ramu had been beaten unmercifully, and now he was very weak. He had great difficulty keeping up with the column.

Yalo swaggered through the ranks of his men, shouting orders and kicking anyone, even his own men, if they got in his way. Over his shoulder he wore a cloak made from the scalps of, perhaps, one hundred men. It nearly touched the ground, the scalps glinting in the afternoon sun. Hopi's mouth tightened.

He did not know what he was going to do, but the Kachinas had assured him they would be at his side. "When the time is right," the family said, "you will know it."

" . . . I will be there in the darkness of the wind."

Allander readied himself to depart. "You have listened well, Zuni. You now possess the knowledge you need to go forth. But before I take my leave and return to my people in the great cavern of the catacombs, I must share with you a last prediction of the Kokopilau."

Amhose sat up in his chair and turned to face Allander.

"The light which swirls over the Second Half of the Fourth World in the reign of darkness possesses a god we do not know. This god has many faces and his people number the Anaa times infinity. This people will find the city of Chaco. They will burrow into the catacombs of the Kokopilau and take all the knowledge we have stored there. The Time Scrolls, the Predictions, the Star Charts, the Weavings and the Parchments; they will have it all.

"These people have more than one heart. Some are of high learning and great wisdom, others are as the traders of flesh and turquoise. The children of your children's children shall have children who will know these people. You must teach the people so they may be aware of them. These new people will speak eloquently of justice and bring injustice in its stead. They will profess to be friends but will steal our lands. They will bring their god and offer our people eternal life. If denied, they will kill. It is their way."

"How will Zuni's children know these people?" Amhose asked.

"They have white faces. They wear clear crystals over their eyes, and they carry their light in their hands."

Amhose raised his eyebrows. He and Allander clucked to one another in the way of the Anaa.

"But, this is not all," Allander went on, "You will know these people because they will sit atop four circles."

"Four circles?" Amhose asked.

"Yes."

"Hmmm," Amhose said shaking his head. "Ahhh, yes! I see it now." He closed his eyes, "Yes, I see this time to come." He turned to Allander, "Remember, when the eagle appeared in the fire during the Abbott's council? We sat on a high plateau and the eagle showed us that one day it would the air in our land would be fouled with smoke from great tubs on the horizon. Tiny silver crosses moved through the sky and left the cotton path behind them. Ahhh, yes." Amhose said, delighted, "Tawa showed us this."

Zuni listened and smiled. He had heard enough this night and he remembered the warning from Allander. He would not question now.

"Before I return to my people in the catacombs to write the end of our history, I bid you farewell and ask you to dance with me one last time."

The three men linked arms and slowly circled the room. Each man gazed into the others' eyes. Soon, their feet left the ground, and they floated above the floor, and smiled until they laughed, and laughed until they cried.

When the dance was finished, Allander said to Zuni, "When you stand on the plateaus surrounded by the pueblos you have built, and the sun disappears, and Yaponcha moves gently around your face, I will be there with you, Zuni. The Kokopilau and I will be there in the darkness with the wind. The knowledge that you seek will be with us, and in the stars, and in the black ocean of the night. We shall not meet again until our Kaa energies combine. You must lead the good people to the place of convergence. Do not worry. You will be led by the word of the Kokopilau and the word of Tawa. I bid you farewell, my son, Zuni." Allander embraced Zuni and then Amhose.

"Ours was the greatest of all times," Amhose said to his brother, Allander. "We have carried the spirit well. I shall pray for our repatriation."

The two men embraced again, and Allander turned and disappeared through the secret passageway in the kiva wall.

CHAPTER

FORTY

A Prayer Candle

At dusk the war drums of del Arroyo stopped. No one was in the streets, and few candles lit the windows in the neighborhoods. Warriors at every pueblo stood ready.

The sunset drew a thin line of orange against the black horizon as the huge doors of Pueblo del Arroyo opened again. The drums beat wildly and the second army high-stepped from the pueblo four abreast. Each man carried a torch in one hand and an ax or bow in the other. It was a beautiful sight; the warriors' faces painted black and their bodies white. Each had a swan feather braided into his hair and crow feathers hanging from his elbows and knees.

The leaders of the army danced ahead, swinging and turning so their long feathered headdresses undulated like serpents. They wore white masks and moved quickly in the direction of Pueblo Bonito. The caterpillar-like army stretched far and did not clear the gates of del Arroyo for a long time. Their torchlight filled the canyon and cast eerie shadows on the canyon walls. When the end of the phalanx had departed del Arroyo, its masked leaders neared the open entryway of Bonito.

The men of Bonito's garrison stood shoulder to shoulder on the wall above the pueblo's open entryway. They were painted bright red, the color of the gods when smiting down non-believers. They held bows and many arrows rested next to them in hammocks. The refugees in the plazas and gardens knelt and prayed aloud. The clerics, medicine men, Ya Ya witches and matriarchs stood on the rooftops of the upper levels, dressed in their finest gowns. They would witness all.

As del Arroyo's army approached the invisible line where Bonito's bowmen lined up to release their arrows, the masked leaders turned sharply away and danced off toward Fajada Butte. The body of the army snaked by until its tail whipped past Bonito's entrance and was gone. As the army neared Fajada, a glow appeared on the horizon above the city of the outcasts. The glow intensified until the source of its light came into view on the cliffs. Torches. Torches held in the hands of the del Arroyo warriors who danced out of the city earlier in the day.

The outcasts knew their fate. Everyone scrambled, ran in every direction and looked for hiding places. Mothers screamed out the names of their children. The elderly clutched each other but made no attempt to escape.

The roiling phalanx from del Arroyo moved up the trail into Galo. When the warriors reached the top of the trail, they ran into the crowd screaming war whoops, axes swinging. They yanked at children's heads and slit their throats. Old people were bludgeoned with battle axes as they huddled together on doorsteps. Prostitutes were dragged by their hair to the cliffs and thrown into the city below. Many outcasts ran to the edge of the cliffs and waited for the inevitable. Some cheated the warriors by leaping of their own accord. There were shouts of "Death to the hypocrites!" or, "Anaa is damned!" People who tried to escape to the higher plateau were slain by arrows from the warriors stationed there.

Amarna and her mother Soya were pulled from their shanty and dragged to the cliff edge. Two warriors took Soya by her hands and feet and flung her over. She screamed Amarna's name as she disappeared into the darkness. Amarna did not struggle. She stood and watched her mother killed. The warriors turned to where she stood impassively and grabbed her by the arms. They took several steps forward toward the cliff. She spat on the warriors and prepared to join her mother. Suddenly, a warrior elder rushed up and ordered the men to stop, "She is to be taken to Ammett!" he said, pointing to Fajada Butte from where Ammett watched. They bowed and immediately dragged Amarna off to del Arroyo.

Hiding behind del Arroyo, Ranal watched his former neighbors thrown from the cliff. He had never seen such violence and was awestruck by its energy. His loins tightened, and he pulled at his trousers. Looking inside he discovered an erection. "Oh!" he shouted. When he saw Soya thrown from the cliff and Amarna nearby, he jumped from his hiding place and screamed out, "Stop! Stop! She is mine!"

When the warriors dragged Amarna away from the cliff, Ranal believed it was his order that stopped them.

The city watched in horror as the killing progressed. In less time than it takes to burn a prayer candle, the screaming and crying died out until only sobs from the crowd were audible. The pueblo warriors of Chettro Ketl watched from the ramparts and cursed their brothers. Clerics and abbotts sobbed, hidden behind their windows. The Anaa and the refugees stood in the streets and sobbed.

One by one the torches burned out. By the time Nuptu, the purple light of creation, illuminated the eastern horizon the warriors had finished their work. The new day found the city of outcasts wiped from the face of the Fourth World. The war drums were silent, and the people awoke fitfully behind their flimsy doors.

Yalo meets Hopi-man

The campfires reflected off the overhang and illuminated the surrounding desert. Yalo sat in a circle with his advisors and planned his attack on Verda. When the strategy was complete, Yalo stood and called his men to attention.

"Come! Listen to me," he shouted. His men were tired, their movement lethargic.

"Do you not hear me, I said, come! This is an order!" Yalo was impatient with his men, "I will not stand for this insolence. Come now or feel the wrath of my whip." Yalo brushed a heavy leather strap on the sandstone.

"I have accomplished much in a short time. From my humble beginnings I have grown so powerful that I can defeat an army of Chaco warriors. My power grows, and soon I, Yalo, will be the ruler of the all Anaa. But there is much that needs to be done.

"In five days we will attack the city of Verda and make it the capitol of my empire."

Yalo's men moaned under their breath. They had no desire to attack the stronghold of Verda. The Anaa who lived there were hunters and trackers. They knew the ways of war, and Verda was well stocked. There were many Anaa warriors to contend with, and an outright attack on the second strongest Anaa city was foolhardy.

Yalo described his plan and Hopi listened from his hiding place. Yalo's men hung their heads, cast resentful glances at each other and shuffled their feet. Yalo sensed this reticence and was furious.

"What is it?" he screamed, "Are you cowards? Are you afraid to tell me what you think? Do you not believe my plan will work? You are swine and it is I, Yalo, who gave you our self-respect. You owe everything to me, and it is your duty to honor and obey me!"

A few of his men shouted out halfheartedly, but this apathetic response was a thin veil for their real feelings, and Yalo was not fooled.

"You are cowards! You are afraid of the Anaa. They have beaten you down like the dogs you are and now you believe they cannot be defeated. Well, I'll show you that the Anaa can bleed and die like anyone else." Yalo ran to the line of slaves and pulled Ramu up by his hair. Two men held Ramu's arms.

"This is Chaco," Yalo shouted, "Look at him. This is the greatest of all Chaco warriors. He is my slave. He lives or he dies at my whim—just like the rest of you. I have the power of life and death over all of you!"

Yalo pulled his knife from his waistband and pointed it at Ramu's chest. Hopi tensed and felt himself standing. He tied a Kachina to the top of his head and moved behind the gathering to the back of the overhang.

"I am Yalo, the powerful. I have the power of life and death. This slave is the city of Verda, and the knife in my hand is my army. I could thrust my knife into the heart of Verda like this!" Yalo stepped back and lunged forward, thrusting his knife toward Ramu's chest but stopped before stabbing him. "If I wish, my army could cut deep into Verda, and it would die quickly. But, if Verda fights back and pushes my knife away? Then, maybe I could be defeated. But, what if my army—this knife—came up behind Verda and cut its soft vulnerable throat when it was not watching?" Yalo moved behind Ramu placed his knife at his throat. "Verda would slowly bleed to death. Like this!" Yalo pulled Ramu's head back and slowly drew his knife across Ramu's throat. Blood rushed down Ramu's chest.

"STOP! STOP THIS NOW!" Hopi commanded, from the center of the amphitheater on a large flat stone. He pointed the Kachina in his hand toward Yalo. Hopi wore a flowing leather gown, covered in ceremonial beads that sparkled and glittered with blue and red light. The Kachinas on his head pulsed with light.

Yalo was caught off guard. He whirled around. The two men holding Ramu dropped him to the ground clutching his neck. Yalo's men stood flat-footed.

"You are not the rightful leader of these souls!" Hopi said, his voice echoing loudly in the amphitheater. "It is I, HOPI-MAN, who lead all people who are abandoned! You, Yalo, are a snake, and you must leave now or die!"

Many of Yalo's men dropped to their knees and bowed to the ground. Yalo, too, could not believe what he was seeing, but he was not so easily frightened—even Tawa himself would not stop him. He would die rather than submit to an apparition.

"Do not believe this interloper!" Yalo screamed, "He is an imposter! Kill him!"

No one moved. Even Yalo's most trusted henchmen stood their ground.

"I command you! Kill him!"

No one moved.

"Cowards and yellow dogs! I shall kill this masquerader myself." Yalo grabbed a bow lying nearby, placed an arrow in its string and drew it back. Hopi did not move. "The Kachinas will protect you," a voice whispered.

Yalo aimed for Hopi's heart but just as his fingers were about to let go, Ramu's massive arm came around his throat and pulled his head back. The arrow soared over Hopi's head and struck the back of the overhang. With his other hand Ramu quickly pushed Yalo's head forward with all his strength. Yalo's neck snapped loudly. He fell limp, and Ramu held him there for everyone to see. Yalo was dead.

"You have seen the gods work," Hopi said, "I am the servant of tomorrow, and I welcome you to freedom and justice you have never known." The words Hopi spoke came from deep within him. "You have searched for peace but have found none. I offer you sanctuary. I am your father. You are my children. For those of you with evil and hardened hearts, leave or shed your thick skins now."

A handful of Yalo's henchmen disappeared into the night. The rest of the men dropped to their knees and bowed, including Ramu, who still bled from his neck.

Hopi commanded, "Bow not to me. Raise your heads and hearts in praise to the gods and to the invisible helpers—the family Kachinas."

CHAPTER FORTY-ONE

Blessed Amhose

Zuni and Amhose slowly climbed the steps from the kiva to the plaza where they heard screaming and shouting. They rushed out to find the refugees facing Galo. Amhose and Zuni turned to see the torches of the del Arroyo army illuminating the canyon around Galo. Giant shadows ran across the wall of the sandstone amphitheater, axes raised. A great struggle was taking place.

"This must be stopped!" Zuni shouted and bolted for the entrance of the pueblo.

"Wait, my son!" Amhose ordered. Zuni stopped and returned to his master's side. "Have you not heard what I have told you?" Amhose asked, "None of this can be stopped by you or anyone else. It is the fulfillment of the prophesy."

"But, father, I cannot stand still and watch! I must do something!"

"There is nothing to be done. It is not easy to witness, but have faith. God will mark the fall of each of his children. It is not for you to intercede."

Zuni stood motionless and watched in horror. Facing Amhose, he told him, "I must go. I must administer to the people."

"Do what you must," Amhose submitted. "The prophecy says nothing of you being in danger, only that you will lead some of the people from the city."

"I honor you, my father." Zuni embraced Amhose, and they held on tightly.

Zuni turned to leave, but when he was only a few feet away, ten warriors from del Arroyo appeared from a hiding place and shot their arrows at Amhose. A shaft struck him, and he fell clutching his chest. The warriors disappeared through the pueblo's entrance. Many onlookers fell to the ground sobbing. A group of Bonito warriors pursued the del Arroyo assassins. They quickly overtook them, but in a short, fierce battle, the outnumbered Bonito warriors were defeated, most mortally wounded.

In Bonito's plaza, Zuni lifted Amhose into his arms, "Amhose! Father. What have they done?"

"Do not worry, my son," Amhose opened his eyes and whispered, "I have fulfilled my duty. I must now bid you farewell. I have one more request, my son."

"Yes, father," Zuni said through his tears, "What is it?"

"Hopi is near—this message is for you both. Please, tell him . . . ."

"Oh, father, please do not go!"

"In my room you will find two sacks of Chochmingwu, sacred seed. One is for you, and the other is for Hopi. Tell him I tried to be here for his return, but Tawa decided it was not to be. Do this for me."

"Yes, my father."

"Thank you, Zuni." Amhose looked at the pueblo, at the sky above, and at the faces of his advisers gathered around. "It is all so good—life and living, loving and caring, duty and obligation. Life is enough. It is enough. The spider's web, the mother land, and the stars . . . so powerful."

Amhose looked into Zuni's eyes, "I shall be with you . . . ." Amhose closed his eyes and his Kaa floated out of his body.

The last confirmed leader of the empire of Chaco and the Anaa was gone.

Pandemonium

Few slept, and when the Morning Cha'tima announced the new day, a sense of doom filled the streets. People who did not live within the protective walls of the pueblos, desperately filled water barrels at Galo creek then barricaded themselves in their houses.

Emissaries from del Arroyo went to all the pueblos with a declaration from Ammett abolishing the Abbott's Council. The Antelope clan of del Arroyo claimed control of Chaco. Criers ran through the streets declaring Ammett the new leader of the empire. Ammett intended this edict to reassure the people, but his announcement only intensified the already palpable sense of impending doom.

When shadows sliced through the city, the drums at del Arroyo sounded again. Citizens stopped and listened. The brutal slaughter of the outcasts was only the beginning. The cleansing of the city would continue. The single war drum of del Arroyo was joined by many drums, beating faster and faster. The exodus from the canyon marked cadence to their beat.

At owl-light, when faces blur at a distance, the army of del Arroyo danced into the streets. They were painted red with black faces. They made their way through the streets toward Bonito, but as they approached they were greatly surprised to find warriors from Chetro Ketl, Kin Kletso and Kin Klizhin gathered around Bonito's entrance.

The del Arroyo army turned away, its serpentine body passing by the entrance as it had the night before. The two armies glared hatred at each other. Had it not been for their training, a tremendous battle would have ensued. But the army of del Arroyo passed Bonito and disappeared into a neighborhood of merchants, traders and the wealthy non-Anaa.

Their orders were to kill the enemies of Anaa—the people who suck on the blood of the empire. Some of the intended victims were already long gone, but those who remained had relied on the civility of the empire to protect them. These were mainly minorities, the non-Anaa, Indians of northern tribes who intermarried with the Anaa, wealthy traders and merchants—anarchists of Toltec heritage, and anyone suspected to be gamblers, loiterers, slavetraders, adulterers, or plotters.

The torches of Arroyo could be seen moving through the city all night long. No one knew if the knock would come to their door. The families of traders and merchants were brought into the streets and forced to watch their husbands, sons and brothers executed and their homes burned. Unfaithful wives were dragged by the hair to a small plaza and burned. People thought to be plotters, many innocent but named by Ranal, were marched to the Impaler—their limp bodies posted for all to see. Many others died too, some simply for being out-of-doors when the army swept by. And there were those who had not been sought out, but who stood in defiance of the injustice.

The Last of the Kokopilau

Hopi and his new people journeyed back to the foothills of the Blue Mountains. From a ridgetop, Hopi spotted a group of hunched-back flute players, the Kokopilau, marching along the horizon approaching them. When they met, Hopi greeted them, and asked, "Are you from Chaco?"

Their leader responded, "We are the last Kokopilau, the teachers and the wanderers. Once, we stayed with the Anaa in Chaco but we have since taken up the trail again."

Hopi said to them, "We are wanderers."

"Yes." The elder replied, "And you are Hopi, the Morning Cha'tima in the last days of the once famous city of Chaco."

Hopi was perplexed, how did they know who he was, and what did they mean by once famous city? "The once famous city?" he asked.

"Why, yes." The elder hung his head, then continued, "We know of you. It was foretold by the stars."

"The stars? Predictions?"

The Kokopilau looked to one another in puzzlement.

"You do not know?" the elder asked.

"I am sorry," Hopi apologized, "I know nothing of which you speak."

The Kokopilau spoke to one another in hushed tones. Finally, the elder spoke, "You are Hopi and these people with you are the Hopis. We wish you long life and great strength on your journey."

The Hopis and the Kokopilaus passed each other on the trail. Later, Hopi fell silent, confused by the Kokopilau's remarks.

Wind through the Pines

When Hopi and his followers arrived at the campsite in the Blue Mountains, Istaqa and the people were no longer there. Campfires smoldered, meat dried in the sun, and clothing hung in the branches. Hopi walked to the center of the meadow and yelled out, "Istaqa! It is I, Hopi, I have returned. Do not be afraid."

Cautiously, Istaqa and the rest of the people appeared at the edge of the forest where they stopped. Istaqa asked, "Who are these men?"

"Fear not, my friend, they are with me."

"Where did they come from?"

"They are what is left of Yalo's band."

Istaqa looked hard at Hopi and then at the men who busied themselves making fires, settling in after the long march. Finally, he burst out laughing, "You have stolen Yalo's men?"

"Yalo has no need of them."

"He is dead?"

Hopi nodded and began to tell Istaqa all that had happened.

Nearby, Tar spotted Ramu being carried into camp by four strong boys, "Ramu! It is I, Tar! You have survived, my friend! Oh, thank the gods."

Ramu turned in the direction of Tar's voice, "I, too, thought you were dead! But here you are, Tar—fastest of all!" Ramu held out his arms and Tar reached out to embrace him. "I am sorry Ramu, but I can no longer stand. My legs do not obey."

Ramu leaned over and took his friend in his arms. "You and I have shared the Great Race, we are brothers," Ramu smiled. "I can no longer see, and you can no longer walk." Tears streamed from Ramu's blackened sockets. "If you will be my eyes, I will be your legs. Agreed?"

"We will be one! Stronger than one!" Tar said joyfully, "It is God's work, my friend. Agreed!"

"Together, we will make our future." Ramu laughed.

Later that night, cool winds came down from the high mountains and set the fire's embers aglow, lighting the faces of all the new people. The piñon and lodgepole pines gently swayed, their boughs making the sound of rushing water. Hopi called to his people.

"Listen . . ." The sound of the trees swept them up. Hopi gestured to Istaqa who pulled his bone flute from his waistband and played. When he finished, Hopi spoke.

"The destiny of each man and wuti is the greatest of mysteries." He moved slowly around the perimeter of the gathering. "Some people believe our destiny is in the hands of the gods, but it takes wisdom to interpret the signs given by the gods and to understand their meanings. Many good people have fallen into the abyss of misinterpretation. And some deliberately misuse the name of God in order to gain personal power and to destroy others. Many of you have suffered at the hands of such people, and the pain cuts deeply into your soul. You are wounded.

"There are others who believe that destiny is in their own hands or who do not believe in destiny at all. These people must be strong, for they carry the burden of creation and destruction. They keep faith in what they feel within. These people acknowledge their own weakness and folly. They are the willows in the wind. They bend, and believe that because they are flexible they cannot be broken. These people lose themselves in doubt. Many of you suffer from this doubt. I, too, have suffered from this affliction of the soul. We have been wounded.

"All of us have been victims of these two kinds of people, of self-righteous men who claim to speak for the gods, and of ourselves by our doubting. All of us gathered here have another thing in common, we have been humbled. Many times we have been humbled, until we believe that humility is defeat. But we are not defeated. Within us lies the true voice, not silenced by humility, but strengthened by it. We cannot see light until darkness surrounds us. We cannot do right until we recognize wrong. We cannot love until we have experienced hatred.

"To all who came with me from Yalo's band, I say forgive yourself for the evil deeds you have done. I, too, might have been among you had I been born an outcast of the Anaa. The past is gone! The new time is here. Never forget what you have done and what you have seen, but allow peace to enter your souls.

"The wuti and boys from the village called Kowawa, The Village that is Always There, have suffered much pain. But, do not deny the humanity still within you. You shall be able to forgive. This forgiveness will give you strength. Use the pain of death to lead you to righteousness, to strengthen your souls, to see the good. Cry if you must, but cry well. Cry for your loved ones who no longer feel the sun, but rejoice when the sun's warmth comes to you. Cry for the separation you feel in your heart until you meet again."

One boy buried his face in his mother's breast and cried out for the father he had lost. A wuti sobbed for her lost son. A warrior from Yalo's band howled at the night. Soon, all the Hopis wept openly, and their weeping was overwhelmed by the vociferous music of Istaqa's flute.

CHAPTER FORTY-TWO

Blind Ambition

Ammett stood at the center of what once was Galo. He surveyed the city below. His warriors stood nearby, and Antelope workers cleared away the ruins of shanties. No sign of the filth that lived there was to remain. As he looked down at Chaco, his satisfaction grew. The troublesome Kokopilau have disappeared, and I, Ammett, control Fajada Butte. Amhose is dead and Bonito has surrendered without a fight, reduced to serving the dregs of humanity. The Abbott's Council is abolished, and without so much as a whimper. Ammett placed his hands on his hips and smiled. Huummph. The city is purged of its impure elements. No longer will outsiders have a say in what happens here. Under my guidance, Ammett mused, the empire of Chaco will rise to greater power than ever before.

Ammett's self congratulation ended suddenly at the sound of war drums. His warriors looked toward the city, and the workers stopped their labor. Ammett smiled, "Ahhh, I have underestimated my opposition," he said, half aloud. Then, from another part of the city, a second set of war drums took up the beat, and a few moments later, a third rumble sounded from another section of the city.

"Hurry!" Ammett demanded of his guard, "We must return to del Arroyo immediately!"

By the time Ammett was safely behind the high walls of del Arroyo, he learned the war drums originated from pueblos Kin Kletso, Kin Klizhin and Chetro Ketl—the spiritual pueblos. Ammett had miscalculated that they could not or would not stand without the support of Bonito.

At Bonito, Zuni assembled the high priests, the Ya Ya witches, the clerics, and even the apprentices. They wrapped Amhose in a beautifully woven carpet and carried him down a long stairway, into the subterranean kiva, and to the tomb of elders. After prayer and dance, Zuni told them of the prophesy of the Splitting of the Fourth World. Many were shocked and dismayed, but a few had already figured out the puzzle on their own.

"Do not be afraid, my friends," Zuni told the clerics. "Fear will not prevent fulfillment of the prophesy. The completion of Tawa's work will not be hindered. Rather, greet destiny with acceptance and ceremony. It is our duty."

Zuni continued, "These are my instructions. The gates of Bonito will remain open. No one is to be turned away. I have told the warriors to leave the pueblo and do what they believe in their hearts must be done. The remaining Chochmingwu and ceremonial wine will be offered. We shall feast and will serve the people of Anaa as we have always served them, with open hearts and conchas. Think not of yourselves, my sons and daughters. We of Bonito will sit at Tawa's side forever."

At Kin Kletso, Kin Klizhin and Chetro Ketl, the warriors of the spiritual pueblos, including a large contingent from Bonito, prepared for war. The abbotts Alluce, Oribee and Tokpa had given their blessing to the warriors. They concurred that del Arroyo had gone too far. A holy war against the pueblo was now a necessity. Del Arroyo had killed Amhose, butchered the outcasts, and purged the city of many respected citizens. Worst of all, Ammett had proclaimed himself leader of the empire.

For the warriors of the spiritual houses, the deliberation over allegiance was over. Ammett had sent their brothers, ill-prepared, to meet their demise at the hands of the outlaw, Yalo. The Antelope warriors had, noticeably, been spared that risk. Ammett had ordered the assasination of the rightful leader of the Anaa, Amhose, and in the process, had slain many honorable Bonito warriors. The warrior caste had been humiliated and destroyed by Ammett, starting with at the equinox massacre six moons ago. Ammett and the Antelope warriors would have to be punished.

Safely behind del Arroyo's walls, Ammett sent runners to Larkin and Shola, at Casa Rinconada and Tsin Kletsin. "The time has come for the clans to unite and bring order to the city," his messengers proclaimed. Ammett reminded them of his storehouses of chochmingwu and of the pipe of agreement they had smoked to seal their alliance. "Prepare your warriors for battle and send word to the city by sounding your war drums."

Ranal Hides

Ranal did not know what to do or where to turn. When the war drums began, he had been surveying the neighborhood where the non-Anaa lived before Ammett exterminated them. He believed that for his help in identifying enemies of del Arroyo he might be rewarded with a villa. I would consider a small house, one where I might compose music, he thought to himself. But when the war drums sounded, his muse was shattered and he ran to del Arroyo for safety.

At del Arroyo's entryway Ranal was stopped and refused entrance. No one but the Antelope may enter, the warrior guard told him. "But I am a helper of Ammett. Surely you must know that," he insisted. Still, the guard refused. Ranal had nowhere to turn so he stood next to the entryway and waited. He could not go back to Galo, because it was no longer there. He dared not go to Bonito. Someone there might know of his complicity in the destruction of Galo. Just when Ranal was feeling frantic, Ammett and his guard rushed by him and into the pueblo. Without hesitation, he fell into the group and passed into the pueblo with them.

Once inside, Ranal did not attempt to plead his case to Ammett. He could see that Ammett was greatly agitated, and in all likelihood would deal harshly with him, so instead he slipped into a doorway and waited. The pueblo prepared for battle. Warriors at the walls gathered hundreds of arrows and placed them at their sides. Great fires were built and animal skins containing flammable fat were hoisted onto the ramparts. Warriors shouted orders and prepared their body paint. Dances commenced, datura was consumed and war pipes were passed.

Partly to Blame

Hopi had only been back at the Blue Mountains for a sukop when a group of refugees fleeing Chaco stumbled into the camp. They had escaped Chaco the morning after Amhose had been murdered.

Hopi was astonished at the hardship the people described. They told him of the thousands of refugees in the city, the shortage of food and water, the starvation, and the mysterious disease. They told him of Amhose's death, Ammett's ambition, and of the disaster that had befallen the outcasts.

"But what of Zuni?" Hopi asked anxiously. "And, the outcast child, Amarna?"

The man lowered his head and said he did not know. Another man had heard that Zuni led Bonito, but he did not know if it was true.

With each story of turmoil, Hopi became more bewildered and filled with sadness. Istaqa sensed this and placed his arm around Hopi's shoulder.

"There is nothing you can do," Istaqa said to him, "Let the Anaa destroy themselves. It is meant to be. The gods have willed it."

Istaqa's words angered Hopi, "You do not understand, my friend. It is I, Hopi, who missed the Cha'tima and set all that has happened in motion. I am partly to blame. What of my friend Zuni and Amarna, whom I promised to return for? What of Amhose's death? What of the good people of Anaa?" Hopi looked Istaqa in the eyes, "What am I to do, my friend?"

Istaqa lowered his gaze, "I do not know, Hopi. It is plain for me to see that the problems of Chaco have been in the making for many, many moons."

Hopi walked to his lean-to, retrieved his Kachinas and disappeared into the forest. Istaqa was worried and followed, but Hopi turned him back, telling him to watch over the people until his return. "I must go to the Green Mask Cave."

CHAPTER

FORTY-THREE

The Warrior Caste Unites

The day surrendered to twilight, the time of Nedder, and the drums stopped beating. The quiet saturated the city as warrior's footfalls danced out of the spiritual pueblos and into the empty streets. The warriors were painted white to symbolize the clarity and purity of their caste and the righteousness of their mission. When the last warrior had gone, the gates were closed and the drums began again.

The three armies paraded from their pueblos to the marketplace where the warriors mingled in cameraderie. The braves numbered more than the leaves in a tree. Their torches and bonfires lit the canyon walls, sending a column of light into the moonless night. Blood ran hot. The warriors of the spiritual pueblos felt united again in this righteous crusade against the Antelope. They would cut out the cancer of del Arroyo no matter the price. The alternative, life without honor, was too heavy a burden to bear.

They danced, howled, chewed datura and smoked war pipes all night long. When the Nuptu tipped the eastern horizon on the plateau above the canyon, preparations were complete and the warriors were agitated into a hypnotic frenzy. Strangely, during the night, Amarna's admirers, more than one hundred of them, ventured out of hiding and made their way to the marketplace. They too, wanted to fight. They were no longer satisfied to sit and ignore what was happening. Normally, the warriors would have sent these well-intentioned citizens on their way, but instead they welcomed the support of all righteous people in this holy war.

Before dawn the elders sent a large company of seasoned men to storm Fajada Butte. The battle was fierce and the Antelope warriors guarding the butte were excellent archers and killed many warriors who scrambled up the butte's precipitous stairways. But, at dawn, when the Morning Cha'tima was to begin the new day, a war whoop sang out in its stead. The Antelope was defeated. The power of the warrior caste prevailed and was strong. They walked the pathway, cobbled with the bones of their fallen brothers.

The elders then sent contingents of newcomers—as well as young, untested warriors—armed with arrows, sling shots and verbal insults to challenge the Antelope braves on Arroyo's walls. The elders watched this game, hoping to discover where del Arroyo was vulnerable. The elders covered their mouths in an effort to hide their laughter—a sign of disrespect—witnessing as these young braves' foolhardy bravado. The young men ran through waves of arrows to del Arroyo's walls where they taunted their adversaries. Many were slain and quickly replaced by others.

Simultaneously, the structures surrounding del Arroyo were set afire. Billowing blue smoke rolled up around the impressive pueblo, choking the Antelope on the parapet. Archers crept under the smoke's protection and picked off many Antelope warriors. Other archers stood behind burning buildings and used long bows to launch flaming arrows onto the pueblo's rooftops.

Inside the great pueblo del Arroyo life went on as usual. Its great walls were constructed to withstand warfare—but the people of del Arroyo, including Ammett, were very surprised by the warriors' attack. The Antelope people believed in their families' rightful ascension to leadership. Within the safety of the structure—in its hundreds of rooms and kivas—the bloodshed outside was not discussed. The work of the pueblo continued as it did in the homes of the Ant people. Like the Ant people, the Antelope had done very well by themselves. The storage bins were packed with enough food to last indefinitely, and it would be nearly impossible for an army breach its walls.

Ammett was arrogant about his part in these history-making events. "How dare they attempt to lay siege to del Arroyo! Don't they know who I am?" After a while, it came to him, "Of course, the warrior caste attacks," he deduced. They realize my true intention—to subordinate them—to have them destroy one another with no sacrifice on my part. But still, Ammett was incredulous, troubled and confused—especially concerning his alliance with the clan pueblos, Rinconada and Kletsin. He sent his messengers to them, demanding them to prepare for war and to relay their intentions with their drums, but not a sound had broken the air.

A Straight Line is a Circle

When Hopi returned from the Green Mask Cave with another Kachina doll he told Istaqa of his decision to return to Chaco. Istaqa pleaded with him to reconsider, and at first Istaqa argued that the risk of returning to the city was far too great. "A new life awaits you only if you turn your back on the past. I have seen great changes during my life, and I have experienced many forms." Istaqa told him, "I have even forgotten some of the people and animals I once was."

Istaqa told him, "The flying spider lays its eggs on top of a pond to sink. On the bottom, the spider grows in its own egg sack. When it is mature, it floats to the surface, unfolds its ungainly wings, and flies to its new life." Istaqa pleaded, "You, my master, Hopi, have received your new wings. Will you fly into your new life or sink backward into the water of your birth? You must fly up the trail, my friend," he told Hopi, "or the circle that is your life cannot continue."

"That is exactly why I must return," Hopi replied, "to complete the circle of my life. Only then can I go forward."

Hopi continued, "We have one life and it should be a line—a straight line that makes a circle—beginning and ending at the same place. You know what I am talking about, my friend. It is the line of integrity that the arrow of life follows. The arrow connects the past and future with its sharpened point always at the present," Hopi pointed to his heart, ". . . here.

"Since I left Chaco, I followed the sage and the flight of the cedar wax-wings. I went from the dunes to the forests. I visited the valleys and mountains. The land called out to me and I followed. But, I know now that my circuitous path was really a straight line, like the arrow's flight, leading me back to the place where I began.

"Perhaps, if it were not for Zuni and Amhose and Amarna," Hopi said, "I would not return to Chaco. I could be satisfied to build anew, with the help of the family Kachinas and all of you." Hopi gestured to the people in the camp and turned and bowed to Istaqa. "This part of my life must begin with a line that is true."

Return to the City

Hopi and a handful of men moved quickly toward Chaco. Ramu followed, struggling, under Tar's weight. The closer they got, the wider the path became, and the more it resembled a dry, dusty river bed than the gateway to the city. Sitting along the path were people who had escaped the city. They had nowhere to go, and even though they were tired and hungry they were happy to have escaped alive. "You are going the wrong way," the people told them. "The streets of Chaco are filled with blood. Death awaits anyone who ventures into the city."

At the insistence of Istaqa, Hopi wore a hooded shroud to conceal his identity. Many people recognized Ramu and cheered. They told him of the war between the warriors and the pueblo del Arroyo. "What of Bonito?" Hopi asked from under his cloak. "Bonito's power is gone," an old man remarked disdainfully. "Its doors remain open, and it cares for the needy and the wounded," others told him.

By the time Hopi and his men approached the canyon cliffs they were filled with anxiety. Hopi felt that he had never left. Though I have traveled far, he said to himself, and have seen much, I feel as though I have not been away at all. He longed to see Zuni and Amarna as he never had before. He imagined finding everyone in the city dead, the same way he found the people of his childhood home of Grand Gulch.

But when they reached the canyon's edge and peered into the city, Chaco appeared calm as though sleeping. Were it not for the burned-out buildings surrounding del Arroyo, the missing cottonwood tree and Galo, the city looked the way it had when Hopi last gazed down from Fajada Butte, the day he missed the Cha'tima.

Before long they spotted fifty or more warriors creeping behind houses and buildings on the far side of del Arroyo. Then, the war drums of Ketl, Kletso and Kizhin sounded, and hundreds of men danced into the streets and made their way to del Arroyo.

The Antelope warriors rushed to the walls of del Arroyo and quickly readied themselves. As they prepared, the warriors behind the pueblo climbed ropes over the back wall without being spotted. Once they were all safely over the wall, they attacked with fury, shooting many arrows and fighting hand to hand against the much larger number of Antelopes. At the same time, the armies from the three pueblos including hundreds more who had been hiding in deserted buildings, attacked from the front. They shot waves of arrows over the walls into the plazas of del Arroyo. Many Antelopes were killed as they rushed to fight the invaders who had breached their walls from behind.

The battle raged and Hopi and his men watched in amazement. Tar described everything to Ramu who sat cross-legged on the stone. Hopi paced, shaking his head. The bloodshed continued throughout the afternoon until the warriors who had scaled the wall were all killed, and the attacking armies retreated or disappeared into deserted buildings near del Arroyo. Afterwards, the clerics from Bonito ran to the battleground and carried the wounded and dead of both armies back to Bonito. Before sunset the battle began anew.

CHAPTER

FORTY-FOUR

Worm Tongue and Snake Eyes

Ranal had little difficulty keeping out of Ammett's way. The Antelope people had seen Ranal going in and out of the pueblo so often, they paid no attention to him, and they had more important things to think about. With the attack going on above, the stockade was unguarded. He had once been held in the pueblo stockade, and he made his way there where he was sure to find Amarna.

"I have come to visit you, Amarna," he greeted.

"What? Who is it? What do you want?"

"It is Ranal, your friend. I have come to see you."

Amarna was quiet. Ranal was not her friend. Deep within the subterranean expanse of del Arroyo in the room where Amarna was confined, there was only darkness and the putrid odor of decay. She could not say how long she had been there. She was disoriented, and the sound of Ranal's voice unsettled her. Since her arrival at del Arroyo, only the recurring image of her mother disappearing over the cliff, and memories of the atrocities she witnessed in Galo marked the passing of time.

"Why do you turn your back on me? I have come to see that you are not thirsty or in pain."

Amarna remained silent.

"Have you heard the war drums?" Ranal asked, hoping Amarna might be curious about what was happening. When she did not answer, he continued, "Amhose has been killed and so have all the non-Anaa of Chaco. They have been hunted down and slaughtered by del Arroyo. My master, Ammett, is the undisputed leader of the empire."

"Impossible!" Amarna shouted, infuriated, "Your master Ammett is a dog with a heart of stone. The people will never allow him to lead."

"Ahhh," Ranal answered, "You do have a tongue, and you know more than you let on. Tell me, how is it that you know of the warriors' attack on del Arroyo?"

Amarna knew nothing of the attack, but played along to get more information. "That is not your concern, ruminator. But you can be certain I know much more than you will ever know."

"That is not true," Ranal screamed, sending a stream of saliva jetting from his mouth and hanging from his chin, "You are nothing but a whore, if it were not for me you would have been killed with the rest of the garbage of Galo."

"You have it backwards," Amarna retorted, "The only reason you have been spared is that you spied on me and Zuni to find out more about Hopi!" Amarna only suspected that what she said was true.

"How do you know that?" Ranal demanded, pounding the stone wall.

"You are a fool. Everyone laughs at you behind your back, but you are so stupid you do not even know it. You know nothing. You are nothing."

"I know that when Hopi returns to keep his promise to you, he will be captured, then both of you will be sent to the Impaler."

"Yes, you may be right this time," Amarna feigned thoughtfulness, "But tell me, little fool, who will be next on the Impaler? Do you really believe that Ammett will keep you around? Ammett will have no further use for your worm tongue and snake eyes. Your days are numbered." Amarna laughed out loud.

Ranal recoiled, and then stood silent for a long while. He had considered what might happen to him, and Amarna made some sense.

"See!" Amarna snapped, "You are nothing without me—a clown, a fool, yes—but not a man! Be assured Ranal, that when I die, you will die along with me."

Ranal was frightened. Ammett had indeed repudiated him and shown considerable disdain the last time they met. Not only that, Ranal thought, even now I hide from Ammett. If he discovered me here who knows what he would do?

"The only way you will survive is by helping me escape and taking me to find Hopi," Amarna said soothingly.

Ammett's Compatriots

At Pueblo Casa Rinaconda, Abbott Shola, stood on a rooftop vestibule and watched the battle progress. Likewise, Larkin, the abbott of Tsin Kletsin, observed from the safety of his pueblo. Neither had forgotten his pledge of alliance with Ammett and del Arroyo, but at that time neither man was aware of Ammett's bloodthirsty ambition. When Ammett spoke of eliminating the impure elements of Anaa they had no idea he intended wholesale slaughter. More importantly, they would never have agreed to the assasination of Amhose. Much had changed since they sealed their pact.

Neither Shola nor Larkin was anxious to throw in with Ammett until and unless del Arroyo defeated the powerful warrior caste to the last man. Even then, they had no heart to participate in an empire run by Ammett, for if they joined del Arroyo and defeated the warriors, they would be nothing more than subordinates to Ammett. Their own warriors were anxious to assist their brothers in defeating the Ammett's tyranny. If the abbotts cast their lot with Ammett, they faced the real possibility of rebellion among their own clan. If, on the other hand, they waited to long to show their support of Ammett, or if they tried to support their own warriors against Ammett and were ultimately defeated—their fate would be the same—they faced the harsh retaliation that Ammett would surely have in store for them.

Family

Istaqa was awakened by the howl of coyotes looking for one of their own. He sat up and answered with his flute and waited quietly. It was silent for a long time. It took a while for Istaqa's music to travel across the forest to where the coyotes waited. The pack, hearing Istaqa's response, quickly answered with a repartee of sharp barks and cries. "No," Istaqa said out loud, "It is not time. I cannot come! You must be patient!" He brought the flute to his lips again, but this time sent a series of short, piercing whistles.

Feast

Pueblo Bonito's doors remained open. Following Amhose's instructions, the remaining bins of chochmingwu were opened, the ceremonial wine tapped, and a great feast prepared. The smell of concha and roasting corn floated through the deserted streets and into the houses and pueblos. Zuni asked musicians to climb the rooftops and call everyone to the feast. *Bonito's Welcoming Song* sounded throughout the city, and people left the safety of their hiding places to gather at the grand Pueblo. "Bonito is alive again," the people said, "salvation is near!" Warriors left off fighting. The warriors fighting the Antelope people gave up their posts and walked arm and arm to Bonito. At the spiritual pueblos, the doors opened and people came into the streets make their way to the home of the seed of the great empire itself. Even the clansmen of Rinaconda and Tsin Kletsin gathered at Bonito to greet their Anaa friends.

Initially, Zuni had questioned the wisdom of Amhose's order to prepare a great feast, but when he saw the people streaming toward Bonito he broke down and cried, "Oh my beloved Amhose, wisest of all abbotts, overseer of our last great dynasty, I love and honor you. Once more the streets of the city are alive with goodness." Zuni fell to his knees, unable to stand. He covered his face and cried like he had never cried before.

From the plateau, Hopi and his men smelled the concha and heard Bonito's welcome song floating on the air. Hopi, too, could not withhold his tears and sobbed uncontrollably, "It is time to enter the city." Hopi said throwing off his shroud and striding down the steep trail into Chaco.

CHAPTER
FORTY-FIVE

Tawa's Voice

Ranal returned to the stockade while the people feasted at Bonito.

"Amarna!" he whispered, "Wake up."

"Ranal, is that you?"

"Yes! Please be quiet, we must not awaken the others."

"What is it?"

"I have come for you." He began to open the door to Amarna's cell but stopped. "You must swear to me that if I help, you will forgive all of my mistakes and never speak a word of this."

"Open the door, Ranal!" Amarna whispered in desperation.

"You must swear to it!"

Amarna was quiet, then spoke, "How do I know that this is not another one of your tricks, Ranal?"

"Tricks? I do not know what you are talking about. I have only done what is been necessary."

A sound came from the hallway behind them.

"Hurry, Ranal! Free me! Someone is coming!"

Ranal opened the door and quickly stepped inside, closing the door behind him. An Antelope guard shuffled down the hallway and disappeared up the stairs.

"We must escape, now!" Amarna whispered.

"First, you must swear to me that you will not tell a soul what you know about me." Ranal suddenly grabbed Amarna around her waist and pulled her close, "Then you must give me what you give so many others." Ranal pulled hard on Amarna's dress.

"We will settle this later," Amarna cried in exasperation, "We do not have time now. We must escape while we have the chance!"

"There is time," Ranal said slowly, "No one will know. I have waited a long time for you, and now I will have you!"

Ranal and Amarna struggled to the floor. Ranal quickly gained an advantage. He groped her breasts with his hands while forcing his legs between hers. Amarna struggled but Ranal easily pinned her. He tried to kiss her, but she turned away and hit him sharply with her hand. He quickly rose up, hitting her again and again with his fists.

"If you do not stop," he hissed, "I will kill you ... just as I killed Vanga!"

"It *was* you!" Amarna said defiantly and stopped struggling.

"Yes, you little whore. It was I," Ranal admitted, laughing gutterally, "I will cut your throat if you do not do as I say!"

"Kill me! I will never submit to you!" Amarna shouted loudly.

"Quiet!" Ranal answered pulling a knife from his waistband and pressing it against her throat. "I will cut your throat, I swear I will! Then, as you die, I will have my way with you!"

At that moment, calling on all of her strength, Amarna twisted violently to one side, sending Ranal rolling off and onto the floor. She got to her feet, ready to defend herself, but Ranal did not get up. Instead, he lay curled up in a ball. His breathing was labored and he cried out, "Help me! Help me! I am stabbed." Ranal rolled over and showed Amarna his own knife protruding from his stomach. She stood over him but did not move. His breathing came in short gasps. He moaned and begged, "Have mercy on me Amarna. I love you. Help me, please!" She did not move.

"The gods have punished you, Ranal," Amarna said standing over him. "They have made you take your own life."

Ranal tried to speak but could not. His breath became more and more shallow and he stopped struggling. Finally, he spoke, "Tawaa seeent meee here to doo what I have done . . . . The voices I have heard are those of Tawa and Sotnang . . . ." Ranal exhaled and stopped breathing. He was dead.

Preordained

The only pueblo to ignore Pueblo Bonito's invitation was del Arroyo. Ammett was outraged. He paced del Arroyo's high wall and watched as the city came alive. "I cannot believe this is happening," he raged.

Ammett had been happy to have the warrior caste attack his pueblo. He knew they had little or no chance of breaching its walls, and now he had ample reason to destroy them. He watched as the warriors who lay siege to his pueblo left their posts to join the celebration at Bonito, and an idea came to him. "This is my opportunity! The gods have ordained it! Yes! Why else would Bonito hold a feast in the middle of battle?" Ammett smiled and sent for his warrior leaders.

Fill your Hearts and Souls

"No, Hopi!" Ramu shouted, "Please master, it is not safe for you to enter the city, not yet."

Hopi stopped on the trail and listened to Ramu's concerns.

"Though the welcome song comes from Bonito, a death sentence has been sent out against you. Many enemies wait for your return. Let me go with Tar to Bonito and make certain that it is safe for your return. It will not take long, and it will assure your safety."

Hopi did not want to wait. He longed to return to Bonito to embrace Zuni and Amarna, and to learn for himself of Amhose's demise. It was difficult, but he conceded to Ramu. "You are right my friend. I will wait, but run with the wind god, Yaponcha, and return to me soon."

Ramu hoisted Tar to his back and descended the trail with Tar guiding Ramu, "Ten more steps . . . turn . . . to the left . . . turn . . . ."

"I know this trail so well," Ramu said in a good-natured voice, "I could run it blindfolded."

"Let me cover your eyes then," Tar joked, and placed his hands over the blackened holes where Ramu's eyes had once been.

The two men laughed loudly.

"Do you remember the Great Race, my friend?" Tar asked.

Ramu laughed, "Yes, I lost my footing on the next switchback and went tumbling into the rocks."

They laughed again. It was good to be in Chaco.

"I wish you could have seen your own face when I passed you," Tar added.

"Ahhh yes!" Ramu smiled, "And I wish you could have seen your own face as I jumped to the trail below!"

Both men laughed harder and Ramu nearly lost his footing. When they reached the bottom of the trail Ramu sprinted toward the entrance of Bonito.

"If you would have run this fast when we raced," Tar joked, "I would have never caught you."

"But then," Ramu said, "I carried more weight, my friend. Now, I only carry you, and you are like a mosquito on my back. During the race, I carried the weight of my clan and that of my own swelled head which greatly slowed me down."

The two were still laughing when they passed under the great walls of Bonito and into the plaza. As soon as the people saw Ramu, a cheer rose up, "Ramu! Ramu! Ramu!" The people chanted. They were greeted by many people, and warriors ran to Ramu's side and stared in disbelief.

"Take us to Amhose!" Ramu shouted, "We have important business."

The crowd fell silent and everyone lowered his head. But then a strong voice rose up, like the wind through a great tree, "Amhose has returned to the father, Tawa. His body is no longer with us, but the spirit of his Kaa remains!" The voice was that of Zuni, and the crowd cheered their new leader. The sound carried through the city, up onto the plateau, to Hopi, and across the expanse of the empire known as Chaco.

The crowd separated as Zuni walked to greet Ramu and Tar.

"Welcome home to Chaco," Zuni said, "What is the business you speak of?"

Ramu's face became serious, "I cannot say with all of these people here."

Zuni stepped closer, "My son, it is I, Zuni. Speak into my ear."

"Yes, master," Ramu replied. As Ramu spoke, Zuni's legs felt weak. He leaned hard against Ramu and his eyes scoured the cliff line above the city.

"Where?" he finally said.

"On the plateau above."

"Take me there, now."

"Yes, master."

Zuni turned in a circle. He spoke to the people. "The greatness that is Chaco surrounds you. Fill your hearts and souls with it! Eat and drink and share one another's company." Another cheer went up and the celebration continued. Zuni bid farewell to Amhose's assistants and high priests. He also retrieved the two sacks of sacred seed corn given him by Amhose.

A Prophesy Fulfilled

As the celebration continued, the doors of del Arroyo swung silently open, and the army of the Antelope streamed out, dashing through the streets to Bonito. They carried many arrows, knives and axes. They were painted black and wore the feathers of the crow. The good people of the city, the warriors who had left their posts to partake in the feast, and the people of the clan pueblos of Rinconada and Kletsin were caught completely by surprise when the Antelope warriors attacked.

Never, in twenty-one dynasties of Chaco, had an attack been mounted without first sounding the war drums. This ritual challenge was honored as truth, witnessed by time and written into the law.

The Antelope warriors streamed into the womb of the Anaa, and many hundreds of people were slain before they could mount a counter attack to drive away the Antelope warriors. Bonito was filled with the bodies of the

Anaa children. The plazas, walkways, storehouses and sacred ceremonial kivas filled with the dead.

As the battle continued, the remaining warriors and guards from the spiritual pueblos were joined by the forces of Rinaconda and Kletsin in an attack against Pueblo del Arroyo. The clan leaders Shola and Larkin joined forces against del Arroyo in the aftermath of the massacre of their own people at Bonito. Many citizen's took up the battle, students, old men and even wuti joined the fight to defeat Ammett and his Antelope warriors.

CHAPTER FORTY-SIX

We Do This for You

Amarna slipped out of her cell and quietly moved up the darkened steps. At the top of the stairway she encountered two hallways. She stopped for an instant, then bolted down one that delivered her to a prayer kiva and some rooms whose doors were locked. The sound of war whoops came from somewhere above. She tried the other hallway, and this one led her to a stairway. Up the stairs she climbed, but halfway to the top two Antelope warriors rounded a corner and rushed toward her. Her heart pounded, her muscles tightened, and she squatted to fight. But the warriors passed without seeming even to notice her. The stairway was dark, but Amarna saw the fear in their faces.

At the top of the stairway she pushed through a heavy door and found herself amidst a tremendous battle on the plaza. Warriors in the war paint of many pueblos fought the Antelope on the Antelope's own ground. Scores of men lay dead around her. Blood flowed down the high walls, and she saw the faces of men as they died. She stood against the plaza wall and did not move. Like the dove chick trapped in long grass by the coyote, she could not move. Suddenly, a warrior from Bonito fell from the wall above and landed at her feet. She screamed and rushed to his aid. Blood streamed from his mouth and he looked into her eyes. He tried to speak, but could not. His eyes rolled back as he fell limp. "Do not die!" Amarna screamed out. He looked at her again, gasped, ". . . we do this for you," and collapsed, dead.

Amarna brushed the long hair from the face of this warrior and looked at his features. He was handsome, strong and righteous. At the warrior's side lay a knife, and before Amarna could think she grasped it tightly in her hand. A sense of tremendous conviction swept through her like a shiver of death. Nearby, an Antelope warrior was about to attack a former brother with a spear. Amarna leapt forward screaming, and thrust her knife deep into the small of the man's back.

Proud Bonito

Zuni reached the plateau accompanied by Ramu and Tar before the Antelope army reached the front gates of Bonito. He turned to look at his beloved home and witness the slaughter. Screaming and shouting intermingled with the festive music of the musicians. At first, many people were unaware of the attack, and the celebration continued as the killing spread from Bonito's entrance into the main plaza.

Nearby, Hopi watched in disbelief. Though the musicians continued to play, the dance of death turned around the walls of Bonito. The laughter died away and was replaced by the angry sound of killing. When the musicians atop Bonito's roof finally realized what was happening, they paused, then quickly began playing *The Song of the Anaa*, the anthem of the empire. The melody floated through the canyon and for a moment, drowned out the sound of death. But, one by one, the musicians were silenced by arrows from the strings of the Antelope's bows.

From the cliff, Zuni took this all in, pained, as he fought the compulsion to run back to Bonito. He repeated Amhose's words, remembering the pathway set out by the gods. "The people of the new world are relying on you," Amhose had said, "You must not fail them."

Hopi did not feel the pain that Zuni experienced. Perhaps, he thought, I have already spent myself on the dead souls of my childhood in Grand Gulch. Soon, only the buildings and the pathways will remain. Our dreams, and accomplishments will fade and be no more. Hopi's ambivalence was due in part to his belief that the scene before his eyes was only one point on the ever-continuing pathway before his feet. What important lessons hide within this slaughter? he wondered.

The slaughter continued through the night. People who were lucky enough to escape made their way onto the plateaus and silently watched as the Antelopes continued their killing.

By Nuptu, tens of hundreds were dead and the warriors of the other pueblos, including Tsin Kletsin and Rinaconada, had regrouped to continue their counter-attack on the bloody criminal of del Arroyo.

The battle exploded at dawn with fury. Warriors and citizens striking against del Arroyo with reckless abandon. They threw themselves into the fight, some without weapons, and drove the Antelope out of Bonito and finally, beseiged behind the walls of del Arroyo. The Antelope did not retreat quickly. They fought with the pride and determination of the righteous, and this conviction afforded them the strength to fight with redoubled courage.

Friends

Hopi and Zuni faced each other. They did not embrace, only their eyes touched.

"If it were not my grief at the destruction of all that I love, I would be so very happy right now," Zuni began.

"Nevertheless," Hopi answered, "It will always be good to see you again. I have missed you my friend."

"And I have missed you, too."

"I have seen much of the world." Hopi explained, "At times I thought I had forgotten Chaco and my life here. Somewhere along the way, I realized that all of life's beauty can be seen in the faces of the people you love and who love you. I needn't have left you and Chaco. I know that now. I could have stayed, and the richness of my existence would have been equal or even greater to anything I have found."

"No, my friend. I disagree. Had you stayed, you would have been killed." Zuni paused before continuing, "It is I who can stand here and tell you what I have been thinking for such a long time. I have been a devoted servant, and I have found strength in my beliefs. But I truly believe that I should have gone with you—to see the stars from the far-off mountains, to experience the desert and the forests, to be on the pathway of Nanapala— with you, my companion and brother. I long for distant places, the world at large. I may never be complete if I do not know these many things."

"You have a point, my friend, but you are wrong. Look into my eyes. Can't you see the pain, the frustration, the doubt? Do you believe that I have answers you do not possess? No. I have learned only a small portion of what there is to know, and it is destined to be so."

Zuni nodded, "The world is filled with mystery and unanswered questions. I have learned that there are many answers and few questions. But look deeply into my eyes. All the teachings of Anaa and witnessing the destruction of my people has not guaranteed me wisdom and peace within my being. I think not.

"I am certain that I have been given many answers by Amhose and Allander, but until I am faced with the questions, the answers do not make much sense. If I had been in your place, perhaps I would find the pathway to the horizon would be more clear."

"Yes" Hopi added, "the pathway to the horizon would be clear, but the journey of Nanapala, from the outside of the person to the inside of the heart, is a pathway you already travel. I have only begun a long journey, and my time short."

Suddenly, each man recognized himself in the other and laughed.

"It is no good to laugh now," Zuni said covering his face, "The city and our people are dying."

"Yes, but our humanity makes us do it." Hopi added ironically, "It is so strange. I have wished that I had stayed in Chaco, and you have wished that you had been with me.

The two men embraced.

"I admit," Zuni said, pulling back and gazing into Hopi's face, "You look much different, much too old for your years. And you have a doll strapped to your head, and you carry dolls in your hands. In a way, you are not the same person I remember."

"I can say the same for you, Zuni. You are still young, but now you carry the weight of witnessing much of life and death."

"I have much to tell you, Hopi." Zuni said, "I bear messages, many songs, sacred dances, lessons and sacred corn from Amhose for you. Amhose instructed me and told me to teach you . . . ." Zuni could not speak, he was overcome by emotion. "There will be time very soon to tell you all I know, but I want to hear everything that has happened to you since you left the city. Tell me, what is your plan?"

"Why, my friend," Hopi looked down perplexed, "I have no plan—except to return to Chaco. I knew that once I arrived, the pathway would appear and the answer would be mine. But what of you? What will you do?"

"My path has many markers. I must fulfill my obligation to Amhose to teach you and tell you the story of the Fourth World. It is my duty and perhaps from this information, you will find the the next step on your pathway."

"Please, do not tell me just yet!" Hopi insisted. "Let us dance together as we have done before." Without another word, the two walked far into the desert to a place where the sandstone is flat and overlooks the four horizons.

"It is good to be with you again," Zuni said, taking Hopi's hands.

"I love you, Zuni." Hopi said as they began to turn.

"I love you, too brother."

"Please tell me, brother, of the girl, Amarna? What is her fate?"

"I do not know, Hopi."

By mid-day the blood in Bonito had dried and the bodies bloated. Some stretched the seams of their garments until they split. The fighting subsided. Survivors fell into a fitful sleep, but by Tasupi the fighting began again. The warriors and their allies would fight until they overwhelmed del

Arroyo or until they were dead.

Inside del Arroyo, Ammett prayed. "Everything I have done," he whispered, "was necessary to cleanse the Anaa and to clear the way for the Antelope clan's ascension to the leadership. If all are killed, my Lord Tawa, we will begin anew. Please allow the rain to return, we are righteous and have done what was required of us. Our world is being restored to order."

More Lessons

Hopi stayed with Zuni for three days before saying farewell. Many people who had escaped the city followed Hopi, leaving their old lives and setting out across the desert to the camp in the Blue Mountains where they were greeted warmly by the people who waited there.

Hopi's followers rejoiced at his return, bowing down and hailing him their leader. He embraced each one of them, and the people loved him as a father. There was plenty of food in the Blue Mountains and Istaqa had just returned from hunting with the young boys. They prepared a great feast, and Istaqa bragged that the deer and pronghorned sheep ran in front of the hunter's arrows to sacrifice themselves for the future of the Hopis. Prayers were offered, and the animals fed the eternal fire of life burning within the new tribe.

Hopi looked for Lakon, but she was no where to be found. "Istaqa," Hopi called out, "where is Lakon?"

Istaqa, who was telling a preposterous story to a group of newcomers, ran to Hopi's side. "Master," he began, "Can you see the crimson robe hanging on the pine tree next to the high cliff?" Istaqa pointed at a stand of pines perched near a steep slope next to an enormous granite rock.

"Yes. Why?" Hopi looked, and then turned back to Istaqa who was looking to the ground in front of his feet.

"When?" Hopi asked.

"It was not long after you left," Istaqa answered, "She would not eat and her eyes possessed the look of a doomed person. I am sorry, Hopi-Man, but when we were not watching she climbed the slope, disrobed and threw herself into the void."

Hopi lowered his head and wept.

"There was nothing we could do, my friend. I am sorry." Istaqa put his arm around Hopi and continued, "I am convinced that the gods sent you to Lakon. The importance of your meeting with her will not be known for many, many moons to come."

"She was so unhappy, and I am sorry that I did not try to comfort her."

"This is the lesson you must learn then," Istaqa added. "Now you must suffer with her memory and the unfinished business between you. From it, your soul will bloom."

"Is there no end to these lessons?" Hopi asked angrily.

"No. There is not. Life is only a series of lessons."

Wait for Me

Zuni camped above the city with his band of refugees for a complete Sukop. The battle in Chaco continued, and many men and wuti escaped to the plateaus, only to return to the city after a short respite. The violence of hatred and the desire for retribution poisoned the blood.

Zuni sat for hours motionless, gazing into the embattled city. When people approached, he did not move or respond. He was consumed by the sight and sound of death. He would remember every detail forever.

Before Hopi departed, they walked for two days into the desert and back again. At Hopi's insistence, Zuni related what had transpired after the Cha'tima was missed and Hopi left. "The day the Cha'tima was missed," Zuni told Hopi, "Amhose said, 'My son, I fear we are on the verge of great change. I believe destiny touches our face. I am not certain what will become of our beloved Chaco, the Sun above us, or the Earth below; but I am convinced that a new day in history has dawned this morning.' So, you see Hopi whether you know it or not, the question you asked that fateful morning was really not your question at all. It was a seed the God Tawa planted within you to grow, possessing its own life."

This gave Hopi peace and equanimity. "You are a very wise man, my friend Zuni," Hopi told him.

"That may be true," Zuni responded, "the cost of wisdom is experience and faith. And you, my friend, have found faith along the pathway of experience. You are the wisest. Your conviction is enviable. Your apprenticeship has been by far the most difficult. "

"I do not agree," Hopi argued good naturedly. "It is easy to run and forget, but it is far more difficult to stay while the world collapses around you. You are the wisest."

They laughed and embraced.

Before they parted Zuni gave Hopi the sweetest of Amhose's gifts to him. "Amhose told me, 'My son Hopi will need this poem, please give it to him.' Here it is,"

Zuni stood erect, looked to the western horizon and recited,

"Wait for me and I will return
Only you must wait very hard
Wait when you are filled with sorrow
As you watch the yellow rain and
when the wind sweeps over the snow drifts
Wait for me when the sweltering heat of summer
brings sweat to your brow and
Wait for me when others have stopped waiting
forgetting all of their grand yesterdays
Please wait for me when from afar
I have not contacted you and when
even the others are tired of waiting.
And when friends sit around the campfire
drinking toasts to my memory, please
WAIT.
For I will return to you
defying every death, every distance, and even time itself -
For by your waiting you have saved me
And only you and I will know that I have survived
Because you have waited as no one else did."

EPILOGUE

No one else escaped the city. All were swept away in the violence. Chaco was lost. Only the pueblos, the footpaths and the spirits of Kaa survive. The sun dried the earth, the moon washed it clean, the wind swept away the doorstep, but the spirit of Kaa lives in the canyon of Chaco, in its bones, canyon walls and in the sage.

The Hopis

From all corners of the world, people sought Hopi. They made pilgrimage to the three-fingered mesatops where Hopi and his people finally settled. He led the Nanapala, the Path to Purify One's Self from Within. Hopi touched them and gave them the true breadth of themselves.

He moved through his people easily, his erstwhile manner winning their hearts. When Hopi was not fighting his own demons, he gave himself to his people. Around the campfire, he told them stories.

"I have told this story many times," he told some of his grandchildren sitting around a campfire, "every one of *The People* know it. When you are old, you will still remember this story. Do you want to know how I know this?" the elderly Hopi smiled. No one ever answered Hopi's questions. Even the children learned to simply dart their black eyes back and forth and wait. "Because you are a Hopi, I will give you this gift. But you must promise to remember it so you can give it to your grandchildren." The children giggled and held their hands over their mouths.

"I will tell you the story of Istaqa, the Coyote Man. Once, when I was young, maybe twenty Kokopilau calendars old . . . ."

"What is a Kokopilau, grandfather?" a small girl interrupted.

Hopi clucked his tongue at her in the way of the elders and opened his eyes like a wise old owl, "You do not know the Kokopilau, the humped back flute players?" he peered down before breaking his gaze, "Haa! But, never mind child, you will learn.

"So, where was I? Oh, yes. Once when I was young and alone in the desert, I drank bad water and became very sick. It was Istaqa who saved my life. I had just escaped the Great Ghost city of Chaco . . . ."

"Why did you escape, grandfather?" another asked.

"That is another story. Let me only say that I escaped because I carried a question in my heart, and I could not ignore it. So, I spoke my question and was forced to leave my home. It was the most important mistake of my life. We would not be here today, if I had not made that bone-headed mistake." Hopi quickly glanced around, then was quiet for a long time.

"What was the question, grandfather?" a beautiful little girl asked.

"It does not matter, little Beetle, my granddaughter. We all have questions inside our hearts." Hopi brought both of his hands to his heart. "So, I asked my question out loud so the world might hear and—it is very important that you should hear this story now because you are worthy and I want to give you its great gift—I was forced to leave Chaco.

"For many days I wandered alone. I had no food or water and was sick with disgust at myself for making such a mistake. Finally, I found a pool of water and drank from it. I did not know it was bad until I became very sick.

"When I awoke Istaqa was with me. He saved my life and nursed me. He offered me clean water and sweet meat to bring back my strength . . . ." Hopi sat up, arched his back to the night sky and yawned, "Let me ask you a question, have you ever eaten a person?" he pointed at a small boy, "Or, how about you?" he pointed to another child. "Or you?" he paused, "I cannot believe this," Hopi said, acting astonished, "Not one here has eaten the flesh of a person! Well, I am not surprised and I do not recommend it . . . ."

Hopi told the children his story, and when he was finished he told them, "Your life is a question, and only you can answer it. It is the Hopi's duty to secure his heart by looking deep within and asking the questions that live there. Only then can he walk with impeccability. Remember, it is not necessary to find answers, it is only important to ask the questions."

A young boy asked, "What happened to the Coyote man?"

"He is out there right now!" Hopi pointed into the blackness of the night. "He is probably watching us and laughing, right now.

"One night when evening stars had disappeared and morning stars still glimmered, the family of coyotes came for Istaqa. Istaqa was very old, but he gathered his strength and went to meet them. Coyotes will not enter a camp of humans, so they waited just outside. Istaqa gathered his things, pulled the strap on his hat tightly around his ears, and walked to them.

"I stood at the side of a campfire wrapped in a heavy winter blanket.

The flames set the world aglow. I nodded politely to the coyotes, and they ran in circles. There was no need for goodbyes between Istaqa and myself. We had said goodbye many times before. When Istaqa reached the coyotes they lifted their feet quickly, licked his hands, smelled his hiney, and wagged their tails. Istaqa, too, was very happy. He kissed them all.

"You see, Istaqa was the last of his kind. Once, 'his People,' his ancestors, numbered many and roamed across the land. They loved the forests and the deserts and the cliffs and the rocks. But they began to copulate with the beautiful and wily coyotes. Well, the offspring of this mating, with few exceptions, were coyotes. In many generations the entire tribe of men and wuti had become coyotes, except for Istaqa.

"When Istaqa was born, a human being among a litter of eight brother and sister coyotes, everyone was very surprised. From the night of his birth until today, the coyotes gather in the forest or desert every night and howl, carrying their news to the far reaches of the Fourth World. A coyote can die in the north and his relatives in the south will know, pronto! So, you see, Istaqa was a one of a kind. He was the first man born to coyotes in many, many generations and he was much more coyote than man. Now that the days of my past outnumber the days of my future, I know that Istaqa and I were destined to find one another."

Hopi told many stories, and he made spirit Kachinas dolls to remember the people the pathway had given him. Long after Hopi's death, the wise descendents of Hopi found the last Green Mask Cave on the three fingered Mesa as Hopi said they would. They set up camp at the cave and waited. Not long after, Istaqa appeared before them. "You have finally found the last of the Green Masks," he told them, "it is good. Now, you dwell on the lands of the family Kachinas where we can protect and guide you. "

Istaqa, too, was a member of the family Kachina. He had the legs and the body of a man but the headdress and heart of the coyote. Istaqa told the Hopis stories about Hopi's life when he was young. He showed the people a secret ceremony which would make the entire family Kachinas visible to them. Among the family were Ranal the Kanis, Ammett the Ambitious, Ramu the Lionheart, Tar the Runner, Lakon the Lost, Amarna the Maiden who gave her body—but who saved her spirit for Hopi, and many more.

Among the survivors of Chaco a great argument developed over what really happened to Amarna. Many believed that she was a candle lighting the pathway for the Anaa, and that she was blessed with an important role in fulfilling the Anaa prophecy. Some believed she that she died in the battle of del Arroyo, that she fought with the courage of a mountain lion but was slain, having served her purpose.

Others believed Amarna survived and made her way out of Chaco with many admirers at her side. Witnesses claim to have seen her with their own eyes, standing on the cliffs, or in Galo. They claimed she carried a spear in one hand, a thick, winter blanket draped over her shoulder. Long after the destruction of Chaco, traders and travelers told of meeting a tribe whose leader was a fabulously beautiful woman who once lived in Galo, the City of the Outcasts.

The Hopis say that many moons after all those who survived Chaco were dead, Amarna was seen walking with the family Kachinas on the mesatop. Unlike the other Kachinas who visited and talked with the Hopis, Amarna never approached but stood at a distance and watched.

Zunis

Zuni and his people, the surviving Anaa, wandered the new world for two generations. They searched until they found the plateau that Adobe had described to Zuni. Adobe said they would find stones and soil for the building of a new pueblo on this plateau, and the people would be renewed, Zuni often repeating Adobe's teachings, telling his people, "Houses can be built and rebuilt, but our most prized possession—our Anaa spirit—lives within our hearts, and when we move on it goes with us. Find comfort within your home, and pray for its protection and warmth. But always remember that your heart lives forever in the place of rebirth."

Before his death Zuni witnessed the rise of a new city on the plateau—austere and small when compared to Chaco—but rich in the songs and ceremonies of the Anaa. The plateau was quiet, and this soothed and calmed the Zunis' souls. "Life offers so much and asks so little," Zuni told his people, "It is best to be humble, to lower the eyes and listen. It is best to have faith."

Every morning for forty solstices Zuni walked from his room to the eastern edge of the plateau. He knelt and prayed in the purple light of the Nuptu. Though none of his people knew, Zuni whispered the Cha'tima of Chaco each day before he rose. But four times every day, the Zuni people stopped and prayed. Some stood alone in the fields, some gathered with their families, and many walked to the plaza and prayed as one.

"We must never forget our heritage," Zuni instructed his many apprentices. "Far away to the north our ancestors built the grandest civilization the Fourth World has yet known. We were born of Chaco, but now it is gone and we must re-align ourselves with the purity it once represented.

You must always remember that the blood of your Chaco ancestors runs in your veins."

From his robe, Zuni brought a dried flower pod and held it tenderly. "Chaco is the pod that opens so that its seeds can take to the air and float in all directions." Zuni pointed to a student, "You, my good friend, are one of Chaco's seeds." Turning to each student he held out the pod and repeated, "You, my good friend, are one of Chaco's seeds.

"We all originated in this one pod," he continued, "and though we are all so different, this is where we all came from." Zuni held the pod out in front of him and gazed at it. He did not move for a long, long time. His students became uncomfortable and squirmed.

"Life in this domain is very fragile," he finally said, "In an instant, it can be destroyed with nothing more than a thought." Zuni cupped the pod in both his hands and crushed it. "This, my friends, is what happened to Chaco. The forces of lust and greed destroyed it. But, if one keeps the hole on top of his head open; if he listens for the voice of God; and, if he lives within his life and not outside of it, the spirit grows, the will strengthens, the dance of life expands and grows more beautiful."

Zuni opened his hands, raised them to his lips and blew the seeds of the dried pod into the air. "If all is destroyed tomorrow, the adobe houses, the plateau we call home, the families we love, we will not lose heart. The essence of our strength is our belief, and it resides within our souls. All can be washed away. But nothing can wash away the belief of a man if he chooses to defend it."

The Hopis and the Zunis returned to cliffs above Chaco many times. To enter the city was taboo. The Kaa energy left by those who lived in Chaco was strong. The people prayed from the plateaus, performed ceremonies and embraced the silence, and only the purest of heart made pilgrimage to Chaco's scared ground.

After many generations the Hopis and Zunis became busy with their own lives and forgot about Chaco. The city and canyon were quiet. But the sun came every day and it did not forget. The sunset cried for the people who once loved it. The sunrise remained purple but no one greeted its arrival with the Cha'tima.

FINIS

CHACO

GLOSSARY

STORY CHARACTERS

Adobe   master stone cutter; pueblo builder

Allander   head astronomer of Kokopilau—also the title

Alluce   Abbott of Chetro Ketl—spiritual house

Amarna   child prostitute; also sign of prophesy

Amhose   spiritual leader of Chaco, and Abbott of Bonito

Ammett   Abbott of pueblo del Arroyo; Antelope clan leader

Bonar   historian, formerly a great artist

Dol   father of Tar; of the Blue Flute clan

Hopi   special student of Bonito and Kokopilau; experiential man

Hous   Abbott of Verda, the empire's 2nd largest city

Istaqa   Coyote man who comes to teach, learn from Hopi

Jule   trader who attempts to push Hopi over a cliff; cruel, evil

Juxz   Amhose's personal servant

Kalo   bandit who kept a tethered mountain lion as a companion

Lakon   from Kowawa, the Village that is Always There

Lama   Kokopilau elder who led his people out of Chaco

Larkin   Abbott of Chetro Ketl—clan house

Nanu   1. Lakon's father; leader of Kowawa

        2. old wuti from Kowawa; one of the first Hopis

Oribee   Abbott of Kin Klizhin—spiritual house

Ramu   the greatest Chaco warrior

Ranal   artist, runinator, outcast; sign of prophecy

Sagg   brother of Tar the Runner; son of Dol

Shola   Abbott of Casa Rinconada—clan house

Soya   Galo prostitute; Amarna's mother

Tar   winner of the last Great Race of Chaco; of the Blue Flute clan

Tokpa   Abbott of Chetro Ketl—spiritual house

Una   del Arroyo chief; member of warrior tribunal;
        committed suicide.

Vanga   stone mason devoted to Hopi and Amarna

Yalo   bandit whose army preys on Anaa

Zuni   special student of Anaa and Kokopilau; cloistered man—
apprentice to Amhose, Allander and Adobe

VOCABULARY, GODS AND HISTORICAL FIGURES

Alo	purity of thought
Anan	language of Chaco and the Anaa
Ankti	colorfully dressed dancer
Bask	builder and intellectual, the first Kokopilau
Bask III	ruler, 3rd Dynasty: during his reign a great astrological event occurs, Kokopilau gain much power
Blue Mountains	1. source of turquoise mines, to the west of Chaco 2. camp sites for Yalo and Hopi
Cha'tima	1. the sacred morning prayer 2. the person who calls out the morning prayer 3. the place referred to as Calling Rock, atop Fajada Butte
Chene	plains Indians
Chochmingwu	corn; sacred Corn Mother
Compo	war and death
Conchas	cornmeal tortilla
Crow	Black Hills Indians
Datura	1. root of; psychedelic used to enhance spiritual enlightment 2. deadly poison
Fajada Butte	free-standing sandstone monolith at the center of the city of Chaco; occupied by Kokopilau astronomers
Galo	1. creek running through the city of Chaco 2. the City of Outcasts
Grand Gulch	1. large Anaa community north of Chaco 2. the childhood home of Hopi
Hohoya	harvest, harvest time, harvesting

Hoodee	owl and Kachina, a spirit god who guides Hopi's path
Huhuwa	total eclipse of the moon
Iroqkuis	empire of the east which included many tribes
Kaa	mysterious cosmic double created alongside the living person at birth, living side by side throughout life, surviving after death; the Kaa spirit guards and protects the burial mound forever; the will and spiritual energy of man
Kachinas	spirit of invisible forces of life; the Kachinas family, cousins of Tawa
Kiva	circular shaped prayer chapel; usually subterranean
Kokopilau	teachers/astronomers; sent into the Fourth World to educate; after many generations settled in Chaco on Fajada Butte; also known as the hump-back flute players
Koritivi	potholes in the sandstone
Kowawa	The Village that is Always There [at the distant horizon]
Kuskuska	to arrive and to depart simultaneously
Mitanna	daughter of Tell, 12th dynasty, who fell ill and was slain by her father who built the City of Outcasts.
Nanapala	the quest to purify oneself from within; Hopi's journey
Narmer	founder of Chaco, its first Abbott
Nedder	Hell; underneath
Nuptu	the Purple Light of Creation, just before dawn
Onowe	Peyote
Palmalma	secret abbott's ceremony, meeting
Piu'u	"I am I" philosophy of will
Senat	board game played for fun and profit; gambling
Shamas	loincloths

Special Ones	students given special treatment, usually the intellectuals, clairvoyants, seers, gifted ones
Sukop	16 day period
Talamuyaw	summer moons
Tasupi	the time when the sun has pulled down all the light
Tawa	GODHEAD
Tawtoma	the place where the sun's rays go over the line
The Great Race	solstice and equinox celebration event at Chaco
Tell	leader, 12th dynasty; anecdote about daughter Mitanna, built city of Outcasts.
Toltec	empire of Mexico
Utta	Rocky Mountain Indians
Verda	a large outlying community of Anaa; mountain people
Vermillion Cliffs	north of Monument valley—the Valley of The gods; an escarpment of cliffs leading Hopi to Grand Gulch
Wuti	female
Yaponcha	the Wind God

CLANS

Antelope	Lizard
Badger	Owl
Bear	Parrot
Beaver	Sand
Blue Flute	Snake
Eagle	Spider Bow
Fire	Sun
Flute	Water

PUEBLOS of CHACO

Spiritual House	Leader
Bonito	Amhose
Chetro Ketl	Alluce
Kin Kletso	Oribee
Kin Klizhin	Tokpa

Clan house	Leader
del Arroyo	Ammett
Tsin Kletsin	Larkin
Casa Rinconada	Shola

For the past twenty years, Mark A. Taylor, a native of Utah, has worked as a writer, editor and publisher in local and national publishing. He has written extensively about Native American rights, and western water and land use issues. He is a past member of the Board of Directors of the White Mesa Institute, an educational foundation seeking to preserve ancient archeological sites and antiquities of the Fremont and Anasazi Indians. His fascination with the Chacoan culture of New Mexico began in 1983 when he stood at the center of the great architectural wonder of Pueblo Bonito in Chaco Canyon under a full moon.